# THE DISAPPEARANCE

# THE DISAPPEARANCE

## A Novel Based on a True Crime

David H. Hanks

THE DISAPPEARANCE
A NOVEL BASED ON A TRUE CRIME

iUniverse books may be ordered through booksellers or by contacting:

iUniverse
1663 Liberty Drive
Bloomington, IN 47403
www.iuniverse.com
844-349-9409

Because of the dynamic nature of the Internet, any web addresses or links contained in this book may have changed since publication and may no longer be valid. The views expressed in this work are solely those of the author and do not necessarily reflect the views of the publisher, and the publisher hereby disclaims any responsibility for them.

Any people depicted in stock imagery provided by Getty Images are models, and such images are being used for illustrative purposes only. Certain stock imagery © Getty Images.

ISBN: 978-0-5954-4860-9 (sc)
ISBN: 978-0-5956-9025-1 (hc)
ISBN: 978-0-5958-9184-9 (e)

Print information available on the last page.

iUniverse rev. date:  07/01/2021

*I would like to dedicate this book to my mother, Hellen Griffin Hanks. Her rock solid foundation in my life has allowed me to pursue a few worthy accomplishments.*

# PROLOGUE

▼

The early tears of Harold's life came from normal childhood events, but when he became a teenager he was left standing alone to sort out hate and love on ground that was molten and moving. Heartbreak became a common frame of mind that captured his young soul, driving him to reach for an answer that would give him peace.

# CHAPTER 1

▼

The summer of 1972 came to a screeching halt when Harold Harmon began eighth grade. Most of his summer had been spent sacking groceries at the pink-block J & I supermarket—the only one of its kind in a twenty-mile radius around Morven, Georgia, a tiny railroad town, population 247.

Every day at 9:00 a.m., Harold would price the produce, drink a tall Coke, and eat a pack of cheese flavored Nabs.

His thirteen-year-old physique was getting ready for a growth spurt and needed a lot of energy. Although quality food was always available at his mother's table, Harold had eaten too many snacks that summer and was carrying a small spare tire around his waist. His height was above average for his age along with the size of his feet. But one could tell that once the baby fat was chiseled away with some good old-fashioned exercise, he would grow into a handsome young man.

Harold loved roasting whole chickens over the spit that Johnny, the "J" in J & I, had installed the previous year. The chickens were basted with a tangy barbecue sauce and placed in the cooker around 10:00 a.m. The field hands who worked the local farms would then scarf them up during their lunch break in the picnic area at the side of the store.

Many of these workers were huge women whose size amazed Harold. He once said to Johnny "I can't believe they don't have strokes or heart attacks, especially in this heat." Johnny nodded and laughed.

On the first day of school that year, Harold confided to his mother how much he preferred working at the market in Morven. "It was a lot easier than the tobacco field last summer."

Helen smiled at her son. "Well, Harold, there will be a time when you'll own your own business or work for a large company that'll allow you to support your family. These summer jobs are gonna help you get ready for those times." Helen turned back to address the dishes she was washing in the kitchen sink.

Harold thought briefly about what Helen said, then ran out the back door to feed Kelly, their albino German shepherd. His mother was always giving him and his two sisters advice.

Kelly wagged her tail and barked happily as Harold filled her dish with dog food. She often hunted with Harold in the woods behind the Harmon property and he thought of her as his best buddy.

Hunting and fishing were popular sports in Morven, primarily because there wasn't much else to do there. Harold took Kelly hunting nearly every day in the fall and winter months, even though she was a terrible hunting dog. She did, however, have a great sense of smell when it came to snakes and there were plenty of rattlesnakes and cottonmouth moccasins around the edge of the pond in the back of the farm. Luckily, Kelly usually found them first, allowing Harold time to get his old 22-rifle cocked and ready to shoot before the snake had coiled to make its strike.

Lisa, Harold's older sister, would be starting school that year in Lowndes County, which had one of the best high school football teams in the state and Lisa, like all the girls couldn't wait to be around the players. His sister, Polly, was youngest, and being close to her mother was still the most important thing in her life. Lisa tried with all her heart to sew and cook just like Helen. She had gradually become a fair cook but the fine sewing that her mother did still eluded her.

Nevertheless, she had managed to carefully stitch two very colourful satin flowers onto her jeans. When she proudly displayed them to Harold, he just gaped.

"Aren't they far out?" Lisa exclaimed.

"Yeah," Harold said, "but look where they are!"

Both flowers were on the rear end of Lisa's jeans. "I just hope mom lets you wear those."

Mom did. Helen, who was quite conservative when it came to dressing herself and the children, was gradually accepting her daughter's wardrobe. Lisa had also gotten hold of a green Vietnam fatigue shirt that was almost completely worn out, but she wore it constantly. But no matter how she dressed, Lisa's natural beauty shone through.

Her skin was dark brown from her summer suntan and the Cherokee Indian blood she inherited from her father Jerry. His German-Indian mix along with the mostly Irish kick from Helen, gave Lisa her wild-eyed beauty look.

"Hurry up, Lisa, I've got to get to work by eight," Helen called out that morning.

"Mama, I just got into the bathroom," Lisa whined, which meant another half hour for hair and makeup.

Helen sighed as she poured her first cup of coffee. She was halfway finished with her usual bowl of Special-K cereal when Jerry walked through the kitchen.

"I've gotta go, it's already past six thirty," Jerry exclaimed while grabbing a cup of coffee for the road.

"Okay, honey. I'll see you tonight," Helen replied as he gave her a peck on the cheek.

Dressed in his uniform Jerry looked especially handsome to Helen this morning as he rushed off for work at the prison. Being a guard had its advantages at times, like the straight eight-hour day shifts that allowed him to get home at a decent time every day.

Jerry had had several police department jobs with most of the surrounding cities. He had even been the Chief of Police of Morven. Harold thought he had the responsibility of ensuring that the police chief's son never got into serious trouble so he worked hard at "doing the right thing," as his mother would say. But when Helen studied law enforcement manuals with Jerry at night until he was ready to take the exams required for his job at the state prison in Valdosta, Harold was a bit relieved. He had borne the task of staying out of trouble for a childlike eternity.

Jerry had been a fine policeman. The Morven Bank was never broken into while he was on patrol around town. However, the year after he left his position as chief and his deputy retired, his replacement gave an interview to the local paper saying that he was the only policeman in town, therefore a perfect target for criminals. It wasn't long after the interview that the bank was robbed and a huge wave of drug-related crimes swept through the little town.

Helen's warm coffee rested in her lap as she sat in the green two-door Montego waiting for her children. The kids were unusually quiet that morning, she thought; maybe the thrill of school's beginning had subdued them, or was it something else? The Harmon family had a little superstition in their blood and that morning felt eerie and distant to them as they drove down the old country dirt road to Morven Elementary.

None of the roads in Morven had names yet, so everyone identified streets by the people who lived on them. They stopped at the intersection of highway 94 and the road Harold and Lisa used to walk to get to the roller skating rink. Harold and Polly got out of the car. The old house in the middle of Morven where Helen and Jerry had raised their children for three years was in the background. The old dentist office made into a home was the first real memory Harold had of life in Morven.

"Polly, be sure to eat your lunch today, okay?" Helen sang out to her daughter.

"Yes, ma'am," Polly replied.

Helen looked at Harold, waiting for him to turn and say good-bye, but he had thoughts of school running through his cluttered mind.

"Harold, aren't you going to tell me good-bye?" Helen asked.

"Yes, ma'am. Good-bye," Harold said quickly.

Helen smiled lovingly at her son. Then, not being able to contain herself she reached out to him. Trying not to embarrass him too much, she said, "It's always important to tell people you love that you love them when you leave, kids," Helen said, looking at Polly and Lisa, too. "You never know when you'll see them again."

Harold felt a cold chill run down his spine, his body shivered. Not knowing why, but suddenly feeling alone, Harold hurried to catch up to Polly, who was making her way to the bus yard where five big Yellow Bird school buses were lined up behind the lunch room. A lush green softball field located near the newly paved bus yard looked inviting to Harold. He had loved the softball season, which was sandwiched in between the football and basketball seasons. Softball would start again each spring and continue until the end of the school year. Harold had been one of the best long ball hitters on the schoolyard for the past two years.

Harold turned around once more to see if his mother had started driving down highway 94 to Valdosta where she worked. A thought of losing her suddenly crossed his mind but then quickly dissipated.

Helen was now driving Lisa to Lowndes County High School. Helen's dark sunglasses shielded her eyes from the intense morning sun, and also concealed the worried look in her eyes so that Lisa had no idea her mother was frightened by something.

Helen's boss's son, Kenny, had been harassing her of late. She was now terrified of him. She hadn't told Jerry for fear of losing her job because of the possibility that her husband would take it upon himself to put out Kenny's lights.

"Lisa, you know I think that our family is the most important thing on earth, don't you?" Helen asked her daughter.

Lisa looked at her mother, and then turned to stare out the car window. "Yes, I think that the family is very important, but I sure wish Harold would grow up. We're always fighting about silly things and he's such a drag," she murmured, watching the passing farmhouses that dotted the landscape. Each miniature "plantation" usually had a pond and several cows grazing in the pastures. Some of the land was covered with cotton and soybean fields that were now in their harvesting season.

"Lisa, do your best to get along with your brother and sister. They're the only ones you have and there's a special bond between blood kin," Helen said her voice firm.

Lisa nodded absently. She was much more concerned with thoughts of Lowndes County High School. After all, Valdosta was a big city compared to Morven. The kids there would be different than the kids she grew up with.

As Lisa got out of the car, Helen called after her, "Good-bye, Lisa, and please remember what I said about the family."

"Yes, ma'am," Lisa said and closed the car door.

Helen drove to work dreading another day of double bookkeeping. Foxy Winkler had made her forge statements for several years against her will, but money was tight at the Harmon house and another job was on the horizon. Neither Jerry nor Helen had college degrees, but Helen had been going to a technical school to learn data processing for the new job she was seeking. A few more weeks here and her nightmare would be over. She would have never stayed after Foxy brought his son into the business if it weren't for the new house she and Jerry had built on the old Grantham family farm. It took both Jerry and Helen's salaries to pay the mortgage and buy the furniture on the installment plan.

But Helen loved the three-bedroom, two-bathroom, brick house with hardwood floors and modest front porch. It was the kind of house that Helen had always wanted and that she felt her family deserved.

As Helen neared the office, she suddenly brightened. Her day would be pleasant after all because Foxy and Kenny were in Atlanta bribing officials, a typical occurrence for the Winkler family. Foxy was heavily involved in the political scene ever since his fight for roadside advertising in the Fifties—those big, intrusive and ugly signs that would soon block trees and landscape all along American highways.

Helen pulled into the small parking lot of Winkler Outdoor Advertising building and locked the car door. The building was adjacent to the railroad tracks and located in a neighborhood that had been recognized for its criminal activities in the past. She was very careful not to walk around too much or flash a lot of money in the convenience store two doors down. While Valdosta in general hadn't had any serious crime in the past few years, there was always the chance of something happening to an attractive thirty-five-year-old female.

Helen was tall and had an athletic body endowed in the right places. Growing up in Morven, she had lived and breathed basketball and softball and had not lost much of her athletic skill as she grew older, not even after having three children.

Helen walked into the building just as Jack, one of the workers, drove up. He gave her the usual good-morning wave from his truck cab and she waved back. Company trucks were only given to three of the employees: Leroy, the longest employed worker, Jack, the company mechanic, and Bobby, the crew foreman. Jack drove around to the gas tank and parked by the pump.

Helen knew that he'd be wanting the key to the company gas pump. She and Foxy were the only two with that particular key. Helen kept hers on a ring in her purse and Foxy had his in a desk drawer in the receptionist area.

Jack came to the window by the side door. "Mrs. Harmon?"

"Yes, Jack, just a minute. My keys are right here," Helen replied. "How's everything with you this morning, Jack?"

"Just fine. Everyone's out of town today except for you and me. Leroy took Nick and Luke to Albany for some work on an old sign that's fallen into the river. Bobby's crew is on I-75 hanging the new Coke sign." Jack walked toward the pump and yelled, "When you reckon Mr. Winkler and Kenny'll be back from Atlanta?"

"Around four o'clock, I think," Helen shouted back.

Jack gassed up the GMC truck and returned the keys to Helen. It was a very strict arrangement that Foxy had ensured his employees abide by. He didn't want them filling their personal vehicles with the 32-cents-a-gallon regular from the company tank.

Helen sat down at her desk, took a deep breath and began to fill out the job application that she had gotten from Moody Air Force Base just north of Valdosta. After taking the civil service exam two weeks earlier she was sure that a job there was in her near future. Her excellent bookkeeping and mathematical skills would surely be appreciated at the Base.

She started the coffeepot on the stand next to Foxy's office after filling out the three-page job application. The percolator soon cranked up its lively bubbling noise that always seemed to amuse Helen.

She thought about the percolator that she and Jerry had in that old dentist-office house in Morven and how the morning coffee would smell so good. She remembered cooking eggs and biscuits for him topped with cane syrup. Occasionally, she would have enough time to make gravy for the morning biscuits and darken it with a little of the coffee. In the small house the kitchen smells lingered.

Helen went back to her desk and began making out the paychecks for the week—it was Thursday and payday was tomorrow. She kept the time sheets available to the crews that were on the road when they returned that afternoon. The checks would be cut early Friday morning.

Around eleven, Daniel Johnson came by for his usual shoot-the-breeze. Daniel worked downtown and had to pick up the mail from the post office every day. It was part of the short list of enormous responsibilities that were assigned to him. Being the boss's son at Johnson Auto Sales, these responsibilities were actually few and far between. He would drop by several offices along the way to the post office and talk to anyone who would listen to him. The longer the conversation the shorter it would make his work day.

Helen paused from her typing and met him at the front desk.

"Hey, Daniel, how're you today?"

"Oh, I'm just fine. Have you seen Kenny this morning?"

"No, I haven't," Helen said with a silent prayer of thanksgiving.

A feeling of disgust and terror enveloped her. It was just the day before yesterday, at the beauty shop in Morven, that she had come to grips with her problem and began to share it with her closest friends.

\*　　　\*　　　\*　　　\*

The Morven Beauty Shop consisted of a single-wide trailer with one chair in the front room surrounded on three sides by mirrors. Tuesday was a big day for Sue, the beautician. She had done Helen, Louise Armon, and Dot Reese all within three hours of each other. But this was not only a beauty shop; it was also the hot seat for gossip and heart bleeding. These women had grown up together and lived in Morven their entire adult lives. Sue, who was in her early thirties, was deaf and lived very near the Grantham farm while the girls were going through school.

Helen had helped her through many of her lessons as they were growing up. She and Helen would write notes to one another once their conversation got beyond the usual sign language that only Sue and her closest friends knew. Sue had learned the proper signs after she developed her own inventory of gestures and murmurs.

The education Sue got was enough to get her started in her own business and all her friends were her customers. The women were close in all things concerning family and local government. The mayor was usually elected from this gathering place. The women would decide and then relate that decision to their husbands when they got back home.

While Sue put rollers in Helen's wet hair, Helen finally confided in her friends that Kenny had made several passes at her. She was extremely anxious about his state of mind when she had slapped his face the week before.

"I cannot believe that bastard would put his hands on you!" Dot exclaimed.

Helen began to weep, "I know. What am I going to do?"

"You should stay as far away as you possibly can, Helen," Louise said, her voice raised over the humming hair dryer.

Sue stood back enough from the group to see who was talking, and then signed to Helen while trying to speak that she should tell Jerry about the incident.

"Helen, I believe Sue is right. You ought to get outta there and tell Jerry," Dot stated.

Helen pulled herself together after a few minutes. "I'm trying to get a job at the Base, which'll give me a chance to get away from Kenny without Jerry knowing what has happened, until later."

"Please don't stay there very long, Helen," Dot said. "I'm worried about you being in that situation."

"I will—it's just that we need the money right now," Helen replied.

The group discussed the event in detail while going through their makeovers. When she left the beauty shop Helen's spirit was high, feeling secure in what she had decided to do for her family.

*       *       *       *

"Helen, you want to ride up to the post office with me?" Daniel asked bringing her out of her frightened reverie.

"You know, I haven't picked up our office mail yet," Helen mused. "Just let me get the keys and my purse so I can lock up."

They returned to the office about thirty minutes later, and Daniel dropped Helen off at the door. Jack had already left for lunch and the office was deserted.

Helen relaxed as she munched on the ham sandwich she had brought that day
and began working on the payroll again.

*          *          *          *

Foxy and Kenny had left the office of their leading advertiser around ten that
morning and headed to Albany. Kenny's new wife, Jane, grew up in Albany
where her father, Oscar Jergen, still lived and owned an auto repair shop.

Kenny hated Oscar for being Jane's father because he knew she would never
give him all her love until her father was dead and buried. The thought of killing
his rival had crossed Kenny's mind a few times, but he could never overcome his
fear of "the man."

"I hope the old buzzard is at his shop today," Kenny said.

"Oh, don't worry, son. There's always time to phone him after we get back,"
Foxy replied.

"I just want to make sure they'll be at the reception tonight. Jane'll really be
bent outta shape if I don't stop by and invite them personally," Kenny said.

Foxy sat quietly in the passenger seat of the big Oldsmobile and thought of
happier times. When there was only Foxy and Lydia his beautiful wife, whom he
loved dearly. Before Kenny arrived twenty-four years ago, Foxy had built a business from nothing into a thriving competitor. He was fifty years old at the time of
Kenny's birth, making him now a tired but contemptuous seventy-four.

Foxy thought of Kenny as his prodigal son while he was growing up. Kenny
thought of his parents as a couple of old farts with no one to leave their money to,
except him. Throughout his childhood Kenny had several nannies to watch after
him, none of whom stayed very long. They said that he was just too hard to handle, but what they really meant was the boy was intolerable. The Winklers
ignored this problem; it wasn't important to them how often they had to find a
new nanny, or any household maids for that matter.

Kenny's friends were usually no more than acquaintances he'd met at military
school or the young fools who became entangled in one of his sadistic games.
When Kenny had met Steve, a young man who worked in the morgue in Valdosta Kenny's perversions really blossomed. The dead greatly intrigued the young
Winkler. He felt powerful and dominant over their lifeless bodies. Kenny visited
Steve around dinner time every evening for several months. Steve would run out
for burgers or pizza and leave Kenny alone in the morgue for almost an hour.

One of these times, Kenny ran into the nearest room and found the most
appealing female body. In only a short period of time he had raped the corpse.

The flesh of the dead woman was cold and rigid, never having to warm to his invasion.

*      *      *      *

Foxy's Oldsmobile rolled into the parking lot of Oscar's auto repair shop.

"Kenny, Foxy, what have ya'll been up to?" Oscar yelled out from one entrance to the ten-bay garage.

"We've been to Atlanta for a meeting with clients," Kenny replied.

"It never ceases to amaze me, Oscar, the way you've turned this ol' one-car shop into a little gold mine," Foxy said as the three men walked into Oscar's office.

Oscar had lined the dark wood walls with several softball trophies his crew had won over the years. He was really proud of his coaching abilities and needed little prompting to begin his endless replays of old games.

He was just about to start regaling his two guests with a softball story when Kenny abruptly said, "The reason we're here, Oscar, is to remind you of the wedding reception tonight and make sure you and Martha are coming."

"Oh yeah, we'll be there around eight," Oscar slowly replied.

He had received the invitation a week ago but had forgotten about it. Martha always thought for the both of them when it came to social gatherings. He couldn't care less.

"Did you see the pre-season game last night, Kenny?" Oscar asked, knowing he hadn't.

"No, we spent the weekend in Atlanta before the meeting," Foxy replied for his son.

Kenny had never answered one of Oscar's questions about a game of any kind. Oscar couldn't understand this either—a grown man who doesn't watch sports on TV.

Oscar met his future son-in-law on New Year's Eve two years earlier and immediately knew he didn't like or trust Kenny the moment he shook hands with him. He couldn't understand why Jane had even considered dating a guy like this. But Oscar never tried to tell his daughter whom she could date, except for the biker friend with the 38-caliber bullet earring.

Kenny had arrived at the Jergen's house to pick up Jane that New Year's Eve with whiskey on his breath and a cocky attitude. Oscar himself had finished a shot of Jack Daniels only moments before, so he couldn't really smell the whiskey, but Oscar's wife Martha did. She made sure he knew about it after their daughter had left the house.

Oscar felt threatened by Kenny but wasn't sure exactly why that fear could not just be turned into dislike. Kenny's sinister eyes and blank expression, combined with a "Southern gentleman" charm, only confused Oscar.

"Well I'm certainly glad ya'll come by to see me and we'll be there tonight for sure," Oscar said.

It was noon when father and son got back in the car and headed out of Albany. The speed limit in 1972 was still 70 miles per hour, but Kenny liked to drive faster. The thrill of speed was another drug for him.

As Kenny drove, deviant thoughts went through his mind about his father's secretary. He wanted her, but she would have nothing to do with him. Being rejected by a "commoner" infuriated him. Helen had more than once pushed Kenny's hand away from her buttocks and he hated the fact it sometimes happened in front of witnesses.

"Kenny," Foxy said, bringing Kenny's internal fury to a halt, "let's grab some lunch. I know this really good barbecue place just south of here," Foxy grunted.

Foxy knew one place well—it was one of his first jobs outside of Valdosta about thirty-four years ago. He remembered how he had made out with the owner's wife in the back seat of his panel van to help him close the deal. She was a decent-looking woman with a hot streak her husband couldn't quench, and although the fling with Foxy was over as quickly as it had begun, she gave him a good recommendation when the time came to choose advertising agencies. Her husband never knew how the advertising deal was really cinched.

He landed five more accounts that afternoon—it turned into the best day of Foxy's career.

Foxy and Kenny scarfed down the lunch special of barbecued chicken and collard greens with cornbread, then left Albany around one o'clock for the drive back to Valdosta.

Settling into the passenger seat with a loud, satisfying belch, Foxy picked his teeth with a sharpened wooden matchstick as Kenny drove. Power poles began flying by Foxy's window like fence post, causing him to lean over and check the speedometer which was approaching 96 mph. The huge beautiful pine trees that were so common in this part of Georgia whizzed by in a blur of green and brown.

"Jesus, look out, Kenny!" Foxy yelled.

A huge buzzard flew up from its sun-fried road kill opossum snack. The bird was munching on the meat when it looked up to see a missile coming its way. All the poor animal could do was to try and vault the weapon before it was too late.

But into the windshield of Foxy's Olds he went. It left a spattering of bloody guts all across the windshield and on the roof of the car.

"Goddamn," Foxy said, feeling a wave of nausea that threatened to bring up all that delicious barbecue he'd had for lunch.

Kenny slowed to 75 mph and turned on the water spray, trying to wash the mess off of the windshield. The wipers smeared the yellow and red-laced remains off eventually. Kenny sped up again, never saying a word about the whole incident.

When they had pulled into Foxy's driveway, Kenny jumped out of the Olds and headed to his own car that was parked there.

"Come inside for a minute, Kenny. I want to show you the new Colt 45 pistol I bought last week," Foxy said.

"No, Pop, I need to get to the office and break in a couple of new projects and put out some old fires," Kenny replied as he opened his car door. Before his father could say another word Kenny had taken off.

Kenny drove a Plymouth GTO that was fast and used an enormous amount of gas. Foxy paid the monthly bills on a stack of credit cards for Kenny and himself. Consequently, gas and insurance were none of Kenny's concern.

At two-forty in the afternoon Kenny walked into the office of Winkler Outdoor Advertising to do what he had planned to do for several days. The scene was set; he had ordered everyone out on jobs. No one who worked there expected Foxy and Kenny back until later in the afternoon.

# CHAPTER 2

▼

Helen looked up from her desk as Kenny walked into the office through the side door. He had parked his car on the same side of the building as she had and walked through the storage—a twenty-by-twenty concrete slab with a tin roof and chicken wire strung from top to bottom on three sides. Lots of old posters and sign-building materials were stored there. Sometimes the rain would blow in and wet some of the signs that were to be posted out on the highway, thus rendering them useless, a fact that always infuriated Foxy, but he never bothered to find a way to keep the area dry.

It was also convenient for storing tools used by the men to put up the signs. Outdoor advertising required numerous tools to build and post signs and having a quick storage area near the parking lot saved time. The men had also set up a two-way radio system that allowed them to talk to the "base station" while out on call.

The adjacent area was a loading dock located just off the main office building. Two wooden boxes were laid along one side of the walkway from the storage area, leading into the loading dock. These boxes were only four feet long, two and half feet wide and about three feet deep, but were able to contain the materials for several signs. They were covered with a sheet metal wrapping that would keep the posters dry. Foxy had converted two boxes that a vendor had sent into neat little supply crates. His men could load them on their pickup trucks and haul materials to different sites. The boxes were labeled Winkler Outdoor Advertising on all six sides and the top of the box was held with hinges that overlapped the frame and metal.

Kenny walked through the loading dock and straight into the main office where Helen had been typing out the infamous second set of books for the IRS. The payroll came out of Foxy's regular account, but the extra monies for family trips and social events had to be transposed into a viable company holding before being tied back into his regular account. Not to mention the large personal checks to his political friends in the Georgia senate.

"What's going on, sexy?" Kenny said with a treacherous grin.

Helen tried to ignore his remark as Kenny moved to the front of her desk in one slow deliberate motion. His body was rigid but he wanted to give the impression of being calm. One wrong move and she'd make a dash for the door before he could block it.

Helen's heart leapt to her throat, but she continued to type—thinking this was another one of Kenny's sick games.

Despite this cunning, Helen still believed that there was some good in his nature. She was a Christian woman, taught to forgive people and give them the benefit of the doubt.

"You're back early, Kenny," Helen said, her tone friendly.

"Yeah, I'm back to show you exactly how a real man handles a woman," Kenny said, leering.

Helen stood up slowly from her swivel chair and backed toward the layout room adjacent to the reception area. The layout room, where signs were pieced together, was just behind and to her right.

"You've been asking for this for a long time. Now there's nobody here to stop me. Not my old man or any other witnesses." Kenny glared at Helen.

"Stop, Kenny! This is not funny!" Helen shouted.

She backed into the layout room just as Kenny rushed her and threw her to the floor. Helen was now petrified and this gave him the slight edge he needed to throw her off balance. She was a strong woman and it would take the element of surprise for Kenny to overpower her.

"Lord help me," Helen cried.

He quickly slammed her into the filing cabinet by the door with such force it knocked the breath out of her. The whole room was covered with old signs and short pieces of hemp rope used to tie the barrels of paper together once they were sorted.

The floor seemed to shift and move underneath Helen's feet as she tried to run back through the open door. Reams of paper caused her to fall face down into a mound of paper and cardboard. Kenny instantly closed in on her.

He grabbed one of the ties, and from behind wrapped it around Helen's neck.

"Now, say your prayer," Kenny said, glee in his voice. But he had misjudged Helen's strength. She whipped him into the wall and then she fell back to the floor on her knees.

"You're going to pay for that one, bitch!" Kenny screamed.

He immediately rose and began another advance. The blow Kenny took wasn't much. It did, however, give Helen enough time to get to her feet. She reached for the nearest object, a pair of eight-inch scissors. "Stay away from me Kenny or I'll—"

Her head was still swimming from the fall and she could hardly catch her breath. She steadied herself with one hand on the layout table in the middle of the room.

Kenny jumped across the room, hitting the table with a force that broke several of Helen's ribs and rammed her against the far wall. The scissors flew from her hand and stuck in a cardboard box, in a corner. His punch came down across Helen's face and left her bloody and nearly unconscious.

Kenny grabbed the hemp rope again and quickly wrapped it around her neck. Helen tried desperately to pull it away. Her strength was now charged with adrenalin and it gave her extra power to fight back, but it was not enough.

Helen's last breath had been labored and then cut short by the hemp rope. A trickle of blood flowed from her mouth as her larynx collapsed. Kenny's sweat rolled down his face; he'd never been so excited. What he could not conquer, he could kill.

Kenny stood over Helen's dead body. "I'm not going to miss this secretary," he said out loud.

He reached into his pants pocket and produced the pocketknife that he'd once been given as a high school graduation present. Its blade was three inches long and made of hardened steel. Kenny had spent many afternoons sharpening the knife on a rough stone first to lower the pitch, then a smoother stone to hone it completely. The knife would shave the hair from his forearm, which he often did to impress his friends. He was careful not to ever use it on anything that would mar the blade though.

Numbness rushed over him as murder made way for lust. He slit Helen's dress on both sides with the steadiness of a surgeon. The blade slid through the polyester, never hanging on a single thread. He lifted the back of the dress off and threw it aside.

Kenny turned Helen over and the front of the dress was taken away from her body with one quick motion. Kenny stood back to behold his prize. He then slipped the knife under the bra, between the cups and pulled up on the blade. Pop! It flew apart.

Kenny could do whatever he wanted now. He proceeded to rape Helen and when he was finished, he stood up and dressed himself. Helen's lifeless body lay there, un-wanting of him. Kenny looked down at her and asked himself why he had done it. "Because I wanted to" he said with satisfaction. He even took pride in the fact that he was now a psychotic killer.

It was three o'clock and Kenny realized that he had to dispose of the body. He knew that his old man would pull him out of whatever he had done, but Kenny was afraid of what Foxy would say about the murder.

Kenny picked up the telephone and dialed his father's number.

"Hey, I've got something here at the office you've got to help me with."

"What is it? You sound so excited," Foxy said.

"Just come on down to the office and you'll see what the matter is. I know this is gonna be hard for you to understand. I can't explain it over the phone, so come down here. Now!" Kenny shouted.

"Okay, Kenny, I'll be there in a minute," Foxy said, confused and nervous.

Foxy had no idea that his son had been hitting on Helen. Everyone at the office always made sure they were not involved in any of Kenny's problems. His reputation for being cold and deliberate in his firing of anyone who ratted on him was Kenny's strong point.

The workers could remember one afternoon last November when Kenny had his father fire an old black lady who cleaned the office building after hours every day. Kenny had brought one of his girlfriends in through the loading dock for a quick drink and a little hanky-panky. The cleaning lady was mopping the linoleum floor in the reception area.

Kenny pulled the girl into the office. He had visions of using the couch in Foxy's office—he had nowhere else to go. This was the only place he could keep Jane from finding out about his affairs with other girls during their engagement.

When the black cleaning woman noticed them on the couch in Foxy's office she was hardly surprised, nor would she have ever told anyone, but Kenny pictured her laughing at him and his juvenile predicament. He leaped up from the couch and rushed toward her, slapping her to the freshly waxed floor. The girl Kenny was with quickly put on her clothes and hurried out through the loading dock's roll-up door.

The poor cleaning woman sat on the floor for a few minutes, then finally stood up and although in pain, she managed to finish cleaning the floor.

Early the next morning Kenny told his father to get rid of the woman; he accused her of stealing money from the office petty-cash box. The same box Kenny frequently stole money from while growing up and blamed the theft on the many fired secretaries who once worked there.

Foxy got out of his car and hurried into the reception area where Kenny was sitting in Helen's chair with his head in his hands. He slowly looked up as Foxy approached.

Foxy's eyes were wide with suspicion and fear. "What have you done, Kenny?" Foxy cried out. Kenny pointed toward the layout room. Foxy rushed into the room where the first thing he saw was the bloodied face of Helen, and then he saw the rope tied around her neck. Kenny entered the room and stood silently by.

Foxy knew his law from personal experiences with the state government in Atlanta. He even knew a little bit about the Bible. Thoughts of condemnation ran through his mind. Had God brought him to this state of horror or was it Satan that forces all evil men to face themselves?

He knelt down and felt Helen's neck to see if by some miracle there was a pulse in the cold stiff body. Foxy jerked his hand from Helen's neck and began to weep. What had Kenny done? Why was his son a murderer?

Foxy stayed crouched there for several minutes, then finally composed himself and dug deep in his prideful inner self.

Foxy had to decide whether to save the family name or turn Kenny over to the justice system. In court his name would be slandered beyond reprieve. And Kenny would be fine meat for the prison gangs up in Reedsville.

Foxy cringed at the thought of having to give up his family's legacy and his life's work for anybody, no matter how beloved this woman had been to her children and husband.

This left Foxy with the most important dilemma of his life: how was he going to get Kenny out of this and save the family fortune? He turned to his son, thinking out loud.

"Well, how should we dispose of this woman's body?" Foxy asked himself.

Foxy was true to his nickname, as Kenny knew he would be. The young man's opinion of himself was important, but the opinion of Foxy was substantially more meaningful to him. Kenny could remember hunting deer in the woods and how pleased his father was if the deer was killed quickly. One shot to the heart he would tell Kenny. He felt powerful each time he held the gun in his hand and shot a deer, sending a lead projectile through its heart and sometimes lungs. He believed his father would then give him the hug he so desperately wanted, but never received.

Kenny knew his father had acquired his nickname by being shrewd and destroying his business competitors. Kenny didn't have his father's business acumen and this failing made him wish for recognition from Foxy for anything that proved he could destroy his enemy using any method necessary. But Kenny now knew that his father would not condone the destruction of Helen Harmon.

"She made me do it," Kenny said pitifully. "She pushed herself on me, then she pulled away. It was all her fault, can't you see that?"

Foxy was only half listening. He thought his son had only temporarily lost control of himself. He wouldn't consider the possibility of Kenny being mentally disturbed.

"Kenny, you've killed a woman here. Can't you see what you've done? Our family's reputation is always at stake in this town and all businesses thrive on having a spotless name," Foxy said as tears rolled down his cheeks.

Kenny, obviously distressed, quickly snatched up the clothing around Helen and rolled them into a ball. He placed them on a counter by her desk in the reception area.

"Oh, Kenny, why? Why did you kill this woman?" Foxy asked his face now red with fury.

Erupting with anger that could only be described as a madman's tirade, Foxy grabbed up a coffee cup with his company logo tattooed across its ceramic surface. "You son-of-a-bitch! I have worked all my life to build this business."

The heavy black cup with the words Winkler Advertising written in silver paint exploded as it flew from Foxy's hand and hit a black framed plaque hung on the dark brown panelling behind Helen's desk.

"I've told you everything. Now help me save our family's reputation," Kenny pleaded.

"Kenny, this is it!" Foxy yelled. "You are the biggest disappointment of my life. If you were not my son, I'd turn you over to the police right now and let them electrocute you."

Kenny stood motionless. He wanted time to pass as quickly as possible, hoping his father would calm down enough to think clearly. Without Foxy's support, Kenny knew that he would never be able to hide what he'd done.

Excruciating moments of silence passed before Foxy finally sighed, shaking his head. "Okay, this is what we'll have to do. We'll put her in one of the gang boxes in the storage shed and figure out what to do with her later. Help me drag her to the loading dock."

Relieved that the harangue ended without his own bloodshed, Kenny jumped at a chance to move on—hoping that Foxy would eventually forgive him.

Helen's brutalized body was limp and very hard for the two men to control. Foxy didn't have much strength and Kenny had never done anything constructive with his hands. His arms were not much bigger at the biceps than they were at the elbow.

Kenny retrieved one of the gang boxes from the storage area and put it on the loading dock.

"Come on, Kenny, lift her into the box," Foxy ordered.

With much heaving and grunting, they dropped Helen into the wooden box. Her body struck the bottom with a loud thump that sounded like one of Kenny's slaughtered deer falling to the ground.

"Oh no, her legs aren't gonna get in there!" Kenny said in a panicky voice.

Foxy nodded. "Take her back out and put her in the trunk of my car. I'll have to hide her while you call the police and her husband," Foxy said.

"Where are you gonna go?"

"I'll just ride around town until I see all the police cars leave, then come back and we can get her into this box somehow," Foxy said anxiously.

Kenny took Helen under the arms as Foxy held her feet. Together they lifted her up out of the box and put her on the floor.

Foxy quickly brought his car around to the loading dock and lined the huge trunk with old paper from unused signs lying around the dock. Foxy was relieved that Helen's body didn't seem to be losing blood—Kenny had been very careful with his knife while removing her dress. The two men struggled to put Helen into the trunk, and Kenny heaved a loud sigh of relief as he slammed the trunk lid closed.

"Now, Kenny, get in there and make those calls. You need to call the hospital, too, in case they check up on us sooner than I expect they will," Foxy said.

"Okay," Kenny said, his tone patronizing as he hurried into his office. He wrote down exactly what he wanted to say to Helen's husband, Jerry. Then wrote down what he would tell the police. He hoped that Assistant Chief Adkins would answer the phone.

Adkins was a good friend of the family and would believe anything Kenny told him. He had gotten Kenny out of several jams in the past and Foxy had always thanked him with a substantial monetary gift at Christmas. Adkins wouldn't be a problem.

Kenny dialed the Harmon residence. "Uh, Mr. Harmon is Helen there?" he asked.

"No, she's not. Who is this?" Jerry asked.

"This is Kenny Winkler, down at the outdoor advertising agency where she works. We came in from our meeting in Atlanta this afternoon and she wasn't in the office. Do you have any idea where she is?"

"No, I don't," Jerry replied.

"Well, I think that you ought to come down here. I'm afraid something must have happened to her," Kenny said.

"Okay, I'm on my way," Jerry said.

Jerry hung the phone up and began to pace around the house, looking for his pistol. He finally remembered it was in the drawer of his nightstand in the bedroom. After retrieving it, he grabbed his keys and headed for his 1970 white Ford pickup truck. Granny, Helen's mother, who was staying with them temporarily, asked where he was going. She had occasionally stayed with Helen or her older brother Don while waiting for her mobile home to be installed across the road.

"I'll be back soon. Something may have happened to Helen. They can't find her at work," Jerry stated as he slammed the door on his way out.

Jerry drove fast but carefully. Having been a cop for seventeen years now, made him think of every possible angle of the situation. Knowing his wife as well as he did convinced him that she had not just walked out of the office. His fears turned to anger as he pondered the possibility of someone kidnapping her.

He thought about the previous night when they were in bed and discussing the kids' futures. Helen said that Lisa had made plans to continue her education at Valdosta Community College. But Harold was still a little young to know exactly what he wanted to do with his life. He was, she noted, much more interested in science than any other aspect of his schooling.

They talked about the chemistry sets their son had earned by selling greeting cards around town. They both chuckled lovingly, there in bed, when they thought about Harold selling anything. He was the worst salesman they knew, but he was tenacious, and thus sold enough cards to buy a microscope kit that he wanted so badly.

Jerry remembered Helen telling him she thought Polly was probably the brightest of the three. That she seemed to stay out of trouble more than Lisa or Harold. Jerry probed every word that Helen spoke the previous night, looking for some hint of what could have led to this predicament. He knew she was trying to find another job because she wanted to better her salary. The computer courses at the vocational technical school were going to waste at Winkler Outdoor Advertising. They still did their payroll and bookkeeping by hand. Was there another reason to leave Winkler?

The pickup moved along about 70 mph. It would now be a matter of minutes before Jerry arrived at Winkler and discovered that it was all a misunderstanding, he hoped.

✳     ✳     ✳     ✳

Kenny waited anxiously for Assistant Chief Adkins to come on the line. When he finally did, Kenny said calmly, "This is Kenny Winkler."

"Oh, Foxy's son?" Adkins asked.

"Yeah, that's right. I need to report a missing person."

"Who's missing Kenny? Not your father?"

"No, it's our secretary—she's run off or something. We can't seem to find her, but her car and purse are still here."

"Okay, I'll send Basset out there to look into it. By the way, how's your father?"

"He's just fine, Chief. I called her husband a couple of minutes ago, but he's in Morven and won't be here for twenty or thirty more minutes," Kenny said.

"I'll make sure Basset is on his way so you won't have to face him by yourself," Adkins said.

"Fine, just take care of it," Kenny demanded.

Adkins knew that Foxy would again ensure he was well taken care of if he kept this whole mess quiet, whatever the circumstances.

Kenny made a call to the only hospital in Valdosta. He asked if anyone had brought in a woman named Helen Harmon or even a Jane Doe during the day. Then he gave his name and business phone number in case she was to show up. Kenny had to make one more call before trying to finish the cleaning up around the office.

"Hey, honey," Kenny said.

"Hey, Kenny," Jane, his bride of three months, replied. "What time did you get back?"

"Oh, about three o'clock," Kenny answered.

"Did you stop by and see daddy?"

"Yeah, we did. Listen, I'm gonna be late getting to the reception. The old man and me have to check out a spot for a new sign on Interstate 75."

"I can't believe you're gonna be late tonight, Kenny," Jane said, sounding perturbed. "Your parents have been planning this for a long time."

"Well it's gotta be done tonight for a proposal due tomorrow," Kenny said. "I'll be there as soon as I can. Love you."

"Alright. Sure love you," Jane said, her voice melting.

# CHAPTER 3

▼

Earlier in the day that Helen "went missing," Jerry had picked up Lisa at Lowndes High because he got off work before Helen that afternoon. The ride home was usually filled with talk of Lisa's day at school, but this day was different.

"Dad, why was Mama acting so weird this morning?" Lisa asked.

"What do you mean?" Jerry asked.

"Well, she kept talking about how we should remember that our family is the most important thing in life. I know that!"

"Lisa, sometimes your parents try to explain things to you from what they have learned through their life. It doesn't always come out in the best way, but they do try," her father said.

A long stretch of silence ensued as the pickup traveled by the farms and roadside car lots. Then Lisa said, "How do parents know anymore about things than their kids? I mean, we all learn the same stuff most of the time."

Jerry glanced at his daughter with a loving smile. "It has to do with how long you've been learning the same stuff, Lisa. Parents have been learning these same things longer than their children. And believe it or not, they've seen a few more things happen than their children."

"What I'm trying to say is that Mama was acting a little funny this morning. It was as if she thought something was going to happen to her," Lisa said with genuine concern.

"I think you're just imagining things, Lisa," Jerry said, but now he too was worried.

The pickup turned onto the old dirt road. They passed between the one-acre plot and their farm when they saw Harold over by the muscadine vines. Every year Harold picked the purple and white grape-like fruits for his mother to make muscadine jelly, his favorite spread on peanut butter sandwiches.

Later on, when Jerry had gotten the call from Kenny and rushed out of the house, Harold came in with a bucket full of grapes and said to his grandmother, "Where's daddy gone to in such a hurry?"

"Your momma is missing, Harold," Granny answered in a weak and questioning voice. She couldn't think about anything but her daughter's safety, while sitting at the Harmon's staring out a set of sliding glass doors into the backyard.

"They said she left the office with nothing but the clothes on her back," Lisa added.

Polly began to cry and asked the same question all three were thinking, "Where is my momma?"

"What do you mean? Where did she go?" Harold asked.

"Nobody knows, Harold. They say she must have left the office sometime this afternoon, but nobody saw her leave," Granny said.

"She probably went down to the store," Lisa said, trying to sound casual.

Harold shook his head. "I just don't understand."

He stood behind Granny's chair looking helplessly at his sisters.

*    *    *    *

Jerry pulled into the Winkler parking lot and immediately jumped out of his pickup. He ran inside the office and found Kenny going through Helen's purse. It was a carpet-type canvas bag that held the handmade leather wallet Jerry had an inmate craft for her at the prison. Jerry also knew that the bag held her birth control pills and numerous items that made it bulge somewhat.

Between the time Kenny had called the hospital and the time Jerry arrived, he had looked frantically all over the office for a key to open the gas pump padlock. Knowing that they would need one of the company pickup trucks to carry tools to bury the box Helen's body would be laid in; Kenny had to find the pump key to fill the truck's gas tank.

Not being able to find a spare key, Kenny decided to use Helen's, but he didn't have enough time to finish looking in her purse before Jerry walked in.

"Hey! What are you doing with Helen's pocketbook?" Jerry asked pointedly.

Kenny looked up, startled. He hadn't even seen Jerry come into the office.

"Uh, well, I need to get her set of keys to the office," Kenny stammered.

"Well, don't be going through my wife's things. Let me have that," Jerry demanded as he grabbed the purse.

Jerry began looking through Helen's purse. The office keys were still in it from her trip to the post office earlier that morning. Jerry pulled the keys out and examined them as Kenny watched nervously.

"Is this where she left her pocketbook, Kenny?" Jerry asked.

"Yeah, and the rest of the office is just as we found it," Kenny replied.

Jerry's eyes narrowed. "Are these the office keys, Kenny?"

Kenny took one look at the keys and his tone immediately changed. "Yeah, this is to the gas pump and this is for the front door and uh, the other one is the key to the green pickup."

Jerry handed the keys to Kenny and continued to look through his wife's purse. He couldn't find anything unusual in it except for the four concert ticket stubs from the rock concert down at Makey Park the weekend before. Helen had taken the kids there because Jerry had to work the weekend shift and the three children loved a live rock concert, especially one that featured Beatles' music.

But Helen hadn't told Jerry anything about the concert. He remembered that she had been acting like she was in another world last weekend. He thought something must have been bothering her during the concert and she hadn't really been able to relax while she was there or she would have mentioned going.

Kenny took a deep breath and said, "I don't know where she could have gone. We tried to leave things exactly where we found them when we got back from Atlanta." But Jerry suspected Kenny knew something.

"I don't know what's going on here, Kenny, but I *will* find out," Jerry said.

Lieutenant Basset drove into the parking lot just as Kenny ended his lie. Kenny went out to meet Basset while Jerry wandered around the office trying to find any clues.

Foxy and Kenny had cleaned up any signs of a struggle in the layout room. Now there was just the purse, the car and a lot of questions. As Kenny and Basset walked into the office, Basset asked what time they had returned from their trip and a few other insignificant questions that Kenny answered quickly with lies.

Jerry knew Basset from the time he had been on the Valdosta police force and he remembered Basset was a terrible investigating officer and wondered why Assistant Chief Adkins had sent him to a case involving a missing person.

Basset walked around like Barney Fife, looking as if he already knew the answer to the case. He did a cursory inspection of the storage area and loading dock, with a quick pass of the offices. He never went around behind any of the buildings or looked into any of the vehicles that were parked in the lot. The only notes that he wrote down about the incident were on a matchbook cover that he had found in his pants pocket. The note read:

"Received a call @ 1630.

Found nothing at the office.

Suspect no foul play at the scene."

When he came back into the main office, Basset said to Jerry

"I can't find anything. Let's walk outside." He motioned for Kenny to join them.

The three men left the building and walked to Helen's car. Jerry checked the Montego's engine to see if it had been used recently, but the engine was cold and the gas gauge indicated three quarters of a tank. Jerry carefully inspected the outside of the car to see if it had been tampered with in any way. Then, to settle in his own mind that the building was clear again, he made another pass around it.

"We'll put out an APB and hope for the best, Jerry," Basset said. "Hopefully, she'll show up soon."

"Is that it? Can't we ask the people around here if they saw anything?" Jerry almost screamed.

Basset shook his head. "I don't know what good it'll do, I think she must have run off with somebody."

Jerry was stunned. Had Basset already closed the case after twenty minutes of "investigating?" Surely there had to be a detective in Valdosta that could do better than this. What Jerry didn't fully realize was that the Winkler family had money and political connections and the Harmon family did not. That made all the difference in the world to Basset and Adkins. If Kenny said she probably ran off with somebody then, by God that must've been what happened!

Jerry shouted at Basset, "You've got to be kidding! Without her pocketbook or birth control pills! A woman never goes anywhere without her purse and the car's gas tank is almost full. Why didn't they use the car?" Jerry's face was red, his eyes blazing.

"Calm down, Jerry," Basset said. "It'll just make it worse in the long run."

Basset got into his car as Jerry pleaded, "Look, just ask the people across the street. Somebody must've seen something."

"Okay, Jerry, I'll ask around," Basset finally said as he drove off.

Jerry turned and looked at Kenny who had already started walking back to the office.

Jerry took one more look through the office, and then got back into his truck and started to drive home. What would be he tell the kids was the only thought in his head.

Pulling into the gravel driveway that led to the house, Jerry looked through his dusty truck window for Helen. The greenhouse out by the shed was in full bloom this time of year and the rock gardens had been weeded last week. Everything looked as if his wife had just left and would be home in a few minutes. Maybe she just ran some errands with a friend and lost track of time. But that thought immediately evaporated because she'd never leave her purse behind.

Jerry parked the truck and went to the enclosure door on the garage. They needed the garage's space during the summer months when the garden crops were harvested, so Jerry enclosed the garage and turned it into a den. The floor was covered with indoor/outdoor carpeting and a window unit air-conditioner had been installed, which made it the most popular room in the house during the summer since it was the only one with cool air-conditioning.

The whole family would sit in the den, watch TV, and at the same time, shell and peel the vegetables they had picked that day. They spent a lot of time in the summer preparing whatever was to be canned and preserved for the winter ahead.

As Jerry walked into the den he noticed that it was spotless and the TV wasn't on. The kids must really be worried, he thought. He quickly looked around the room and he gazed at Helen's sewing machine, realizing it seemed more still than ever.

The muffled sounds of his children in the kitchen finally got his attention. He opened the den door and stepped up two stairs into the kitchen.

Everyone was still sitting at the kitchen table. Granny had made roast beef, fried okra and fried squash but neither she nor the kids ate much of anything. The food smelled delicious to Jerry, but he, too, had no appetite.

"What happened, daddy?" Lisa asked.

Jerry looked confused and sad as he sat down at the table. "I don't know, honey. She's just gone," Jerry said. "The police are looking for her now, but there aren't any clues where she might have gone or what could have happened to her."

Granny stood from her chair. "Where could she have gone? I just don't understand!"

The weather had been threatening rain all day and finally the drizzle gave way to a downpour, accompanied by thunder and lightning. It only added to the Harmon's anxieties.

"Where could she be?" Harold began to mutter to himself.

Harold was famous for muttering to himself as he left a room. He left the kitchen and went back to his bedroom, still muttering.

It was dark outside his window and the rain frogs were getting drenched. The little green varmints would eventually seek the safety of the side of the house and inevitably crawl onto the double-paned windows. They would then sit there and croak to beat the band. Harold had caught plenty of them over the last five years, but tonight he had no desire to try.

Harold sat down at his desk and cleared away some of the chemicals he had used on an experiment the day before. It included a testing of the effects of sulphur and soda combined together and wrapped in newspaper. The mixture was taken outside and set on fire with big red kitchen matches. From what Harold could remember it worked great. Smoke billowed from the paper and chemicals. The smell was atrocious—a perfect stink bomb.

Harold was bewildered. Surely God didn't want this thing to happen to him. He wrote down his thoughts on his chemical stained loose-leaf paper; the most prevailing of which was that it had to have all been a mistake. The next statement was a concept of hatred without direction. Harold tried to decide who was to blame for his mother's disappearance. The rest of the night was spent deciding what he was supposed to do with his life if his mother was gone forever.

Every thought Harold had was overshadowed by confusion. He knew there were plenty of people in the world who knew what it felt like to have one of their parents die, but was there anyone out there who knew what it felt like to *not know* where his or her parent was?

Harold's paper was soon overrun with questions, some of which had a list of answers. The answers were riddled with vague expressions of faith and prayer. Harold thought that if he could come up with a resolution to this dilemma, he would be able to sleep for a little while. Until then, however, he would not rest. Lightning cracked and thunder roared outside, while rain hammered against the asphalt-shingled roofing.

Harold turned over a page in his stack of loose-leaf paper to find a hand written note his mother had left for him earlier that week. It was a list of chores that he was supposed to complete throughout the week with each day listed separately.

He was to begin the week by watering the flowers in the yard and green house both morning and evening. Harold had completed that task last Monday. He read the next chore for Monday: pick the tomatoes. Harold loved the sandwiches Helen would make for him with luscious steak tomatoes fresh from their garden.

Tuesday's chore list: take out the trash and burn it. This was one of the easiest chores of the week—and there was something about burning trash that he really liked. He would take the small kitchen trash can out to a 55-gallon drum and dump it in. That particular drum was old and had been used for at least two months of trash. Harold had knocked several holes in the bottom of it with an axe to allow rainwater to drain.

Harold remembered this week's trash and its hairspray cans that usually came with the bathroom trash on Saturdays. The hairspray cans sounded like grenades in the big drum when they exploded from the heat of the rest of the burning trash. There had been one left over from the weekend in Tuesday's trash and Harold witnessed a special explosion.

When the hairspray can blew, the explosion caused trash fragments to spew from the can's mouth for at least ten feet. It was truly a sight to behold for Harold. Living in the country did have its advantages when you were looking for a cheap thrill.

After the hairspray can explosion, the burning trash blown from the can began to ignite the grass surrounding the drum. Harold recalled running to get a hose connected to the deep well and spraying the dry grass down to put out the many small blazes.

He looked at the list of Wednesday's responsibilities. The first thing for him to do, after watering the flowers, was to wring the red rooster's neck and pluck his feathers.

The old red rooster had been with the family for about two years now and Harold was truly fond of it, despite its temperament. He had run the rooster out of the greenhouse more than once and scolded it for eating Helen's plants. Harold even made the rooster work for him from time-to-time by having him eat tomato plant worms in the garden.

He remembered the day the rooster attacked his basketball in the backyard. The goal was located about twenty feet from the chicken coop, where all the hens usually stayed. But the rooster would come and go from the coop as he pleased.

On that fateful day, the rooster had escaped from the chicken coop again. Harold was out shooting a few baskets and occasionally the ball rolled toward the coop after bouncing off the square plywood backboard. The basketball and the chicken met by a small goldfish pond Jerry had tried to install but never finished. The red rooster decided that the orange basketball that came rolling his way was indeed the enemy, leading him to engage in combat with it, spurs fully cocked and armed. When the rooster hit the ball Harold recalled an instant of glory for the bird as it flapped its wings once. But then the explosion of the ball made him tumble topsy-turvy over himself, trying to get away from the orange nemesis.

It amused Harold to recall the scene, but he felt disappointment in losing a perfectly good basketball. On the other hand, Wednesday's other chore was not amusing whatsoever.

Harold had gotten the .22 caliber rifle from the den where it sat in a home-made gun rack. It was a single shot Remington bolt action that had sent many a squirrel to the stew pot.

He would imagine shooting a squirrel from an oak tree at that distance each time he read the label. Could anyone really shoot something at a distance of one mile? He would ask himself.

The old red rooster had it coming to him, Harold thought. But he knew that he would never get close enough to grab him and ring his neck like Helen had instructed him to do. He would use the rifle to kill him, and then throw the rooster's head far out into the peach field to hide the evidence.

He found the red rooster out of the coop as usual, pecking the grass, looking for bugs. Harold put the bird in his sights and began to follow its body up to its jerking head. He squeezed off the round in his rifle just as the bird hesitated a moment from its pecking. The round eye of the rooster had been lying perfectly in the sight when Harold's shot went off, but he seemed to duck before the projectile left the barrel of his gun.

Harold quickly looked to see where the bullet had hit the rooster. It had struck the top of his head and glanced from the sight carrying a small chunk of brain matter. The rooster flung himself violently about the yard, flapping his wings and bleeding profusely.

Harold froze for a moment to watch the unnerving action of the half dead rooster. Then he impulsively stepped over to the fowl, grabbed him firmly by the head and began swinging it in quick clockwise circles. He felt the neck give way on the third twist, but gave it one more for insurance.

The great red rooster was dead now and ready for the pot of boiling water that Lisa had heated up. Her chore list included heating the water that was used in the de-feathering process. Harold brought the pot out into the yard and dumped the bloody chicken carcass into the steaming hot water.

After all the feathers had been removed, Harold had to singe all the small hairs from the rooster's body. A piece of newspaper was lit and used like a torch under-neath the limp carcass to rid the meat of its tiny hairs.

Harold remembered carrying the chicken into their kitchen for Lisa to clean after ridding it of small pieces of paper ash left behind from the singeing process. What a disgusting sequence of events, he thought to himself. It would have been a lot easier to just run down to the J & I and buy a chicken. But Helen and Jerry both grew up doing that sort of thing and thought it best if Harold learned to do it too.

Harold put the list back under his notes and continued to write about what had happened earlier that afternoon. He thought that if he could write it all down, later on he would be able to talk about it to someone.

After he finished writing everything he could think of, Harold went over to his closet to find something to wear to school the next morning. Jerry had told him and the girls that they were going to school on Friday. He said it would help take their minds off what had happened. Harold thought that nothing could take his mind off what had occurred, not school or anything else. But he would go to school without a complaint. He knew that his dad had a lot on his mind.

He stared at himself in the mirror on his dresser for a moment. He saw a heavy-set, sun-tanned thirteen-year-old with a clean haircut. The hair was long, but it was in style and Harold wanted to fit in with the crowd.

Harold briefly thought about losing a few pounds before too much longer. He decided he would have to get himself in shape in preparation for his mother's return. She was really big on physical fitness and he wanted to show her that he had been working out while she was gone. During that moment he had subconsciously faced the fact that Helen was going to be away for a long time. He had no idea why he felt that way, but he did.

Harold thought about building a workout bench for the Sears plastic weight set that he had in the den. That would constitute some serious exercise.

"Let's see," Harold mumbled to himself, "There's enough wood under the shelter near the chicken coop to build a workout bench."

Quickly he ran back over to the desk, grabbed his pencil and drew the plans on a piece of loose-leaf paper. The bench drawing looked pretty good for the ambitious thirteen-year-old and would probably safely function for a couple of years. Harold left the drawing on top of his stack of papers that contained his inner most thoughts about his mother and got ready for bed.

He set his radio alarm clock for school, lay down and began the most power prayer he could think of—trying to remember the preacher's words from Sunday's service. "Our gracious heavenly Father. It is because of your incomprehensible wisdom that your glorious work on Earth is done. We have done so little to warrant your gift of everlasting life and the love of one as great as you, Father. It is only by your grace that we are saved from certain eternal death. However, there is one question I would like to ask you, our Father. And that is, would you please let me know where my mother is and when will she be home? Amen."

Finally, Jerry came by Harold's room and told him to turn out the light. It was midnight and there was still no word of Helen's whereabouts. Harold lay in his bed that night and the tears came. He prayed for hours to have his mother returned. Polly and Lisa cried most of the night too, but Polly cried hardest and longest. Jerry and Granny never went to bed, still hoping for some word of Helen's predicament. But there was none.

# CHAPTER 4

▼

Foxy drove to the office around 6:30 p.m. with Helen's body still in the trunk of his car. He had been driving around waiting until the "investigator" left the scene. The drive gave Foxy enough time to think about how to hide the evidence of his son's brutal crime.

The thought of turning Kenny in to the authorities wasn't part of his scenario. He just couldn't let the world know what kind of monster Kenny was or how he had failed in raising him.

Foxy drove past Five Points shopping center on the north side of Valdosta. Helen had done her shopping there for the kid's school clothes a couple of weeks earlier. Foxy rode by the fields where Helen's uncle Joey grew tobacco, then traveled on to Hahira and stopped to get a cold drink at the gas station that had once been owned by Jerry's father. Harold's granddaddy used to sit on the front stoop of the station and chew tobacco.

Jerry told Harold a story of how granddaddy had fallen asleep in his chair there on the stoop one day. The chair was kicked back into a reclining position and granddaddy was catching some serious snooze time when a "nice-looking lady" walked by. Not noticing her in his drowsy state, granddaddy leaned forward and spit chewing tobacco directly between her legs. The station's attendants were in an uproar from the comical occurrence, but granddaddy never woke up and the lady never broke stride.

As Foxy drove to Valdosta on the Hahira Road, he passed the Harmon T.V. Repair Shop that Glen, Jerry's oldest brother, had opened up many years before. Glen only sold American-made Zenith television sets and worked on vacuum tube motherboards. "Don't want to get into all that solid-state crap from Japan," he would say.

Foxy drove slowly, watching the time, until he felt it was safe to return to the office. He certainly didn't want to rush things and be seen driving by in a car that was familiar to everyone.

When Foxy finally pulled into his company's parking lot, Kenny came running out.

"Where on earth have you been?" Kenny asked.

"I wanted to make sure that the coast was clear," Foxy replied.

"Okay, let's get her into this damn box," Kenny demanded quickly.

Foxy backed the Olds up to the loading dock and opened the trunk. Helen's body was now so stiff with rigor mortis it would never fit into the wooden box they had designated as her coffin.

Father and son removed Helen's body from the trunk of the car and laid her on the loading dock floor. They grabbed the paper Foxy had used to line the trunk and burned it in an old fifty-five gallon drum. The two men then stood there on the loading dock looking at Helen for a moment.

"Okay, Kenny, you're gonna have to cut her legs off to get her body in the box. We'll never get the lid on unless you do," Foxy stated. He was all business, his voice emotionless.

Kenny nodded and reached into his pants pocket to retrieve his freshly sharpened knife. Kenny squatted beside Helen's lifeless body and slowly drew the blade across the surface of the side of her right knee joint. The skin parted and blood began to stream from her knee, eventually becoming a large puddle under her body.

Kenny had cut the flesh from around the joint of her right knee when he realized that the ligaments had to be severed before the bottom part of her limb could be removed.

"We'll have to cut them off with something else, Kenny. Get the hacksaw out of the tool room," Foxy ordered.

"Okay," Kenny replied and returned a couple of minutes later with a green-handled hacksaw.

As he severed Helen's once lovely legs just above the patella, his mind wandered to the reception that was scheduled for that night. He blocked out the loathsome act he was performing by thinking about his wife and her long, beautiful legs. He couldn't wait to get home and make unbridled love to her. Ironically, it was because the cold dead body had aroused him.

Kenny liked to simulate the coldness of the dead bodies from the morgue he still visited by making Jane take cold showers before getting into bed with him. He now envisioned Jane lying very still and cold with the same expression Helen had on her face.

After finishing the right leg by cutting the strong ligaments with the hacksaw, Kenny moved to the left leg. He performed the same operation, but much faster this time. The loading dock's concrete floor was covered with bright red blood.

"Open the box, Kenny, and let's get her in there," Foxy ordered.

Kenny, covered in blood from the elbows down, reached over and opened the box's lid.

They grabbed Helen's body, Foxy at the head and Kenny at the severed knee joints. Both men struggled to put her in the box. Eventually they succeeded and began to look around again for their next order of business. The lower parts of Helen's legs still had to be put in the box and the blood on the loading dock had to be cleaned up.

"Kenny, get the hose from behind the storage shed. I'll wrap these legs up. We can wash down this area and scrub it clean with the stiff broom," Foxy said.

As Kenny headed to the storage shed Foxy grabbed two burlap bags from the broom closet and put each leg in a bag. He placed them behind the counter of the reception area on a piece of plastic, to get them out of the blood and out of the way. Foxy noticed that Helen's clothes were still on the counter waiting to be removed. He then went over to the box, closed the lid and slid it back from the bloodied area.

Kenny returned with the pressurized hose and gave it to his father who began wetting the area down. Kenny used the stiff broom to push the water and blood from the loading dock off onto the ground.

Foxy was beginning to worry about the reception scheduled for eight o'clock that night. "We'd better hurry or we're gonna be late and questions might be asked."

Kenny, without checking, thought that his father had made the box ready to be buried. He had only glanced at it and saw that it was closed. He assumed that the severed legs and clothes were in the box, therefore, all the evidence was ready for burial.

But Foxy was in such a hurry to get rid of all the blood, he forgot about the leg segments and Helen's clothes. He went over to the box and drove two nails into the top to secure it.

Foxy planned to take the body out to one of the old trails by the airport where they used to park the work truck and put up billboards on the side of the highway. The trails ran through the woods and were easier to use than parking on the highway and taking the chance of being seen.

"Back the green truck up to the loading dock," Foxy said impatiently.

Kenny went over to the pickup and pulled the keys out of his pocket that he had reclaimed from Helen's purse a few hours earlier. He backed it close to the gas pump, unlocked the padlock on the pump handle and tossed it into the back of the truck. He was in a hurry and didn't have time to put it back on the gas pump.

Once the truck was gassed up, he pulled over to the loading dock and backed up to Helen's coffin. Kenny jumped out of the pickup and helped Foxy lift the heavy box onto the truck bed. The tailgate was let down and the two men lifted one end of the box onto the truck, then the remaining end and slid it back against the cab.

It began to rain intermittently and Kenny cursed the wet weather.

"Come on, Kenny, get two shovels and a pick. We need to bury the box out by the airport," Foxy said. Kenny hurried to the storage shed and picked up the tools. "Don't forget a flashlight, it's getting dark," Foxy yelled after him.

The tools were thrown into the back of the truck and the two men were ready to bury what they believed was all the evidence of the murder. Foxy got into the truck with Kenny and they drove off to what would be the final resting place for Helen.

It was an old logging trail used last year to put up the latest First National Bank sign. Kenny backed into the little trail as far as the truck would go, then the two men climbed out of the truck and quickly began to dig in the soft topsoil.

Occasionally, Foxy would ask Kenny if he needed a break from the digging, but Kenny shook his head. He was determined to get this over with. However, not being strong enough or in very good shape, Kenny was soon exhausted. And he had only made an outline in the ground from what they could tell. The Q-beam flashlight that Foxy held was very bright but also narrow. It wasn't as much help as they had hoped.

"I can't dig anymore, ol' man," Kenny pleaded with Foxy, who had already begun thinking of another way to get this job done. "It's just too much work for the two of us to do before going to my wedding reception tonight. Let's go get the niggers and let them dig the hole. Besides, it's raining."

The downpour had slackened to a misting rain, but another storm was on the horizon. Kenny tossed the tools back into the truck and moved through the tall grass and cocklebur bushes to reach the cab.

When the two men got into the truck they removed handfuls of the cockleburs from their pants and socks. They were quiet as they drove back, thinking of the predicament they were in. Foxy also had a new worry: the company would surely be in worse shape now that the records would have to be kept by Kenny or a new trainee who could keep up with two sets of books.

As they turned into the Winkler parking lot, Foxy noticed that the truck used by Wren and Maynard had returned. Foxy was relieved. He knew that he could trust Wren to keep whatever he had to do quiet if he told him to. Kenny backed the mud covered green truck into the loading dock.

"Okay, Kenny, here's what we're gonna do. You go get ready for the reception and I'll call Wren and Maynard at home. I'll tell them to meet us tonight around eleven o'clock here at the office," Foxy explained.

Kenny frowned. "What about there being two extra witnesses?"

"We'll pay them two niggers' salaries for the rest of their lives, with bonuses every year. They'll never have to work again and I'm sure they can live with that," Foxy said with his usual arrogance.

Kenny agreed, then walked to his car and drove home. Foxy went into the office. He immediately noticed the clothes on the counter. Suddenly struck with a sickening gut feeling he stepped around to view the leg segments in the burlap bags behind the counter.

"Crap!" Foxy said with disgust. "We forgot the legs!"

Foxy felt it was reckless to leave that kind of evidence in the office while he was at Kenny's reception. But it was the safest place he could think of in that moment of haste. Adkins or Basset wouldn't be back that night to do any more investigating in the pouring rain—he knew how lazy they both were.

Foxy stepped into his office, reached for his black rotary desk phone and dialed Wren's number. Wren answered after the fourth ring because he had already gone to bed in the rundown shack Wren called home. It was one of many built years earlier for the cotton gin workers.

The roof under which Wren, his wife and four kids lived, was rusted tin in some places and galvanized tin in others. Surprisingly, the roof had not leaked lately because of the tar Wren's boys had put on the nail holes. Foxy had given him the leftover tar from construction of the storage shed.

The house did have running water though and an indoor bathroom. Light bulbs hung from the ceiling by the wires they were connected to and an old TV sat in a corner of the big room used by the family for meals and socializing. Wren had to have a phone installed because he was on the road so often. It was costly, but he had to have it if he wanted to keep his job at Winkler Outdoor Advertising.

"Wren, this is Foxy Winkler," Foxy said.

"Yessir, Mistah Winkler, I's glad to be hearin' ya," Wren said.

"We've got some serious business to do tonight at eleven o'clock, Wren. And I need my most reliable men to help me."

"Watsever you be needin', I'll help. Uh, what is it you want to do, Mistah Winkler?"

"I need you to get Maynard and meet me at the office tonight," Foxy said.

Wren had little education and had worked for Foxy over twenty years. Maynard had worked for Foxy about fifteen years but had little allegiance to him. Foxy, however, knew that Maynard would do anything for money. Wren, on the other hand, was one generation above slavery when it came to an employer-worker relationship. Foxy knew that Wren would call Maynard and convince him to help them that night.

"Me and Maynard'll be there," Wren promised.

Foxy heaved a sigh of relief as he hung up the phone, and headed to his car, and home.

Foxy and Lydia Winkler had a beautiful, two-story house in the heart of Valdosta. Four columns supported the roof at the front of the house. The veranda on the second floor was attached to the columns from the rear. Along the edge of the veranda was an imported latticework wrought iron railing that Foxy had installed at a great expense.

Foxy arrived home and immediately went to clean up for the reception. Lydia was already dressed and had been waiting for him. She was frail and it usually took her a couple of hours to get ready to go somewhere, especially a fancy, dress-up affair.

Lydia had met her husband during his heyday of experiences with the Georgia State Legislature. She wasn't aware how he had accomplished his goals in business and it didn't matter to her. She could only see his success and wanted to be part of its financial glory. Her mother once told her, "Stay dumb, but be smart about money." She always listened to her mother.

"Where have you been, Foxy?" Lydia asked in a whiney voice.

"We hit a deer on the way out to a sign site," Foxy quickly replied.

"Looks like you cleaned him, too," Lydia said.

"Yeah, he was a real mess, but Kenny and I cleaned him as best we could."

"Well, you know you've made us late for the reception." Lydia was clearly annoyed.

"Yeah, I know. Lay out my suit, will you and shut up," Foxy said, equally aggravated.

By the time Kenny got home Jane had already left for the reception. He gathered up his bloody clothes and put them in a garbage bag as he undressed in the kitchen. The dirt and blood was caked on his pants and shirt so thick that he could hardly move without dropping some of it onto the clean floor. Once his clothes were in the bag, Kenny quickly wet-mopped the kitchen, then threw the bag in the trunk of his car to dispose of later.

Kenny showered, dressed, left the apartment and arrived at the extravagant party, being held at the local Moose Lodge, at 8:45 p.m., forty-five minutes late. Foxy and Lydia pulled into the parking lot in time to meet Kenny at the entrance.

"I guess we're a little late, but still respectable, ha!" Kenny said to his father under his breath.

Foxy whispered back, "Just talk as little as you can to the guests, but be polite tonight. We don't want to draw any extra attention to you."

They entered the reception hall and began to mingle with the guests. Kenny stayed with Foxy, while Lydia went to greet Jane and Oscar at the punch bowl. Lydia then moved on to visit with some friends.

"Kenny sure is quiet tonight, Jane," Oscar said. "Without that overbearing ego he seems almost human."

Jane looked hurt and a bit angry. "Daddy, I love Kenny, so please stop saying those things about him." With that Jane went off to look for her new husband. She knew that he was probably with Foxy somewhere and she eventually found both of them drinking and talking at the prime rib table near the bar that had a never-ending champagne fountain.

She tugged on Kenny's sleeve and pulled him politely away from Foxy. "Where have you been all afternoon? I started calling the apartment after I left around seven o'clock. I even tried calling the office but—"

"I've been running around all day, Jane," Kenny said, cutting her off.

She knew better than to push the issue. More times than she cared to remember Kenny had embarrassed her, and tonight was not the time to start an argument.

A guest suddenly waved and called out to Jane. She turned, waved back and started walking toward the guest, a smile pasted on her face. Foxy never skipped a beat as he talked to the mayor and a city councilman. His poker face never belied the fact that he had just tried to bury a woman's body in the woods. However,

Kenny looked as if he'd been slapped by a fat woman in public for making advances.

The reception lasted until ten o'clock and then guests began to trickle out. The band had played their last song and were starting to pack up their instruments.

"Let's go, Kenny," Foxy said. "Wren and Maynard are supposed to be at the office by eleven."

"Okay, let me tell Jane I've gotta finish up some urgent work at the office."

Kenny kissed his wife as he told her that he'd be a bit late getting home, but wanted her to wait up for him.

Jane finished saying her good-byes to the last of the guests and her family and was on her way home when she decided to stop off at the King of the Road lounge. She had spent many nights there during the years she and Kenny had dated. It would be like old times. A stop by the King of the Road for a little Ted Nugent and the Amboy Dukes would pass the time away until Kenny got home. Then a rendezvous with her new husband would top off the evening.

∗     ∗     ∗     ∗

The rain had worsened and most of the dirt roads in the rural areas of Lowndes County had become pits of shotgun mud—the kind that made balls of sticky goop that clung to the underside of a car or the wheel wells of a truck.

Mud on the red clay roads was different than shotgun mud. It was much slicker. The red clay would cause a car to go into a power slide—no bogging or slowing, it just slammed the car into the ditch. Many of the local routies would go out on nights like this with a case of beer and begin pulling stranded motorists out of the ditches with their four-wheel drive trucks and jeeps.

Wren and Maynard were already at the office when Kenny drove up. He got out of his car and walked into the storage shed to get more shovels and picks. He brought them to the roll-up door and then waved for Wren and Maynard to come into the loading dock. Both men got out of Wren's old Ford pickup, walked to the door and stood there in the rain while Kenny went around to open it.

The door slowly rolled up and the two black men looked inside. There sat the green pickup with the box in the back. Nothing really looked unusual to Wren and Maynard.

"My father will be here in a few minutes," Kenny told them. "We've got to bury this box out in the woods. It's pretty heavy and we need to get it buried tonight."

"Yessir, Mr. Kenny, but what fer?" Wren asked.

"Don't ask any questions and we'll make sure you never have to work again," Kenny told them.

Foxy drove up and parked near the loading dock. He lifted his umbrella as he walked toward Wren and Maynard.

"How're you men doing?" Foxy asked.

"We's doing fine," Wren replied.

"Step in here and I'll show you what needs to be done," Foxy said as he led the two men to the rear of the pickup and knocked the top of the box loose with a hammer. Foxy lifted the lid the box and motioned for the two men to look inside. They crawled up onto the tailgate and quickly looked into the box.

"I don't need no trouble like dis here," Maynard said nervously.

"Me neither," Wren said, shaking his head.

"You boys are already in trouble just for knowing this," Foxy warned. "And if I have to take care of you two, I will. Now remember that I'm gonna pay you boys the rest of your lives if you'll just do this one thing for me and Kenny."

Wren and Maynard recognized Helen Harmon. They remembered how she had always treated them with kindness. But it was the money that cleared the two men's consciences.

"Well, sure, if'n you need this here box buried, I reckon we's can do that," Wren said.

Maynard nodded. "Yeah, I reckon so. But I wants my money every week on Fridays."

"That's not a problem," Foxy said.

The men stepped off the tailgate and stood back from the truck. They were afraid of the dead woman's body, but they were even more afraid of Foxy and his friends. Wren and Maynard had grown up during a period in Southern history when the black man was used as a tool. To deny the white man was a mistake in these parts. Being told that they would be paid for the rest of their lives also gave them a little more courage.

Foxy didn't forget the severed legs this time. He ordered Wren to get the two burlap bags from behind the counter and put them in the box. Then he turned to Maynard.

"You pick them clothes up on top of the counter and ya'll throw that stuff in the box."

Wren wondered what could possibly be in the burlap bags. Then he remembered seeing Helen's body in the box, and realized it didn't have the bottom part of her legs attached.

He reached down and lifted the bags, then quickly made his way back to the truck and put them inside the box.

Foxy and Kenny had brought some work clothes with them to the office, and they quickly changed as Wren and Maynard did their jobs.

Maynard, still a little rebellious about this situation, took Helen's clothes off the counter and threw them in the back of the truck instead of into the box as Foxy had instructed. The rolled-up garments landed on top of the lock for the gas pump that Kenny had thrown in earlier that afternoon.

Foxy and Kenny returned to the loading dock. Foxy stepped up on the tailgate, dropped some other items into the box and hastily nailed the top closed.

"C'mon Wren, you and Maynard get into the truck. Kenny, you drive," Foxy yelled. The three men silently did as ordered.

Foxy closed the roll-up door behind them, and then got into his Olds to follow them to the burial site.

The rain was letting up as Kenny backed the truck up into the little logging road. The three men got out and Kenny put the truck keys in his pants pocket. The men made their way through the cockleburs to the tailgate. Wren and Maynard lifted the shovels and pick out of the truck bed. Then they began to dig the hole for the box in the same place that Kenny had started. The ground was softer now that the rain had soaked into the topsoil. As the men started digging Foxy drove up, stopped behind the truck, and got out of his car. He nodded approvingly to his son and the two black men.

When Wren or Maynard took a break, Kenny got down into the hole and continued digging. His old tattered clothes started to give way from the stress of his movements. A hole in his pants pocket relinquished the keys that had once been in Helen's purse. The keys slipped into the hole, but Kenny was digging so frantically he never realized what had happened.

"Okay, let's put it in the ground," Foxy said.

Remembering that Foxy had ordered him to put the rolled-up clothes into the box, Maynard moved slowly to their side of the truck bed. He reached over and retrieved the soaking wet clothes, not noticing that the gas pump padlock was mixed in with the clothes. He went over to the hole and tossed the items in which landed on top of Kenny's dropped keys. Not seeing the keys, Maynard kicked a little dirt over them from the edge of the hole and went back to help with the box.

Occasionally grunting from the strain, the men lowered the box with Helen's body into the ground. The box also contained the rope used to strangle Helen, and a petty cash box. Foxy shrewdly thought it would add to the mystery if there had been some property that appeared to have been stolen from the office.

"Is that it, Kenny?" Foxy asked.

"Yeah," Kenny said.

Wren and Maynard filled the hole in with the Georgia topsoil. They had worked for the last two hours and were tired, but they knew that this would be the final day of manual labor for them. Foxy Winkler and his family would always take care of them as long as they lived.

They didn't know why Kenny and Foxy had killed "Miz Harmon" and they never wanted to know. Each felt Kenny was somehow more responsible for the murder, but they agreed that it would never be talked about again.

"Alright, Wren, you and Maynard take the pickup back to the office. Kenny and me will drive in my car," Foxy told them.

As Wren and Maynard got into the truck, Maynard asked, "Wren, what you reckon hap'n to Miz Harmon that they put her in dat dare sign box? It shore is a terrible thing, ain't it? But dat's white folks fer ya."

"I ain't got no idee, Maynard," Wren said. "But we are done with working for a livin'. Dem Winklers don't want anybody knowin' about any of dis here diggin' or buryin'." He suddenly looked around frantically. "We ain't got no keys, Maynard," Wren said. "That stupid boy done took dem keys wit him!"

"Here, let me hot-wire dis thing and get us out of here," Maynard said. "This place gives me the spooks."

Maynard pried the key switch out of the dash and snatched the wires off the backside. With one swift toss he nonchalantly threw the switch into the bed of the truck. Five minutes later, the motor started and the two men drove back to the office.

The evidence was gone now and the case was just another missing-person file in the Valdosta police records.

# CHAPTER 5

▼

The following day Harold slowly got out of bed. Granny had already cooked their breakfast and was sitting at the table with her morning coffee. She had made her usual eggs, ham, huge biscuits and red-eye gravy. It looked really good to Harold, because he hadn't eaten since yesterday at lunch. And he had only picked at his food.

Granny always cooked plenty when she cooked meals. Probably because she had raised four farm boys and a big eating husband. She had fried a dozen eggs and baked fifteen biscuits, enough to feed everyone twice.

Polly and Lisa began their morning ritual: hair, makeup and clothes selection. Lisa always got to the bathroom first and today was no exception. Both girls slept in the same room, with all their things separated evenly in their own closet. They shared the only mirror in the room, which was on Lisa's dresser. But more often than not, Lisa camped out in the bathroom, leaving Harold little time to wash his face.

Harold's clothes matching was easy enough—his mother always separated the clothes and put them in their respective drawers. She had just done the washing on Wednesday so his task of matching was simple.

"Morning Harold," Granny asked as he came into the kitchen. "Did you sleep any last night?" Harold shook his head. "Your daddy and me never went to bed. He's already gone to the police station this morning looking for that Basset character. I think he wanted to go back out to the Winkler office and search for some more clues."

"Where do you think she is, Granny?" Harold asked as he sat down.

"I don't know, Harold. Let's just eat and carry on with our usual chores today, okay?" Granny said and drank her coffee.

Lisa and Polly came in and sat down at the breakfast table, which gave Harold a chance to hit the bathroom.

"Have they heard anything yet?" Lisa asked Granny.

"No, honey, not yet," she replied.

Lisa looked sad and disappointed. Polly began to cry again and couldn't eat her breakfast.

"Polly, you need to eat, honey," Granny said.

"I can't eat, Granny. I miss my momma," Polly whimpered.

Granny wrapped her arm around Polly and tried to comfort her while Lisa finished her breakfast. Lisa was determined to stay strong and try not to cry anymore. It had been a long night for the two girls—when one had stopped crying, the other one had started.

As a grandmother, Granny was best at comforting younger children; her ability to communicate with teenagers was obviously less honed. Spending her life with little education, other than what she had learned from her mother while growing up on a backwoods farm. She felt somewhat intimidated by how quickly Lisa could think through problems, solving mathematical equations with a general ease. But Granny loved her only daughter with an eternal love, and grieved over Helen from the moment she disappeared.

Harold gathered his notebook and school books from his room and with his sisters, climbed into the Montego. Granny drove the children to school, but Harold, Lisa and Polly knew that this arrangement was not going to last much longer.

The clouds were hanging low again and only added to gloom that fell on Harold, his stomach aching from sleepless fatigue. Depression for him was a new and terrible feeling. To make matters worse, Harold was now in a new school located in Quitman, adding another hour bus ride from Morven.

Harold got off the bus and walked to his first class with his eyes steadfastly focused on the ground. As he sat down at his desk the room began to fill with loud excited sounds. It was the first week of school and friendships lost during the summer were being rekindled.

Eighth grade classes were not going to be difficult for Harold—he'd always done well in school, and was especially good in science. He loved playing with chemicals and creating the desired effect. By the time the rest of the class had reached the experimental problems, Harold had already found their solutions and was working on another "great chemical discovery."

Harold thought no one knew of his trauma from the events of the day before and he wasn't going to talk to anyone about it. Even his old girlfriend from last year, Lynn Wilson, wouldn't get it out of him. He would have told her any secret in his heart last year, but this year was different.

Harold went to his first class and saw Lynn sitting at her desk. A strange feeling came over him. He remembered writing letters to her all summer; each one drenched in puppy love statements of how he couldn't wait to see her again. But today, Lynn somehow looked different and all he could do was give her a little wave. Today, the only thing Harold cared about was whether he would ever see his mother again.

By the end of class Harold had loosened up enough to chat with a few of his buddies from Morven. It was then that one of the boys said, "I heard about your momma last night," His parents had told him that Harold's mother was missing.

"Yeah, we haven't heard anything yet," Harold said.

"Well, she'll be comin' home soon. Don't worry," the boy said, trying to sound encouraging.

Subjects changed so rapidly that Harold only heard part of what everyone was saying. His mind wandered back to last night's vigil. He hoped that his next teacher would have a message for him to go to the office for a phone call. Jerry would be on the other end of the line telling him that Helen was alive and well and back home.

Lunch was the event of the day for the kids in junior high. They had forty-five minutes to eat and hang around outside the lunch room talking to their girlfriends, boyfriends or whomever they wanted to.

Harold ate his pizza and fries, and left the lunch room. The kids outside had already gathered into their peer groups. Harold didn't know his peer group yet. Was there anyone there with a missing mother he might talk to? Probably not, he thought.

Harold found his friend Jack playing football behind the shop building with a gang of hoodlums. He watched the game, hoping it would be a distraction from his intolerable thoughts.

What good are your friends if you can't talk to them he asked himself. It was at that moment when Harold began to lay the foundation for a brick wall around his feelings. He thought that he could build a wall high enough and thick enough to prevent the most diligent intruder from entering his thoughts. It wasn't as hard as he thought it would be; it felt natural under the circumstances.

Harold finished out his day with a Social Studies class and band practice. He had learned to play the saxophone fairly well and would begin playing with the marching band soon. At three o'clock Harold rode the bus from Quitman to Morven for the bus exchange. The long drive on roads that were still muddy from the rainstorm the night before gave Harold too much time for his fears and sadness to wash over him again.

The Harmon driveway was full of cars, more than Harold had ever seen at his home. His heart began to pound and he started to sweat as he hurried through the front door.

In the den he saw his mother's brothers and Granny, as well as close family friends who lived in Morven and had come over to find out what they could do to help.

"Hey, Harold, how was school?" his uncle Hugh asked.

"All right, I reckon," Harold replied.

"Polly, how was school for you today?" her uncle Don asked.

"Just fine," Polly replied.

The presence of Helen's brothers and their families made Harold very uneasy. He liked all his uncles, each were characters out of the old country farm scenes he read about in school, but today he felt confined and isolated in his own house.

Harold realized it was comforting when relatives came over; some even brought food and cleaned up a little. But since no one there could explain the feelings he was now experiencing, their visit seemed irrelevant—a well intentioned but futile gesture in comforting him.

Harold left the den and made his way through the kitchen full of aunts and cousins and escaped to his bedroom. If only he could stay there and do homework until everybody left, distracted by his chemicals and telescope until his mother came home. Maybe she just lost her memory like people with amnesia, and was wandering around Valdosta. Isn't anyone looking for her?

Harold's thoughts turned gruesome. Maybe his mother was lying somewhere, bleeding to death after being taken prisoner in some kind of unrelated crime. There must be some reason the Winkler business would be robbed. The robbers might have taken her captive and the Winklers not reported the theft. The fears that reeled through Harold's head intensified with each passing moment, until he had to get out of his bedroom or go crazy thinking about what could have happened to his mother. He grabbed the drawing he had made of the bench he wanted to build and headed to the shed. Polly was outside by the old shed where he had decided to take refuge. She had already been told to go out and play while the grownups discussed important things, things she didn't need to hear.

"Polly, why do you think everyone is still here?" Harold asked as he reached for a board and some nails.

"I don't know, but the grownups are gonna find out what happened and tell us later," Polly stated with confidence.

Harold searched the shed and found two boards already nailed together that would make the perfect horizontal platform for his exercise bench.

"Who brought momma's car home?" Harold asked.

"I think one of the policemen inside did; at least that's what I heard Granny tell Aunt Alice," Polly said. "Her pocketbook is still at the police station."

Harold nailed a couple of two-by-four boards to the horizontal platform to make the uprights. Then put two short two-by-fours at the other end to make the horizontal piece level. Once all the legs were on the bench, he cut a V-shaped notch in each upright section with a hand saw.

"I'm glad Uncle Hugh came," Polly said.

"Yeah, me too. Everyone else too, I guess," Harold said.

"You think momma would have left us without telling us where she was going?" Polly asked as she jumped from stone to stone in Helen's flower garden.

"No, I don't," Harold replied.

"Then what happened to her, Harold?" Polly asked as she stopped jumping.

"I don't know," Harold replied, exhaling deeply.

"Momma is gonna come home, I just know it," Polly insisted as she smelled the roses she and Helen had planted the previous spring.

"Who did you see at school today, Polly?" Harold asked, moving his workout bench into the light to get a better view of his work.

"Oh, Rhonda and Iva," Polly replied a little excited. "But who is gonna help me with my homework now?"

"We can work on it together, I know a little bit about your stuff," Harold said. "Just ask me if you have a problem and I'll try to help you, okay?"

"Yeah, okay."

Harold and his little sister stayed out of the house and played together around the shed for the rest of the afternoon. Cousins came and went, but by the time supper was ready everyone had left except two of Jerry's sisters. Both aunts tried to show Lisa how to cook fried chicken, hoping to take her mind off Helen's disappearance. Lisa felt the way Harold and Polly did except she had the added burden of being the oldest and was expected to cope with the problem like an adult.

When Jerry came home, his sister Edna took one look at him and ushered all three children into the living room. Jerry slowly came in with a solemn, tear-stained face. Harold, Lisa and Polly stared at their father, uncertainty and fear in their eyes.

"You kids are gonna have to take on a lot more of the responsibilities around here now," Jerry said, trying to keep his voice steady. "Your momma may never come back. I hope that she will, but chances are looking pretty slim. We have all our family with us to help, but the chores of daily living rest with each of you."

Jerry flicked at a tear and cleared his throat. "Harold, you'll take care of all the outside work and help around the house when Lisa needs it. Lisa, you'll have the responsibility of running the house like your momma ran things.

"And Polly ..." Tears began streaming down Jerry's face. His voice faltered.

Edna put her arm around her brother. Another sister, Laverne, made a motion for the kids to leave the room. Jerry broke down and cried. Unpractised as he was, his tears flowed like the Colorado River in June. His wife had just disappeared off the face of the earth. He couldn't understand why it was happening to him. Jerry felt overwhelming confusion and pain.

Had he sent her into the arms of another man, with such frantic excitement that she left her entire family behind? He could not believe that. Jerry also doubted that he could keep his head above financial water—he had depended on Helen's income. He felt an ineffable sadness that she was probably dead, which he was sure was the only way she would ever leave her children.

Harold could sense the pain in his father, deeper than he had ever seen pain in another human being this close to him. He had been herded into the den with Polly and Lisa where they sat while everyone else stayed with Jerry in the living room.

"Lisa, how are we gonna do everything around here without momma?" Harold asked.

"Listen, Harold, Polly, we're a family and daddy needs us to help him hold his world together. Now, start helping out all you can 'cause momma would want it that way," Lisa said in a shaking voice.

"Lisa, you know that I'm gonna help with everything I can do," Polly cried. "But I miss momma so much!"

"Just remember, Polly, we're always gonna be together," Harold said, suddenly confident. "Daddy said that we'll stay in this house and things'll be tight but we have enough money to live as a family."

Everything calmed down, eventually and the relatives left, including Granny who went to stay with her son Stan, Helen's favorite brother. Jerry and the three children sat down together at the dining room table—down to the fried chicken dinner that Lisa had helped Granny to prepare earlier.

In the early evening the police arrived to question the Harmon children. They were trying to find out if Jerry had been mean to Helen or had ever hit her. The kids answered all their questions with an emphatic "no."

In the following days, Harold's responses when asked about his mother's disappearance were always, "I don't know" or "we haven't heard anything from her." It was his reply to everyone's questions pertaining to Helen's whereabouts. What else could he say? He wondered.

The children were longing to talk to someone about the incident, but no one in Morven was a psychologist. Besides, Jerry didn't believe in psychology. No, his children would be okay. He could minister to their needs, he thought.

*         *         *         *

Helen's brothers Don, Stan, Carl and Hugh, had families of their own, but she was still their baby sister. Each one loved her very much and wanted desperately to find an answer because their vengeance was undirected. They decided to put up a $5,000 dollar reward for any information that might lead to Helen's whereabouts. They had contacted the local television stations to help them get her picture into public view.

The next day a group of volunteers came to the Harmon house with Helen's brothers. They consisted of firemen, policemen and friends of Jerry's. A search pattern was established: each group had an area around Valdosta to look for Helen's body. Jerry was asked to stay home, to be the "base" for the search parties—utilizing his military and police background to their fullest.

Harold was asked by Stan and Hugh to go with them on the search. He was ecstatic about being able to finally do something. The boy wanted to search every corner of Georgia for his mother.

The two men and Harold drove Stan's pickup to the east end of Valdosta and began slowly traveling down every dirt road, stopping to look in dumpsters and creek bottoms at the bridges along the roadside. Harold got out to open a few dumpsters, which was frightening for him, but he knew he needed to do it.

The men searched for two days but they couldn't find any sign of Helen's body. The road Foxy and Kenny had chosen out near the airport, was traveled by the group, but they never saw any of the tracks leading down to the old logging road where her body was buried.

Several television newscasts covered the story, and there were many newspaper articles, all asking for information about Helen Harmon. The story had reached as far north as Atlanta and as far south as Jacksonville, Florida. If only Foxy and Kenny hadn't covered their tracks so well.

School and work started back on Monday. The search had stopped and would be resumed the following weekend. Volunteers from all around Georgia would search for several weekends, to no avail.

∗        ∗        ∗        ∗

Along with the tragic disappearance of his mother, which was driving Harold crazy, he was also dealing with the onset of puberty. Harold had decided that he was really interested in girls and that he could use them to block out some of his soul-destroying grief.

But it was an elementary school geography teacher who had sexually intruded on Harold's life back when he was in the seventh grade. Harold was aware of Samuel Murdock's existence the summer before in Morven but only a few kids were invited to visit Murdock in his two-story wooden framed house near the school. A classmate of Harold's, Evan Foster, had been one of those few that summer, along with some other "in town boys."

As the school year progressed Evan and other boys began to congregate at Murdock's house after school and on weekends. Harold wanted to know how anyone could get that friendly with a twenty-four-year-old teacher. To him teachers were just one small step below parents in authority.

One afternoon Harold, Evan and a couple of the other boys went over to Murdock's house. He had remodelled it in a strangely appealing antebellum style—ivory paint outside and gardens perfectly trimmed. He had created a secluded retreat for himself in the small town of Morven to which he had recently moved.

Inside Murdock's house, the wood panelling and high ceilings created an atmosphere that appealed to the boys. Santana records were stacked near the cheap stereo, along with a few strange looking water pipes; the kind you see in Turkey or India, not Morven.

Harold thought the house was "a neat place" but didn't understand why a teacher showed so much interest in this group of boys.

Murdock brought the boys into a back room, off his kitchen, that was filled with toys from all over the world. He picked up a few toys, explaining their function, then made a few unnatural jesters with a balloon. Harold began to withdraw.

"Feel the balloon, Harold. It has a wonderful texture, doesn't it?" Murdock asked.

Harold reached out and touched the balloon.

"Uh, yeah, I guess so," he replied uncomfortably. "Look, I've got to get home."

Before Harold left Murdock invited him and the other boys to go on a river camping trip the next weekend. Camping was Harold's favorite pastime and he didn't want to miss a chance to go with his closest friends. He couldn't wait for the weekend to arrive

After school on Friday, Harold drove his father's old Ford pickup, along with his friend Levi, to the river using back roads and cutting through fields. Like most very young farm boys in Georgia, Harold had already learned to drive tractors, trucks and small motorcycles. Harold and all his close friends prided themselves in community leniency when it came to underage driving around the Morven area in old farm trucks.

They met everyone at a sandbar on the river, where Murdock had already put up his eight-man tent. A campfire had been started and several boys were sitting around it talking about their day at school.

"Hey, ya'll, we finally made it! What a crappy road that was gettin' down here, it was full of potholes and sand pits," Levi exclaimed.

"Man, you guys are just in time, Murdock is going to take us skinny dipping," a boy named Tim shouted.

Harold thought to himself that he didn't want to go skinny-dipping, but he wasn't about to chicken out and never be able to camp out with "the boys" again.

The next hour was spent running naked up and down the river. It was only knee deep during certain times of the year because of the dry weather. The water was a translucent blackish color, cool and inviting to the romping boys.

Eventually Harold and Levi came back to the campsite, leaving the other boys to play. Harold didn't feel comfortable without any clothes on; besides, people fished these river waters late in the afternoon—a boat might be coming up the river at any moment.

When Tim and another boy got back to camp, Levi and Tim began to talk, moving away from the tent and campfire. Harold couldn't hear what they were saying but knew something was wrong.

When everyone had eaten their hot dogs Levi came over to Harold. "Hey Harold, you know what Murdock did to Tim?" Levi whispered. "He grabbed his private place!"

"Aw, get outta here, Levi. Nobody is that gross, man," Harold whispered back. He kicked some dirt into the river.

"I'm serious, Harold, that's what he told me. You know what else? Evan told me Murdock was a queer."

"Really! What are we gonna do tonight? There's only one tent," Harold said panic in his voice.

"Just watch out. And if something happens, yell out," Levi said.

Harold had never been exposed to a child molester before and didn't realize that Murdock was dangerous. Each boy tried to shrug off the idea that Murdock might attack one of them during the night and felt that as a group they could handle anything that he might do. However, Murdock exploited the boys' closeness.

The boys yelled and ran around until midnight before crawling into their sleeping bags, trying to enjoy themselves by ignoring the problem. Unfortunately, Tim had put his sleeping bag on one side of Murdock and Levi was on the other when they arrived that afternoon.

Waking up after dawn the next morning, Harold discovered that everyone had already left the tent. He took for granted that they were swimming in the river, so he quickly got into his cut-off jeans and made his way down to the spring.

An underground stream ended very near the campsite creating an 80-foot deep hole. Its water that flowed into the river was crystal clear and ice cold. The air temperature was a pleasant 85 degrees and just right for swimming. Tim, Levi and Evan dove into the spring water.

"Hey, where's Murdock?" Harold yelled.

"Oh, Anthony and him went up river fishing. I think," Tim shouted.

Evan climbed out of the water and came over to where Harold was standing by the spring.

"Anything happen last night, Evan?" Harold asked.

"Yeah, I think something happened to Tim."

"What was it?" Harold asked.

"I'm not sure, but I think he tried to feel him again last night," Evan said.

"What did Tim do?"

Levi joined the conversation, ice-cold water dripping from his hair.

"He said that he rolled over and made him stop," Evan said.

"Murdock tried to feel me too," Levi said.

"What's wrong with this guy?" Harold asked. "I'm gonna find Anthony."

Harold ran up the sandy old road looking down the embankment toward the river. The further he ran the higher the ground was above the river. Trees had grown along both sides of the bank between the road and the black water river, but Harold could still see the water churning from his viewpoint high above its surface.

Suddenly Harold was staring in shock at what he now saw. Anthony and Murdock were lying on one side of the bank facing the river; they never heard Harold's approach. Murdock had pulled Anthony' pants to his knees and was playing with his penis. Harold froze in his tracks.

He tried to think of a way to get their attention without letting them know how long he'd actually been there. He had moved back only far enough to be out of view, but if he tried to go back down the trail, he'd be seen.

Harold decided to throw a clump of dirt into the river just down the road and continue to throw one every few feet or so. That way they would think he was coming this way for the first time. It sounded like a good idea—in his head.

Harold made his first two throws and called out to Anthony. But he was too close with the last toss and saw them as they turned around to see who was there.

Harold jumped back out of sight and yelled, "I'll see ya'll back at the spring. We're all ready to go."

He knew that this would never be something he and Anthony could talk about, yet he wanted to tell Anthony that his secret was safe. The shame and completeness of Murdock's intimidation kept the boys from reconciling their feelings. Maybe one day the two boys would grow to be men and face that problem, but not while they were young.

Harold and Levi had loaded everything in the old Ford by the time Anthony returned to the camp. With few words passing between them, Anthony packed his things and Murdock pulled down the tent.

It was almost Christmas before everyone learned that Murdock was leaving town. Somehow the Board of Education had gotten word of some other kids being fondled by Murdock and they asked him to leave. Evan was extremely upset about the matter and tried to get Harold and the other boys to stand up for Murdock, but no one did.

Although Harold never said anything to Evan, he did think it was strange that his friend was so anxious to keep Murdock in the school. But he liked Evan and didn't want to question his motives.

＊　　　＊　　　＊　　　＊

Three months had passed since Helen's disappearance. Neighbors stopped coming over and the family would only visit on Sunday afternoons occasionally.

Harold became withdrawn. He just wanted to hang around with a few of his closest friends and that left him spending a lot of time with Evan and a new friend, Randy, who had recently moved to Morven.

Harold and Evan never knew exactly where Randy's parents were—he and his mentally retarded brother were living with their aunt Juanita in her trailer.

One day after school Evan invited Randy to play chess with him.

"Yeah, sure, Evan," Randy said, then joked, "but you know I'll just beat you again." Evan was not as good a chess player as Harold and Randy, but he loved to try and win a game.

Evan knocked on the door of Randy's aunt's trailer—he could hear Randy rumbling around inside.

"Whoa!" Evan yelled as Randy opened the door. There stood Randy with a 38-special in his hand. Evan was frozen to the spot and wide-eyed.

"Check this out, Evan," Randy said, showing Evan the gun butt first.

Evan took the gun from Randy and stepped inside the very unkempt trailer.

"Man, where'd you get this beauty?" Evan asked as he admired the varnish that made the gun shiny.

The gun felt heavy in Evan's hand. It was hard to control its bulk, yet it gave him an awesome sense of power. Evan swung the gun toward Randy. The hammer had been drawn back. It was a dangerous position and Evan knew it, but he felt he was only playing a joke on Randy.

Randy had leaned over to retrieve the chessboard which was stored under his aunt's sewing machine. Randy turned around with the chessboard in hand and saw Evan on the couch with the gun pointed right at his head.

"Come on, Evan, stop playing around with that thing. Besides, it's not even loaded," Randy said.

"Didn't it scare you though? I mean even though there are no bullets in the gun it still gives you the willies, don't it?" Evan said as he lowered the gun and un-cocked the trigger.

"Here, give me that thing and I'll show you what scared really means," Randy replied as he took the gun from Evan and turned to the bookshelf where Juanita kept it and the bullets.

Randy took out a box of solid point 38's and put one into the chamber. He then spun the chamber like an actor in a film about to play Russian roulette.

"What do you think of this?" Randy sneered as he wheeled the gun toward Evan's head and quickly pulled the trigger.

Randy turned back around to the bookshelf and opened the loading latch of the gun. Five empty chambers stared at him with expected gleam in the light.

The one chamber with the .38 shell somehow looked very queer—not only was it full but the firing pin had also made a small round indention in the end of the casing. Randy loaded five more live rounds into the gun, hoping that the used round would somehow change its present state. Closing the loading latch Randy turned around to see Evan's expression.

Randy had never heard the gun go off nor seen the explosion on the back of Evan's skull as the bullet exited his brain. The expression Randy saw was a blank stare from crystal blue eyes. A hole in Evan's forehead had the blackness of a horrible cavity.

Randy fell to his knees and begged Evan to hold on, but Evan was already dead. Randy ran into the yard, across the road and to the old principal's house. He frantically beat on the door and yelled for help, sobbing. The old principal's wife came to the door and in seconds Randy spilled the whole story, and then ran back to the trailer, but he couldn't go back inside.

The principal's wife called the Morven police and the sheriff's office in Quitman. The police were there in a matter of minutes. Randy stayed in the front yard of the trailer, pacing back and forth. He was crying and praying that what had happened was all just a crazy dream.

The Morven cop was new to the town and didn't know the boys that well.

What happened, son?" the cop asked Randy.

"I killed Evan. I didn't mean to, the gun just went off," Randy replied, wringing his hands and pacing the little yard.

The cop went into the trailer and made his way down its hall past the messy bedrooms. He found Evan lying on the sofa in the living room, his head hung lifelessly over the back of the couch and against the wall. A window just to the left of his body was covered with blood. The cop tried to find a pulse but knew instantly there was no need for CPR.

He left the trailer and went back to his patrol car, radioed the Brooks County Sheriff to come to the scene. But the sheriff was already on his way, and the principal's wife had already called the hospital to send an ambulance. The cop got out of his patrol car and went over to Randy. He was afraid that Randy would try to kill himself if he couldn't calm him down.

The sheriff arrived shortly and brought Randy's aunt with him. She tried for hours to calm the boy down, but to no avail. The sheriff suggested Juanita call one of Randy's friends; maybe if he could talk to someone about the incident he might calm down. Juanita agreed and immediately went inside and dialed Harold's phone number.

Darkness had fallen over the Harmon farmhouse—encouraging crickets and frogs to launch into their nightly concert. Harold slowly made his way to the phone as it rang. He listened to Juanita as she cried and told a horrified Harold what had just happened.

Harold immediately drove the two miles to Juanita's trailer. Pulling into the driveway he could see Randy sitting in the back seat of the sheriff's white car. Juanita and the sheriff hurried over to Harold, who had just gotten out of the pickup.

"Harold, I know you're friends with Randy and that you were close to Evan, too," the sheriff began, "and Juanita felt that you would be the best person to call because of the hardships you've tolerated the last few months. You could really help Randy if you would just ride up to the gas station with him. Evan's body is still in the trailer and we need to get Randy away from here while we remove him. We can't get a straight word out of Randy, just a bunch of mumbling and praying."

"Okay, I'll try to calm him down," Harold said. "He really looks shaken up though."

Harold climbed into the back seat of the sheriff's patrol car next to Randy.

"I'm glad to see you, Harold," Randy said. "Evan is dead and I killed him. I can't believe what I've done. The gun was in my hand when it went off and I turned around to see Evan lying on the sofa. Dead!" Randy started sobbing and moaning.

"Try to calm down, Randy. The sheriff needs to know exactly what happened," Harold said as the patrol car pulled out of the driveway.

"Well, one minute we were talking about guns and how dangerous they were and the next he was laying there with the most distant look you have every seen in a person's eyes," Randy cried as he buried his head in his hands. Harold put an arm around Randy's shoulder.

"Hey, Randy, you remember all those Friday nights we used to go over to Valdosta and skate? Do you remember how the blisters kept us from walking right for two or three days?" Harold asked.

The question sounded feeble as Harold listened to himself ask it, but miraculously, Randy responded and continued the conversation until they reached the gas station.

"Randy, what really happened today?" Harold asked bluntly.

"I think it was an accident, Harold; I mean, it just went off," Randy said.

They sat at the gas station with the sheriff and Randy went over the story again, this time conscious of what he was saying.

"Okay, boys, we'll go with what we've got," is all the sheriff would say as they drove back to the trailer.

Harold left there feeling sorry for Randy, but he also knew that his friend Evan, had lost his life that day. The thought of a person dying was foreign to Harold because he wanted it that way. He could not possibly think of his mother as being dead.

When Harold got home he went straight to his room and prayed for Evan, then thought about how great it would be to see his friend and mother in heaven. Harold had not been to church in a couple of months and was beginning to think about going again.

Evan and Harold had been friends since the fourth grade, so Evan's mother asked Harold to be one of the pallbearers for his casket. Without hesitation Harold agreed.

The funeral took place on a rainy Thursday. Clouds were suspended from the blackened sky, low and threatening when the hearse brought Evan's casket to the church. His sisters wept openly and inconsolably while Evan's mother and father were numb with grief, but held themselves together during the somber event.

After the service, Harold helped lift the casket from the church table and place it in the hearse. Until then he had been able to stay the tears, but now he couldn't hold back any longer. Somehow the sobbing for his close friend was easing his own never ending sadness. Finally, he could release some of his pent-up pain in public.

Randy attempted to attend Evan's funeral, but collapsed while walking from his aunt's car to the Baptist church. The mental institution near Valdosta said he was suffering from suicidal tendencies—his aunt Juanita had placed him there under observation for several weeks.

Grieving Evan's death was a feeling Harold could understand but the disappearance of his mother couldn't yet justify mourning because they still didn't know what had happened to her. Nor could the abuse of his friends by the sexual pervert who had molested them be recognized. Harold mourned all the things that had happened to him recently—a soul-cleansing that lasted several minutes—while the funeral procession was forming.

At the gravesite Harold regained his composure. Knowing that he would someday see both his mother and Evan in heaven made him feel better. His faith had helped him realize that there was life after death and if his mother were dead, he would see her again. The casket was lowered into the grave and the family left for home. Harold stood there for a while, hoping that this was all a bad dream and he would soon wake up.

The sheriff presented Randy's case to a tri-county judge when his court date finally came around. Ruled an accident, Randy was released and lived with his aunt a very short time before she signed for his early enlistment in the U.S. Army.

On the way home from Evan's funeral Harold thought about getting right with God. But then he remembered why he had stopped going to church in the first place. Jerry didn't like the way people looked at him and asked him every Sunday about Helen. The Valdosta Police Department released their version of what had happened to the media shortly after Helen's disappearance. When word got around that the police thought Helen had run away with someone, Jerry was gradually blamed by the community for his wife's untimely departure.

Jerry had given up the search for Helen and was deeply disappointed and hurt that people blamed him for what had happened. Little by little, he was building his own walls of defense, one of which blocked out the church and God's guidance, taking his children with him.

He would tell Harold, "Those people down there gossip more than they learn about the Bible." Harold didn't quite believe this, but how could he disagree with his father. It was the same for Polly and Lisa and so, eventually, the children stopped going to church once Jerry stopped taking them.

The first Christmas crept up on the family of four. All the magic was gone from what had always been a wonderful holiday. Granny had left them just before Christmas. She packed up her trailer across the road and took off without even telling Jerry she was going. Living on the Grantham home place without her daughter was too sad for her. She cried constantly.

Christmas Eve came upon the Harmon household with presents as always, only this year they were only from daddy. The famous fruitcake that Helen loved to bake and enhance in her own way was replaced with one from the Piggly Wiggly market.

The meal that Lisa and Jerry prepared for Christmas dinner contained everything Helen would have cooked. Turkey, green beans, potato salad, fried squash, fried okra and store bought rolls. The vegetables were the frozen ones that Helen had put up the summer before and still reminded everyone at the table that her spirit was there.

The meal began with Polly asking the blessing. She had asked the blessing ever since she started talking. The food was passed around and eaten, but not much conversation accompanied the clicking of the knives and forks as the Harmon Christmas dinner ran its course.

The table was cleared and the dishes were washed by Harold and Polly. The meal was concluded and what everyone had dreaded was now over.

# CHAPTER 6

▼

"Come on, Frank, push!" Harold yelled as the barbell slowly moved upward from his friend Frank's chest.

The wooden bench Harold had constructed began to creak and moan but held its ground. The lockout at the top of the push came at last and Frank racked the weight.

"Man, Harold, this is a lot like work! The weight feels good though, kinda like pushing an accelerator on a 454 with a six-pack, y' know?" Frank exclaimed.

Harold and Frank had been doing bench press exercises for the last half hour. Both boys were feeling the burn of the lactic acid pumping through their veins.

"Yeah, man, I known exactly what you mean," Harold replied.

Harold positioned himself under the barbell. He gripped the weight with an intense hold that expressed his attitude for getting the job done. He began his "psyching up" deep breathing. The steel bar felt good in his hands.

"Give me a lift-off, Frank," Harold gasped.

That was Harold's last command before powering into the bar with all his impact strength. The metal bar and concrete-filled plastic weights moved off the uprights swiftly. Harold lowered the weight to his chest with slow and methodical struts. Every fiber in Harold's pectorals and frontal deltoids began to flush with the issuing blood with each upward movement. Soon Harold's muscles began to scream for relief. Yet he insisted that they do one more bench press movement. The bar lowered to Harold's chest and he began to push from the pit of his hatred for whatever it was that caused his mother to disappear.

Harold was fatigued but determined. "I've got it," was all he could grunt.

"Okay man, push it," Frank replied.

The bar moved through his breaking point into his lockout position. Finally, his arms were completely extended. He relaxed.

"Alright!" Frank yelled.

"Yeah, I'm okay," Harold replied.

Each boy felt weight-lifting would help them achieve their goals. Frank was trying to get in shape for his summer job, delivering refrigerators and washing machines.

Harold, on the other hand, wanted to be able to overpower other players on the football field. He was going to play first-string football and nobody was going to keep him from doing what he came to do.

He worked hard in spring practice just to keep up with the guys who knew all the right moves required to tackle and block in those cumbersome pads. After it was over he had decided that he wouldn't be pushed around in the fall when the games started. After all, he was now six foot two, weighing in at about two hundred and fifteen pounds. And all wall-to-wall muscle now that he had been watching his diet and paying attention to his exercise regimen. He had even begun to run through the nearby peach fields, making laps around the field until his sides split with cramps.

The bench in the den had been used at least once or twice a week for the last two and a half years. By the spring of 1975 he and Frank were lifting every other day, ensuring Harold wouldn't have much trouble keeping up with the boys on the football field in his first year of high school.

"Well, Frank, what are you gonna do tonight?" Harold asked. "It's Tuesday and everything around here will be dead, as usual."

"I reckon we can ride up to Quitman again. Some of that old crowd'll be hangin' round. Yesterday I heard people were hangin' out at the courthouse again," Frank replied.

"I guess we can get a couple of eight packs and nail signs from Hahira to Quitman," Harold said.

The two boys had been notorious for hitting road signs with beer bottles while speeding down the highway. It had taken them awhile to perfect the technique, but Harold was especially good at it. He had practiced hitting signs on his dirt bike with Jack back in the ninth grade. Hitting them now from a car window was not really much different.

Frank would cruise along in his Charger RT with the 454 and Holley 4-barrel, while Harold hung from the passenger side of the car and tossed the small pony bottles at the sign. The bottles were perfect for nailing signs, because they were about the size of a baseball. Harold had played high school baseball for the last two years, which helped his pitching arm.

"Well, I'll see you about seven o'clock then," Frank said as he pulled out of the driveway and peeled off down the dirt road.

"Okay, seven o'clock," Harold said.

They would take Frank's car that night because Harold still didn't have a decent ride. Jerry had let the Montego go back to the bank after Helen had disappeared, along with some of the furniture they were paying off. Jerry's salary alone just wasn't enough to pay all the bills.

The house payments were always top priority, but the last couple of years had brought home the realization that Jerry not only spent money on essentials like food, clothes and gas, but on booze and women, too.

*       *       *       *

Harold would never forget the day Betty moved in with them. It wasn't long after Helen's disappearance. Jerry had lasted less than a year without a woman in the house. He just couldn't stand the limits that had been placed on his life. He was angry with the people around him and wanted his old life back, or some version of it.

Jerry was just too lonely; he began drinking a little heavier after his first Christmas without Helen. Back in the spring of 1973, Jerry began to visit places around Valdosta that he and Helen had gone to during their marriage.

One Saturday afternoon, Lisa took Harold and Polly to Valdosta to see a movie. When they returned the house had a new guest, Betty Thompson. Jerry said that she needed a place to stay for a little while. She was only going to stay with them until she could figure out what she was going to do.

"What do you mean?" Lisa said furiously to her father.

"Lisa, calm down now. Betty's ex-husband made her leave and she doesn't have anywhere to go," Jerry said, his voice slurring a bit because he and Betty had finished off a six-pack of beer since they had come home.

"There ain't gonna be anybody living here that ain't my momma!" Lisa shouted.

"This is my house and what I want to do, I'll do," Jerry yelled back at her.

Harold and Polly stood in the kitchen doorway and watched in amazement. They had never seen Lisa so upset. She was already upset that her father was going out in Valdosta in the first place. She wanted her mother's memory to last several years before another woman tried to take her place. Besides the fact that

Helen had not even been found yet. Harold and Polly agreed with their sister. Tensions were on the rise in the Harmon household.

When Betty moved her things in from her ex-husband's house Lisa called her closest friend in Valdosta and asked if she could move in with her and her family. The late night arguments Lisa and Jerry had after Betty moved in led to Jerry agreeing that Lisa should move out, at least for the time being. Betty cried the day Lisa left and said to Jerry, "Honey, I didn't want for this to happen. Please don't let her go."

Jerry brushed it off. "It's better this way." And that was the end of that conversation.

This left Polly and Harold to deal with the new presence in their home by themselves. Harold was thrown off balance, and at thirteen he didn't have much say in Jerry's affairs. He just ignored his situation and the looks everyone gave him in Morven where the gossip lines were extremely hot for several months.

The Harmons did not celebrate Christmas during Harold's ninth-grade school year. Lisa came and went during the following year, Harold and Polly trudged along through their school work and summer jobs that followed. When tenth grade started for Harold he was fed up with the current state of his life. He began to drink beer that fall. He remembered how nasty it tasted at first, but when he started feeling the alcohol buzz after a few drinks he forgot about the taste. He was now exploding with rebellion. He quit the school band and became interested in only one thing: weight-lifting. He'd gotten big enough for the football coach to ask him to try out for the team at spring practice, so he began his workouts again in May for the fall. And he knew he'd gain more muscle mass working in the tobacco fields that summer.

\*     \*     \*     \*

At seven o'clock, Harold had just put on his last pair of clean jeans and was heading out the door when he remembered, no money! He drifted back to his father's room where Jerry and Betty watched TV constantly from the bed.

"Dad, I'm leaving now—do you have a couple of bucks for Cokes and gas?" Harold asked in his best pitiful voice.

Jerry lifted a five-dollar bill from the night table and held it out to his son. "That should be enough."

Harold said thanks as he quickly exited the room. He couldn't stand seeing Betty next to his father in the bed where his mother once slept, and god knows where she was sleeping now.

Harold drove to Frank's house, got into his friend's Charger RT and by seven-thirty they were cruising to the Hahira bridge liquor store to pick up the eight packs of Miller ponies for their sign-hitting operation. They hit a few signs and talked about everything from loud music to loud girls. Finally, they arrived at the Burger Barn, the only joint in Quitman for young people to hang out. The restaurant atmosphere never appealed to them, but the parking lot was akin to an ant pile someone had just stepped on.

After about an hour of hanging out, and eating burgers, Harold and Frank headed for the courthouse where the older kids always gathered.

The courthouse had a large fountain in front with huge goldfish swimming around in pea green water. Jeff, Frank's cousin, and his girlfriend Debbie, were in the parking lot when Harold and Frank arrived.

Debbie and Jeff had been arguing as usual, except tonight Debbie's car window was open and one of the guys from the Westbrook private school yelled to Debbie about the need for a real man whereupon Jeff burst out of his car.

The eight-track tape case Jeff had been looking through—no doubt the object of the argument—flew into the parking lot and tapes went flying in every direction. Jeff never slowed down, reaching the car door of "Mr. Westbrook," and snatched the teenager right through the window. He grabbed him by the crotch and neck and carried him directly to the algae-infested fountain.

The surprised look on the goldfishes' face was nothing compared to the look on "Mr. Westbrook's" face when he was tossed into the fountain like a worthless coin.

Jeff and Debbie had already gathered their tapes and gone home before the local police came by to see what the commotion was about. Harold and Frank left the parking lot laughing uncontrollably just as the patrol car pulled in. On the way home that night they picked up two more ponies each and nailed four more signs.

*       *       *       *

When summer rolled around it was back to uncle Joey's tobacco fields for Harold and Polly, working from daybreak to dusk, 7:00 a.m. to 7:00 p.m. At ten dollars a day, the pay was not commensurate with the work by any means. It was steady though, from June to mid-August, and gave the kids some money for school clothes.

The tobacco barns were composed of four rooms spaced about four feet apart that ran the length of the barn. Six tier poles were spaced about three feet between each elevation so that the tobacco could be hung on them in layers. Using twine, workers strung the tobacco on a long stick that was hung on the tier poles. Gas heaters were placed in the bottom of the barn to cure the tobacco.

The mornings would always start the same: muster at the barn, followed by a pickup truck ride to the field. Once in the field, the girls would ride the harvester seats in front of the boys and string the tobacco on the sticks. The boys would crop the leaves from the stalks and hand it up to them. It was a hot and dirty job in the afternoons, but the mornings were worse. In the mornings the dew was usually heavy on the large leaves of tobacco. It wet everybody in the crew as they traveled through the first set of four rows. By the end of the first round, up the row and back, everyone would be cold and miserable.

Around ten o'clock, Uncle Joey brought out cold drinks and a pack of crackers to everyone in the field. He had a comedy routine worked out for the field crew when he intercepted the harvester. He thought he could knock the chill off the morning with a few quick jokes. Then he would collect the drink bottles and carry one to Harold at the barn. It was like having a coffee break at the stock exchange as far as these field hands were concerned.

By noon Harold was usually so hungry he could feel his stomach gnawing at his backbone. Leaving the harvester in the field, the crew would drive up to the tobacco barn in the black and dusty Ford pickup. Everyone would jump out of the open bed truck to wash up. Black tar that came off the green tobacco while the croppers were picking the leaves, stuck to the hair on their arms and heads like glue. It would stain black any exposed skin and had to be bleached off on Saturdays before going out. Tobacco tar reacts to water like tar used by road hogs repairing highway asphalt in the summer.

Harold realized that the tar on everyone's arms and hair was the same tar that the cigarette companies listed on their packs. It made Harold realize how important it was to clean this carcinogen from his body. He also knew that the tobacco had been sprayed with strong chemicals to kill insects and prevent suckers from growing from the stalks and stunting the growth of the leaves.

Surrounded by cigarette smokers in the fields and barns Harold tried to learn the habit of smoking, but it never appealed to him. Maybe it was the harsh taste of inferior tobacco leaves used by big companies to make the cancer sticks, or the burning sensation in his lungs when he breathed the poison. But each time he tried, Harold recognized a tobacco laced morning dew flavor that field workers unintentionally drank as they harvested the leaves.

*     *     *     *

Jerry and Betty were unable to get married as long as Jerry was still legally married to Helen. And Jerry wasn't ready to file for a divorce; he thought there was still a chance—even if remote that Helen might come home. However, he knew that by law after seven years she would be considered dead anyway. Maybe then he'd marry Betty, maybe.

Although Betty was very easy to get along with and obviously made Jerry happy, Lisa refused to return home as long as this "other woman" was living in her mother's house. She never trusted Betty, and believed that she was there only because she had nowhere else to go. Harold wasn't sure he agreed with Lisa, but he was sure of one thing: The day in June 1975 that Betty's daughter Maxine moved into the Harmon house, was a very important one.

Harold and Polly had walked in from work and there she was in the yard, wearing a pair of cut-off jeans that tightly clung to her sixteen-year-old body. For Harold this wasn't a bad addition to the household.

Maxine stood there, looking at the two tar-stained tobacco field hands and just smiled. Jerry told Harold and Polly that Maxine was going to stay the summer and maybe part of the next school year. Harold wondered why people were moving in and why his old man never said anything about maybe marrying Betty. But Jerry had no intention of telling his kids what he was up to because he didn't know himself.

"Hey," Polly said.

"Hey. You must be Polly and you gotta be Harold," Maxine said by way of introduction. Harold just stared and nodded. Maxine smiled flirtatiously at him.

Although Betty had really been an asset to Harold and Polly at times, cleaning the house, cooking and washing clothes occasionally, there was still a lot of animosity between the children and Jerry about Betty moving in suddenly, without any warning. Now Harold and Polly had to deal with her daughter too.

As Polly reached thirteen she tried to look to Betty for guidance. She needed a mother's support, but Betty never attended any of her school activities or took her to church on Sunday, like Helen would have done. So Polly regarded her as more like a friend rather than someone older and wiser whom she could talk to about her problems.

The Saturday that Frank came over on his trail bike, Harold got out his old Suzuki 90 and the two began riding around the maze of dirt trails in the surrounding peach fields and jumping the terraces built for the peach trees. It was a follow-the-leader chase and they had gotten good at dodging the tree limbs—all of which was meant to impress Maxine who stood in the driveway in her summer shorts and halter top. She looked very sexy in her skimpy outfit, but Harold tried not to admit that he was falling for his almost stepsister and he couldn't do anything about it.

"You want to go for a ride, Maxine?" Frank asked, as the bikes came to a sliding stop.

"Yeah, sure," Maxine said, smiling as she got onto the back of Frank's bike.

The bike wheeled out of the driveway and sped down the road, whining with each gear change. Frank spun around at the dead end, where the dirt road met the pavement. The two figures on the bike came back just as fast as they had taken off.

"Whoa, that was great! Let's go for a ride, Harold," Maxine exclaimed breathlessly.

"Okay," was all Harold could say.

Maxine climbed on the back of Harold's bike and put her arms around his waist. He started slowly down the dirt road; his riding style steady as a rock. He'd had a lot of dirt-bike riding experience and had taken several falls over the last couple of years to prove it.

About halfway to the end of the road Maxine moved her hands from the tight grip around Harold's waist to the top and then back of his thighs. Harold felt a thrilling sensation as she began to rub the back of his legs.

"How does that feel?" Maxine asked with enough volume to be heard over the sewing machine engine of the Suzuki.

"Uh, well, feels pretty good," Harold finally sputtered.

He had always thought that boys were supposed to be the aggressors, but he'd discovered that this was definitely not always the case. By the time they had reached the end of the dirt road Harold had fallen in love with Maxine.

Harold worried about his father's reaction. He knew that dating a girl from school was fine with the old man, but his soon-to-be stepsister? Harold thought Maxine obviously liked him, but he was convinced his old man wouldn't approve of this situation.

Maxine and Harold made it back to the house and turned the bike off. Frank said he had to get home and exited with his usual wheelie.

As soon as they were alone Maxine said, "You know what a fling is, Harold?" Maxine asked with a slow smile.

"Yeah, sure, I know what it is," Harold said in a monotone voice with little confidence.

In the back of his mind he dug for some hint of what kind of a fling she was referring to. He couldn't relate to the swift and easy way she was operating.

"Let's have a fling this summer, Harold," Maxine chirped with a perfect southern belle accent. "It'll be great fun and nobody has to know about it but us. Maybe we can write a book about it when we get older." She giggled and cocked her head to one side.

"Okay, Maxine," was all Harold was capable of saying at that decisive moment in his life.

The two of them walked into the house where Jerry and Betty were fixing supper and drinking beer. Polly was in her room and the Grand Ol' Opry was blasting away on the TV. This Saturday scene had become a ritual since Betty had moved into the Harmon house.

That night Maxine went to bed in the den where the fold-out couch and lone air-conditioner resided. Harold decided to sleep in the den that night too, but Jerry and Betty never realized what Maxine and Harold intended to do in that den, which was on the opposite end of the house from their bedroom. After a couple of six packs of Miller High Life it really didn't matter anyway.

Harold and Maxine were both virgins, although Maxine exuded experience. "Harold, what do you like in a girl?" she asked.

"Uh, I guess I like a tight body and a good personality. You know, fun to be with." Nodding his head Harold replied, "Yeah, that's really what I like, somebody I can talk to, that looks good."

"Do you like the way I look?" Maxine asked. Harold couldn't believe the lucky way that things were turning out for him.

"Yeah, Maxine, I really like the way you look in your cut-offs and the way you smile."

Maxine had opened the fold-out couch and turned off the lights. They were lying on the two-inch mattress across a squeaking metal frame. The question that Harold was waiting for was offered.

"You want to get naked?" Maxine asked.

"Yeah, sure!" Harold replied.

They took their shorts and shirts off and lay on their separate sides of the creaky bed. Then Maxine reached over and met Harold reaching to her. The two lay there, naked in each other's arms the whole night.

They woke up early and were dressed before Jerry and Betty had time to start breakfast. Harold relaxed now, knowing that the ice had been broken between them.

The two were inseparable that summer. They met almost every night in the den. They also used the same excuse every time Jerry questioned them about sleeping in the den together. "The rest of the bedrooms are too hot to sleep in," they would say.

That excuse allowed them to accomplish their nightly rendezvous without further questions. Harold discovered that romance for two teenagers already living together was great—no chase, no waiting for the phone to ring, just together all the time. Harold came home from work and there would be Maxine, waiting for him with open arms.

During the summer Harold took on an extra job because it supplemented the days he was off when working for his uncle Joey. And it also kept him out in the tobacco field instead of inside the barn. The field work was hard and paid only twenty dollars a day, but Harold needed the money for clothes and lunch next year, so he kept working, especially since Jerry was supporting two more people on his one pay check.

Harold worked so hard on those extra days that often he would come home and vomit up his supper right after eating it. The world would become a blur and would spin from the partial heatstroke he suffered during the day. But it didn't matter how hard he pushed himself in the field or at the barn because he knew that when he got home, Maxine would be there for their exciting sexual encounter and a night of sleeping in each other's arms.

Then, one evening, as they lay in the darkness, Harold said, "Maxine, we've got to start school in two weeks."

"I've been thinking about that a lot, Harold, and I need to tell you something," she said. Here it comes, Harold thought as Maxine sat up on the old box spring and mattress.

Maxine took a deep breath. "We need to break this off. The folks are beginning to ask too many questions and momma wants to know if I'm seeing you in this kind of way. Ha," Maxine said with an unseen smile on her face.

Harold let out a sigh. "I knew it wouldn't last forever, but I can't believe the summer has ended so soon."

He tried to respond to her strength with what he felt was a courageous statement. But in truth, Harold was heartbroken and needed to talk to somebody. To break their "fling" off was best and Harold knew it, but he wanted more.

"I leave for football camp tomorrow and won't be back for a week, Maxine," Harold finally said.

"Okay then, this is our last night together," Maxine said bluntly.

Harold never questioned or tried to change her mind because he knew she was right. It wasn't proper for an almost stepbrother and stepsister to have a relationship like this one. They had spent their whole summer together with no other contacts, not even a date with a school friend.

The next morning Harold left for football camp and the fling was history. Coach Griddle and the other coaches were signing guys up and handing out equipment when Harold got to the gym. The high school seniors were scoping out the fresh meat as the sophomores and juniors came into the locker room.

Harold never tried to hide his intentions; first string was all he could think about. And from the first hit on the first practice, he tried to bury the guy in front of him. Partly because he wanted to play first string, and partly because he had just been "divorced" from his steady.

Harold knew that his mother would want him to push himself to the limit anyway. "Always try," she would tell him. "Quitters always lose and God doesn't like losers."

The week that Harold spent in summer football camp made him want to play more than ever. He felt part of an organization that had a common goal. Coach Griddle was hard on his backs and receivers, but the lineman Harold worked with were animals. Several of them had failed at least two grades. They grew up around Quitman in the bad section of town, where shootings and knifings were common Saturday night practice. He learned from them that beating an opponent was just the beginning of the game. They taught Harold that you had to hurt him, so that he would avoid you the next play.

The big seniors intimidated the new sophomores and juniors—the standing rule that everyone learned quickly was, don't walk! The seniors would catch someone walking from one play or place on the practice field to another and blast them from their blindside.

Harold never walked. He was in great shape from his weight lifting and tobacco-field work. He would run from play to play. He'd run from the two-by-twelve-inch pine board, to the steel cage, back to the Oklahoma tires.

The "board," as the coaches so affectionately called it, put a defensive lineman against an offensive lineman. Each would straddle the board and fire off at each other from their three-point stance.

Harold's first acquaintance with the board came on the third day of summer camp. He had been put heads up with Danny, a tough senior. Danny had always won his matches on the board. He was quick and stayed low. Harold had to beat Danny to be able to show how serious he really was about playing first string. Everyone knew this was Harold's first year playing football in pads. The other players gathered around to watch the senior lineman wipe the board with this rookie.

The coach blew the whistle and Danny came after Harold with blood in his eye. Everyone thought that he would be just another rookie that was blasted off the board. Harold came out of his three-point stance with all his might and power. Thoughts of bone-cracking sounds went through his mind as he drove forward.

The two boys hit and Harold stood his ground as Danny began losing his footing. Then Harold felt a great pain shoot through his left shoulder. Danny had hit him hard enough to jam his left arm back into his shoulder and pull every muscle in it backward. But he couldn't push Harold off the board. Finally, Danny went down.

Harold walked back to the end of the line with his temporarily paralyzed arm hanging by his side. Soon the pain began to shoot through his shoulder and down his arm like a cold needle that had been slowly pushed into its core.

The line gradually went forward as each of the seniors and grade-failing juniors were blowing new players and juniors off the board. It was a cruel game of survival of the fittest. Harold's arm had finally begun to move some and he was next.

Danny had repositioned himself in line so that he could hit Harold again. Nobody had ever beat Danny twice, not even another senior. Harold held his left arm back away from the expected blow he was about to receive. The coach blew the whistle again and the two boys fired out at each other.

Harold swung his good right arm with all his strength under Danny's chinstrap. It lifted him up enough for Harold to get under his head and drive his helmet into his chest. The blow caused Danny to reel backward, tumbling as he fell into the crowd behind him. Harold didn't realize that he could wield such a blow. The hit was the greatest feeling Harold had ever felt, even if it cost him the use of his right arm.

Both shoulders were aching from the battles he had just won, but it didn't matter—he had definitely gotten the attention of the coaching staff.

Harold worked hard to be on the team that week at summer camp. He made the cut and was put in the defensive lineman's line-up. Harold lettered that year as a defensive tackle and then swapped to a tight end position his senior year where he won the most valuable offensive lineman award. There was no one from his family at the annual sports banquet to watch him receive the award, but he felt his mother would have loved to see it.

Harold was still having a hard time getting over his summer romance with Maxine, who was now sleeping in Polly's room. She was a hard act to follow for the girls of his high school, so he'd brush a lot of them off with a fictitious girl-friend in another town and keep his secret to himself. Maxine had left him alone with his raging hormones.

Sitting together for dinner was avoided at all cost—each making an excuse when feeling that there might be an exchange of words between them. It was especially difficult for Harold living under the same roof as Maxine; Polly could sense the riff between them growing and steered clear of Maxine.

Jerry seemed oblivious to what was going on with his son, escaping into a six-pack of beer almost every afternoon and twice on the weekend. Betty finally found time to start working as a waitress and Jerry welcomed the extra income.

Lisa began attending Valdosta State College and had moved back in with the family during the Thanksgiving holidays and planned on staying through Christmas to save a little money. Jerry informed Lisa that she'd have to drive Maxine, now sleeping in the den alone, to school every day. Lisa felt extreme resentment taking Betty's daughter anywhere, but she did it anyway.

One morning, the kids loaded up Lisa's car and started for school. The Volkswagen Beetle had a small back seat, which caused Harold much discomfort while he and Polly rode to Morven to be dropped off by Lisa and Maxine.

"Jerry said you've gotta get a board outta the shed for my project, Harold," Maxine stated.

"Oh no, I'm not!" Harold replied.

Harold had conditioned himself by now to detest Maxine and the cruel games she would play.

"Okay then, I'll tell your dad about you not helping me," Maxine said.

Harold knew that Jerry would make him get her board out of the shed so he sat back in his seat.

"All right, Lisa, take us down there," Harold said in a sheepish voice.

But as they rode down the one car path to the shed, Harold began to regain his entrails. He would go in and get Maxine's board for her, but he would show her that he wasn't happy about doing it. Harold was sitting behind Maxine in the car that had been equipped with a side release on the front bucket seat.

The car arrived at the shed and Maxine opened the door. Harold quickly lifted the release on the seat and pushed it forward rapidly. The seat hurled Maxine forward causing her neck to whiplash back. Harold heard a loud crack as she rebounded forward and her head hit the windshield very hard. Polly and Lisa were unaware of the damage to Maxine's forehead because their attention had been focused on the shattered windshield. Although Maxine cried a little after she realized her head had been used as a battering ram, she hadn't sustained any permanent injury.

The incident brought about new respect for Harold from Maxine. She even realized and acknowledged that she had hurt him. Although they were never as close as they had been the summer before, their relationship was finally tolerable, and they even became friends.

The Harmon house was operating on instincts that no one there could quite comprehend. Harold was disappointed that Jerry didn't come to any of his football games during the fall, but he was more concerned about his mother not being able to attend. Harold had somehow begun to dedicate his workouts and games to her memory. He felt that if she ever were to return, he would have kept himself in good shape. That was one of the things she wanted for her children, along with a good head on their shoulders.

# CHAPTER 7

▼

Another Harmon family Christmas passed without Helen. Harold had kept decent grades in his junior year and by the time the school year ended, he had learned most of what he needed for college.

Summer vacation began in June 1976 as it did every year. The tobacco fields were calling him again. Uncle Joey had increased his tobacco crop that year and established a different routine for curing the tobacco at his new barns, which were designed for bulk loading of the tobacco on wire racks.

After loading barns all day Harold was exhausted and very hungry. He would come home around seven o'clock to the supper Betty had fixed for the family around five o'clock. It was usually cold and the Harmons hadn't gotten around to buying one of those new modern microwave ovens everyone was raving about. Harold would eat the fresh vegetables that Jerry and Betty had grown out in the garden, along with the cornbread she would make in their iron skillet. The meals during that summer had gotten progressively better. Betty had definitely become more competent in the kitchen—she had learned how to really scald a chicken with the best of southern cooks.

\*     \*     \*     \*

Harold left his house every Friday night by himself to play football with the Brooks County Trojans only to be humiliated by another team from another county. He wanted so badly for his dad to see at least one of his football games during his two years of playing, but Jerry never had the interest, the time or the energy to go to the games. At first Harold was very hurt, but by now he had gotten used to being out on his own.

When the ball was in play he would give all he had, playing both tight end and punter. When the season ended Harold brought home the most valuable offensive lineman trophy, of which he was very proud. When he showed the trophy to his father, Jerry said, "Congratulations" and then turned back to his beer and TV.

During this time Jerry had turned down an assistant warden job and Harold supposed that his father didn't want the responsibility of a supervisory position. Jerry just wanted to work his eight-hour day, come home, drink a couple of beers and pass out watching TV. Harold couldn't understand why his father had given up on the world with such unwavering determination. From the moment Helen disappeared, Jerry was a very different man than the one Harold remembered.

$$*\qquad*\qquad*\qquad*$$

During his senior year Harold applied for acceptance into Georgia Tech and prayed that they would send an offer for a full scholarship into their engineering degree program. They never did send the scholarship offer, but he did get accepted to the school. Of course, Jerry was happy for Harold, but there still wasn't enough money coming into the household to pay the expensive tuition.

Harold made applications for several grants and loans on his own, but because of the lack of guidance provided for the students at Brooks County High, he became quickly frustrated. Jerry was making just enough money in 1977 to prevent Harold from qualifying for several low-income grants and wasn't about to provide for his son's college education. This catch-22 made Harold angry and unhappy. He and Jerry barely spoke to one another.

Harold decided that he would have to earn the money for tuition by working on the railroad with the husband of his older half-sister Carol. Harold barely knew the young woman because she had been mad at Jerry for years and hardly ever visited them, even though Helen had invited her many times. Jerry never took Harold and his sisters to see Carol in Atlanta because he felt guilty about abandoning her so early in her life.

While still in his early twenties, Jerry had had an affair with a girl from a small town northeast of Morven. She became pregnant and Jerry married her to ensure the baby had a last name; then within two months filed for divorce. Carol had the Harmon name until she married. She was now a young adult with two beautiful children.

Harold prayed for guidance about the changes he was going through. He even hoped that his mother would come home to help him decide what to do now that high school was over—he knew she would have the right answer. She always did.

Jerry, on the other hand, had been pushing Harold to find a job and get out on his own. And if there was one thing Harold wanted, it was to get out of his father's house and make some money. Thus Harold moved to Atlanta and began driving railroad spikes with a sledge hammer for the contracting company that Carol's husband managed.

The company had been hired by the city of Atlanta to move railroad tracks that were laid many years before in order to install a new monorail system for MARTA, the mega public transportation system that the city was building.

By the summer of 1977 Harold had accumulated enough money to start college, but the tuition at Georgia Tech was still well beyond his means.

It was in September that a Navy recruiter called Harold. He didn't have anywhere else to turn but the armed services and was ready to investigate his military options, specifically focused on engineering.

"I want to be an engineer, I guess," he told the chief petty officer at the U.S. Navy recruiter's station in Valdosta.

"You're in luck today, Harold, because we need engineers. Have you ever heard of the nuclear power program that the Navy has?" the salty chief asked.

"No, I haven't."

"It's a great opportunity to work in engineering and see a lot of the world while you're at it. Nukes never have trouble getting jobs when they get out either," the chief assured him.

"Okay, I'll try it I reckon," Harold said, not too enthusiastically.

Harold explained how his dream was to go to Georgia Tech, but there wasn't enough money and his father was pushing him toward a vocational decision. The recruiter understood and now jumped at the chance of making his monthly quota with Harold's enrollment.

About a week later Harold was in boot camp and playing the military game of rank and file. Eventually, he arrived at nuclear power school in Orlando, Florida. By then he realized the huge effort he would have to put into this school. The entire program lasted two years and was full of mathematical calculations, none of which Brooks County High ever taught.

Harold had taken the highest-level math courses that his small high school had offered. He remembered his physics teacher, Mr. Craig, telling him that he had a long way to go if he wanted to become an engineer.

Craig liked Harold and admired the boy's motivation to be the best at whatever he did. Craig would give the class of five physics pupils, problems that were meant for college students. Then he'd sit back in his large chair and let Harold figure them out for the class.

Harold learned everything he could from Craig. However, it didn't prepare him for the Navy's nuclear power school as well as he had hoped it would. When he signed up for the program he thought that he could do a good job and hoped that he would come out of the Navy with a skill.

Harold studied two hours every night; weekends were spent mostly in Daytona Beach, two hours away from "nuke school." Harold had befriended a wild Californian named Mike Larson, nicknamed Stoner, which more aptly described his state of mind on weekends.

Stoner and Harold caroused at many local establishments and occasionally met girls that weren't "Navy bias." Most of the girls Harold's age were not interested in "squids" or their nuclear power. Besides, the girls knew the Navy nukes were only going to be in Orlando for six months—too short a term for a meaningful relationship.

After six months in Orlando and eight hours a day sitting in a classroom studying physics, chemistry, thermodynamics, and nuclear engineering-related subjects, Harold was sent to Idaho Falls, Idaho for prototype training. The Navy wanted everyone to know how to operate their nuclear powered vessels before they got out to the fleet. Harold spent the next six months at one of their nuclear power prototypes in the Idaho desert.

Harold and Stoner rented a five-bedroom house with Charlie Sioux. He was a true party animal who learned his trade in the hills of Tennessee. The house was used as a crash pad for the guys between their twelve-hour shifts. The shifts were bad enough, but the 2-hour bus ride to the nuclear reactors located sixty miles through the deep snow drifts was worse.

Harold would stand at the bus stop near his house surrounded by snow drifts that would be over his head. It was true misery for the country hayseed, tobacco-cropping kid straight from a peach farm in the warmer parts of Georgia.

"Hey, Stoner, you and Charlie want to head over to the Cut and Shoot tonight?" Harold asked his roommates. The place was a cowboy bar on the outskirts of Idaho Falls that the guys frequented about once or twice a week.

"Yeah, I need to get Red outta my head," Stoner replied.

Red was how Stoner referred to the teenage beauty with long auburn hair, that he left behind in Petaluma, California almost two years earlier and was apparently still in love with.

"Hey, Harold, are you gonna back me up when I start a fight tonight at that shit-kicker bar?" Charlie said a look of determination on his face.

Harold could tell that Charlie had already been drinking. It was five o'clock in the afternoon and he'd already put down a pint of tequila and was ready for some action.

"Of course," Harold replied. "But give us a chance to meet some chicks before you start fighting. And don't yell out that lame expression you like!"

"What are you talking about?" Charlie asked, feigning innocence.

"You know the one—'I smell sheep shit!'" Harold replied. "It always brings the cowboys to their feet."

Stoner started laughing and that set Charlie off too. Harold was mad but couldn't help cracking a smile. The threesome got into Stoner's 1971 Dodge 4-wheel drive SUV about nine-thirty that night. Stoner had recently repaired the rear end, which had been broken while trying to pull a tractor out of a nearby pond. Luckily, all three were fairly good mechanics and weren't afraid to get their hands dirty if the repair job didn't hold up as well as they had hoped.

The Dodge was like a tank and not intimidated by the two feet of snow on the ground as Harold, Stoner and Charlie made their way to the cowboy bar and pool hall. A huge crowd was already there, leaving only one table available as they paid the two-dollar entry fee.

"Did you see that chick looking at us?" Harold yelled over the loud music to Stoner.

"Yeah, but she's not Red and I ain't interested," Stoner stated. "I'm heading to the pool table. Catch you guys later."

"Okay, man," Harold replied. "Hey, Charlie, you want a beer?"

"Does the Pope wear a funny hat?" Charlie replied.

Harold made his way over to the bar through a thick crowd of local cowboys, peppered with a few Navy guys here and there. The cowboys were never in the mood to put up with the Navy hanging around their drinking hole and talking to their women. Friction between the two groups generated a thick smell of burning brush.

As Harold turned around to bring the two beers back to the table, he caught a glimpse of Stoner near the pool table. He had just been hit in the back of the head with a beer bottle. Luckily, the bottle broke upon impact, allowing him to remain conscious. The cowboy who decided that he wanted to play pool on the table Stoner had staked out by placing his quarter on the edge near the coin slot was only tall enough to deal the blow from his tiptoes.

"What are you doin'?" Stoner yelled, loud enough to be heard over the live music being played by the Lynrd Skynrd tribute band.

Harold couldn't believe that he hadn't even tasted his first beer before the fireworks had started. He looked briefly over to where Charlie had been sitting at their table and realized that he had already made his way over to Stoner. The two were engaging at least six cowboys in some kind of Indian war dance, which seemed to drive the cowboys crazy.

"I can't believe this is happening already!" Harold mumbled to himself.

Harold dropped the beers on the nearest table and headed over to his buddies. But before he could get through the growing crowd, the bar's bouncer came charging through the group right beside him.

The bouncer quickly grabbed Stoner, who was the loudest of all the contenders.

Stoner had broken a pool cue over the edge of the pool table and had the fat end in one hand, yelling to the gang of cowboys that it was time to meet their maker. However, the bouncer was well ahead of Stoner and grabbed him from behind, placing a butter knife to his throat. Stoner stopped struggling; following the bouncer anywhere he wanted him to go.

The bouncer and Stoner stopped just by the door and the band took a break. Over the noisy crowd the bouncer shouted, "Alright, all you guys, out! That's right, you three guys and you six cowboys. Get out!"

Without hesitation, the fist fight moved outside into what had become a snowstorm. Wind and snow were blinding all the players. Rules were quickly established: it was to be a fight between the two starters. Stoner made quick work of it and everyone, including the twenty or thirty onlookers, was glad to see it end in minimal bloodshed.

When Harold, Stoner and Charlie piled back into their SUV, Stoner said, "Red would've been proud of me tonight." And then he passed out.

\*     \*     \*     \*

Prototype school felt familiar to Harold, much more so than the classes in nuke school. While growing up in Georgia, Harold had worked around machinery at the peach shed and had had to work on cars and tractors constantly to keep them running. And so he had scored well on the entrance exam for the Navy in the mechanical abilities section. Although every aspect of operating naval nuclear reactors was learned at this hands-on training, not all of it would be used in the fleet.

Harold survived the winter months in Idaho and was grateful for the warmer weather that finally arrived in May. Three of his buddies from prototype school had planned a camping trip up to the Blackfoot Reservoir one weekend and they invited Harold to come along.

The camping trip involved some cross-country skiing through the surrounding mountains of the reservoir. Harold had never been on a pair of skis in his life, but that wasn't about to stop him.

Harold and Steve Zimmerman knew each other from Orlando, but Bobby and his brother Zack Erwin he had met in Idaho Falls. The four sailors arrived at the reservoir on Friday afternoon with plenty of daylight to spare. Harold had never seen scenery this beautiful in his entire life. The lake was still frozen and the surrounding mountains had partially melted snow hanging from its sheer faces. Snow sparkled and dripped from tree branches like the hanging moss he remembered in the Okefenokee Swamp back in Georgia.

They packed up tents and supplies rented from the Navy's sports equipment store into four separate backpacks. Each took one pack that they would carry up the five-mile trail to the mouth of the river. But the mountain trail added a couple of extra miles to the trip because of its winding path. The tents and supplies didn't weigh much at first, but Harold knew that they would eventually become very heavy.

Steve was the leader of the group. He was the only one who had actually been to river's mouth and was a "prototype commando," the nickname given to someone who had been assigned instructor duties in prototype school. The Navy used its own people to train the men who were coming through the program.

Harold followed the pack of skiers—only one of which had been on cross-country skis before—up the trail toward the first large mountainside. The trail was narrow and made Harold very nervous as he tried to control his cross-country skis.

It took Harold about an hour for his body to heat up from the exertion. Feeling very uncomfortable Harold stopped and removed his shirt, thinking that he would just cool down a bit, and then put it back on. The surrounding mountains still had plenty of snow on them that reflected the bright sunlight back onto his skin, making him feel warm as long as he was moving.

The group made it to the mouth of the river after several hours of hard skiing. None of these men in their late teens and early twenties wanted to admit that they were tired, so it was full speed ahead during the entire expedition. But when they had reached the mouth of the river they were exhausted.

Their tents went up fairly easily and as the sun went down, they built a fire
and tried to stay warm. Unfortunately, the shadows of the mountains around
them made their campsite very cold, very quickly.

The next morning they awoke to a flurry of snow falling rather quickly.
Harold's eyes felt as though he had gotten his head caught in a belt sander. He
had heard of snow blindness, but never knew until that morning how painful it
could be. He hadn't worn any protective eyewear or even a shirt during the entire
afternoon trip the day before. Bright sun reflecting off glistening white snow had
caused his eyes to swell. They were almost closed. Cold snow falling around them
had made it a miserable morning for everyone. They were unanimous in their
decision to pack up and leave.

The trip across the mountains was out of the question for Harold. He couldn't
see the trail or the drop-offs caused by landslides that occasionally occurred during the rainy season, destroying parts of the trail. During their trip to the mouth
of the river he had been able to avoid the treacherous drop-offs, but now he
couldn't even see them.

Luckily, Harold realized that the ice on the lake was still probably thick
enough for them to cross on their skis. The long fiberglas skis would distribute
their weight over a larger area and hopefully prevent them from breaking
through. They began the trek across the thin ice near the running water at the
mouth of the river and made their way quickly to the center of the lake. The
Blackfoot dam down river, where the group had started their trip, had formed the
lake.

They decided to space themselves about twenty-five feet apart and travel single
file. Snow was still falling and visibility was about twenty-seven feet. As they
turned the first large bend in the river, the four could tell the ice had thinned due
to the centrifugal effect of the water moving faster on the inside of the bend
where they were.

Harold thought that someone was hunting off to his left as he continued to
travel across the thinner ice. He could hear gunshots close to the shore of the river
as the four persisted in their traveling—there could be no turning back. Suddenly
Harold realized that no one was hunting; it was the ice cracking underneath his
skis!

He tried to look down at his feet, petrified that he would see them partially
submerged. The group was about fifty feet from the bank and Harold knew that
the water was deeper than he wanted it to be. All he could think about was the
movie "The Omen" where Damien killed his brother by causing the ice to break
underneath him, and then was swept under the ice by the river.

Harold kept moving, hoping his skis would keep his weight distributed enough to give him time to reach deeper water and thicker ice. His three buddies all heard the ice cracking, and had moved toward the center of the lake and began to lose sight of the water underneath their skis.

Finally, after the heart-stopping ice trek, they reached the shore where, for the first time, they all breathed a collective sigh of relief, congratulating themselves with hand slaps and cheers. They all agreed this was their first and last such outing.

When Harold arrived at the prototype site in the middle of the Idaho wilderness the following Monday, his co-worker Joe Conner asked him the frightening question. "Did you hear about the nuclear accident out at Three Mile Island?"

"No, what happened?" Harold said, feeling his pulse race and his heart pound.

"It sounded like they lost control over the reactor or something and it blew sky-high!" Conner replied.

Conner was working on the same reactor as Harold, one of three different types located at the training center. He and Conner had met in nuke school and became good friends while working the same shift at one of the three reactors located on the site.

Harold also knew that Conner wanted out of the nuclear power program, because he was tired of the constant studying and qualifications. Prototype school was conducted as a self-paced program that allowed everyone to finish at their own rate, as long as it only took a total of six months. Conner didn't want anything to do with qualifying on a nuclear reactor and the Three Mile Island (TMI) accident was just the excuse he needed to send home to his parents.

"I don't think that the plant blew up, Conner," Harold said.

"Well, the news on TV said that it's the worst accident that has ever occurred on U.S. soil," Conner replied defensively.

"Maybe that's true, but we ought to ask the Chief about what happened."

"Okay, let's go. And when he tells us it's true, I'm outta here!" Conner was adamant.

TMI was a terrible accident that seriously affected the nuclear power industry. Although the building of new nuclear facilities had already slowed down substantially during the 1970's, TMI caused a complete re-thinking of laws and regulations that forever changed previous approaches used by U.S. electrical companies utilizing nuclear energy as their heat source.

The U.S. Nuclear Regulatory Commission (NRC) instilled a new urgency into the industry that forced companies into redesigning their nuclear facilities. A stronger code of federal regulations was passed and implemented, creating new requirements for Reactor Operators to obtain licenses to operate nuclear power plants. The code of federal regulations had many aspects to it other than Operator's license and Senior Operator's license. For Harold, the civilian Operator's license and working in a control room was his ultimate goal.

"Hey, Chief, what do you know about TMI?" Harold asked the man in charge of his guidance through the nuclear power program.

"Yeah, it's true," the chief said, "but it won't affect our business here in the Navy too much. We're already regulated to a much higher standard than the civilian utilities."

"Well, that's good to know," Harold said and then went about his routine of tracing pipes and getting system knowledge checkouts from training instructors.

The instructors made the trainees recite from memory all the starting and trip-set points for each component of a particular system connected to the reactor. This method of verbal checking also included a required drawing of the system on the white board in the instructor's office. A satisfactory pass was signified by a signature on his qualification card for that system and meant that Harold was one step closer to going to the fleet.

Harold finished prototype training and said his farewells to Stoner and Charlie. His orders had him assigned to a ship stationed on the east coast. He had hoped for something out of Florida, but that was his dream-sheet request, not his orders.

# CHAPTER 8

▼

The USS Nimitz was an aircraft carrier ported out of Norfolk, Virginia and Harold's new home. The Nimitz was known as a "showboat" for the Navy. It had been commissioned in 1975, which meant it would be doing a lot of sea time before coming back into dry dock for inspection and repairs. The ship held around six thousand men when it was fully loaded, and it traveled in excess of thirty knots.

The Nimitz had made two cruises to the Mediterranean since its commissioning. Its first cruise was about four months and the second was six months. She was still very fresh with lots of life left in her nuclear reactors in 1979.

Harold pulled up to Pier 12 in Norfolk and saw the largest piece of grey metal he had ever seen. It was about six stories high and a quarter of a mile long. As he stood there, gaping at the ship's size, the crew of the movie "The Final Countdown" walked down the gangway. The whole scene overwhelmed Harold and his small farm-grown imagination.

After putting his gear on board in his assigned rack, Harold went to the mess hall for lunch. It was located about halfway to the reactor rooms from his berthing area.

As Harold passed the potato peelers and dishwashers assigned to "crank" duty, he heard.

"Aye, captain. Yuk, Yuk, Yuk." It was the crank yelling in the best Popeye imitation Harold had ever heard.

"Shut up, Olive," the crusty first class mess cook grunted back.

The conversation carried on over the mumbling crowd of some fifty or sixty sailors trying to eat. Even though the voices sounded blurred by constant mess hall chatter, Harold laughed to himself at the irony of it all.

"Hey, man, where you from?" asked a third class nuke who was standing in front of Harold in the chow line.

"Georgia," Harold replied.

"I'm from Rhode Island, name's Rob."

"Harold, good to meet ya."

The air was dead for a few seconds as Harold looked at what was in the reddish stew that the Filipino cook was dishing out.

"What kind of meat do you think that is, Rob?"

"I heard one of the guys up front call it Red Death," Rob declared.

"I think I'll go for the slider," Harold said as he pointed to the hamburgers cooking on a large steel grill.

"Yeah, me too," Rob said.

After gathering their food and locating a scenic table between the milk-machine and the huge trash cans, they began to talk.

"How long you been on board?" Rob asked.

"Just arrived today," Harold replied with a bit of hesitation.

He had learned from his previous assignments that by just being the "newbie" you would be first choice when it came to picking a target for the next practical joke. He had seen a couple of guys targeted back during a temporary assignment aboard a landing vessel in Norfolk. Old salts in the engine room would challenge them to the vice test. Two guys would set up the joke by having one put his thumbs into a vice, which was bolted to a workbench. Jokester number two would slowly tighten the vice and count the turns to test the first joke player's pain endurance. What the target didn't know is that when he was challenged to put his thumbs in the vice, it was only to capture him.

After the unwitting victim had yelled that his thumbs could no longer take any further tightening of the vice, the two jokesters would pull his pants to his knees and cover him in axle grease. The grease was hard enough to wash off, but occasionally, the game would be played with Prussian blue, which was a dye used to find defects in smooth metal surfaces after machining. When applied correctly to an unsuspecting rookie, his testicles would be blue for weeks.

"I just came on board too," Rob stated.

"Are you a nuke?" Harold asked.

"Yeah, I start pre-qualification training next week," Rob replied.

"Well, I suppose we'll be in the same classes then," Harold said.

The training department was a first stop to qualifications necessary to becoming a Reactor Operator. Harold's ultimate goal was to become a Chief Reactor Watch, which would give him the experience that he needed to get a good job when he got out of the Navy.

Letters from Sheila, an old girlfriend to whom he had starting writing out of sheer loneliness when he was in Idaho, was the first mail he received. Lisa also began writing to Harold about their mother's disappearance and how it was time to put up a memorial—it had been seven years, and as the law stated, Helen Harmon was considered legally dead. The family had to come to grips with the finality of that fact.

Lisa designed the memorial to include an epitaph, but left the wording up to Harold. He searched for several weeks looking for just the right thing to say. He wondered what his mother's last words would have been if she had had a chance to speak to them.

It was then that he remembered one of his favorite Bob Dylan's songs. He found a phrase buried in the song that resembled a Bible verse in Joshua 1:6-9.

## *MAY YOU ALWAYS BE COURAGEOUS, STAND UP RIGHT, AND BE STRONG. FOREVER YOUNG.*

Lisa set up a memorial service for family and friends of Helen in the autumn of 1979. Helen's old pastor conducted the service, while the three children sat in the front row of the congregation.

Harold came from Norfolk in his Navy whites. Polly arrived there straight from college. Jerry had decided not to attend the memorial, thinking it would be too emotionally hard for him.

"How did the service go?" Jerry asked his three children as they walked into the Harmon house.

"It was very nice," Lisa answered in a solemn voice.

"Who was there?" Jerry asked.

"Well, all of momma's brothers, and all of your brothers and sisters. As a matter of fact, everyone was there but you," Lisa said, the sarcasm evident in every word.

"I just couldn't go; please understand," Jerry said. "It's too painful for me to do those kind of things."

Maybe he was just too full of sorrow, Harold thought. But since no one yet knew what had actually happened to Helen, Harold concluded that Jerry must also have been embarrassed by the event.

Without his children knowing it, Jerry had actually divorced Helen a year earlier in order to marry Betty. They had kept it a secret from Harold, Lisa, Polly and Maxine, who had moved back down to Florida to live with her real father. Jerry and Betty planned to let their children and everyone in the Morven community know about their marriage when an opportunity presented itself, but it never did.

Two days later, Harold took the train back up to Norfolk, Virginia to report back to his new command. The U.S.S. Nimitz was soon leaving for the Mediterranean on what was to be a six-month cruise. But that would change dramatically in a matter of weeks. It was November 1979, and the Iranian hostage crisis had begun. Sixty-six American hostages were being held in the U.S. Embassy in Tehran and President Jimmy Carter wanted some action taken right away.

In response, "Operation Eagle Claw" was created by the U.S. military command. Naval forces were dispatched to the Indian Ocean, which included the Nimitz battle group.

The news came as an incredible shock to the crew, but patriotism swelled among them as the word spread like wildfire. Harold was in the reactor room, standing the 2400 to 0300 watch, when he heard what had happened and realized that he would be out to sea for much longer than he thought was possible for a ship the size of the Nimitz.

Mid-watch was a very difficult one to stay awake through, but the 0300 to 0700 watch was much more demanding on the human body. Off-going operators usually made fresh coffee for the relieving watch. Harold tried to resist too much caffeine; however, lack of sleep was a never-ending battle that demanded coffee cannons on the early watch.

After getting off watch there was just enough time to eat, meet with the chief for the daily assignment and get back down to the plant to work until 1600 hours the next afternoon. Work included Harold's favorite, machinery maintenance, but also painting and occasionally deck grinding had to be done.

Harold was still going through his early qualifications, but he had left the training department and was now working as a lower level watch on reactor support equipment. Lower level areas were hot because of the steam-driven equipment, but also because of the high temperature of the ambient air, which coursed its way through the ship as they traveled through the Straits of Gibraltar and south.

The Nimitz cruised around the tip of Africa from the Mediterranean to the Indian Ocean because it was much too large to traverse the Suez Canal. When the ship crossed the equator Harold thought that he would catch a few rays on the flight deck. Sunbathing was a typical pastime for some of the young single guys who went to Virginia Beach when on shore leave. A suntan always looked great against a white uniform.

The ship was traveling through winds up to thirty knots an hour, making its head wind about fifty mph or more. Harold felt the wind blow him backwards as he made his way to the bow of the ship. He was wearing a pair of shorts and carrying a towel to sit on when he arrived on the best section of "steel beach."

The wind whipped his short towel so violently that he decided to go back downstairs after only about ten minutes on the bow. It was then Harold started to feel hot on all the exposed skin of his body. His face began to burn and swell. He had sustained a terrible sunburn from the hot winds that moved over the ship. Traveling across the equator aboard an aircraft carrier, he discovered, was not the place to sunbathe. Harold's face and ankles had second-degree burns on them that took several weeks to heal.

Workouts on the ship had been a great opportunity for Harold to monitor his diet in order to sustain his six-day, three-way split routine.

The weight room on the Nimitz was a small enclosure one level below the flight deck. At times there would be a line of guys waiting to get in because only ten men were allowed inside at any one time. Adjacent to the weight room was a sauna that would accommodate about four guys. The sauna was a chance to escape reality for a few minutes in a relaxing, dry-hot atmosphere.

Harold always took Sunday off. He eventually revisited his upbringing by going to the ship's chapel while he was at sea. He knew that by learning more about heaven and God, it would help him to remember his mother. He felt closer to her whenever he was in the chapel.

*          *          *          *

Eventually an order was given to develop a plan to rescue the hostages using a specially formed group called Delta Force. This was about six months into the crisis and failure to negotiate a release. The Navy's largest vehicle, the USS Nimitz, was assigned the task of carrying the special forces into the Persian Gulf off the coast of Iran. They were to rescue the fifty-two U.S. citizens from the Iranian students holding them as a political statement in opposition to U.S. foreign policies.

The Nimitz is a huge steel stingray that stays afloat due to its hull design and enormous water displacement along its massive sides. Anyone standing within a mile of a vessel with the height and width of the Nimitz would be in awe of its ability to traverse the sea. Harold was in awe of how gracefully she cut her path through open waters, leaving a white water plume behind her that resembled a raging river.

The Indian Ocean, on an incredibly calm afternoon, became a theater for an extraordinary show of man's ability to construct a seaworthy ship and nature's ability to bring animal grace to a flat blue-green seascape. The ocean was like glass, something very unusual to see at those depths. But all winds from every direction had ceased, leaving the open waters beautifully wave-less.

Flight operations had been suspended due to the lack of head winds for the day, so deafening noises normally experienced by the constant launching of jets, had temporarily ceased. Almost silent, the ship cut through quieted seas.

Harold gazed over the starboard side and suddenly saw three dolphins launch themselves into the air, leaving the still water surface slightly rippled about six hundred meters from the ship's side. Two other dolphins followed quickly behind, obviously, part of the same family unit. Unexpectedly, the five dolphins lifted themselves out of the water on their tails and began to move away from the ship's wake, reminding Harold of a Sea World show he had once seen in Orlando. But this was so much better—dolphins played and danced on the calm waters of the Indian Ocean for almost two hours. Harold and many of his ship-mates watched nature's show, in awe the entire time.

The Nimitz was now abuzz with rumors of the rescue attempt being planned for the American hostages. Everyone was talking about how the plan would unfold, but no one actually knew how things would develop. Even if someone on board did know some of the details, it would be impossible to send anyone a message. All mail carried by airlift was stopped from leaving the ship for several weeks. Even the ham-radio operators were not allowed any unauthorized personal radio communication to shore.

Several helicopters landed on the ship and were quickly placed inside the hangar-bay so that they could be repainted a sand-brown color, making them harder to spot when traveling across the desert. Vietnam-war aircraft, equipped with jungle battle gear, had to be refitted with extra equipment for the desert. However, some important aspects of the navigational equipment were overlooked.

Directional navigation was impaired when the helicopters flew low and near the sand of the desert. Sand is the brutal enemy of intricate electronics used to determine positioning of aircraft. Thus, the pilots got lost enroute to their refueling destination, and two of the helicopters were disabled completely.

Post-Vietnam war equipment was prevalent throughout the military. Most Army and Air Force transports were still painted khaki and jungle green, which would not provide camouflage for a vehicle traveling across the deserts of Iran.

Special forces walked around the ship, eating in a separate area of the mess hall. Blankets were hung from the ceiling to cordon off their designated space in order to prevent them from mingling with the regular crew.

The mission was deemed "Evening Light" and on the night of the rescue attempt in April of 1980, Harold was standing the 1900 to 2400 watch. Ship's movements were critical to successfully positioning the Nimitz at the proper launch site, and on schedule. The entire crew wanted this mission to succeed at any cost.

Maintaining the reactors in excellent running condition was vital to the ship's support and most importantly, propulsion. Watches were doubled in some cases, two men for each station.

Reports from the bridge to the Officer of the Watch were transmitted to the Chief Reactor Watches in the reactor rooms to maintain propulsion at all times. Anxiety ran through Harold's body when he heard the orders. He had never been in a situation where his actions could ensure the success of a mission that the whole world was watching.

Dave Danielson was standing auxiliary watch on Harold's crew when the orders came down. He had been on the ship longer than Harold, but still hadn't qualified as a Chief Reactor Watch, so Harold was in charge.

"Hey, Dave, they're very worried about the reactors tonight," Harold said.

"Yeah, I know." Dave said. "I've been watching our steam production, this ol' girl must be maxed out. She can really move when she's ready."

"You see those guys in the helicopters, on your way down to the reactor room?" Harold asked.

"Yeah," Dave replied. "The air crews were all over those helos, gettin' 'em ready for their trip into Tehran."

It took thousands of men performing their jobs with precision in order for a ship as large as the Nimitz to get within fifty miles of the Iranian shore and launch helicopters in the middle of the night. Should the reactors trip off-line while on their run, the ship would be an easy target for gunboats manned with small arms and shoulder launched missiles.

Harold finished his watch after the Nimitz completed her part of the mission and was back in the open waters of the Indian Ocean. He hit his rack and caught a well deserved six hours of sleep, before waking for the crew's debriefing.

Naval operations were flawless during the first leg of the mission and the Delta Force was dispatched as scheduled. However, by the time they arrived at the designated refueling station in the Iranian desert, many delays had occurred. The cover of night was fleeting—too much time was lost due to the misdirection caused by the sand in the aircraft navigation equipment.

The helicopter pilots were too hasty in taking off for the final phase of the mission after refueling, causing one helicopter to collide with a C-130 plane upon takeoff and several essential personnel were killed in the tragic accident. The rescue mission was, unfortunately, scrubbed on orders from President Jimmy Carter.

Word of mission failure was devastating to the crew of the Nimitz. They had been very proud of their part in the effort to rescue fellow Americans. At first, everyone was hopeful that another attempt would be made before going home, but that never happened. And the failed mission would, ultimately, cost Carter his presidency.

The Nimitz and its battle group stayed in the Indian Ocean, performing flight operations almost every day until relieved by the USS Eisenhower, dubbed "The Ike."

It was like a twin to the Nimitz and carried the next successive hull number. The turnover took a few days and the Nimitz finally began its long cruise around the tip of Africa again and back to home port in Norfolk, Virginia.

"Hey, Harold, do you smell that aroma?" his buddy Rob asked one day as they stood on the flight deck

"Yeah, it kinda smells like grass," Harold replied. "Can you believe that we've been at sea so long we can actually smell fresh cut grass three miles from shore?" Harold was exhilarated.

Rob sighed with genuine longing. "I just want to get on land and ride my bike."

It was May 26th 1980 when the crew were finally able to reach port for the first time in many months. Tugs began to nudge their way into positions that allowed them to help navigate the ship through more shallow waters near the piers at the Navy's largest naval station. Main engine propulsion shafts stopped while one of its reactors maintained life-supporting power as the Nimitz glided into position along its moor at Pier 12.

With sailors stationed along the railings and edges of its flight deck, the Nimitz was an awesome sight for the thousands of people gathered near her home. Everyone looked to the men dressed in their white uniforms, hoping to see their loved ones or buddies returning from their over nine-month-long cruise.

Many of the people along the shoreline were there just to see a floating city come home and to welcome the men who had attempted to rescue the American hostages that still remained in Tehran.

An exercise in appreciation was scheduled for the crew of the Nimitz, which included among others, a speech by the wife of one of the hostages. President Carter and members of Congress each gave a welcome home speech to the men and confirmed the nation's gratitude.

Of the original sixty-six American hostages held in the Embassy from November 4th, 1979, thirteen were released on November 19th and 20th. Fifty-three were to be rescued during operation "Eagle Claw" in April of 1980. And after the Nimitz had returned to the States, another hostage was released in July of 1980. But it wasn't until President Ronald Reagan was sworn into office that the remaining fifty-two were released on January 20th, 1981.

Harold went below to change out of his dress whites and into his Navy denims to help with the final shutdown of reactor number one. As he worked to put the power plant in a safe operational condition, Harold made a final decision on a question he had been pondering for a long time about his career in the military—whether or not to stay in for twenty years and retire from the Navy. Harold now felt that the Navy had too much control over his life and decided on that very day not to re-enlist.

When he stepped off the ship, it took several minutes to adjust to his surroundings. The ground felt strange as he stepped onto the pier—it wasn't moving. He had felt the sway of constant motion from the moving decks of the Nimitz for over five months. Harold was glad to be back on land again.

During the first day on shore Harold and Rob went to Virginia Beach for a day of sun and parties on the beach. Several of the guys from the Reactor Division decided to meet on the beach and play football and volleyball all afternoon.

Between games Rob and Harold sat down to drink cold beers.

"What're you gonna do this summer, Harold?" Rob asked.

"I think I'll go home to see my sisters in Georgia, and then find Sheila," Harold replied. "She wrote to me almost every day that we were out in the Indian Ocean."

"It sounds like she's serious about your relationship," Rob said.

"Yeah, but we've had our go and no-go episodes," Harold said, then brightened. "But you should have seen how many letters I got when we finally were able to get mail!"

"Well, good luck. I've been writing somebody, too. But it hasn't developed into anything serious yet," Rob said wistfully. "Anyway, my bike comes first."

They both toasted each other with their beers.

\*　　　\*　　　\*　　　\*

Sheila and Harold met again for the first time in over ten months. Although they had written letters back and forth, their first phone contact was tense and awkward.

"Sheila, it's me, Harold," he said nervously on the phone in his father's house.

"Harold, I'm so glad you called," Sheila said with nervousness in her voice too. "Can you come over?" she asked hesitantly.

"Yeah. I can be there in about an hour," Harold replied.

Harold's apprehension about seeing Sheila was unwarranted, considering the things that they had written about in their letters. Nevertheless, the uneasiness was still there the evening they met.

"Harold!" Sheila exclaimed as she came running out of her family's modest wood framed home in Valdosta. They hugged each other.

"It's been a long time," Harold said.

"I've been waiting for you since you left last summer," Sheila said.

"You wouldn't believe how much your letters helped me make it through that long cruise," Harold said.

"I know," Sheila acknowledged. "What happened during the last few months? I didn't get any mail at all."

"All our mail was stopped during the rescue mission and I didn't get any of your letters until we were almost back in Virginia."

The conversation continued into the night as they sat in her father's kitchen where he had prepared several delicious Egyptian dishes that he had learned from his parents when he was growing up in Egypt. Sheila's mother had died of cancer several years earlier and her father had never remarried, so he especially enjoyed having his daughter around.

During Harold's stay, he and Sheila would meet somewhere in Valdosta each night to get to know each other all over again. The separation had given them time to realize how much they believed that they loved each other.

Harold's leave time ended after only three weeks and he returned to Norfolk and to continue his work aboard the Nimitz. But he called Sheila almost every day during the summer. She started to cry and complain that her father was too strict with her and he was also hoping she would marry a boy of Egyptian descent. Sheila rejected this notion and told Harold that she had to get out of the house as soon as possible, so when Harold invited her to live with him in Norfolk, she quickly accepted.

By August, Harold had found an apartment that was affordable on his skimpy military salary. Apartments within his means were not very nice, but it didn't matter to him or Sheila—they were together and that's all that mattered.

# CHAPTER 9

▼

November is a good time to clear land—most of the vegetation is dry and snakes are starting their winter hibernation. Cleared trees and brush piled high in long rows burn like crazy once started with an old tire or gallon of kerosene.

Two farmers living near Valdosta and clearing land in 1980 could feel the chill of the autumn morning.

"Hey, Bo, start the tractor up and let's get going on these roots," Nathan shouted. He was standing near a sparsely cleared opening that led to a new field.

"Okay, Nathan, I'll meet you on the other side," Bo said. He climbed onto his tractor, which was carrying a root rake attachment.

Bo usually drove the 4-wheel-drive Case tractor while Nathan followed behind to pick up roots and limbs buried just under the earth's surface. Using their rig they'd remove old stumps and roots from the new field. It was a hard job for the men, but they loved the feeling they got from working their land.

Time passed quickly while they worked and morning soon turned to late afternoon. Bo pulled the tractor around to Nathan's side of the field and dropped the root rake into the ground.

"Watch out, Bo, there's a lot of big roots around this old rotten stump," Nathan called out.

Bo waved his hand in acknowledgement and started pulling the attachment through the field. It was hard to hear someone yelling over the tractor's loud and obnoxious engine.

"Whoa!" Bo yelled. He felt the tractor pulling hard against something. Whatever it was, it was deeply imbedded.

"Hold up!" Nathan shouted back to Bo.

He changed to a lower gear and popped the clutch on the big Case. They heard a loud crack as pieces of tin and boards flew into the air.

"I'll get it, Bo," Nathan called out.

He jumped into the hole and began pulling out pieces of board.

"Looks like some kind of box, Nathan," Bo said.

Bo jumped down from the tractor after shutting off the noisy engine. When Bo reached the hole where Nathan was standing he could see the first signs of bone and clothing lying in the bottom of an old crate of some kind. Inside it Nathan saw a skull and all the bones of a human skeleton.

Nathan immediately jumped out of the hole when he realized what he had found. "We've got to call the police!" Nathan exclaimed.

"Absolutely. You go and I'll wait here," Bo said.

Bo walked around the hole where he saw pieces of the box's lid still partially buried. He brushed away some of the loose soil from a piece and held up another thinking that together they might hold a clue to the origin of the box. He was right. The pieces, when placed together, revealed three words in large black letters: **"Winkler Outdoor Advertising"**

*     *     *     *

Helen's disappearance was no longer a mystery. She had been found. The question of abandonment versus murder had been answered by this grim discovery. It was clear she had been put in this box and buried in a shallow grave from 1972 to 1980.

The hole was only a few yards from the Valdosta airport road and if not for Bo and Nathan clearing these five acres of land, her body would never have been found. Bo stood above the hole wondering whether or not he was going to build his house near the site, as he had planned.

Nathan's call came into the Valdosta police department where officers were immediately dispatched to the area. They roped off the area and waited for the crime investigators to arrive.

Detective Starnes of the Valdosta police department was assigned to the case and was called to the scene. Starnes was a very thorough investigator in the eyes of Collier Dosier, the current district attorney. He watched carefully as his team began to excavate the hole where Helen's remains were. Each article was logged and photographed using a methodical process.

"Detective Starnes, this plank of wood has a name on it!" shouted one of the officers at the scene. "Says Winkler Outdoor Advertising."

"Let's do a good fingerprint check on the whole box, gentlemen," Starnes stated.

Chief Adkins finally made it out to the scene. He had been promoted to Chief of Police and couldn't afford to stay away—he knew it would be a high profile case. Little did he know that this was the crime scene of a murder he had deemed an "abandonment case" eight years earlier.

When Adkins heard Winkler's name mentioned his recollection went instantly back to 1972 and Helen Harmon's disappearance. He immediately radioed the station house and had them contact Foxy Winkler, in hopes that he could shed some light on the mysterious box. Adkins' stomach churned with an anxious pain as he thought about the day the Harmon woman went missing.

Detective Starnes continued to watch the crime lab gather evidence and slowly remove Helen's remains. Constantly walking around the hole the boys from the lab were digging in, he suddenly spotted an object under all the dirt and debris. He reached into the grave, and removed a lock; discovering a set of keys that had rusted and stuck to one side.

Not knowing the importance of this clue he put the items into a silver metal box after they were checked for fingerprints and bagged. Starnes pulled out his memo pad from his jacket pocket. He jotted down notes as he shivered a little from the chilly air. The sun was starting to set as Starnes scanned the surrounding landscape. He could see Bo's turnip field across the two-lane road that Kenny and Foxy had driven down to bury Helen's body and he began to imagine a sequence of events.

Kenny showed up a couple of hours after receiving a call from the station to come to the crime scene. Chief Adkins met him there. Kenny looked quickly into the hole and turned to the group of men standing by the piece of wood labelled "Winkler Outdoor Advertising." Kenny's thoughts raced. Why didn't he bury this thing deeper was uppermost in his mind.

"Looks like one of the old boxes we used to carry signs in several years ago," Kenny said.

"Do you remember any boxes like this missing from your business?" Adkins asked.

"Uh, yeah. I reported one missing a few years ago. Don't you remember?" There was no reply from the Chief, who felt browbeaten for fouling up this investigation. Adkins had dreaded the day that any evidence of Helen Harmon's untimely death might be found.

Kenny reported the box missing back in the fall of 1972 when one of his men discovered it missing and suggested that it might be a clue to Helen's disappearance. His arrogance made him believe it would never be found, buried deep into a wooded area with no houses around for miles. It was now the fall of 1980 and Kenny was still confident that no one would find out the truth.

Valdosta's crime lab worked all night sifting through the dirt that surrounded the box. It was a careful and laborious excavation. They knew that all evidence would be needed if they were to find and convict a killer.

Kenny went home around midnight to wait for the investigators to call him back in for an official statement, probably in the next few days, he thought. But Starnes decided to wait until all the evidence of the box was completely checked out, especially that lock and set of keys.

Daybreak rolled around, bringing a stinging frost. Starnes believed that this was Helen Harmon's body, but had to be sure. He verified his suspicion by finding her dentist and using her old dental records he provided—the body was Helen's.

Starnes went back to his office about ten o'clock and called Jerry at the prison camp where he was working his dayshift, still unaware of the finding.

"Jerry, I've got some news for you about your wife, Helen," Starnes said in a deliberately gentle and calm voice.

"What is it? Have you heard something new?" Jerry asked.

"I believe we have found her body," Starnes said.

Starnes could hear a swallow in his earpiece that was dry and difficult, then silence for about thirty seconds. Finally, Jerry's pained and raspy voice said, "Where was she found?"

"Near the airport, off an old dirt road, where a couple of farmers were clearing some new land. I'll come out to the prison and pick you up. We can ride out there if you want," Starnes said.

"Yeah, uh, sure. I'll be here when you get here. Just let me check out," Jerry stammered. In fact, Jerry was very hesitant to go out to where his wife had been buried for the last eight years. It frightened him to think about Helen, but he felt that he had to at least satisfy his curiosity.

When Starnes arrived at the prison, Jerry had already checked out and turned in his gun to the armory. Staring from behind deeply tinted sunglasses, Jerry got into Starnes' car with a handshake and a quick hello. He had been in many squad cars during his long career in law enforcement, but his wait for this ride was too long in coming.

"Jerry, I'm really sorry about all this," Starnes said.

"Well, I just hope that you catch the lowlife that killed Helen," Jerry said.

Jerry began to loosen up as Starnes tried to question him.

"What do you remember about the day Helen disappeared Jerry?" Starnes asked.

"I remember Kenny Winkler calling me that afternoon and telling me that they couldn't find Helen anywhere. So I drove down to the office to see what was going on. When I got there Kenny was going through Helen's purse. I asked him why he was doing that and he said he was trying to find the office keys."

"Did ya'll find the keys he was looking for?" Starnes asked.

"Yeah, I found them and gave them to that little bastard," Jerry said.

"You think you could remember what they looked like if you saw them?"

"Yeah, I think I could."

Starnes's imagination ignited and he began to attach some meaning to the set of keys. He listened closely to the rest of Jerry's recollections as they drove to the gravesite.

When they arrived, Jerry couldn't bring himself to get out of the detective's car. His grief gave way at the sight of the dirt piled beside the hole. Jerry broke down and cried, until Starnes finally realized that this was a mistake and drove Jerry back to the prison.

Jerry slowly got out of the dark blue Impala and said nothing as he shut the car door. Starnes shook his head sadly as he watched Jerry walk back inside the prison.

Back at the station Starnes went into the evidence room to examine all of Helen's remains. He took the garments that were found in the hole where the box had been and positioned them out on the floor by his desk.

The dress Helen had made with polyester material held up fairly well during its eight year entombment. But it was obvious, that the dress had been slit on either side by a sharp blade of some kind. Starnes examined the costume jewelry that Helen had been wearing. Her wedding ring was still on her finger when the bones of her hand were removed from the grave. Starnes had it now in his stack of evidence. He continued to examine the dress on the floor until he finally decided to have it pinned to a mannequin.

Jerry left work around lunch time that day; he needed time to recover from the morning with Starnes. Later that night he asked Betty to call all the kids to tell them what had happened. Lisa was still living in Valdosta, Polly was in college and Harold was home-ported in Norfolk for a few months.

Dave Danielson was standing the midnight watch that night and came down for his cold iron watch around 21:00. Harold went back to his berthing area where Rob met him at the bottom of the ladder leading into the small lobby.

"Harold, Sheila called you earlier."

"Thanks, Rob. I wonder what she's bought with my money this time," Harold said half under his breath.

"Uh-oh, a high-maintenance wife," Rob said. Harold nodded.

It was an instinct of Harold's to think that Sheila had emptied their checking account on something useless. He went back up the ladder and made his way to the divisional office to phone her, just in case it was important.

"Hey Sheila," Harold said.

"Harold, you need to come home right away. There's something I've got to tell you in person," Sheila said emphatically.

"Okay, I'll be there in a few minutes," Harold said and hung up the phone.

Harold checked out with his Division Officer and drove about fifteen miles from the pier to their little apartment near downtown Norfolk. Sheila was waiting for him at the door when he opened it.

"What's wrong?" Harold asked. Sheila's face was ghost-white.

"They found your mother's body," Sheila replied.

Harold just stood and stared for what seemed like an eternity, then slowly walked over to the J.C. Penny stereo positioned on two boards and four cinder blocks, and started a Neil Young album that he had left on the turntable the day before. He turned back to Sheila where she could see the tears rolling down his face, but no sound came from him. Sheila took him in her arms and held him tightly.

When Harold's tears had finally stopped, Sheila said, "I don't know all the details, Harold, but someone found her buried out by the airport in Valdosta."

"I've always hoped that we would find her one day," Harold said. "I prayed that she would be alive though, not this way." He paced around the apartment for several minutes trying to decide what to do. "I've got to go back to the ship and request emergency leave. I want to see where they found her body."

"Okay, I'll get everything packed," Sheila said.

Harold went back to the ship to find that day's duty officer and requested emergency leave. Then he drove back to the apartment and picked up Sheila to begin the fifteen-hour trip to south Georgia. He drove for hours before taking a short break—adrenalin coursing through his veins kept him going.

Harold jumped out of his Mustang when they arrived at the Harmon house the next afternoon. He ran inside and found Betty sitting in the living room reading the newspaper.

"Hey, Betty," Harold said. "How're you doing through all this?"

"I'm fine, Harold," Betty replied quietly.

Sheila came into the house and hugged Betty's neck as she sat her overnight bag on the floor. Harold watched the exchange in pleasantries, but was barely able to contain himself.

Harold finally blurted out. "Where did they find the box? What did it look like? Who found it?"

"You'll have to let your daddy tell you all the details, Harold."

"Okay." Harold replied. "Where's daddy at?"

"He's still down at the prison," Betty replied.

Harold and Sheila would have to wait for Jerry to get home later that afternoon in order to get directions to the site. Harold calmed down after an hour of waiting. Betty made some tea and brought a tray of homemade cookies into the living room. Sheila said thanks, but Harold had one more question.

"Betty, have you been out there yet?" he asked.

"Yeah, me and your daddy went out there yesterday," Betty answered. "But, I don't know how to get back there; it's down some old winding dirt roads by the airport."

In the late afternoon, Jerry's old white Ford truck pulled into the driveway. Harold walked over to meet his father as he got out of the truck. Their greeting was perfunctory—the years of anguish and resentment had created a deep chasm between father and son. As soon as Harold elicited the directions to the site from Jerry, he and Sheila were on the road, heading toward the airport.

Parking the Mustang on the old dirt road's shoulder, Harold and Sheila walked slowly through the plowed field toward the hole. Harold couldn't help thinking of all the times he had speculated on where his mother might be over the past eight years. A flush of anger rushed through him. He gritted his teeth and walked toward the cavity in the ground, far from the road's edge.

The Harmons always suspected the Winklers had something to do with Helen's disappearance. However, even at this point no hard evidence linked Kenny or Foxy to the murder, except a newly unearthed wooden box with their name painted across its surface.

Harold stepped up to the hole, now only a squared off five-foot depression surrounded by a huge mound of powdered dirt, twice sifted over with a backhoe front pan.

"Do you believe this, Harold?" Sheila said awkwardly, shaking her head.

Harold just starred into the hole, seeing nothing and thinking about the ridicule he had lived with through years of conjecture by local residents.

"I don't know what to think, Sheila," Harold finally stated. "The lives of our entire family have all been affected by this murder. How can we ever change that?"

"Who do you think could have buried her out here?" Sheila asked.

"Winkler, of course. But we can't prove anything yet," Harold flatly replied.

Harold walked around the perimeter of the crater while mentally logging every possible aspect of how his mother's grave could have been constructed by her killer. He scanned the surrounding area from his viewpoint atop a small mound of dark brown powdered dirt.

He could see a small dirt road running from where he was and out to a paved main road that led to the Valdosta Airport. When he turned to look back at the yet uncleared wooded area behind him, he could see through a small opening Interstate 75 and a large outdoor sign that read,

## Support UNICEF and Save a Child's Life

Underneath the large sign mounted on six tall telephone polls, held in a wide black frame was a small advertising company telephone number and the words "Lamar Advertising." Lisa had once told him that Lamar Advertising had bought out Winkler Outdoor Advertising a few years ago.

Harold realized that servicing this sign would be easier when approached from the main road in this direction. The tree clearing activities by the two farming brothers had erased all traces of an access road to Interstate 75 and the outdoor advertising sign. Harold thought that this area must have been familiar to Kenny, who was in charge of the maintenance of outdoor signs like this for Foxy.

They left the grave site, Harold still contemplating various scenarios for Helen's murder, and returned to the house where Polly and Lisa were waiting for them. Jerry and Betty had cooked supper for everyone that night—peas, fried okra, squash in onions, fried chicken and cornbread—and although there were awkward silences, the food was good and the Harmons all tried hard to relax a bit.

"What did you think about the site?" Lisa asked Harold.

"It was a very depressing place," Harold said. "I could feel evil all around me."

"I'm not going out there," Polly stated. "It'll be too hard for me to handle."

"I don't think I'll go there any time soon either," Lisa said. "I want to remember momma the way she was, not buried in some hole."

Harold couldn't blame his sisters for feeling this way. Everyone around the table was eating silently again.

Later that evening, the Harmon family was gathered around the television set in the living room as local newscasters announced a "special report." A reporter stood near the grave site and told of Helen Harmon's remains having finally been found.

"I think we should know soon who murdered her," Harold finally said.

"It's Kenny," Jerry stated.

"Yeah, I think so too, daddy," Lisa quickly confirmed.

"Well, we'll see," Harold said.

# CHAPTER 10

▼

"When do you have to go back to Virginia, Harold?" Polly asked the next morning as the two stood in the kitchen sipping cups of freshly-made coffee.

"I think we'll have to go back day after tomorrow," Harold replied. "But I want to see Hank first."

Hank was Harold's cousin, a son of Jerry's brother Gary, who lived near Valdosta. Hank was like an older brother to Harold—they saw each other at Harmon family reunions all of their lives and when they were old enough to go places they traveled together.

Harold returned to Valdosta with Sheila where they spent the night at her father's place. At noon the next day Harold left alone to meet with Hank.

Hank had been sleeping off an all-nighter when Harold arrived but he greeted Harold with his best 'glad-to-see-ya' voice.

"What's up, hoss?" Hank said, opening the door of his mobile home.

"Same ol' crap," Harold replied. "You got a beer?"

"Of course, Miller or Bud?" Hank answered. "Come on in."

"Bud," Harold replied. "I guess you heard the news?"

"Yeah, that's really unbelievable," Hank said. "But I knew they'd find her one day, hoss." Harold nodded as Hank handed him the cold beer.

"I believe Kenny had something to do with it, don't you?" Hank asked.

"I don't know what to think yet, man," Harold replied. "But I believe they have a good detective on the case, this time. Not like that jackass that said she had run off with some guy from Alabama."

"Gary said Jerry is drinking too much, and this might push him over the edge," Hank said. The cousins liked to talk about their fathers using their given names; it felt more real to them.

"I don't think he's drinking any more, or less, than usual," Harold said with a smirk.

Hank's sofa was made of automobile exhaust pipes that he had bought new and then bent into a couch shaped frame. His coffee table was of wood that Hank had also planed from a tree that had been blown down by a near miss tornado one spring.

"How long you gonna be in town?" Hank asked.

"Sheila and I are leaving tomorrow," Harold said as he took a swig of beer.

"Oh yeah, congratulations on getting married. I guess our rambling days are over, huh hoss," Hank said.

"Yeah, I'm trying to be respectable now," Harold replied, laughing.

"Hey, I've got an idea," Hank said. "Why don't we drive down to the river, and cook us a mess of fish? I've got some mullet in the fridge."

"Okay, let's go," Harold replied, brightening up.

They drove from Hank's mobile home to a favorite place where they used to take Hank's purple jeep river-road riding.

"Let's cook some fish here, whatd'ya think?" Hank asked.

"Sounds great," Harold responded.

Harold needed some down time, away from everyone and everything that reminded him of where his mother had been buried for the last eight years. While Harold phoned Sheila to let her know he was going to be late getting back, Hank packed the fish and some cornbread and a couple of beers into a freezer chest. He loaded another small cardboard box with peanut oil, a deep steel fryer and a small gas burner.

When they got to the river and found a good spot, the cousins got out of Hank's jeep and within minutes Hank was heating the oil and frying the sweet fish. Soon the delicious smell filled the air. Harold didn't want this part of the day to end.

When Harold and Hank finished eating the sizzling fish and some hush puppies, Hank had also fried for an extra treat, the two reminisced for a couple of hours. Recalling the good times when they were kids racing Hank's Can-Am with its tail-fin airfoil design resembling Indy 500 stockcars, on a strip of road near the Valdosta airport.

Finally, Harold said he had to get to Shelia's dad's house. The two cousins packed up the cooking gear and were soon on the road to Hank's mobile home. Gary was pulling up just as Hank and Harold arrived.

"Uncle Gary, it's great to see you," Harold said, jumping out of the jeep.

The two men gave each other a quick bear hug. "I heard the news, and I'm really sorry about your momma," Gary said.

"Thanks," was all Harold could say.

"I spoke to Jerry today, and he was very upset. But I think now he has some closure," Gary said.

"We've all had some closure. At least, about where she's been all this time," Hank added.

Gary turned to Harold. "You'll have to face this with a lot of patience. Remember that there are some good detectives working on the case now, and I hear that the Georgia Bureau of Investigation is also involved."

"Yeah, I heard they brought in one of their forensic specialists," Harold said.

"It'll take a while to figure out all the evidence—it's been a long time since she was murdered," Gary said.

"I hope it doesn't take too long." Harold said. He paused. "You know, there's been a lot of reporters hanging around."

"It's better to just stay away from the press," Gary said. "Besides, her brothers are speaking out enough."

"You're right about that one," Hank said, nodding.

"I know, I intend to go back to Norfolk tomorrow and avoid being interviewed altogether," Harold said.

He hated saying goodbye to his cousin and uncle, but Harold felt a little less depressed than when he first arrived at Hank's mobile home.

"Be patient!" Gary called out as he waved goodbye to Harold who was pulling his car out of Hank's driveway.

"I'll try," Harold called back.

Sheila met him at her father's door with a hug and kiss. They loaded everything into the trunk of the Mustang along with a few things that Shelia had forgotten in her haste to leave Valdosta the previous summer.

On the trip home to Norfolk, Shelia asked, "Harold do you think it was Kenny. Your father sure does."

"I don't know, it's too early to tell," Harold replied.

They drove in silence for a long while passing huge multi-colored signs along the interstate announcing "South of the Border." Harold hated the fact that they blocked out views of the hills and valleys. "Those damn billboards," he muttered.

"Harold, I have something to tell you," Sheila said softly.

Harold pulled into a gas station to fill up the car and check the oil. "What's that?"

Sheila hesitated for a moment, long enough for Harold to jump out of the car, not waiting for her answer. He finished pumping gas, checking the oil and paid the attendant.

"What were we talking about, Sheila?" Harold asked as he jumped back into the car.

"Well, I need to tell you something and I'm afraid to talk about it now." Sheila replied. "I mean after everything that we've been goin' through the last couple of months. Well, it's just unbelievable timing!"

"What is?" Harold asked, annoyed.

"I'm pregnant!" Sheila blurted out, tears coming to her eyes.

"Are you sure?" Harold asked. He was both excited and fearful.

"I'm sure. I took a pregnancy test twice," Sheila said.

"Well, I think that's great!" Harold exclaimed.

"I'm not ready for a baby, Harold," Sheila stated. "I don't know anything about raising children."

Sheila began to cry. Her mother had died when she was very young. She had always felt alone without a mother's comforting voice to promise her that everything would be fine.

"Harold, you're twenty-one and I'm only eighteen—that's too young to be parents.

"I know it'll be tough, but can you imagine, a son or daughter to raise as our own." Harold patted Sheila's hand.

"Maybe you're right," Shelia said and closed her eyes. She slept for the rest of the drive home which took four more hours.

Sheila and Harold put together a scrapbook of newspaper articles written over the next few months sent to them by family and friends. The scrapbook helped Harold put all his memories and anger into one physical place that could be closed and put away when he was through thinking about it for that day.

The scrapbook grew as many articles were published over the winter months and the narrowing of suspects in Helen's murder case continued. Television news and newspapers reported on every aspect of the investigation as it proceeded from its beginning through the tightening of the case.

Helen's body was exhumed twice during the course of the investigation from her grave in front of the Harmon monument, in Morven. Each time she was removed from the grave her demise was broadcast again and Harold would receive a clipping from someone back home.

# CHAPTER 11

▼

Six months after the discovery of Helen's body, Harold left Norfolk, aboard the USS Nimitz, for Cuba.

Tugboats pushed the great vessel out into the channel where its screws were engaged and it began moving under its own power. Nuclear power heated primary coolant systems, transferred their heat energy to steam generators, creating enough power to provide a medium-size city with all its electricity.

Steam from the reactor's systems supplied four catapults, each generating enough power to launch a multi-ton fighter aircraft from the ship's deck. To retrieve these aircraft, several large steel cables were laid out in succession across the rear end of her very wide flight deck.

The Nimitz cruised through the warm waters of the Gulf Stream in the early morning hours of May 25, 1981, while her crew prepared for a routine EA-6B Prowler night landing, on the shifting seas of the Atlantic Ocean.

As the pilot approached the fantail of the Nimitz, he felt his aircraft dip slightly below the height of the flight deck. Seasoned Navy pilots, with numerous at-sea landings on an aircraft carrier expect a sudden drop in altitude when approaching a carrier. But the pilot of this Prowler hadn't made very many arrested landing, on a ship in open waters.

When the pilot regained his composure and corrected his altitude he located what he thought were to be the proper row of landing lights.

"This is Prowler one-fifteen," the pilot squawked. "Permission to land aboard the USS Nimitz?"

"Clear, ready for your landing Prowler one-fifteen," a voice replied.

The pilot saw three rows of landing lights dotted along the flight deck from stern to bow. He knew he was supposed to use the lights to line up his aircraft in order to catch one of the arresting cables laid out across the flight deck.

Flag-off lights placed on the far port side, were used by a flagman to tell a pilot to "fly by," at night if he wasn't aligned correctly with the middle row of landing lights. If the flagman flashed these flag-off lights at the pilot he was supposed to give his aircraft full throttle at touchdown. He'd need the power to take off again, when he missed the arresting cables.

The ship's constant rolling and pitching in the medium to large sea swells created a moving target that the Prowler pilot had seldom seen prior to this landing. His exhaustion and effects of a head cold impaired his judgment even further causing him to align his aircraft to the starboard row of landing lights, closest to the Conning tower, instead of the middle row. A deadly mistake.

Slamming his aircraft onto the deck, the pilot ignored the flagman's constant flashing of the flag-off lights. His wheels hit the deck and he immediately realized that he had made a terrible mistake; he was misaligned. But it was too late for him to correct his trajectory. He was on a disastrous path of destruction that quickly created panic at all levels of the on-duty flight crews. Life seemed to slow to half speed as eyewitnesses watched the crash unfold. The flight boss heard the last clear words of the Prowler's pilot, "Oh, my God," over the radio.

The pilot's right wing tip hit an F-14 parked along the starboard tail section of the flight deck, normally out of reach of landing aircraft. He felt a sudden jolt and tried to veer his airplane left, but it was too late to correct the error and his wingtip hit another F-14 parallel to the first. The Prowler began to spin clockwise into bystanders, now running for cover.

A crewman sitting in a flat-top starter cart couldn't move his vehicle fast enough from the right wing's path. He was decapitated within a split second of seeing its leading edge. It was his second cruise aboard the Nimitz, a father of two small children who would never see his return.

Noises coming from the Prowler's brake-locked wheels couldn't be heard over the screaming jet engines that had now turned one hundred and eighty degrees and were momentarily pointed toward the bow of the ship. Just as quickly as the pilot had seen the white waters of the great screws behind the Nimitz, he rotated clockwise to see that his aircraft was headed to the port side at near flight speed.

Screaming for God's mercy the pilot slammed his Prowler into another EA-6B tied down between two other aircraft, fueled and ready for launching. The crashing Prowler exposed its underside to the nose of its parked partner, causing a tremendous explosion. Ripping through the thin sheet metal skin of the pilot's aircraft, the parked EA-6B sparked a lesser explosion that quickly propagated to the adjacent tied down aircraft.

Momentum of the crashing Prowler forced the parked EA-6B backwards and over a gangway that was mounted along the angle's outer side, slightly below deck level. The parked EA-6B was now temporarily suspended over the gangway, leaking jet fuel.

Steel safety netting mounted below the gangway acted like a human flesh strainer when the EA-6B finally exploded above the two men stranded beneath its belly, blowing their bodies through its two-inch square holes.

Fuel tank explosions of the fully loaded EA-6B also leveled an eight-inch jet refueling station, used for fighter jets preparing for launch. Pressurized jet fuel, released by the shearing of its above deck cut-off valve, shot flames from the open-ended pipe into the air. Isolation of the spewing fuel was made impossible by another explosion.

Harold finished his last watch by 22:00 that night and jumped into his rack for some shut-eye. His sleep was abruptly interrupted by the sound of a 1MC announcement coming over a damaged speaker in the overhead near his rack.

"General Quarters, General Quarters! All hands man your battle stations. Traverse the ship down and aft on the port side, up and forward on the starboard side."

The announcement was repeated over and over as everyone in the Reactor Department berthing area jumped to their feet and got into their dungarees as quickly as possible.

Passing by Harold's rack, jumping on one foot trying to put his left boon-docker on, Rob turned to Harold. "What's going on?"

"I don't know, but it sounds serious!" Harold exclaimed.

Both men ran into many others trying to negotiate the ladder leading up and out of the berthing area into the passageway, back to the reactor rooms and their repair parties. Harold's repair party was located above the hatchway to reactor room number one, directly across from medical triage, where corpsmen and doctors dressed in the first thing that they could find to wear, were buzzing around.

Harold arrived on station at number one reactor room hatch and put on his fire-fighting gear. He listened to a First Class Machinist Mate brief his repair party, while checking his self-contained breathing-apparatus air supply canister.

"Listen up, guys. There was a crash on the flight deck and there are several aircraft on fire," the First Class stated. "Set condition Zebra when ordered."

Harold knew there were televisions in the berthing areas within his repair party's zone; he could hear some guys talking about the fire, one deck down. He climbed down the ladder leading to the closed circuit T.V. and couldn't believe what he saw.

Cameras mounted in the Conning tower were trained on a huge fire located near the front angle of the ship, at the end of catapults three and four. A mainline jet fuel station was spewing flames into the sky as high as the camera could see. It was a terrifying site.

One of the men wearing a Navy issue ball cap and standing in front of the T.V. grabbed onto his buddy's arm. "That's unbelievable, man!"

"I've never seen a fire like that in all my life," his buddy replied.

Looking over several heads, Harold could see that all the aircraft anchored within a hundred yards of the jet fuel mainline were in flames.

They watched as a four-man hose team moving from the Conning tower toward the spewing fire, sprayed a full water stream from a fully charged fire hose toward the flames. The hose team also tried to cool an aircraft near one of the F-14 fighter jets that had two large fuel tanks mounted under its wings. It was clear to the observers that the hose team was losing the battle, but it was also horribly obvious that the team was not going to back down from the fire.

Suddenly a flash of bright light blanked out the small television screen, its closed circuit transmission from the Conning tower interrupted for a split second. The men watched in shock as the screen slowly came back into focus. Harold could see that a bleve of the F-14's fuel tanks had created a huge explosion near were the hose team once stood; they were no longer on screen. Left behind was a madly whipping, unmanned and charged canvas fire hose, now fully visible in black and white.

The blaze continued to engulf the angle of the ship as they watched for a few more minutes, then headed up the ladder again to rejoin their emergency repair parties.

"Everyone upstairs! We have to help with the wounded," the First Class shouted.

Elevators near the mess hall just down the passageway from Harold's repair party began bringing down injured sailors from the flight deck in wire mesh gurneys. He stepped up to the elevator doors and grabbed one end of a gurney as it passed from the flight deck emergency repair party crew. Together, with three others, they brought the injured sailor into the medical triage. A doctor dressed in a lab coat, pair of skivvies and tennis shoes yelled over the noise of the crowd.

"Bring that guy over here, he needs anesthesia," he said, pointing.

Harold put the man down and then waited in line at the elevator entrance for a chance to carry another gurney, with an injured firefighter. The group of guys waiting ahead of him parted, so he stepped forward and grabbed one end of a gurney. Not expecting to see it holding a black plastic bag, he was temporarily confused. But he kept moving with three other guys, helping to carry a motionless plastic bag toward triage.

A commander stopped them and without a word, pointed the way to a bathroom. The men lowered the body from shoulder height to their waist and then put it on the floor by a shower stall inside the small head. Several more plastic bags were laid next to the first body. A Navy chaplain came into the room and began praying over their bodies.

Harold had never been so close to so many corpses in his life, but he tried to stay focused on the events surrounding him. Everyone in the repair party knew that the carnage would continue until the fire was extinguished at its source.

He made his way through the crowed passageway to a local command station where a lieutenant was following a schematic of the ship's JP-4 mainline routes. Harold followed the piping schematic, along with the lieutenant; suddenly they both realized that the fuel pumps were in the engine room just below them.

The lieutenant immediately called down to the number one engine room and ordered the watch to secure all his JP-4 fuel pumps. It took some time; there were a number of mainlines and pumps that had to be disabled, but after a few minutes they heard the announcement that the JP-4 mainline had been isolated. And the fire was out.

Harold's repair party leader announced to his team that an EA-6B Prowler had crashed into the flight deck of the ship, killing fourteen good men and injuring at least forty-five others. The toll of dead and badly wounded was devastating.

As Harold and Rob began stowing some of their gear, Harold said, "Rob, I felt like a trapped rat, watching the ship burn on the T.V. downstairs." Rob nodded solemnly.

The last gurney was being carried through the passageway beside them, followed closely by a doctor in tennis shoes. The sailor on the gurney was face down but conscious, with eyes open as he listened to the doctor.

"You'll be alright, my friend," the doctor said in his most reassuring voice. "We're taking you to Houston."

Slightly exposed flesh on the sailor's right shoulder was barely visible between the ice packs keeping his body cooled. His skin was burned away and the muscle tissue, which looked as though it had been in a deep fryer, was swollen and pulling away from the bone. The sailor turned his eyes upward at the doctor for a second, emotionless, morphine obviously taking effect.

About daybreak, everyone was released from General Quarters and went back to their normal duties, exhausted from the previous night's traumatic tragedy. The ship's flight deck was heavily damaged; the Nimitz would have to leave her post off the Cuban coast and return to Norfolk.

Damaged aircraft were hurriedly removed by crane from the ship and flight operations support equipment was quickly repaired. All refueling depots around the flight deck were checked for damage and refitted.

Harold went home to Sheila the first afternoon of the short forty-eight hours the Nimitz was back in Norfolk.

Sheila was in her ninth month now, ready to have their baby at any moment. As painful as it was, they knew that Harold couldn't stay in port to be with her. Making it back to the ship in time for his duty was much more important to their continued survival.

Two days later they said their goodbyes and Harold left her alone, to await the arrival of their baby.

# CHAPTER 12

▼

Detective Starnes' new partner, Lieutenant Sparks of the Lowndes county Sheriff's Office, was assigned to help the city's detective perform the rigorous task of investigating the evidence found in Helen's clandestine grave.

Starnes and Sparks drove out to Lamar Outdoor Advertising where they would begin a survey of the property. If there were to be any long lasting clues, they felt they would probably find them somewhere on the Winkler's business lot.

Kenny now managing the office for Lamar met the two detectives in the reception area. He had gained some experience in disguising himself in a shroud of deceit by now. Kenny was cool as a cucumber.

"Hello detectives, can I help you?"

"Hello, Mr. Winkler. My name is Detective Starnes and this is Detective Sparks. We're here investigating the murder of Helen Harmon."

"Well, I'll answer whatever questions you have. And you're welcome to look around all you like," Kenny said, with as much courtesy as he could muster. He was shrewd enough not to want to become a possible suspect. "You fellows want any coffee?"

"No, thank you, Mr. Winkler," Starnes said.

"How 'bout you, Detective Sparks?" Kenny asked. Sparks shook his head.

Starnes felt uneasy in the building where he believed Helen's murder and dismemberment had taken place. He and Sparks would try to reconstruct the actual layout of the office building at the time of Helen's death. Several walls looked new and the paint was fresh on the ceiling.

Starnes walked through the building making a mental note of the floor plan. He wanted more evidence to help him determine the motive for Helen's murderer to take her from this office put her in a Winkler Advertising box and bury her in the woods.

Starnes would not give up as easy as Basset or Adkins had in 1972 when Helen first went missing. He knew that he'd have to work very hard to eliminate all the irrelevant possibilities in a case eight years old.

Starnes walked onto the loading dock at the rear of the building and stood in the middle of the floor. His eyes wandered across the opening that led outside and over the storage shed that had served the company for many years. Nothing looked unusual at first glance, but Starnes had a disturbed feeling in his bones.

He stepped into the storage shed thinking that there had to be some overlooked clue still in the Winkler place of business. All he had to do was to recognize what that clue was. What was the lock and key he found at Helen's burial site used for around here? The storage shed had no evidence of ever being locked by a hasp.

Valdosta's first cyclone fence encircled the Winkler property and had been there for at least the last ten years, but its hasp was too small for the lock's shank. Foxy must have used the lock to secure something very valuable to him inside the fence.

Starnes knew that the small padlock couldn't be used on a water meter cover or electrical box. It was too big to fit through the latching mechanism. He knew there had to be another use for the padlock. He continued to walk around the perimeter of the property, then unexpectedly Starnes came upon a company gas pump behind the shed. Starnes found that its handle was locked with a padlock using the same gauge shank.

Foxy Winkler's continued distrust of his employees had forced him to hang a padlock on his gas pump years ago and it was locked that day with a padlock identical to the one Starnes had found. He now had identified the most probable possibility for the lock's use.

At that moment, Sparks came out to join him, followed by Kenny. "Kenny, is this gas pump always locked?" Starnes asked.

"Yeah. The old man taught me to use a lock to keep the niggers from stealing company gas," Kenny replied. Starnes gave Kenny a hard stare but said nothing.

Kenny wondered why Starnes had asked such an off-base question. His mind raced, trying to remember every detail of the night he and Foxy committed the heinous crime. He decided that this possibly insignificant question wasn't going to rock his confidence.

Starnes continued to tour the area and Kenny continued to tag along, constantly talking about the terrible incident and how he hoped that the law would take care of the "scoundrel" who had killed Mrs. Harmon.

"Well, Kenny, is there anything else you might be able to tell us about the day Mrs. Harmon disappeared?" Sparks inquired.

"No sir, that's all I remember," Kenny replied politely.

Sparks asked a few more questions, giving Starnes time to move away from them and look around some more on his own. Not finding any other evidence, he walked back to where Sparks and Kenny were standing.

"Starnes, you got anything else?" Sparks asked.

"Yeah. Kenny, I'm lookin' for a key. Do you know if there are any old keys around here? You know, most of us have a bunch of old keys that don't fit anything, but we like to keep 'em around, just in case," Starnes said.

"Yeah, I know what you mean," Kenny chuckled. He walked over to what had once been Helen's desk, now behind a partition in the reception area, and opened a drawer that was filled and cleaned many times over the last eight years. All the stray keys that had been found in the office were put in a glass jar in the drawer. "Here's all the spare keys we've got," Kenny said, handing the jar to Starnes.

"I'd like to try a few of these on this lock I've got here," Starnes said.

He pulled the lock from his pants pocket. Kenny didn't recognize it right away, but tried desperately to remember anything about the padlock. It had been lubricated and was in working order even after all those years underground.

Starnes tried the keys in the lock one at a time, until he finally came upon a match for the lock.

"Here we go," Starnes said.

"Looks like a match, Starnes," Sparks stated. He deliberately withheld his real feelings about the importance of this discovery.

"Yeah, I think this lock was used around here for somethin'," Starnes said, matter-of-factly.

Starnes was fishing for a reaction from his suspect, but Kenny controlled himself with great effort, now realizing that something significant had just happened. He suddenly felt his stomach knot up and his heart pounded.

"I think that'll be all for today, Kenny. Let's go, Sparks," Starnes said.

Kenny watched nervously as the two men exited his company's building.

Detective Starnes's office was simply furnished with one wooden desk, but overcrowded with filing cabinets. His practice was to collate his evidence in bundles he called "Files." The drawers of his filing cabinets had become small safes for various case items. Filing cabinet number one was labelled "Helen Harmon."

The mannequin he used to "wear" Helen's last dress and her costume jewelry was placed next to his office window, close to his desk—it inspired him to carry on with the investigation.

Starnes and Sparks worked over the next few days to gather all their suspects. On a corkboard in Starnes's office, they posted the faces of the original twelve suspects. Most had iron-clad alibis for the day Helen disappeared, reducing the number to six.

Newspaper articles from Sheila's sister came to Sheila in Norfolk, usually two or three days after they were published. After reading them Sheila would forward them to Harold, at sea. Betty also sent the bulk of the material being published to Harold, but she never read any of it first.

Statements from Chief Adkins in the articles were obvious smoke screens, to keep the press at bay. Adkins knew he had made a mess of the first investigation, so he worked hard to direct the focus away from himself and toward Detective Starnes. Harold hated reading Adkins' statements and self-serving comments. It would make him sick to his stomach and Rob once jokingly said, "Hey, bud, haven't you got your sea legs yet?"

Since all the employees of the former Winkler Outdoor Advertising company had left their jobs years earlier, most of the evidence that the detectives had to work with was found in Helen's burial box.

A list of previous Winkler employees arrived in Starnes's office in December and the cumbersome task of identifying witnesses began. Starnes and Sparks spent the next seven months tracking down all the employees who worked for Foxy Winkler the day Helen disappeared and interrogating them.

One employee lived in Los Angeles and was located through his parents still living in Valdosta. Starnes few out to L.A. to question the man. He was given a lie detector test, but he was unable to provide any helpful information. Except for the mention that he once heard an argument between Kenny and Helen.

Starnes brought Kenny into his office and connected him to the lie detector equipment.

"Did you plan the murder of Helen Harmon?" Starnes asked.

Kenny believed that he didn't plan the murder. He thought that if she had not resisted his advances, he would have let her live.

"No," Kenny replied.

Results were inconclusive from the test, but Starnes knew that Kenny was somehow involved. He spent several days studying Kenny's every response to the questions he was asked during the test.

Harold read about the lie detector test in one of the articles that Betty had sent to him. In the letters, she asked him what he was doing and how his marriage was going. Morven was buzzing with talk of the case:

*Dear Harold,*

*Things here are going good, how are things with you? I am sending you the newspaper articles from the last week. You'll see that the Atlanta Constitution had the best coverage, but they are not saying much. It only says that the investigation that Starnes and Sparks are doing will narrow the suspects down to three very soon. I know that Kenny will be one of those three, but it's taking a long time and we're getting anxious.*

*The whole Harmon family had a fish cooking the other day, wish you could have been here. Your cousin Hank asked where you were, I told him you were still in Norfolk. What are you doing now? Will you go back to sea soon?*

*Love you,*

*Dad and Betty*

# CHAPTER 13

▼

On June 7<sup>th</sup> 1981, Harold was sent a ship-to-shore message from a ham radio operator on the Norfolk Naval Base. Local ham operators in Puerto Rico received the message and forwarded it using a two-way communication link with the Nimitz. The ham station had been setup in Guantanamo Bay for personal calls to sailors who were sailing off Cuba's coast and near enough to the United States base to pick up the signal.

The Chief Petty Officer of his division called down to the reactor room where Harold was rebuilding an air compressor.

"Hey, Harmon," the Chief growled. "You've got a message in the forward communication room."

"What kind of message?" Harold asked.

"I don't know," the Chief replied. "Just get on up there and get back as quick as you can. We need that compressor."

"Okay, Chief," Harold said.

Harold ran up the ladder from the reactor room and went to the forward communication room. He had never heard of a ham radio on the ship or its ability to make phone calls through a system of relay stations.

The message read:

"Congratulations, it's a boy. Sheila."

Harold and Sheila had decided early in her pregnancy that they would wait to find out its gender until the baby was born. Knowing its gender before its birth wasn't as meaningful as the baby's health. The ham radio message left some amount of uncertainty about the newborn's health, but Harold believed in his heart that everything had gone well.

Although he had just returned to sea, following the massive cleanup effort after the Prowler crash, he really wanted to go back to Norfolk to see his new son. Harold went immediately to his division officer to ask for leave to return to Norfolk.

Harold's division officer recommended emergency leave to the Reactor Department's senior officer, who also realized that sending Harold back to be with his infant son was important. Morale was low in the division ever since the Prowler disaster and the men needed some personal attention. His leave was instantly approved.

Harold's buddies congratulated him when he returned to his berthing area and within an hour of finding out that he had just become a father, he was scheduled to travel on the next mail delivery aircraft to Puerto Rico. From there he could catch a military airlift to Norfolk.

Harold climbed six decks of ladders before reaching the flight deck with his one small bag of civilian clothes. Blue skies, brightened by the sun, made Harold's eyes hurt for a moment as he felt the light winds blowing across the deck from the bow.

Flight crewmen briefed him and two officers flying off the ship that day about their passage through a torturous path of aircraft tie-down chains and roaring jet engines. Their warning to avoid jet engine intakes was taken very seriously by the small group of travellers. Harold knew well the story of a flight deck crewman who forgot a cardinal rule on an aircraft carrier: never stand-up in front of an aircraft engine.

Images of a vacuum-dragged and screaming crewman flashed through Harold's mind as he ducked his head and followed his guide through the maze to the prop-jet mail plane.

The seats Harold and the two officers occupied were facing the rear of the plane and that was somewhat disconcerting to him.

Prop engines roared as the plane screamed forward from its position on the stern of the flight deck. Harold's heart jumped into his throat when the black deck that he could see from his six-inch square window turned to bright blue-green water. The plane's sudden dip in space as it left the flight deck was terrifying for Harold and the two officers sitting backwards aboard the craft. But the pilots felt right at home—going over their plans for the night in Puerto Rico.

The plane landed in San Juan after a fairly short flight and smooth landing. Harold grabbed a taxi and made his way to a hotel in town for the night.

The next morning Harold's military transport plane finally arrived at the airport after a two-hour delay. He boarded it with fifteen other people of different ranks, including some military family members. Luckily, this aircraft was for personnel transport, and the passengers could sit facing the cockpit in comfortably cushioned seats.

Exhausted from his traveling when he arrived on base in Norfolk, Harold tried to figure out what hospital Shelia might have gone to for the delivery. Since they couldn't afford an answering machine on their telephone, he began calling every hospital in the Norfolk phone book. Eventually he found her at the women's hospital. Walking into her hospital room, Harold rushed over to his half-asleep wife.

"Hello, Sheila. How do you feel?" Harold kissed her awake.

"Harold, you came!" Sheila exclaimed, reaching up and putting her arms around his neck.

"Yeah, I got your message by ham radio," Harold explained. "How did you know to contact me that way?"

"I didn't, it was the hospital," Sheila said.

"That was the best news I think I've ever had," Harold said. "Where's our baby?"

"I named him Scott. It was one of our choices, remember?" Sheila said.

"Yes, yes. Where is he?" Harold repeated.

"He's fine and he's down the hall," Sheila replied.

"How are you feeling?" Harold asked.

"I'm fine, just tired and sore," Sheila said. And then without warning, "I don't know if I can do this, Harold."

"What do you mean by that?" Harold asked. He was truly stunned.

"I'm just having a hard time adjusting to the fact that I'm a mother."

"I don't understand what you're talking about. Shelia you need to get ready for that responsibility," Harold stated.

"Okay, okay," Sheila said. "I just had a brief moment of doubt. I'm all right now." But Harold wasn't so sure.

Harold walked quickly from Sheila's room to the hospital nursery. Two babies were behind the viewing window, one wrapped in a blue blanket and one in pink. Both babies were beautiful, but Harold's eyes went directly to the nametag for Scott and for the first time called his son by his name through the thick, soundproof glass.

He went into the nursery and held the infant until the nurses decided that he needed to rest and asked Harold to come back in a couple of hours, which he did.

After his last visit to see Scott, Harold reassured Sheila that everything would be fine. He said he was proud of her for going through her pregnancy and the baby's birth on her own. "You're stronger than you think, Shelia," he told her before he left her room. But doubt sill gnawed at Harold.

✳    ✳    ✳    ✳

After Sheila and the baby came home, Harold was issued temporary orders while waiting for the Nimitz to arrive from its Virgin Islands cruise. His orders called for him to serve as a Master At Arms on base in the maximum-security wing of the restricted barracks. Harold had been assigned this duty almost every time he had a layover on the base, but never in the maximum-security wing. Criminals housed there were usually waiting to be sent to military prison.

Harold arrived at the restricted barracks one morning as a boatswain mate first class, hurried up to him and another petty officer, frantically. "You two guys come with me, right now!"

Harold and the petty officer ran to the second floor of the maximum-security wing. About halfway down a row of racks, Harold saw a group of sailors standing around a man who had tied himself to his bedpost with a sheet. The man had overdosed on some smuggled acid that he took earlier that morning.

Harold grabbed his feet and the other two officers grabbed the man's arms. They strapped him to a gurney and everyone stepped back. Vomit suddenly erupted from him like a spewing geyser, pressurized chunks of pizza hitting the concrete sidewalk, as they carried him to a waiting ambulance at the bottom of the stairs.

All Harold could think about was getting back on board the Nimitz as soon as she returned.

Sheila and Scott saw Harold every night after his eight hours shift on the naval base was over. Sheila was very happy in the small flat—it seemed much cozier with a baby living there with her. Her attitude had improved dramatically since Harold was home and they were together as a family.

The Nimitz finally pulled into Norfolk Naval Station and two days later the prime suspect in Helen's murder case was announced back in Valdosta, Georgia.

# CHAPTER 14

▼

The Harmon murder continued to be investigated for several months after the announcement was made that Kenny Winkler was the prime suspect. In total it took almost a year from her body's discovery until all the evidence was identified and investigated by Starnes and Sparks. Harold never forgot his uncle Gary's words, "Be patient." Starnes wanted to make sure their case was as airtight as possible because the district attorney needed all the ammunition there was to prosecute the murderer.

District Attorney Collier was assigned as head prosecutor. He insisted that all leads be traced back to their origin and be either confirmed or shown to be false. Collier knew how tough it would be to prove a case with very old evidence, so he continuously preached to Starnes and Sparks about the importance of eliminating all false accusations before ever stepping into a courtroom.

Investigative work had advanced a great deal from 1972 to 1981 and the detectives were using every resource. Although DNA testing of certain evidence would be possible in the future, its reliability at that time was untested in court. DNA tests seemed to be as much guesswork as it was science. Therefore, it was unusable.

Early in the investigation the Georgia Crime Lab determined that the green dress, beads and all the other items left in the grave were void of any fingerprints. Everything found with Helen was greatly affected by the elements, and had deteriorated too much. This left them the rigorous job of evaluating each item's place in the sequence of events leading up to the murder.

The detectives meticulously examined the wooden box that once held Helen's body. The box had suffered a great deal of damage during the eight years it was in the ground. Its wooden frame and slats, however, had maintained their shape while ground water rotted most of the natural elements contained inside the box.

Helen's polyester dress and costume jewelry were still recognizable, along with the cashbox found inside. These items were below par evidence for the prosecution, but Starnes felt the set of keys and padlock found under the box would be essential to the case.

Kenny was arrested for Helen's murder on the third of July 1981. Foxy was also arrested for hindering the apprehension of a criminal. The detectives knew that Foxy had to have helped his son with the concealment of Helen's body because of what the detectives two best witnesses had told them. Both Winklers were released on bail in a matter of hours.

Starnes and Sparks brought Wren and Maynard in for questioning. The two old black men admitted that they helped Kenny and Foxy bury Helen in the woods one rainy night near the Valdosta airport.

Collier had little trouble convincing the grand jury to take the case to court with Wren and Maynard's testimony documented. Kenny's defense lawyers pleaded with the judge not to allow the testimonies of such unreliable witnesses to be introduced. Both men were in their late seventies now and could be easily confused by Kenny's defense attorneys, but the judge decided in favor of the prosecution and the case went to trial.

Immediately after the judge's ruling the Winkler's defense lawyers called for an examination of Helen's remains.

Harold and his family had buried their mother in their minds once, in their hearts once, and now her body would have to be raised and buried again. It was heart-wrenching news for Harold when Jerry told him what would have to be done. Harold held his baby son that night in his arms and fed him his bottle. Scott cooed and burped as Harold walked back and forth, and wept.

\*     \*     \*     \*

Harold was to begin another six-month cruise that would probably be the toughest stint of his enlistment. He and Sheila put all their belongings in storage except for what she needed to support her and Scott in Valdosta. She was going to stay at her father's place for the half-year that Harold would be away at sea in the Mediterranean.

Sheila stood among thousands of Navy wives on Pier 12, many of them crying as the Nimitz was pushed out into the channel by the tugs. Each of the fatherless families were left on their own to defend themselves against the challenges they would surely face.

Sheila whispered to the baby in her arms, "Scott, now you're gonna have to be the man of the house." She giggled for a moment, then tears formed and ran down her cheeks as she waved at the ship taking her husband away from her for so long.

Harold received his first letter from Sheila when they reached Naples, Italy.

---

*Hey,*

*We made it to my dad's house okay. I miss you terribly, but Scott and me are gonna be okay. Everyone here is talking about your mother's murder and Kenny's arrest. I hate him!*

*Love ya,*

*Sheila*

---

Harold received and read six more letters during the same mail-call, but his reminiscing was soon interrupted by another crew briefing.

Shortly after arriving in the Mediterranean in August 1982, President Reagan's troubles with Colonel Khadafi, the Libyan leader were coming to a head. The Colonel wanted to establish Libya as a world power at any cost, including the destruction of the United States.

In mid-August the Nimitz and the USS Forrestal began open missile exercises in the Gulf of Sidra near Libya and Colonel Khadafi's so-called "Line of Death."

This "Line" was an imaginary boundary drawn two hundred nautical miles off the shores of Libya, in the Mediterranean. Extremely unreasonable limitations on shipping through Khadafi's "territorial waters" caused interruptions in shipping lanes vital to numerous free countries. International law only allows up to twelve miles of claim to waters offshore from a sovereign nation—Khadafi was testing the world's resolution.

Open missile operations from two aircraft carrier battle groups within the boundary threw Khadafi into a rage, which he decided to act upon at a most inopportune time. President Reagan had just backed down the Iranian leadership in Tehran and the American hostages were released after 444 days of captivity.

Flexing American military muscle was well within Reagan's plans to rebuild faith in the free world, and put an end to tyranny by leaders like Khadafi.

Operations by the Nimitz crew were successful on the first day of various drills connected with the planned war games. On August 19<sup>th</sup> several air squadrons were performing flight operations above the battle group and behind the infamous Line of Death, with little regard to Khadafi's threats to destroy anything that entered its air space.

Two F-14 Tomcat fighter jets were performing normally scheduled routine flying maneuvers when two Libyan fighter-bomber jets shot a heat-seeking controlled air-to-air missile at the F-14's in an effort to demonstrate the Libyan resolve to protect their territory behind the Line of Death.

Harold and Rob had taken over their watch about an hour before they heard the announcement: "General Quarters, General Quarters! All hands man your battle stations. Traverse the ship down and aft on the port side, up and forward on the starboard side."

"What's going on?" Harold asked.

"I don't know, man, but we aren't supposed to be having any drills today," Rob said.

"Yeah, I know," Harold said. "We're having a problem with one of the turbines back aft and we're supposed to finish the repairs tomorrow."

"Maybe we'll get more information from the control room," Rob said a worried look on his face.

Another announcement rang out: "Attention all hands. The Nimitz is experiencing a threat from a hostile force. Maintain your battle stations."

Harold's battle station was no longer in a repair party, but in the reactor room, which is where he really enjoyed being on days like this.

Radio communications from pilots of the Tomcats came quickly as they executed avoidance measures, one peeling off to the right, the other peeling left. Seconds later, both Tomcats were at 06:00 position on the Libyan bomber jets when they announced over the radio that they had locked on "two bogies."

The Captain himself had reached the command center by that time and was listening intently to constant radio communications between his flight boss and the pilots. The Captain immediately gave the orders to his flight boss to "Splash two."

The order to shoot down two Libyan-owned Soviet-designed SU-22's was executed by the two F-14 Tomcat pilots by firing one sidewinder each. Without any delay the pilots reported, "Splash two complete." They had eliminated the threat without hesitation and with little difficulty.

The next announcement was loud and clear. "Attention all hands. Two Libyan aircraft have been destroyed by VF-41 F-14 Tomcats."

"Do you believe that!" Rob exclaimed.

"That's incredible!" Harold said. "It's the first time that the Nimitz has been engaged in actual combat."

Debriefing of the two F-14 pilots was held within two hours of the incident and news of military action became world news quickly. Crewmen aboard the Nimitz immediately began designing the next big T-shirt logo: US 2—Libya 0. There were handwritten signs posted throughout air squadron berthing areas replicating the logo using many designs.

Sheila wrote to Harold describing what the Valdosta newspapers were saying about the murder investigation as well as sending him articles about Libya's backing down their Line of Death to one hundred miles off shore, then again to fifty miles.

Weeks of a letter a day kept Harold entertained, along with reruns of old sit-coms played over and over on the closed circuit television set in the lounge of the Reactor Department's berthing area. Harold would answer letters as soon as he could in order to keep news coming from home about the new clues that were being brought forward in the case.

The ship pulled into Naples, Italy toward the end of October for a short break. This was when Harold received news from Sheila that Kenny's lawyers insisted on exhuming Helen's body again.

Harold was beginning to realize that he couldn't keep up with events unfolding back in Valdosta. He was so far from home and news was too slow in arriving to the ship. Naples was on the other side of the world from where he needed to be. The situation made for many a sleepless night.

Harold could not have been more grateful when he was able to go ashore for a quick one-day liberty. He and Rob took a cab from Naples' port landing to a downtown restaurant that they knew about from their last Med cruise before traveling to the Persian Gulf. Buffet style seafood platters looked enticing as they entered the out of the way restaurant.

Rob and Harold enjoyed their meal and conversation. Being off the ship gave them an opportunity to relax and talk about their problems at home. But Harold couldn't open up to anyone yet about his mother's body or it having to be exhumed.

After eating the tasty seafood, both young men drank a small glass of Italian port wine. They grabbed a cab back to the landing where everyone mustered to catch a "liberty launch" back to the ship.

The size of the Nimitz and its nuclear capabilities kept her from ever getting close enough to tie up to a pier overseas. Consequently, she was anchored two miles away from shore to ensure that her condenser intakes wouldn't pull in a lot of mud, while maintaining one nuclear reactor on-line for electrical power. The liberty launches would sometimes have to transport sailors long distances to get them to and from shore.

The queue to get back onto the liberty launch was long and loud by the time Harold and Rob reached the pier. One launch only carried about sixty sailors to the ship, thus it was taking forever to get the seven or eight hundred men back on board.

Harold and Rob stood in the chilly weather amongst the drunks and loud-mouthed squids who frequently made their way to the bars near the pier. Some of the worst of the lot would travel out from the pier about a mile and drink their way back, hitting every bar along the way.

Harold was deep in his own thoughts and concerned about the upcoming trial when a drunken sailor from his division jumped him.

Harold was now six-feet-four-inches tall, and weighed about two hundred and forty pounds. When the Harley-riding sailor grabbed Harold by the collar of his jacket, Harold didn't have time to think about who had attacked him or that it might have been a joke. Rob yelled for Harold to stop and tried to pull him back but was outweighed by a hundred pounds. Harold stopped when he realized that Rob was trying to pull him backwards.

Suddenly the drunk's face came into focus—it was one of the men from Harold's watch the night before. Harold didn't recognize his colleague until he had driven his face into the concrete road underneath their feet.

Shore patrol came quickly to the scene and hauled the drunken sailor, now scared out of his wits, along with an angry Harold, to the Shore Patrol shack. When they arrived the sailor claimed complete responsibility for the incident and vowed never to attack anyone again. Harold reassured him that he wouldn't hold a grudge and apologized for his reaction.

Sheila sent Harold six more letters, which he received one morning at mail call. The mail included one letter with a recent newspaper clipping from the Valdosta Daily Times and another from the Atlanta Journal Constitution.

Sheila wrote:

*Harold,*

*I miss you, and can't wait to see you soon. Here are some newspaper clippings from the Valdosta and Atlanta papers. It looks like they'll put Winkler on trial starting January 4$^{th}$.*

*Scott has been sick lately and had to spend a few days in the hospital. He is okay now, but cries a lot still. I am having a very hard time with him and no one here is helping me.*

*Please write back as soon as you can and let me know what you think about Winkler and the trial.*

*Love you,*

*Sheila*

In fact, Scott had been very sick, according to Jerry's letter that he received the same day:

*Harold,*

*How are you doing? Scott has been very sick. Betty and me went to see him in the Valdosta hospital yesterday after Sheila called for some help in staying with him.*

*I was very surprised when the doctor took me aside and said that he had been neglected for some time now and that I needed to report Sheila to someone or at least contact you about her behavior. I believe that we can take care of this ourselves for now though, but please try to come home as soon as you can.*

*Winkler is going on trial in January. Here is a newspaper clipping from the Jacksonville, Florida paper.*

*Love,*

*Dad*

Sheila was exposed to a little notoriety around Valdosta, because she was Harold's wife and close to his family. Her high school friends called her to go out to a pub or party somewhere, almost every day. Sheila scheduled babysitters to stay with Scott at night three or four times a week, and occasionally for an entire weekend.

Scott had difficulty sleeping—he hated being moved from house to house, wherever Sheila could find a sitter. His crying spells got worse, and eventually Sheila took him to a local doctor who prescribed paregoric to help with the baby's stomach gas. Sheila used the paregoric to force him to sleep when she dropped him off at a babysitter's house.

Ultimately, her neglect led one of her babysitters to recognize Scott's problem and took him to the hospital. He was weak and terribly dehydrated and required an IV drip to regain his strength.

Sheila finally contacted Jerry who immediately went to the hospital. He was furious that his grandchild had come so close to death. The doctors told him that a few more days of his drug-induced existence would have killed Scott before his first birthday.

Sheila and Scott moved in with Jerry and Betty so that Jerry could keep an eye on the baby. After about a week, Sheila started traveling back and forth from Morven to Valdosta to see her friends. Jerry jokingly told everyone that she was working for the county, "compacting the fresh pavement with her car."

After Harold learned about Kenny's imminent trial and Scott's near-death illness, he began to take out his frustration on the surrounding equipment in the reactor rooms. He knew his feelings were getting out of hand when he found himself using a sledgehammer to vent his frustrations on a defenseless bench and vice late one night.

"Hey, Harmon!" Rob yelled. "What the hell are you doing?"

Harold couldn't believe he was pounding the top of the bench with a two-pound sledgehammer until he exhausted himself and a crowd gathered. The pristine metallic bench was fine, but Harold's psychological wellbeing, was definitely in jeopardy.

"I've got to get outta here," Harold sighed breathlessly.

He walked down to the lower deck of the reactor room and stared at four gauges, each showing a vital parameter of the reactor's health. Harold wasn't thinking about the reactor's temperature or pressure, but about how he had waited nine years to see his mother's killer on trial. And now he wouldn't be able to attend the proceedings.

It happened more than once on his shift in the reactor room that he found himself mad as hell, with no port for release. He finally realized that he'd have to be at the trial to maintain his sanity.

Harold explained his frustration concerning the murder investigation and trial date to the ship's chaplain who immediately issued a statement to the head of the Reactor Department to release Harold under hardship circumstances. He was ordered to return to the United States as soon as possible. Harold's anger subsided a bit and his depressing thoughts were replaced by the anticipation of seeing home again.

It was a week after Christmas of 1981 that Harold was on a cargo flight back to Virginia. His division officer, concerned about Harold's state of mind, escorted him through the process of checking in at the airline terminal near Naples, Italy.

There was very little heat in the passenger/cargo area of the plane, which made the eight-hour flight extremely uncomfortable. Harold paced around the huge cargo bay of the craft trying to warm up and thought about his return to Morven.

Arriving in Norfolk, he disembarked the cargo plane, called Sheila and caught the next Amtrak train to Savannah, Georgia where she met him, with baby Scott. Amtrak's southbound passenger train stopped briefly in Savannah on its journey to Miami and was only a few hours drive from Morven.

"I'm so glad to be home, Sheila," Harold said hugging them both. "I thought that I was gonna loose my mind over in the Med."

"I know, Harold," Sheila replied. "I've had a very hard time here too. Scott was so sick that he almost died."

"Yeah, I know. Dad wrote me about it," Harold stated.

Sheila quickly tried to defuse the situation. "Valdosta has been buzzing about Winkler's trial. It's been on the six o'clock news and in all the papers."

Harold tired to concentrate on the upcoming jury selection scheduled for Monday morning and to forget about Sheila's bad behaviour that led to Scott's terrible illness. He was home now, where he wanted to be, and that was all that mattered.

# CHAPTER 15

▼

The courtroom filled quickly on the first day of the trial, after the Harmon and Helen's Grantham family members were seated.

A line of people waited without complaint to get in to watch the trial, including some of Helen's closest friends. Most were granted access into Lowndes County's largest courtroom, including members of the press from Georgia and Florida.

Harold could see several defense attorneys sitting at their table with a number of giant file cases strewn about. District attorney Collier, Starnes and Sparks sat on the opposite side of the courtroom, waiting patiently for everyone to be seated.

Kenny sat amongst his covey of attorneys expressionless. His stiff posture and plain black suit gave him a statue like appearance to the people packed into the courtroom that morning. Kenny's eyes were narrow, conveniently concealing his focus and maximizing his poker face stare.

Foxy was sequestered to the defense witness room, where he sat and pondered over his situation. Lydia had died a few years earlier leaving him alone to face his humiliation. Determined not to let anyone send his son to jail, he continuously reminded himself of the coached responses Kenny's defense had planned.

Solemn jury members filed in as the audience's murmuring slowly died down. They had been selected from one hundred and twenty-five potential candidates, a week earlier. Local residents of Lowndes County, some from Valdosta, others from surrounding cities, made up the twelve-person jury.

Kenny's defense team consisted of five attorneys led by Clay Lee Barker, representing one of the best law firms in Atlanta. Clay Lee's elegant, expensive suit and grey goatee set off his "Southern gentleman's" style, typified by his holier-than-thou demeanor.

The assured stride Clay Lee used to approach the jury with his opening remarks reminded Harold of Foxy Winkler's political power.

"Ladies and gentleman of the jury. During the proceedings of this trial it will become evident that an innocent man has been part of a witch-hunt and accused of killing Mrs. Helen Harmon. Kenny Winkler is a victim of circumstance. His accusers are sitting here expecting you to believe that evidence nine years old can be used to convict a man of murder. Not even good evidence I might add. I only ask that you listen with questioning ears as this unbelievable case is laid before you.

"The district attorney was pressured into finding a scapegoat for the murder of Mrs. Harmon. Everyone here is aware, I'm sure, of the risk that comes with trying a person on circumstantial evidence. You will always have a reasonable doubt about the innocence of that person. The prosecution will have you believe that this man, *without* a reasonable doubt, killed someone he knew and respected.

"In closing I only want to say that Kenny Winkler did not commit a murder eight years ago, or at any time in his life." Clay Lee looked quickly at each and every juror, then boldly made his way back to his table of lawyers who chattered and smiled with content.

"Is the prosecution ready for their opening statement?" Judge Johnson asked.

"Yes, your honor," Collier said.

Collier stood and walked over to the jury box. His down-to-earth style and plain clothes were in stark contrast to the foppish-looking Barker.

"Ladies and gentleman of the jury," Collier said in a strong voice, "we should begin this trial with the truth, instead of the ineffectual rambling of this high-powered defense. The *truth* is that Kenny Winkler killed Helen Harmon, in cold blood, one day years ago. The truth is that he was infatuated with her and demanded that his desires be met, by whatever means necessary. The truth is that he has a profound belief that he is above the law.

"With the evidence we will present, you will be able to recognize that there are too many incriminating circumstances surrounding the murder that point to only one person. That person, beyond a reasonable doubt, is Kenny Winkler.

"You, people of the jury, are tasked with one occupation these next few days. That is, to listen to all the evidence presented here and decide for yourselves whether Kenny Winkler is guilty of the murder of Helen Harmon. Keeping in mind that no person on God's earth is above the law."

Collier sat back down at the table next to Starnes and drew his witness list from the top of a collection of papers.

Harold now felt a little more confident that the high powered defense team Foxy had selected for Kenny wouldn't be able to save Foxy's soon-to-be destroyed reputation. After all, he too, had been arrested for assisting in the concealing of a murder.

The first day of Kenny's trial was interrupted by Clay Lee's next motion.

"Your honor the defense requests a recess before calling their first witness," Clay Lee stated.

"Any objections from the prosecution?" Judge Johnson asked.

"None, your honor," Collier stated.

"This court will be in recess until 0900 tomorrow morning," Judge Johnson proclaimed.

"All rise," shouted the bailiff.

People filed out of the courtroom through two sets of twin doors. Jerry's sisters sat directly behind Harold, on one of the sixty long benches. He turned to speak to them, but his aunt Laverne couldn't contain herself.

"That defense attorney looks like an old goat," Laverne stated. Several people who overheard turned around as Harold, Polly and Sheila began to chuckle out loud. For a brief moment Harold felt some relief from the stress of being in the courtroom.

Lisa and Jerry were sequestered to the prosecution's witness room, until the jury had been relieved for the day and were not interviewed by the media. But reporters from various news affiliates, performed ad-hoc interviews with many other Grantham family members and friends of Helen's. The Grantham and Harmon families had become well acquainted with each other over the years of dealing with Helen's disappearance. They stood together at her memorial service one year earlier in Morven.

Harold and Sheila left the courthouse together and traveled to her father's house where they were staying during the trial. Lisa decided to stay with Jerry at home and Polly was staying in Quitman with a friend. Sheila's sister was babysitting for Scott.

"Do you want to eat something, Harold?" Sheila asked.

"No, not now. Maybe later," Harold replied.

"I think I'd like to ride to Morven. Do you want to go?" Harold asked.

"No, I'm too tired to go all the way out there today," she replied.

Harold drove down North Valdosta highway toward Hahira and took a look at the old Thunderbowl speedway where he had spent so much time during his high school summers, watching stock-car racing on Saturday nights.

Pulling away from the racetrack Harold smiled a little, enjoying his momentary escape. But by the time he reached Hahira Bridge all the weight of the trial had come back. He drove on to his mother's memorial stone—her bones now lay in the crime lab until after the trial.

Investigators agreed to maintain the body outside Helen's grave, in case there might be another question about the knife marks on her femur bones and around each patella on both legs. But her memorial stone was enough for Harold to focus his thoughts and memories of his mother on, that afternoon.

Watching the attorneys gathering for a battle during the first day of the trial created a sense of separation between his feelings for his mother and the science of putting together a case against her killer. Without saying anything, Harold stared at the stone and remembered his mother playing basketball with him behind their house when he was a little boy.

She had made Jerry put up a wooden-backed basketball goal out by her greenhouse, allowing her to challenge her children occasionally to a game or two. Stones and red clay around the old style basketball court made it very difficult to dribble the ball, but it really didn't matter as long as she was able to play.

Harold took a deep breath and got back into his car. He drove up highway 94 to Valdosta; reminded of the many times he and his mother drove the same route to go shopping on Saturdays when he was a kid—with Lisa and Polly in the backseat talking about the latest rage at school.

His arrival back at Sheila's father's house was uneventful. Scott was already in bed for the night and Sheila was sitting on a very uncomfortable sofa in the living room.

"How are you feeling?" Sheila asked.

"Not bad, a little tired," Harold replied.

"I've been thinking," Sheila said, not looking at Harold. "I don't think I want to go to the trial anymore. I just can't take it."

"Fine. Whatever you want to do is fine," Harold retorted. "I'm gonna go to bed."

Harold suddenly realized that his wife was far too self-centered to just be there at the trial to give him moral support. "She only cares about herself," Harold muttered softly under his breath as he walked into the bedroom.

# CHAPTER 16

▼

Waking from a nightmarish dream in a cold sweat the next morning, Harold, wondering what to make of his visions that night, felt a sharp pain in his neck; a radiating pain from the bottom of his brain through a thick trapezius muscle to the tip of his right shoulder blade. Every time he tried to turn his head left he experienced an electrical shock shoot down a corridor of fire—it caused him to jerk back immediately.

Harold dressed slowly, preparing for what he knew would be a nauseatingly long day of trial proceedings. Detective Starnes had probably put together some very sound evidence for Collier to use, Harold told himself, which made him relax a little.

Sheila, true to her word, stayed home with Scott while Harold got into his Mustang and drove to the courthouse, listening to Rush playing on his cassette player.

Swerving into a freshly asphalted parking lot near the Lowndes County Courthouse, Harold was parked and sitting next to his sister Polly in a matter of minutes.

District Attorney Collier began the day by calling Lisa to the stand; she was the last family member to see Helen alive. Lisa, tall, with long brown curly hair, looked a lot like her mother and several family members wiped tears from their eyes as they watched her take the stand.

Collier began his questioning with dates and times, identifying her relative time of departure from her mother on the morning of August 31st. Type and make of car Helen drove was quickly mentioned.

"Lisa do you remember the dress your mother was wearing the last morning she dropped you off at Lowndes High School?" Collier asked.

"Yes, I do. I remember the exact dress she was wearing. It was one of three matching dresses she had made. One for Polly, one for me and one for herself," Lisa replied.

"Bailiff, please bring in the evidence marked exhibit A," Collier said.

The bailiff left the courtroom long enough to walk to the evidence room and retrieve several items for the prosecution. He re-entered the room with a headless mannequin wearing a light green polyester dress, opened along the seam on both sides, and now tinted a dingy brown. There was also a string of green costume jewelry beads draped around the neck of the mannequin.

"Do you recognize this dress, Lisa?" Collier asked.

A hush came over the courtroom as Lisa turned to look at the dress she had been avoiding up till now. Her face was pale as she viewed the last garment her mother's body ever wore.

Harold felt suffocated with grief as he stared at the mannequin. He felt a scalding sensation of loss and distrust. Tears of anguish filled his eyes, but he stopped them before anyone could see what he was feeling. Mental walls were thrown up, blocking out everything except the science of finding out the truth about what had happened.

"Yes, I remember this dress," Lisa said. She began to weep.

"Your honor, I would like to take a recess, in order for the witness to recover herself," Collier said.

"Yes, of course," Judge Johnson said. "This court will be in recess for one hour."

People waited outside that morning in the rain, hoping to get a seat in the packed courtroom, some were Helen's closest friends, some were law students and others were merely curious.

Harold noticed that Kenny's new wife—he was now long divorced from Jane—was seated alongside Kenny's Aunt Hilda. It was now common knowledge that Aunt Hilda's "old money" paid for his defense attorneys. Kenny's blonde wife looked very self confident and didn't look like the type to be married to a maniac, but looks are deceiving, Harold thought.

Courtroom chatter began to quiet down as the bailiff brought the jury back to their seats. Lisa was brought back to the stand, having composed herself somewhat. Harold, sitting beside Polly, watched their sister intently.

Without moving from the prosecution's table, Collier said, "Your honor, the prosecution has no more questions for this witness."

"Defense may question the witness," Judge Johnson said.

Clay Lee rose from his chair, dressed this day in a pin-stripped suit with wide lapels. His strut of confidence was deliberate and aimed at his opponent's witness.

"Well, Lisa, do you remember everything that happened that morning over nine years ago?" Clay Lee drawled.

"No I can't remember everything that happened on that particular day. But I do remember more about that day than I would normally recall, because it was the last time I saw my mother," Lisa replied.

"In other words, most of the other things going on at the time of your mother's disappearance, you don't remember. Is that right, Lisa?" Clay Lee asked.

"Well, maybe," Lisa replied.

"I believe that will be the case in all the testimony we will hear in this deliberation. That people only remember small parts of what was going on during that period of their lives. Don't you believe that is so, Lisa?" Clay Lee's voice rose as he spoke.

"I remember a lot about my mother, mister, things that I will not *ever* forget. Things that only a daughter or son would know. I loved my mother when I was a teenager," Lisa replied.

"Do you recall your father ever hitting your mother or shouting at her, maybe even cursing her?" Clay Lee taunted.

"No," Lisa replied abruptly.

Clay Lee looked at the judge. "I have no more questions for this witness, your honor."

Lisa returned to the witness room. Harold was proud of how his sister stood up to Clay Lee's questioning. He knew she despised talking about her mother to the defenders of Kenny Winkler, a man who had taunted her throughout her life.

Kenny had seen Lisa out at night in Valdosta several times during the period of time that Helen was missing. He had walked right up to her and tried to talk to her about Helen. His boldness would totally vanquish her self-esteem, making her feel soiled to have even acknowledged his existence.

Harold didn't know if he could have performed as well as Lisa had, answering questions from behind his thick brick wall. Fortunately, neither he nor Polly had to answer questions about the tragic day. Collier felt they only needed one child to testify and Lisa was the oldest of the three.

Collier stood up. "Your honor, I call Jerry Harmon to the stand." As soon as Jerry was sworn in, Collier asked, "Mr. Harmon, would you tell us what you remember about the day your wife Helen Grantham Harmon disappeared?"

"Yes, I arrived home as usual after leaving work about five o'clock. When I got home Kenny called me and said that Helen was missing. He said her purse and car were there, but that she was gone, and they couldn't find her anywhere. So I got into my pickup truck and drove to Winkler Outdoor Advertising"

"Please tell us what you found when you arrived at the Winkler offices," Collier inquired.

"Well, when I walked into the office, I saw Kenny going through Helen's purse. So I grabbed the bag from him and asked him what he thought he was doing. He said that he was looking for her office keys," Jerry declared. "I found the keys in her purse and handed them to Kenny,"

"Bailiff, please bring in Exhibit B," Collier said.

Various remnants of the wooden box, once clad in tin that held Helen's body were brought in, along with a cashbox and a set of keys.

Allowing Jerry to hold the set of keys, Collier asked, "Mr. Harmon, is this the set of keys that you pulled from Helen's purse?"

"Yes, these are the keys," Jerry proclaimed.

"Thank you Mr. Harmon. No more questions for the witness, your honor," Collier said.

"Defense may question the witness," Judge Johnson stated.

"We have no questions for this witness, your honor," Clay Lee said.

There were surprised murmurs in the courtroom but Harold figured the reason Lee wouldn't cross-examine his father was because he knew that Jerry Harmon had been an expert witness in many cases while working as a police officer and a few while a corrections officer at the Lowndes County Correctional Facility.

The next witness came to the stand after lunch. It was Sue, Helen's deaf friend who owned the Morven beauty shop.

Sue was an essential witness for the prosecution to establish Kenny's motive for murdering Helen.

A sign-language interpreter was brought in from Georgia's School for the Deaf to translate the information that Helen's lifelong friend recounted. The prosecution went through all the details of how Helen had described her situation at Winkler Outdoor Advertising. Sue kept up with everything the signing interpreter was asking her and replied quickly to Collier's questions.

Helen's friends from the beauty shop continued to be put on the stand, each remembering what Helen had said about Kenny's advances toward her, his ugly comments when she rebuffed him, and how afraid of him she was. Questioning for that day lasted until about four o'clock. Judge Johnson then released the jury and court was recessed for the day.

Polly followed Harold from the courtroom, along with other family members. She left her brother standing beside his car, after saying her goodbyes and drove off in her small station wagon. Harold went down to Little River that afternoon—he needed desperately to unwind after the day's events.

$$*\qquad*\qquad*\qquad*$$

Harold drove to the Adel Bridge and down the sandy little road that fell off the two-lane highway, steep and rut filled. It would take someone without the "know-how" a long time to commute the pass, but Harold drove down the ditch like he had been doing it all his life, which he had.

Driving up to the edge of the bank of the river he looked from the car into the muddy light brown water. River currents were strong and shaded the color of chocolate milk. Leaves floated through the water as it churned and rolled southward toward Valdosta. The debris would eventually pass by the prison where Jerry worked as a guard.

Harold got out of his Mustang and walked to the edge of the steep embankment of the river. The river was about fifty yards across and fairly shallow at the turn where Harold was standing. Its bank had an incline below his feet that was at least twenty-five feet from the water, but he knew he could walk along this edge to the beginning of the turn in the river. He'd then be on the same plane as the surface of the churning black water.

His mind began to clear as he continued to walk along the riverbank. He felt positive about the way the trial was going. Clay Lee was putting on a good show, as everyone expected he would, but Collier was also proving himself as the trial moved forward.

Harold recognized the sandbar on his left where he and Jack parked their trail bikes after their ride through knee-deep water. When the water level was at its lowest they could ride along the river bed, making sure the bike's tailpipe stayed clear of the water.

Harold and Jack spent much of their free time in junior high riding motorcycles down old dirt river roads that went several miles back into the woods. Roads laden with old trees and giant potholes that'd flip trail bikes over and toss riders into palmetto bushes.

Jack performed more dynamic stunts than Harold had the guts to try including one where he would stand on his motorcycle's seat. Harold chuckled to himself remembering Jack standing straight up with out stretched arms, balancing himself perfectly as he traveled down a paved road between Harold's house and Jack's farm.

Jack's luck ran out one fateful day when the Kawasaki he was riding, standing with his arms out for about fifty yards, began to drift. Realizing that the road was bending, leading away from his current trajectory, didn't seem to bother him. Harold had no idea what Jack was thinking as he watched in horror until Jack reached the pavement's end.

The county had made a great ditch during the road's construction about a year earlier, a ditch that rolled away from the asphalt and up into high brush. Seeing Jack go straight as the road turned left was a thrilling sight. While maintaining his upright pose he went out of sight, vanishing into an abyss of matted brown, neck-high grass and weeds. Harold quickly drove his Suzuki over to where Jack had left the pavement and ran into the brush to locate his friend.

It was awfully quiet, as he approached Jack's dead bike. Harold saw Jack lying face up, smiling.

"Did you see that?" Jack exclaimed.

"Yes, I did," Harold said. Seeing Jack alive was a real relief.

"I felt like, if this was gonna be it for me, I wanted it to at least look good," Jack said with a loud laugh.

"Well, it was awesome!" Harold screamed at his friend.

The two laughed and talked about each detail of the amazing jump while gathering Jack's bike parts, strewn all over. Both boys were stunned to realize that the bike, too, like its owner, was still in good shape except for two broken mirrors and a bent foot peg. Jack started his bike and they rode back to Harold's house for some terrace jumping through peach fields.

Junior high school summers were confusing to say the least for Harold. Between working in the tobacco fields and riding motorcycles, he kept himself very busy in order to avoid thinking about his mother. Little River was a haven, however; he could come here and escape long enough to allow himself time to sort out what his next step in life would be. Most of his steps were just to make it through another day or another week in life.

Snapping out of his daydream, Harold saw broken beer bottles at the base of the embankment he was standing on, at the water's edge. He and his father had spent a lot of shells, shooting bottles and even some beer cans. Most of the beer Jerry drank in those days came in bottles and made great targets, floating in the water like partially submerged "Nazi U-boats," as his father referred to them.

Looking downstream around a slow curve, Harold could see an old rope swing that he and Hank used when swinging into the river on Georgia's hottest days. Somebody delivered a refrigerator to the middle of their landing zone one day, ending great summer fun for the boys.

Walking back to his car Harold let out a sigh of relief, his anxiety now calmed. Harold's brief reverie of times past, even after Helen's disappearance, had given him a much needed respite from the trial.

# CHAPTER 17

▼

Harold didn't sleep very much that night; he still felt that strange electric pain in his neck, and baby Scott woke up crying several times. Harold came into the courtroom looking tired and sad. Polly was running late so Harold sat next to two of his mother's close friends.

Collier's first witness of the day was Jane, Kenny's ex-wife. Kenny had treated her like trash for as long as she could stand it before divorcing him in 1975. Ironically, Kenny introduced her to the man she later married. His name was Bill Johnston, a patrol officer for the Valdosta Police Department.

Bill Johnston became friends with Kenny when he decided to join the policemen's auxiliary of Valdosta in 1973. By joining the auxiliary, Kenny thought he would be closer to the investigation concerning Helen's disappearance. As their friendship grew, Kenny often asked Bill to travel with him and Jane to the lake for water skiing, or go to parties with them.

On many occasions Kenny would become so obnoxious during these outings that Jane couldn't bear to be around him. So, she would often catch a ride home with Bill, and one thing led to another before long.

Kenny believed that Bill had stolen his wife from him. It hurt his arrogant pride so much that Kenny began spying on them from a distance. He would follow them around town, taking notes on their activities. Kenny created a log of Jane and Bill's movements, and put them in a timetable.

One warm autumn night Jane and Bill opened the windows of their bedroom, to catch some fresh cool breezes.

Suddenly, the two heard a noise outside. Bill leaped from the bed and ran the culprit down in the backyard before he could escape. It was Kenny. Bill blackened both of his eyes and reported him to the night watch down at the police department.

One month later Bill was found dead in his house with a rope around his neck. The police determined that Bill had been exercising a little known form of masturbation that included gasping techniques. Jane and the rest of the town believed that Kenny had murdered Bill, but there wasn't enough evidence to bring charges against him.

Collier walked up to Jane where she sat on the witness stand nervously fidgeting and clearly unhappy. But undeniably ready to testify against the man she hated.

"What can you remember about the night Kenny and you were to meet for your wedding reception?" Collier asked her.

"I recall Kenny coming to the reception late, with Foxy, his father," Jane replied.

"Did you notice anything out of the ordinary, Jane? What I mean to say is, was he acting strangely, in any way?" Collier asked.

"Yes, he was. He came into the hall and stood near his father the whole night. He only spoke to me when it was politely necessary.

"There was something else too, that night. He and I left the reception in different cars around ten. He went back to the office, said he had to finish up some paperwork. I decided to go out for a little while before going back to our apartment. When I got there he wasn't there, so I decided to go to bed. He got home around three in the morning, covered in mud and wouldn't tell me why or where he had been all night," Jane said.

"Do you think he was with Foxy that night?" Collier asked.

"Yeah, because I overheard Foxy tell his wife that he, too, was going back to the office that night," Jane said.

Kenny glared at his ex-wife as she spoke. His current wife sat stone-faced a few feet behind Kenny. Harold thought Kenny's lawyers would have their work cut out for them. It almost made him smile.

Prosecution questioning continued until the early afternoon. Jane painted a clear picture of the timeline that Starnes and Sparks had worked out during their investigation. Kenny's whereabouts the night Helen was murdered were becoming clear to the jury; he had the opportunity to bury Helen's body after the heinous crime.

Clay Lee began his belittling interrogation of Jane's story when Collier finished. He couldn't find any holes in her story though and she wound up reiterating what she had said a couple of times over. Clay Lee returned to his seat, not letting anyone see his annoyance and bewilderment.

Harold thought that Clay Lee's team acted like they knew everything they needed to know to have the jury bring back a not guilty verdict. Maybe the Perry Mason showmanship worked in Atlanta, but they were not pulling it off in Valdosta too well.

After Jane was released to the witness room, her father Oscar was brought to the stand. District Attorney Collier validated the timetable Starnes and Sparks described for the day of the murder, including Kenny's availability at the time of Helen's disappearance. It was obvious from the testimony of Jane and Oscar that Kenny came back from Atlanta earlier than expected and that he was out late that night doing some muddy business.

Jury members retired as Judge Johnson called for a recess until the following day. Everyone filed out, this time with little hesitation in the lobby. Trial proceedings were taking their toll on everyone on both sides of the aisle. Granthams and Harmons took their leave quickly after cordial goodbyes. Winkler family members and lawyers moved outside even faster.

$$* \qquad * \qquad * \qquad *$$

An announcement by the bailiff for everyone to rise as Judge Johnson approached his bench started things off the next morning. Collier brought in a locksmith from AAA Lock and Key in Valdosta.

Detective Starnes had been able to track down the truck that Wren and Maynard used the night they helped bury Helen's body in the woods. The truck was registered to somebody south of town, who used it for hauling hogs to and from stockyard sales.

Searching for several days through Department of Vehicles records, Starnes and Sparks eventually found a link that tied the truck to Winkler Advertising. Vehicle records were recorded on microfiche film in the '70s, categorized strangely according to a clerk's personal system. She took that system to her grave, creating a massive overhaul of records by the DMV around 1980.

Lieutenant Sparks saw the truck first as the two investigators arrived at a farm belonging to a man named Denepheu Jackson. The old truck had never been washed or cleaned out since the days when it was used at Winkler Advertising. They checked its vehicle identification number against their printed copy of the old clerk's microfiche scanned document. It was a match, but when Starnes looked inside he noticed that the ignition switch was missing from its mounting spot on the dashboard.

After a short discussion with Jackson, Starnes searched for the ignition switch through hog crap and loose hay lying in the bed near its cab. If found, Starnes thought that he would try to match the switch to the key found in Helen's grave. He could then tie the truck, used by her killer to transport her body in a make-do casket, to Kenny Winkler. Sparks searched through the glove compartment, behind the seat and beneath Jackson's gun rack that held a 12-gauge Remington automatic shotgun and .22 rifle.

Starnes discovered the ignition switch under a few corncobs at the bed's cab end. It had been left there by two gravediggers, who removed it while hotwiring the truck's ignition on that rainy night in Georgia.

Starnes handed Collier the switch from the table of evidence at the front of the courtroom. Collier began his questioning of the locksmith.

"Your honor, I'd like to present as evidence this lock found in the truck of Mr. Denepheu Jackson as Exhibit C."

"Evidence noted, Mr. Collier," Judge Johnson stated.

"Mr. Watson, could you tell me the maker of this ignition switch?" Collier asked.

"Yessir, it's a switch from a vehicle made by GMC," Watson stated.

"Can you approximate the year that this particular switch was made, Mr. Watson?" Collier asked.

"It seems to be from around 1970, but it's hard to give an exact date of manufacture," Watson replied. "But I know from its serial combination that this particular switch was installed in a 1972 GMC pickup."

Collier turned to the judge. "Your honor, the prosecution would like the court to recognize that this switch was linked by CID number to a 1972 GMC truck, registered to Foxy Winkler on June 4, 1972," Collier said. "Mr. Watson, would you attempt to fit this key to the ignition switch?"

Watson, a middle-aged locksmith who needed glasses, tried to fit the keys found buried along with Helen's body into the lock. The same keys that Jerry had held in his hand the day Helen disappeared. They were now too old and too corroded for the locksmith to use for the ignition switch. Expecting this would happen, Collier had previously asked the locksmith to bring the necessary equipment to make a key for this specific ignition switch when asked.

Judge Johnson ordered a recess for half an hour, just long enough for the locksmith to produce a key from serial numbers stamped on the original GMC key.

Everyone stayed very close to the courtroom waiting for recess to end and results to be presented.

Operating the ignition switch with his freshly-made key, the locksmith demonstrated that the rusted old keys found with Helen's body were indeed made for this switch, once installed in Winkler's GMC pickup. There was no doubt in the locksmith's mind that the keys were identical.

The locksmith was presented with the padlock, the key from the office, and the key from the gravesite. He made the connection between the padlock, the rusted key, and the key Starnes discovered in Kenny's glass jar of stray keys. Linking the gas pump key with the truck key helped to reassure the jury that these were the very keys Kenny had taken from Jerry the day Jerry caught Kenny going through Helen's purse.

Major components necessary to commit Helen's murder were introduced to the jury: Opportunity—by establishing a timeline that allowed Kenny to commit the murder and bury the body. Motive—when Helen's friends from the beauty shop described her genuinely frightened frame of mind. Means—to hide her lifeless body was also becoming evident, using the keys.

When court recessed for the day, Harold left the courtroom mentally drained. His relief valve had to be manually lifted before the automatic one went off.

\*     \*     \*     \*

Harold left his father-in-law's house that afternoon to work out at a weight club that was just down the street from a movie theatre that Harold and Sheila used to go to when they were dating. The weights seemed heavy at first as he began with his usual warm-up on the bench press. Then a sudden rush of blood entered his pectoral muscles as he intensified his sets by adding fifty more pounds.

He lifted the bar over and over, reaching exhaustion somewhere around his fifteenth repetition of that set, settling the bar on its uprights. Then he added another one hundred pounds to the bar. This much weight would take him into an abyss of the burning sensation in his deepest muscle tissue, which he required to quell the conflagration in his mind.

A beautiful body builder with the physique of a pageant contestant was the only other lifter in the place.

Their eyes met briefly and Harold said, "Hello."

"Hi," she replied.

"Would you mind giving me a spot, I don't seem to have a partner today?" Harold asked.

"Sure," she said.

"I think I can get it off the rack and I'll let you know when to lift, Okay?" Harold said.

She nodded and walked over to the rear of the bench, as Harold lay down underneath the bar.

The bar came off easily, Harold's mind again burning with the hatred he felt for Kenny. He lowered the weight to his chest and exploded it upward, blood pumping through his pecs again. He lowered the bar and his mind drifted into the pit of anxiety he hid beneath his conscience thinking. It felt good to press the bar back to the top of his reach as he completed another repetition.

"Come on, you can push it," she shouted.

This time the weight began to feel as though he was pushing on a giant sponge with a stone center. Heavy, but he could still bear it.

Weights and bar slowly moved together toward the summit of his mental wall, a wall he was constructing with each and every repetition he forced himself to push.

"I've got it," Harold grunted.

"Come on, babe. Make it burn," she said.

His next arduous lift required her touching the bar, not helping as much as just feeling confident that she would give it a boost if needed. Harold lowered it quickly and began to push his next stone. As unimportant as it might have seemed to his unknowing partner, this might be the move that released his frustration today. The blast of energy required to push it to the top was fueled by the loathing he had for Kenny Winkler.

Blood flooded into his torso, making him feel sick and ready to throw up. With very little air left, he whispered, "One more."

"Okay, give it to me this time," his beautiful partner said. She leaned over the bench to grab the weight.

Lowering the bar to his torso Harold knew that he was burned out and the weight would crush him if his gracious partner didn't pull it off his chest. There was a thud as it hit him upper chest level. He grunted and she grabbed for the bar.

Harold pushed with what little strength he had left and she did the rest. Slowly moving the bar upward Harold finished his last lift and finally rested his efforts by placing the bar in its uprights, his eyes still watering from the effort.

The set was good for him. "Thanks. For a second there, I didn't think we were going to get that one up!"

"Yeah, me neither. It was a tremendous set, though. I've never seen anyone work out like you do. Are you a bodybuilder?" she asked.

"No, not really, just a lifter. I love the feel of the steel in my hands," Harold said. "These weights always give me back what I put into them."

"Sure, I know what you mean. Hey, are you doing anything tonight?" she asked.

"Afraid so. See, I don't wear my wedding band while I work out. It gets bent around my finger. Sorry," Harold replied.

The rest of Harold's workout consisted of exercise after exercise with more weight than he had ever lifted. Dumbbell work caused blisters to form on top of his thumb knuckle. Bar work left his chest and shoulders so weak and tight he couldn't reach above his head.

Harold left the fitness center physically exhausted, but at least his mind was finally relaxed enough to forget about the trial for a while. After a sauna bath and shower he drove to his father-in-law's house and dove into bed, saying very little to Sheila who was in the living room watching T.V. with her father and brother.

In bed, Harold thought about the young woman at the fitness center, how he'd have loved to take her out, talk to her about what he was going through—it would be so different than his limited communication with Sheila. It dawned on Harold that he was unhappily married.

*       *       *       *

Court was back in session the following morning, with crowds gathered at the entrance. Newspaper reporters were humming through the crowd, interviewing some family members while waiting for the doors to open to the public.

It was Friday and District Attorney Collier wanted to spend his day questioning employees of Winkler Outdoor Advertising. He called two former employees to the stand, both stating there had been a lot of tension between Kenny and Helen. One even stated that he saw Helen slap Kenny's face near the water cooler two days prior to her disappearance.

Collier thought it was time to bring in a weatherman from the Valdosta Airport to testify that weather conditions for August 31, 1972 included rainstorms.

The weatherman stated, "Rainstorms started about 18:00 that night and continued until the following afternoon."

"Several inches of rain fell during that night, according to the airport records," Collier said. "Enough to change dirt roads into muddy quagmires. Rain enough to stop men from burying a body in the woods."

"Objection, your honor," Clay Lee shouted. "The weather's got nothing to do with this case."

"Objection overruled." Judge Johnson said. "Continue your examination, Mr. Collier."

"I have no further questions for this witness, your honor," Collier stated.

"Your witness, Mr. Lee," Judge Johnson said.

Clay Lee stood up and came to the center of the courtroom. There was a pregnant pause and then Clay Lee said, "Your honor, I have no questions for this witness." He slowly walked back to his table of supporters, looking for some help.

The prosecution's case was building effectively against Kenny, but his defense attorneys relied on jurors throwing out testimonies, based solely on memories over nine years old. Kenny's attorneys used a defense strategy that rested on Clay Lee's reputation. He repeated several times that memories of witnesses were clouded by time and couldn't be blamed for wanting to find a killer. He stated in many different ways, time and time again, that Kenny was just a victim in the community's witch-hunt.

When court was recessed until Monday morning, before departing, Judge Johnson admonished the jury, "not to discuss any part of this case or the trial with anyone."

Harold arrived at his father-in-law's house late that afternoon and Sheila told him she wanted to go out into town for a quick dinner and movie. Harold didn't object so they left Scott with Sheila's older sister, and headed to town and a restaurant named Shoney's which always had an adequate salad bar and the food was reasonable enough for a sailor on E-5 pay. They sat in a back booth and unwrapped their silverware from the paper napkin blanket.

A waitress came over to the booth. "Can I hep y'all?"

"We're just gonna go to the salad bar," Harold replied.

"Okay then," the waitress said. "Anything to drink?"

"I'd like iced tea," Sheila said.

"Me too," Harold added.

As soon as the waitress walked away, Sheila looked at Harold. "Who was questioned today?" she asked, but without interest.

"Employees from Winkler Advertising; they were good witnesses. One even stated that he saw Kenny get slapped by my mom," Harold said.

"You know everyone is talking about this case," Sheila said. "Seems like every conversation I overhear ends up with some kind of comment about it."

"I know. I heard someone on the phone at the fitness center while I was work-ing out talking about the trial," Harold said. "But they were on Kenny's side. People are divided by whose side they believe is telling the truth."

"I am overwhelmed by it all, Harold," Sheila said. "I cannot explain to you how hard this is for me to cope with."

Harold tried to calm her. "Yes, it's very tough for all of us to think about every day."

Sheila had tears rolling down both cheeks. "No, I am really having problems thinking straight!"

The waitress came to their table with two glasses full of crushed ice and sweet tea. "Here's y'alls sweet tea," she said, putting the tea down and walking away.

Harold sipped his tea. "Why don't we go to the salad bar?"

Sheila ignored Harold's suggestion. "Fact is, I want to leave," she said through pursed lips.

"You know that I can't leave now," Harold retorted.

Silence between the two was so thick that Harold thought it felt like a change in atmospheric pressure, before a storm.

"Okay, let's just finish our supper and talk about this at home," Harold said. He wanted to avoid talking about leaving Valdosta until the trial was over.

They ate in silence, with Sheila picking at her salad and Harold wishing every-thing was different than it was.

Harold was up before dawn on Saturday morning. He made a strong pot of coffee, then woke Sheila and Scott. They were going to spend the entire day at the Harmon house with Jerry, Betty, Lisa and Polly.

Soon after their arrival, Jerry suggested that Harold put some chicken on the grill in the backyard. Jerry was still using his 55-gallon drum grill. It was cut lengthwise at the prison camp by prisoners trying to make cigarette money. Also welded to its frame was a small shelf that he could use for barbecue sauce and other paraphernalia needed for grilling.

Lisa and Polly played with their baby nephew while the others laid out the pic-nic table with plates, and bowls of potato salad, cole slaw, and cornbread. It took about an hour to get the charcoal red hot and ready for cooking chicken halves, then another hour to eat the succulent meal. Sheila looked uncomfortable around the Harmons and was glad she had the excuse of needing to get Scott home and to bed. Hasty goodbyes were said and soon Harold was driving his family to the house in Valdosta.

The front page of the Sunday Atlanta Constitution was plastered with a long article about the trial. Inside, the Sunday magazine section's cover was a picture of Clay Lee standing in front of his home in North Georgia. The magazine had a four-page description of his legal accomplishments and personal information.

Harold poured himself a cup of coffee and read the article, then called Polly who was staying at the Harmon house during the weekend. She had already picked up a copy from Quitman, after church.

Lisa got on the phone and said, "Harold, I'll bet this article and all that Clay Lee publicity was paid for with Winkler money."

"You're probably right," Harold agreed.

Clay Lee was a prominent lawyer in and around Atlanta, with a strong reputation for winning cases. He usually didn't leave the Atlanta area, but took the Winkler case thinking that it would be his last one before retirement—one more feather in his cap of distinction.

"Well," Lisa said, "with any luck he'll lose his last case."

"He will, Lisa," Harold reassured his sister.

# CHAPTER 18

▼

Monday's procedures began by allowing statements from both the prosecution and the defense. The jury listened as Collier went back over evidence presented so far by the prosecution, then Clay Lee tried to dispute its validity, proclaiming that most of the evidence was hearsay and the rest was just too old and therefore, too unreliable, to send a man to prison. "No one should be convicted if there is a reasonable doubt of his or her innocence," Clay Lee concluded as he stared at the jurors.

When the statements were finished, Judge Johnson said, "Mr. Collier, call your first witness."

"Your honor, the prosecution calls Elijah Maynard," Collier said, his voice firm and confident.

The bailiff escorted the frail black man in his seventies into the courtroom and up the two steps to the witness stand. With one hand on the bible, Maynard swore to tell the truth.

"So, Mr. Maynard, what do you think caused the death of Helen Harmon?" Collier asked.

"I don't know anything about her dying," Maynard said.

Harold looked over at his sister in shock and horror. Kenny had a smug half-smile on his face. Maynard was recanting his entire confession that detective Starnes had worked months to get out of him. It had been recorded on tape by Starnes but the tape couldn't be brought into the courtroom for the jury to hear. It was considered inadmissible evidence.

"You remember Detective Starnes sitting right over there, Mr. Maynard?" Collier asked, pointing to Starnes seated at the prosecution table.

"Yeah, shore I 'member him," Maynard said.

"Do you remember telling Detective Starnes that you helped carry a wooden box to a secluded area out near the airport and burying it in 1972?" Collier asked.

"Dat ain't what I said. But dat detective kept on axing me until dat's what I told him," Maynard said.

"Do you know what perjury is, Mr. Maynard?" Collier asked.

"Yeah, I know, but I ain't perjurin'!" Maynard exclaimed.

Maynard had been on the Winkler cash payroll for the last nine years, without working for a dime of the money. Harold knew that he would never admit to what he had done now. Maynard blamed his confession on badgering and coercive questioning by Starnes.

Collier knew it was hopeless for the moment. "No further questions, your honor."

"I have none, either," Clay Lee said, knowing when to leave well enough alone.

Samuel Wren was then bought into the courtroom. After his swearing-in Collier approached him. "Mr. Wren, would you state your name for the court?"

"Samuel Wren."

"Mr. Wren, do you remember digging a hole with Kenny Winkler nine years ago near the airport and burying a wooden box in it?" Collier asked.

"No sir," Wren said with a questioning tone.

Wren looked totally confused as he glared down at his shoes. He was the picture of an uneducated man who had served his employer like a slave. This slave knew he hadn't worked in years though and that the Winkler family still paid him his salary, in cash. But he, too, had confessed to Starnes during questioning the previous July. It was now January 1982 and Wren was trying to remember back to the last time he was asked these questions.

"Now, Mr. Wren, listen to this question very carefully. Do you remember digging a hole one rainy night back in 1972 out by the airport?" Collier asked.

"Yessir, I do. Me and Maynard buried a box dat Mr. Kenny told us to. I axed what had happen to dat poor woman, but he wouldn't tell me. Just told me to keep my mouth shet," Wren said.

"Did you put Helen Harmon's body in that box, Mr. Wren?" Collier asked.

"I didn't put her body in dat box," Wren said.

"Did you put anything in that box, Mr. Wren?" Collier asked.

"Yessir, I put her legs in dere," Wren said.

"No more questions, your honor," Collier said.

Collier sat back down at his table a little relieved that Wren had come through with the same confession that Starnes had gotten out of him.

Clay Lee arose from his chair and sauntered to the front of the witness stand.

"Mr. Wren, did Detective Starnes threaten you with going to jail if you didn't say you remembered burying a box in the woods?" Clay Lee asked.

"Yessir," Wren said.

"Why do you think that he asked you to say that, Mr. Wren?" Clay Lee asked.

"Well, I reckon he know'd Maynard might lie," Wren said.

The courtroom broke out in restrained laughter. Clay Lee turned away from the jury and composed himself; he was getting furious. His body language was speaking loudly, warning of his attack.

Smirking a little, Clay Lee turned to Wren. "Do you honestly remember going out nine years ago and burying some box in the woods?"

"Na sir," Wren said.

"Did you hear what I said, Mr. Wren? That is, do you remember going out nine years ago and burying a box in the woods with Maynard and Kenny Winkler?" Clay Lee asked.

The jury suddenly seemed visibly shaken by what Wren was saying. Wren lost his perspective and was beginning to answer questions the way he thought Clay Lee wanted him to answer.

"Yessir," Wren said.

"Did you understand what I said or are you answering the question?" Clay Lee asked.

Wren was obviously confused.

"Yessir I's understand," Wren said.

Clay Lee slowly sat back at his table, amazed at what had just happened. "No further questions, your honor,"

"Your honor, I'd like to question the witness again," Collier said.

"Yes, Mr. Collier," Judge Johnson said.

Collier walked up to Wren and smiled gently. "Mr. Wren, think carefully now and answer this question to the best of your memory. Did you help Kenny Winkler bury a big wooden box in the woods nine years ago?" Collier asked.

"Well, yeah I 'member burying that box. Yessir I do," Wren said again.

"Are you sure that you remember burying a box like the one sitting right over there." Collier pointed to the leftovers of the box that held Helen's body.

"Yessir, I heped Kenny and Maynard bury that box," Wren said.

"Okay, Mr. Wren, that's all," Collier said and sat back down, relieved that the story had been straightened out again.

The prosecution rested after Wren's testimony, sensing that Clay Lee's attempt to confuse Wren had been curtailed. It was difficult to see any reactions from the jurors after Maynard and Wren finished their testimonies. Collier had depended on them bringing their stories to light, thereby exposing Kenny's murderous actions and Foxy's efforts to protect his heir. It wasn't a complete and clear victory, but he felt that enough had been recalled by Wren to sway the jury.

Clay Lee began his witness list with one of Kenny's friends who stated that he believed Kenny was not guilty. It was a weak witness and didn't mean much to the case. Three other character witnesses were called to testify to Kenny's personality traits. Most who actually knew him thought him to be strange and unpredictable.

Clay Lee decided to bring Foxy Winkler to the stand in the afternoon. Clay Lee opened the questioning with, "Mr. Winkler, would you describe what you remember about August 31, 1972?"

Kenny's father told his version of how he and Kenny had arrived back in town and went to his office around four o'clock in the afternoon. His story contradicted Oscar's recollection of the times of arrival and departure, but it all sounded convincing the first time through.

Clay Lee released Foxy to Collier who immediately started breaking down Foxy's story. The details of their stop at Oscar's garage that afternoon began to confuse him; times of arrival and departure became muddled. By the end of Collier's cross-examination, Foxy was no longer contradicting Oscar's story. The case became stronger for the prosecution as Foxy continued to testify for over two hours.

Kenny's expression never changed as Foxy began to change his story. One would say, "the truth bell rang loudest," during his attempt to outwit Collier. Kenny could not have known that his own father would be the witness to take him down. After all, Foxy had always covered for his son through all his years of criminal and immoral behaviour.

But now Foxy was a broken man, ill and frail. He could probably still be "foxy" in his business dealings and when manipulating politicians, but now he was the hen in the hen house waiting to be sacked, with nowhere to hide.

Harold felt a swell of relief come over him as Foxy's questioning continued through the afternoon. In spite of all that was happening, Clay Lee couldn't break his façade to express his outrage. He was a master at looking victorious in the face of defeat.

Foxy was excused by Judge Johnson and slowly stepped down from the witness box. His head hung low as he stumbled back to the witness room. He knew that he could be next on the prosecution's list for charges of aiding and abetting in a murder.

Ending the day of testimony early, Judge Johnson dismissed the jury and recessed court.

✳    ✳    ✳    ✳

Kenny's testimony was last in the proceedings. Sanctimoniously coming to the stand, Kenny sat down in the witness chair around nine a.m. that frosty morning.

Clay Lee must have realized that he was commanding a sinking ship. He elected to go back to North Georgia the previous night, and didn't come to court on that day. He could not imagine sitting at the defense table watching one of his team of lawyers try to explain why Kenny shouldn't be convicted by a jury of his peers. Clay Lee's law firm's work was done.

George McMillan, a long time attorney on permanent retainer with the Winkler family, opened Kenny's questioning by allowing him to describe his version of his actions on the day he killed Helen.

McMillan paraphrased every utterance that Kenny made, trying to convince the jury he was telling the truth and give them some reason to feel little doubt about his innocence. McMillan wasn't as flamboyant as Clay Lee, but a decent local lawyer with local respect. Kenny finished his story and McMillan released the witness to Collier.

"Mr. Winkler, would you say that you are a passionate man?" Collier asked.

Kenny shifted his position and looked directly into Collier's eyes. "I appreciate life. Yes."

Collier walked nearer to Kenny and asked him, "Will you explain why you returned to your office early from your trip to Atlanta the day Mrs. Harmon disappeared?"

"I remember getting to the office at four o'clock," Kenny said, his posture stiff and practiced.

"Mr. Winkler we have witnesses that saw you in Albany the day of the murder and have testified that you left that city at one o'clock," Collier said. "That'd give you plenty of time to get to Valdosta and to your father's office by say, two forty-five."

Kenny sat still with an expression of repugnance on his face. "I have told you the truth—I got to the office at four o'clock."

"But Mr. Winkler, why did you call the victims husband?" Collier began, "It seems odd that you would've suspected Mrs. Harmon left her job, without taking her purse or car. Why do you think she would do that Mr. Winkler?"

"I don't know why she would leave her purse, but I called Mr. Harmon to see if he had heard from her," Kenny said, now looking toward his lawyers.

"And, Mr. Winkler, why were you going through Mrs. Harmon's purse when Mr. Harmon arrived at the office that day?"

Kenny shifted in his seat again before answering Collier's question. "I was looking for the office keys."

"Do you believe that you can search someone's personal property without their permission, Mr. Winkler?" Collier asked. "What were you doing?"

Kenny had thought about his response to this question for many years, his words seemed automatic. "I had an emergency on my hands and I needed to get the office keys from Mrs. Harmon's purse."

"What keys were usually kept with that set of keys, I mean on the same key ring, Mr. Winkler?"

"There was a key to the office in addition to some other miscellaneous keys," Kenny answered Collier with a scripted response.

"Isn't it true, that a key to the company's gas pump was also on that key ring, Mr. Winkler?" Collier asked.

Kenny tried to focus on every question Collier was asking him. "Yeah, I believe a key to the company gas pump was on that ring."

Collier came back at Kenny. "But don't you think that if Helen was gonna leave the office she would have locked the door before leaving? There were no signs of a struggle in the office. I believe that Mrs. Harmon would not have left that office without her keys or her purse. What do you think Mr. Winkler?"

"Objection your honor, the prosecution is asking the witness to speculate," McMillan called out.

"Sustained," Judge Johnson said.

"I will rephrase your honor," Collier said, stepping in front of jurors briefly and speaking more in their direction than Kenny's. "Why did Mr. Harmon find you going through Mrs. Harmon's purse?"

Harold watched Kenny answer questions about his actions the day of the murder, hanging on every word, hoping Collier would find a crack in his story. Everyone knew that Kenny had had years to prepare for his day in court and a prosecutor's questioning. Harold prayed for an exposed lie.

Kenny appeared aggravated now with Collier. "Like I said, I needed to get the pump key—uh, office keys."

The short stumble was the closest Collier got to confusing Kenny; he was well prepared for his testimony and kept himself focused on his script.

Collier knew that Kenny would never relinquish the truth about what happened that night in 1972, but he attempted to at least show the jury what Kenny was thinking during the trial. No matter what was said during the past two weeks of testimony by witnesses and evidence brought against him, Kenny felt that he was above it all and would walk away. His "holier than thou" attitude came out in his testimony with blinding illumination.

Final statements began with George McMillan. He tried to explain to the jury how detectives and the prosecuting D.A. had not put together an airtight case against Kenny and attempted to convince them that there was reasonable doubt and to convict a man with any doubt of his innocence was unacceptable.

Collier allowed the support attorney Helen's brother had hired to give a rather mismanaged closing statement to the jury, before giving his own powerful final statement. The supporting attorney's point finally made its way home, save several mistakes, and then Collier arose from his chair.

"Ladies and gentlemen of the jury, please let me begin by explaining to you that you have been awarded the task of deciding the fate of a man's life. Remember that you are charged with listening and examining all the information presented for and against this man during his trial, then deciding his guilt or innocence based on the facts.

"I contend that this man has committed the horrendous crime of killing Helen Grantham Harmon, a woman only thirty-five years old, for his own pleasure. Helen left three teenage children and a loving husband who was burdened with raising his children without their mother.

"You have heard eyewitness testimony from the men who buried her body in a tin-covered wooden box from Winkler Outdoor Advertising, easily accessible to Kenny. Friends and family came forward to defend Helen's character, describing her as a loving mother and good employee. And for her hard work at Winkler Outdoor Advertising, Kenny sexually harassed her to the point where she had to slap his face to stop his advances.

"But Kenny would not stop, he would not let someone that he thought was beneath him in social status embarrass him in public. Kenny became a killer, a killer who came back to his father's office early after a meeting in Atlanta. Then he took up his frustration and hatred toward all women and released it on a young mother of three.

"Kenny Winkler found a piece of rope lying around the office and strangled Helen with it, then had his way with her. When he was done with her body, he tried to put it into a box that was obviously too short for a woman of her stature. Therefore, I believe that Kenny cut Helen's legs off at the knee, and stuffed her into the box piece by piece."

At this point there were low gasps and moans from numerous people in the courtroom. Even one or two jurors looked like they were about to throw up and one woman kept dabbing her eyes with a handkerchief.

Collier went on, "He and his father then rounded up two trusted employees to help them carry her lifeless remains in her improvised casket out to a wooded area near Valdosta's airport. Kenny and Foxy then forced these two men to dig a hole and bury her remains in a hidden grave, where she stayed for eight years.

"What kind of a man would do these things? I ask you to remember testimony from people who know him and have testified about his behavior the night of his wedding reception.

"I solicit you as a jury to take these things into account and conclude that Kenny Winkler is guilty, of murder."

As Collier went back to his seat he noticed for the first time how many people in the courtroom were visibly shaken. Harold glared at Kenny who sat stone-faced and unmoving.

Harold figured there would be several hours of deliberation by the jury before their final decision would be reached. His mind was burning from the stress and he felt that some kind of distraction to pass the time would be a relief. He needed a trailer-hitch mounted to his Mustang so that he could carry Sheila and Scott's accumulated belongings from Valdosta back in a U-Haul so he gathered the notes he had been taking and made a call to the nearest Ford dealership before leaving the courthouse.

Radio stations in Valdosta were constantly monitoring the trial and broadcasting updates each time a major witness came to the stand. When he turned on his radio that morning Harold heard the announcer say that the jury had retired for their deliberations.

Langdale Ford's shop supervisor was ready for Harold, stretched out in his bay was a trailer hitch waiting for a free mechanic. Harold walked around the showroom looking at cars and listening to the latest promotional crap that a nearby plaid suit peddler had to offer him when he overheard a phone conversation taking place in the manager's office.

"Yeah, we're all upset about the trial here in Valdosta," the manager said, listened to the voice on the other end, and then went on, "But that Winkler has always been in trouble. His old man has bought and paid his way out of more wrongdoing than anyone can imagine," the manager stated. "Take my word for it, he's going to jail for a long time."

Harold smiled knowing that a complete stranger felt the same as his family. All the newspapers, radio and television stations were slanting the stories in different directions, every other day. It seemed that no one had a clue which way the jury would decide that morning.

Walking around, pretending to notice price listings pasted on rear passenger windows of cars, Harold thought about what would happen if Kenny were found innocent. Could he deal with knowing that his mother's killer was on the streets of Valdosta, conducting business as usual.

The hitch was finally on his car and Harold drove away, thinking only about the jury and their deliberations. It had been two hours since he left court to go to the shop, when he pulled into the courthouse parking lot. He wanted to be in the courtroom for the reading of their verdict, but when he arrived everyone was inside, including Sheila, who had said she wanted to be there for the verdict. She was standing in front of the huge, richly stained doors of the courtroom, smiling and crying. Harold had missed the reading of the verdict by about ten minutes.

Witnesses were now out in the hallway, along with all of Harold's family. Everyone was shocked that the verdict had come so quickly.

Guilty. It was unanimous. Judge Johnson had told Kenny and his attorneys to please stand. An immediate sentence was passed down. "Kenny Winkler," Judge Johnson intoned, "I sentence you to incarceration in the state prison for the rest of your natural life."

Clay Lee provided instructions for McMillan to immediately ask for an appeal before leaving for Atlanta the evening before.

# CHAPTER 19

▼

Harold left the courtroom with Sheila, Lisa, and Polly. Jerry had already left with Betty without delay right after the verdict was read. Detective Starnes had only spoken to Harold in passing during the trial—it wasn't in his character to socialize much. But as the group was leaving the courthouse, Starnes called out to him. Harold went over to the detective and shook his hand with tears in his eyes.

Starnes smiled. "I just wanted to say that I'm so glad we put Winkler in prison today. With the evidence that we had there was no doubt in my mind that he was going to be convicted."

"You're absolutely, right Detective Starnes," Harold said. "And we want to thank you for all the work you put into this case."

"It's my job," Starnes replied.

Helen's vindicated children, now in their twenties, continued on their way outside the courthouse and into the parking lot. Everyone decided to head back to Harmon farm for a visit with Jerry and Betty before going home. Harold rode with Sheila to her father's house to pick up Scott and then to Morven for one last supper before going back to Virginia and the Nimitz.

They were all waiting on Harold to arrive so that he could start the steaks on Jerry's old grill. Harold dumped about five pounds of charcoal into the big grill and lit the fire with lighter fluid. After about twenty minutes Harold placed the T-bone and rib-eye steaks on the wire mesh that lay across the hot charcoal.

"I'm so glad the trial is over," Lisa said.

"Yeah, me too," Polly said.

"I believe that he's gonna use all three of his appeals. His lawyers were planning the first appeal before their closing statements were even read," Harold said cynically. "That's why Clay Lee didn't even show up for the closing arguments. He was probably out working on the first one."

Jerry smiled. "His appeals will be turned down, you'll see." He paused. "If he ever got out, I'd kill him with my bare hands."

"You won't have to do it alone, dad," Harold said, and raised his can of cold beer in a toast.

About an hour after their meal Harold sat on the front porch with Polly. "I'm glad that we sat together during the trial, Polly."

"Me too, Harold. I don't think that I could've made it through without you being there with me," Polly said.

"I haven't told anyone yet, but I called the district attorney's office this afternoon and spoke to Collier," Harold volunteered. "I wanted to know when he would prosecute Foxy."

"Oh, what did he say?"

Harold took another sip of iced tea before answering. "He said Foxy was an old man and trying to convict him would take too much effort." Harold paused briefly. "Collier told me that I should forget about Foxy and be glad that Kenny was going to prison."

Polly turned to look at Harold. "Do you think Foxy still has friends in high places?"

"Of course, but he'll be in hell soon enough," Harold said and changed the subject to avoid his building anger.

Harold's little family left for Norfolk the next morning after saying their farewells to Sheila's father. Scott was cranky for most of the drive, but at least Harold noticed Sheila was taking better care of the baby.

Sheila and Harold stayed with an uncle of hers until they found an apartment in a duplex near the naval base. The small apartment was close to a beachfront known as Ocean View and was within bicycle range of the ship for Harold—he was thinking about summer living in Norfolk already. But he was also planning on leaving the service the following year.

Ocean View was not as nice as other beach areas because it was located in a harbor area with little open water circulation. Ships leaving the navy piers would pass about five miles offshore from the beach, depositing oil and trash trails behind that would eventually wash up onshore. But being close to the sea was relaxing no matter how dirty the water seemed to be.

Bicycling to work every day kept Harold in very good shape during the spring months. Sheila would drop off Scott at day-care and go to work at the Navy

Exchange. Her job as a salesgirl kept her busy and the extra money helped with their bills.

Harold was assigned Master at Arms duty again on the naval base until the Nimitz returned from its Mediterranean Sea cruise in February. His job was to watch over hardened criminals awaiting transfer to federal prison—they were being held in a barracks with bars on the windows.

It was a stressful assignment, but it went by quickly and soon the Nimitz arrived at Pier 12 as scheduled. Harold was glad to hear the news that she had moored and within two days he made his transfer back aboard.

Harold's way of thinking had changed soon after the jury's verdict was read. Although his confidence level was high, he couldn't communicate with the men in his division the way he had before the trial. Harold had completely closed the brick wall surrounding his feelings. Only Sheila and Scott were inside, everyone else was on the outside.

He traveled to his job aboard the Nimitz every day in Norfolk, but never said more than two extraneous words to anyone. He was able to continue his daily duties as a watch-stander, avoiding any small talk—he was constantly thinking about the trial's outcome.

Actually, Harold really didn't need to say much about his personal life to be a good reactor operator. The commands he received and gave were flat line directives. He could not find a reason to pull himself out of the deep depression he was sinking into. Depression was also beginning to take its toll on his waning relationship with Sheila.

She was unable to understand what was happening to Harold—she only knew he had changed in some strange way. He was talking to her, but not communicating anything of substance.

Surviving his mental state of disconnect was easier for Harold than it might otherwise have been, had he not spent years avoiding talking about the disappearance of his mother. He'd had a lot of practice at not saying anything about his personal life to friends and acquaintances. Sheila had been the only one whom he could actually discuss his thoughts and feelings with at any length. But she was losing patience with him. It never occurred to her that her husband might need some outside help.

His shipmates also recognized Harold's changes. Rob asked him several times how he was feeling, but Harold couldn't tell him because he truly didn't understand what was wrong. He made himself believe that it was normal behavior for someone who had just gone through one of the toughest ordeals that anyone could face. And, in fact, that was partly true. But keeping this kind of pain bottled up inside could carry a terrible toll.

However, Harold didn't seek help from outside because he was afraid that psychiatric evaluations would somehow influence his promotions through the nuclear power ranks.

During the following four months the fortress Harold built around him blocked the sunshine from his marriage. Sheila had gotten herself into every kind of extra activity she could think of that allowed her to talk to people.

In June, beaches were in full swing and Harold loved to take bike rides down Ocean View near his duplex. Riding his bike invigorated his determination to overcome his melancholy. He really loved to feel the sea breeze as he rode the Raleigh ten-speed that he bought secondhand from a hobbyist repairman in Virginia Beach. The beachfront roads permitted him to ride along and view the pretty girls with their boyfriends tagging along behind them.

Harold pulled over to a beach park one day having ridden his bike over eight miles—he needed a short break.

He sat looking out over the ocean's wavy surface. There had been a storm the night before and the swells were still noble in their cresting height. Harold could see ships treking their course to and from the piers at the naval base, about five miles north.

Harold suddenly noticed someone entering his peripheral view, coming rapidly up on his right side. The man had come toward him from a covered patio near one of the many other bike racks.

"Is this your bike?"

"Yeah, it is," Harold, replied.

"It's nice. Looks fast too," the man said.

Harold thought that he could be in his late twenties or early thirties. Harold was only twenty-four himself.

"You looking for a good time?" the man asked.

"I'm always looking for a good time," Harold replied with a cynical chuckle.

"My friend and I are having a party over at our place," the man said. Pointing to his partner, he asked, "Why don't you come with us?"

Harold realized the man was probably gay, and looking for a kinky threesome with his partner slinking nearby.

"No, I don't think so," Harold replied as he got up from the bench and back onto his bike.

He'd heard stories back on the ship of sailors who had been invited to parties with guys like this. Somehow they'd find the sailors left for dead on some deserted road, somewhere out in the country.

As Harold rode back to the apartment he noticed that a car had been following him through his last two turns. Harold decided that he would make a couple of unnecessary turns, in case the "queers" were following him. After the first of his turns he realized that they were on his tail and starting to pull up on him.

After making the second right, the car pulled up beside him and the man from the park bench leaned out the window on the passenger side.

"Come on and join us. It'll be fun," the man said.

"Sorry. My wife is expecting me," Harold said and pedaled away as the car turned and drove off in the opposite direction.

Harold was indeed relieved that the whole incident had not gotten messy. All he could think about was the guy pulling out a gun and forcing him into the car.

In all Harold's experiences he'd always been able to accept the outcome with faith that God was in charge. God was in charge of his life as well, he had to face that and let his depression go. He had to remove the demon that was suppressing him, drowning him in the venerated ocean. A comforting feeling came over him—he could regain control of his life. He pedaled his ten-speed home with renewed vigor.

A couple of days later, the Nimitz pulled out of Newport News Shipyards for a two-week cruise to Cuba and sea trials around Guantanamo Bay. Feeling better about life Harold accepted his duty and didn't mind that the reactor rooms were so hot and steamy that he could hardly breathe. Adjusting to their sea legs again, the crew set off.

Sheila was left behind to care for Scott for the two weeks Harold would be away. Scott was now one year old and developing quickly, since Harold had been spending time every day with him.

While Harold was at sea, he again worried about Sheila's ability to be a good mother to their son. He remembered his father telling him that when Scott had gotten so sick, the doctor told Jerry that she was not fit to raise a child. But Harold didn't really want to confront Sheila when he came back for the trial.

He still loved her and was so preoccupied by unfolding events of Kenny's trial that he overlooked the incident. But now he had private time to think about it, he became quite distraught about Sheila's very meager maternal instincts. His gut was telling him something was wrong back home.

Sheila had only written him twice while he was out this time, very unusual for her. Normally he would get at least five or six letters when he was out for longer than a week. Somehow Sheila had not seemed as lonely as she had been on all the other cruises that they had gone through as a couple.

Returning on the high tide to Norfolk after the cruise, Harold was in port for a three-week stay. Sheila met him at Pier 12 with Scott in her arms. She seemed fine and Harold was very relieved. He listened as she explained that she had been very busy, keeping up with Scott's everyday routine.

They drove back to their small apartment and Sheila pointed out the used furniture she'd bought at a garage sale, sprucing up the living room somewhat. Although not too comfortable, the furniture was functional and included what would soon be Harold's favorite chair. Dishes were piled high in the sink as usual, but it didn't matter—he was home.

"When do you go back out?" Sheila asked as they sat down to a dinner of tabouleh, rice and another Egyptian dish called Kebi bil Sanieh.

"We have to go back out to sea to finish flight qualifications for some new pilots in about three weeks," Harold replied.

"I really hate it when you have to go. I get so lonely here by myself," Sheila said.

"Just remember, I'll get out of the Navy next year and we can move back to Georgia," Harold said, feeding a spoonful of mashed carrots to Scott, who was banging his bowl of baby food on his high-chair. "I can get a job with Georgia Power at the nuclear power station in Baxley,"

"It's not just the Navy—" Sheila began to say, but then stopped.

"What do you mean?" Harold asked.

Sheila avoided his question. "I don't know."

Harold left the conversation open ended; he couldn't think about anything except how happy he was to see his little son. Scott was beginning to respond to Harold's voice and play catch with a small rubber ball.

Harold and Sheila spent the next three weeks trying to improve their communication. Harold stood a full 24-hour duty day, every three days, where he would have to spend the night on the ship. His duty included maintaining the nuclear reactor aboard the Nimitz in a safe and sub-critical state.

He would usually call Sheila sometime during the night while working his long hours. It had become routine for them over the past two years that they had been married. But things were different now because more often than not, Sheila would not be home until after ten o'clock at night.

Harold couldn't figure out what on earth she could be doing out that late. He began swapping shifts with his duty partner and coming home on his duty nights. The apartment would usually be empty when he arrived. The next day

Sheila would come home with Scott in her arms and tell Harold that she'd spent the night with her girlfriend. "It's hard for me to sleep alone in the apartment," she told her rather naïve husband who didn't notice the signs of a cheating wife, so he believed her.

The Nimitz pulled out to perform one more sea trial before the next Mediterranean cruise. This was a two-week cruise to Fort Lauderdale, running flight operations twenty-four hours a day.

Harold attempted to write Sheila his first letter of the cruise, but he couldn't finish it. He realized there was no point to write Sheila letters that he knew she wouldn't answer. He could no longer avoid the feeling that something was happening back in Norfolk, something that he hated—he believed that Sheila was being unfaithful to him.

Harold called Sheila while he was in Fort Lauderdale and told her that the ship was behind schedule. Instead of coming in on Friday night's high tide, they would have to wait till Saturday morning's tide. Because of the Nimitz's size, the ship needed the high tides for a safe entry into Norfolk's harbor.

However, flight operations and sea trials went better than the captain had anticipated and the ship would make its Friday night high tide after all. Harold wanted to contact Sheila about the change in plans, but there was no way of getting a letter to her in time.

"It's gonna be nice to be back in Norfolk," Rob said to Harold as they stood in the hangar bay, watching more and more of Virginia become visible.

"Yeah, I guess," Harold said.

"What's up?" Rob asked.

"I don't know, Rob, things just don't seem right," Harold replied.

"Don't worry, Sheila would have contacted you if something was wrong," Rob said. Harold shrugged but said nothing.

Harold volunteered to be on the reactor shutdown crew before leaving the ship, mainly because he dreaded going home to Sheila. Harold was almost grateful when the Reactor Division Officer told him that the shutdown valve line-ups had to be done over, because someone screwed them up.

A safety valve line-up must be completed on every vessel's power plant each time it comes into port. A nuclear vessel has many more safety systems than a conventional ship, therefore more valves to line up. The Nimitz was no exception.

Al, a nuke from New York, had taken the valve line-ups that everyone was supposed to help in completing and filled them all out. He had worked feverishly on line-up documents for the last two days of the cruise.

Official documents, such as the line-ups, were not to be treated lightly. However, Al used the names of every cartoon character he could think of to fill out the blanks. Donald Duck finished the plant electrical line-up, while Mickey Mouse completed the circulating water valve line-up. It was a funny stunt, until everyone in his department was denied liberty in order to re-perform the line-ups.

Harold was relieved by the duty shutdown watch about nine o'clock, when everything was completed. He put on his civilian clothes and headed to the pier to call Sheila to come and pick him up. Harold got a busy signal on the phone, so he decided to surprise Sheila by catching a cab to the apartment. When he arrived he noticed a truck in the driveway, but never thought about it belonging to another man.

Harold tried to open the front door, but it was locked. That seemed odd because Sheila didn't usually lock the door until she went to bed around midnight. Harold knocked several times.

Sheila opened the door with a very surprised look on her face. Behind her, Harold could see a man sitting on his sofa.

"Harold, what are you doing home?" Sheila asked.

"The ship came in a day early," he said coming into the living room.

"This is David," Sheila said, pointing to the man on the couch. "He's renting the apartment while you're away."

"Why is he renting our apartment?" Harold asked, his voice rising with anger.

"Uh, his wife threw him out and he didn't have anywhere to stay," Sheila said.

"You're a lousy liar," Harold said, his voice low and menacing.

Harold went into the bedroom where he dropped off his bags and the gifts he had brought home. He noticed David's shoes and clothes on the bedroom floor.

Harold was not at all prepared for this situation. All his life he had wanted to have the perfect home. A happy family life for his son, that, he himself couldn't have because Kenny had killed his mother when he was a boy.

Harold looked under the bed and saw his twelve-gauge Remington shotgun. He had bought it right before traveling out to Idaho for nuclear prototype school. He knew he would use it to go hunting for birds when he returned home on leave. Doves were his favorite game, but he also loved to hunt quail that sometimes found their way onto the backfields of the Harmon farm. Now he kept it around for Sheila's protection when he was out to sea.

As he stood in their bedroom, Harold asked himself if she was worth it. Maybe this whole thing was just some kind of mistake, he told himself. It was a possibility that this guy is renting the apartment and everything is okay. But, in his gut he felt otherwise.

Harold left the gun where it was and went into the kitchen where Sheila was busy hiding the marijuana that she and David had been smoking that day, while her son was asleep in his bedroom.

Sheila had made one of the most common mistakes of a cheating Navy wife— not expecting a change in plans based on ocean tides.

Harold watched Sheila for a moment, shaking his head the whole time. Then he headed to the living room to throw David out, but David was already hauling ass out the front door.

Harold went back into the kitchen. "You want to tell me about you and David?" Sheila avoided looking at Harold, pretending to clean an already clean table.

"I told you, he was only renting the apartment for a couple of days, Harold."

Harold just wanted her to admit what she had done so that maybe they could carry on with their lives. But she'd never admit to cheating on Harold—the truth would disgrace her.

Over the next few weeks Harold continued to stand his assigned duty night-shifts, while Sheila spent the night somewhere other than their apartment. Then, one day when he arrived home early in the morning, Harold entered his apartment with his key, but Sheila was nowhere to be found. His bike parked outside Delores, a neighbor of theirs, could see that he was home early, so she came over.

"Harold, listen," Delores started. "I can't stand to see this happen to a nice guy like you."

"Do you know where my wife is?" Harold snapped.

Delores nodded. "Sheila's with David at a hotel in Ocean View," Delores said. "The Beaumont, I can take you there if you want."

"Thanks, Delores," Harold said.

Delores drove Harold to the Beaumont Hotel where he saw his Mustang in the hotel parking lot. Harold thanked Delores and jumped out of her car.

Harold went into an office located in front of a row of rundown hotel rooms.

Pointing to his Mustang parked outside, Harold asked the man behind the desk, "Excuse me sir, do you know where the owner of that car is?"

"Naw, sure don't, but I'll bet she's in room 209 with that guy."

If he found anyone in room 209, there was gonna be hell to pay, no weapons needed this time. Harold jogged over to the nearest stairwell and jumped every other step until he was on the second floor standing in front of room 209.

He knocked on the door, but there was no answer. He knocked again and waited. No response. Harold went downstairs and asked the man at the desk for the key to room 209. "I think my kid is in there asleep and alone!" Harold exclaimed.

"Yeah, sure. But don't tell nobody that you got this from me," the man said, handing the key to Harold.

Harold walked briskly into room 209, but as he expected it was empty. Disgusted, he returned the key to the man at the front desk and then headed to his Mustang which was still in the parking lot.

Harold opened the car door and there in the back seat was a pile of a man's clothes. He grabbed the pile and with one smartly executed swing deposited them into the hotel's partially drained swimming pool.

Smirking a little, Harold started his car and drove back to his apartment, which was still empty. Exhausted from stress and being awake for forty-eight hours he finally collapsed on his bed and slept until late in the afternoon when Sheila finally came home.

"Where have you been?" Harold demanded.

"Don't start on me Harold, I don't want to—" she replied.

Harold interrupted with, "Why was my car out at that hotel and where is Scott?"

"I was helping David move, and of course, Scott was with me. He's now out in the yard."

Harold went outside and found Scott playing with his yellow dump truck in their little yard. He seemed okay, so Harold went back inside, leaving the front door open in order to keep an eye on Scott.

"I've had it," Harold said.

"What do you mean?" Sheila asked.

"You need to either straighten up or go home to Georgia," Harold stated.

"I want to go back to Georgia," Sheila retorted.

"Fine, that seems to be the only way that I'll be able to focus on going back out to sea next week," Harold said. "If you stay here, I'd end up missing ship's movement and reported AWOL." If that happened, Harold could've been sent to Captain's Mast for discipline under the Uniform Code of Military Justice. Maybe decreased in rank and probably a fine of two-month's pay.

Harold went to see a stockbroker in Virginia Beach that he had once used to invest a little money in RCA stock. He told the broker to sell everything. He had accumulated a little extra money for a rainy day by making a quick investment before RCA developed their first digital DVD player. Right now he needed all the money he could get his hands on.

Packing all their belongings into a short U-Haul trailer, he drove Sheila and Scott to Valdosta, to live in a small apartment near her father's house. It wouldn't be ready for a couple of weeks, so he left Sheila at her father's house with enough money to set things up.

He kissed his son goodbye, trying to hold back tears, but couldn't say anything more to Sheila than, "Stay well. Take care of yourself."

Sheila's father and Jerry helped her set up the apartment in Valdosta while the Nimitz pulled out for the Mediterranean that September. Harold wrote to Sheila to find out how Scott was doing, but never received any reply. In November Harold received a letter from Jerry saying that Sheila had left the apartment in Valdosta and moved back to Norfolk as far as he knew.

Harold couldn't believe that Sheila would agree to move to Valdosta just to get him out of the way. But it was true, and he couldn't do anything about it from three thousand miles away. Stress was beginning to consume him when he headed to the gym for the first time in several weeks.

He started his workout with free weights and barbells then went to a chest machine and began to pump the hydraulic pistons attached to its levers. Because of the machine's design, resistance was added according to the lifter's speed of acceleration. Harold worked hard enough to feel the blood rushing through his chest and arms, thinking all the while how cruel Sheila was to punish him with the one thing that hurt him the most. Not knowing where his son was reminded him of not knowing where his mother was for eight years.

Although he felt that Sheila would probably take care of Scott, the aching memory of what Jerry told him about her neglect was impossible to get out of his mind.

Arriving at muster that morning on time as usual, Harold made his way over to one of the many chairs stacked into a briefing room designed for thirty people. Many stood around the room and by the time everyone was inside the count was fifty-two men.

Divisional Senior Chiefs briefed everyone about daily work, upcoming destinations and when to expect the next General Quarters drill. It was a boring uneventful meeting until a listing of new assignments was distributed. Harold had made E6 a couple of weeks into the cruise and was now a First Class Nuclear Machinist. He was put in charge of about half of the number one reactor room machinists that morning. His job was to ensure that men assigned to work under him carried out necessary tasks, essential to maintaining the reactor in a safe condition.

As they broke from the meeting, he was congratulated by many of his peers that he had worked with on the Nimitz for over three years. He was scheduled that morning to operate as the Chief Reactor Watch. It was a position held by a senior person, responsible for all operations of on-watch nuclear machinists in his compartment. Naval Nuclear Power School training was used to its fullest when standing this particular watch. Reactor safety, performance, and casualty control were responsibilities shared by everyone on watch—the Chief Reactor Watch coordinated their activities.

Ships' operations demanded a significant load on the reactor over several weeks and daily SCRAM recovery practice was essential to re-qualifications for the crew. Harold knew that while operating near Guantanamo Bay, the day would be full of normal operations, plus the bonus SCRAM recovery drill.

SCRAM is a term first used by Dr. Enrico Fermi's team during their nuclear pile experiments, conducted in Chicago in 1942. SCRAM today still describes an immediate shutdown of a nuclear reactor should an unsafe condition exist that could threaten its continued safe operation.

Fermi's team of scientists built a contraption above their small uranium and graphite geometrically designed pile, with neutron absorbing control rods attached to shut down its self-sustaining chain reaction of nuclear fission. The contraption was normally inserted to shut down the chain reaction, but was withdrawn by a scientist standing behind a thick lead shield using a long rope, when Fermi gave directions to start up the reactor. An axe man stood adjacent to the rope operator in order to immediately chop the rope and drop into the nuclear fissioning reactor core, a bank of control rods attached to this contraption. Thus the term "Shutdown Control Rod Axe Man" or SCRAM was coined to describe what they might need to do if their fissioning pile went prompt critical and out of control.

Multiple SCRAMs of large nuclear reactors is something that military reactors can handle, without a problem. Ruggedly engineered mechanics keep everything in a safe operating condition even when exposed to repeated drills.

Harold's day was slow to start but as he made hourly tours of his responsible area, stopping to talk to watch standers at every station, he felt uneasy. He noticed that there were a lot of men working that day who had only recently qualified their stations. He reminded them of their listing of assigned valve cleaning and deck painting that had to be done during their watch and then continued his tour.

About halfway into his watch the SCRAM drill started out like any other drill, everyone reacted as they had been trained to and the reactor was shut down in an orderly fashion. Training teams watched the nuclear machinists perform their activities and adding additional insight from their own experience.

When it was over, the order was given to restart the reactor and everyone went to work restoring equipment as usual.

Abrupt changes in plant conditions suddenly created a surge in steam flow and power fluctuations caused by steam generator level swings. Harold immediately took control of his crew's actions and ordered them to determine the cause of steam generator level swings and pressure spikes. His crew went into action to mitigate effects of the level swings, but could not stop automatic makeup and draining that was occurring from a large feed tank designed to feed water to the steam generators.

Harold looked at the large tank's level instrument and noticed that all the water in it had flashed to steam, leaving nothing for its electronic components to grasp and transmit to a level controlling circuit. As water re-entered the instrument electronics, it tried to compensate for the flashing, but time was an enemy to these perturbations and the hot water flashed before automatic electronics could make mechanical components respond.

Harold wondered what could have happened between the SCRAM and reactor start-up. Although it had taken about an hour between reactor shutdown and recovery, it was unlikely that anyone could have changed a level instrument setting. Harold started going from station to station, quickly interrogating each watch stander about their actions.

As he slid down the ladder to the main steam generator feed water pump area he noticed something out of the corner of his eye. He had made that downward sliding movement a thousand times, holding onto handrails and lifting his boon-dockers high enough above the stairs to miss all but the last two, but today a small change in a stainless steel label connected to a even smaller instrument valve was oddly turned backwards.

Normally, Harold could see the shining label to his right as he hit the last step on his ladder slide, so he took a closer look and found that the valve had been recently cleaned. Just then, an officer from the control room peered down from the deck above at him as he reached over and closed the small instrument valve that cross-connected feed tank level instrumentation.

As abruptly as the huge steam generator level swings started, they ceased. Harold looked up at the control room officer who gave him a "good-job" nod and then left number one reactor room.

Harold looked over at the main feed pump watch and just shook his head, as if to say don't let it happen again. Men working and living together as these men did when at sea knew each other's demeanor very well. Today's watch acted guilty and grateful that Harold was on watch that day as he climbed back up the ladder.

His day ended that afternoon when he met Rob and they both went to the mess hall for chow. Red death was on the menu again, so they grabbed a baked potato and a salad of brown tipped lettuce and olives.

"Hey, it's Sunday," Rob said with a smile.

"Yeah, that means ice cream, right?" Harold said.

"You know it," Rob replied.

It was a small tradition they had come to enjoy on Sundays. Even though ice cream was available almost every day, they tried to limit themselves to one on Sunday—it felt more like a treat that way.

"I'll buy you fly," Harold said.

"Okay," Rob said.

Rob returned with ice cream sandwiches from the ice cream store near the barbershop that tasted like heaven after being at sea for a few weeks.

"How's things at home?" Rob asked as they ate their ice cream sandwiches, savoring every bite.

"We're going our separate ways," Harold said.

"Ouch," Rob said, then paused. "Want to tell me about it?"

"Nope," Harold replied.

"Okay," Rob said. "I'm here if you want to talk."

"Thanks, buddy," Harold said.

At first Harold's new position seemed to be too much for him to handle, but instead of resisting more responsibility he embraced it and buried himself in the work. He made schedules and plans for machinery preventive maintenance, filing systems, and cleaning schedules in preparation for the next major inspection. His new position also gave him responsibility for various ventilation spaces and voided storage areas outside of the reactor rooms. He used one of these void spaces to put together a small free weight room that he and a couple of his close friends used every day except Sunday.

The void space was directly off the port chow hall line below deck, which meant that the guys would have to drop down through a manhole to get into the makeshift weight room, earning a few strange looks from sailors eating chow because they were in workout clothes.

But the small room down in the void was ideal for a bench and free weights. Barely enough room was left over for anything else so they would have to move the weight bench when they wanted to do squats or dead lifts. Eventually, word got around of their private gym, leading to groups of four to five guys working out at different times.

It had been four months that Christmas since Harold had heard from Sheila. He continued to send his paychecks to her through automatic deposits at the bank in Valdosta. Finally, he'd seen enough letters and unopened packages he had sent being returned to him "addressee unknown." Harold stopped the money that he was depositing into their account. About two weeks later he received a letter from Sheila asking for money. Harold filed the letter with a Norfolk return address, under his bunk.

He couldn't believe how self-centered and selfish Sheila had become. She had decided to move back to Norfolk as soon as the Nimitz pulled out to sea because she knew that Harold would never miss ship's movement. He was too responsible for that and smart enough to know these six years in the Navy would establish a great beginning to his career in nuclear power operations.

Christmas was an especially lonely time for him, but to relieve some of his stress he decided to go into Naples with some of the guys who were invited to attend a country square dance. Several sailors stationed permanently at the Naples, Italy naval base with their families, would sometimes invite other sailors from ships ported in Naples during Christmas, to join their celebrations.

Arriving on base about noon Harold and five other men were invited to a recreational hall, decorated like a barn for a square dance. Some single girls from the military hospital had been invited to meet and dance with the young sailors. But Harold wasn't interested in any involvement as long as he was still married to Sheila.

When the square-dancing began, Harold moved around the floor according to instructions given by a caller speaking over a microphone and shouting out the moves. Harold didn't really know how to square dance, but tried like everyone else to make the best of their time on shore. At least, it took his mind off more painful thoughts about his personal life.

Christmas of 1982 came and went quickly and Harold was anxious to do only one thing: get home to see Scott. He had definitely decided that his marriage to Sheila was over.

Harold wrote Jerry a long letter in late January to ask him if he would try to find a used Harley Davidson motorcycle, maybe a low-rider for around two thousand dollars. Since Harold had always loved motorcycles and enjoyed riding them in high school, he felt that now owning one again would be fun and cheer him up. He promised he would pay his father back when he picked up his bike that coming March.

Jerry had had two Harleys when he was discharged from the Army after serving two years in Hawaii in the early '50s. There were even old videos Helen had taken with a Kodak video camera of Jerry riding his motorcycle that were still in Harold's memory. One was a pearl white police special and the other a black hog.

Stories about those Harley Davidsons were plentiful after Jerry had a few beers. One story involved him riding his pearl-white police special in Homestead, Florida one afternoon and having to lay it down when an eighteen-wheel semi pulled out in front of him. His motorcycle slid underneath the truck. Luckily, Jerry was thrown from it in time enough to see it crushed by the rear wheels.

The Nimitz was now anchored two miles off the coast of Livorno, Italy, which was close to Pisa. Harold had two day's of shore leave coming up, so he decided to rent a motorcycle at a shop in Livorno as a temporary gift to himself. Although it was still very frigid weather, Harold decided he would take the sleek Italian bike up to Pisa for a long awaited ride. Besides a trip from Livorno to Pisa would be an ideal chance to relax a little and get away from six thousand other sailors.

When he arrived on shore from his long travel by Italian supplied ferry, he jumped on the red Moto Guzzi and headed north towards Pisa along the SS1 highway, which was a two-lane road that wound its way through Tuscany along a winding path of lovely hills, toward one of Italy's oldest cities, Pisa.

Harold arrived in Pisa after his ride invigorated, revived from months of stale re-circulated air aboard the ship. Clean Mediterranean breezes blew through the surrounding forest, leaving the air he was breathing charged with positive ions.

He rode through the city along the Lungarno Galileo adjacent to the Arno, running directly through city's center. Painters, sightseers and tourists were thick through his touring path.

Harold found an older, small hotel along the Arno that had a room for about fifteen U.S. dollars, no frills, but close to city's center. After checking in, he left the hotel to walk toward the leaning tower, about ten minutes away.

Shops filled with chic clothes, jewelry, electronic equipment and all sorts of imported and domestic goods, caught Harold's eye as he walked. It saddened him to think that under happier circumstances he'd have gone into one of these stores and bought a gift or two for Sheila.

Harold's ride back from Pisa to Livorno was bone-chilling and hazardous. Sleet conditions made the small two-lane road slippery and he wasn't wearing a warm enough jacket. Still, Harold felt more relaxed than he had in months. He now thought that he could find enough strength to finish this last Mediterranean cruise. Getting back to the States, finding a small apartment off base and finding Scott were his clear priorities.

Harold's six-year enlistment contract would be up in September of that year and he had already begun to type up his work history to give to head-hunters in Norfolk who were paid by civilian utilities to find Navy-trained operators for civilian nuclear power plants. Personnel managers knew that Navy trained operators came into an organization prepared to start operating immediately. Nuclear power school behind him and experienced as a Chief Reactor Watch, Harold was an excellent candidate for a new facility putting together its operational staff. He was genuinely excited about starting a new career, independent of the Navy.

# CHAPTER 20

▼

Harold landed in Norfolk and spent his first day in port shutting down the reactor and placing it in a safe "cold iron" condition. As soon as his assigned duty was finished Harold went in search of Sheila and Scott.

He traced an address from one of two letters he received during the six-and-a-half-month cruise, back to a beach condo Sheila was renting in Ocean View, near the Norfolk Naval Base. Grabbing a taxi he gave an Asian driver a piece of paper with the address and in fifteen minutes was standing in front of her door.

He knocked and she opened the door of her apartment.

"Hey," Sheila said.

"Hey! Is that all you've got to say?" Harold asked.

"Yeah, that's it," Sheila answered.

Harold stood in the doorway of her condo. "I want my car and my son," he demanded.

"You can have the car, but you don't have a place to keep Scott," Sheila said.

"Where is he? I want to see him," Harold said.

"He's inside, but you can't come in—just a minute," Sheila replied.

She left Harold standing at the door and returned with Scott in her arms. Harold was relieved to see him healthy and talking about his day at the beach. He took Scott from Sheila, and they sat together on the top step of the second floor staircase leading to Sheila's apartment.

"Scott, did you miss me?" Harold asked tentatively.

"Yeah," Scott replied.

"Well I'm home now. Do you want to come live with me?" Harold asked.

"Yeah," Scott said.

Harold knew that he would have to leave Scott until he moved into his own apartment. He spent a few more minutes with his son before taking him back to Sheila, still standing in her doorway. Scott ran back inside, where it was warmer and his toys were waiting for him.

"Okay, I'll be back to pick him up later," Harold said. "Right now give me the keys to my car and good riddance to ya!"

Sheila handed him the keys to the Mustang and Harold left her condo. He was determined to find an apartment and make his life in Hampton, Virginia until he was discharged from the Navy the following September.

Hampton was located across a large bay inlet from Ocean View and was connected to Norfolk by a long bridge, about an hour drive from where the Nimitz was moored. Traffic was usually tolerable unless you were negotiating the bridge on weekends, when everyone traveled back from Virginia Beach.

Harold found a place near a man-made lake, which was built about two years earlier. Apartments near the lake were in much better shape than his duplex flat where he and Sheila lived. Scott would now have a nice place to ride his little red tricycle, but Harold needed to find someone for him to stay with while he was at work.

Harold discovered that a couple of his mates from the ship also lived in his apartment complex and one of them had brought a French-born girl named Maria from Monaco back to the States. They were to be married very soon, and were just waiting on approval for her to stay in the U.S. Harold liked the couple but best of all was the fact that the young French woman was willing to make extra money babysitting Scott.

Sheila was satisfied with the new arrangement. She had to move in with one of her co-workers from Knickerbockers, a bar where she was working. Her hours were long and it didn't pay very well, but she never wanted to go back to school and further her education. All she wanted was to leave Harold and Scott, allowing her the freedom to do as she wished.

Sheila explained to Harold one night on the phone that she had never been out on her own and she wanted to spend some of her life not answering to anyone. "Either you or my father always wanted to control my life. I've never had real personal independence."

"Well, now you've got all the independence you want, Sheila," Harold said sarcastically. "I hope you enjoy it."

Sheila quickly and willingly gave up Scott. "You're the better parent," she told Harold. "Scott will be safer living with you." Harold agreed and took his twenty-two month old son back over the bridge to Hampton and their new place. He rented enough furniture for him and Scott to have beds, dressers and even a few pieces of living room furniture. Nothing fancy, but enough gear to make their place liveable for a few months—until he was discharged from the Navy.

He had one more piece of business on his "things to do when back in the States" list and that was to pick up his Harley Davidson from Georgia. Harold gave Jerry a call the following weekend, standing at the end of Pier 12, shouting loudly over an overused pay phone.

"Hello, it's me."

"Hey, son," Jerry replied.

"How is everything going?" Harold asked.

"We're all fat and happy," Jerry replied. "I bought you a motorcycle."

"I'm so glad you were able to find a Harley. How much was it?"

"Well, it's not a Harley. It's a very nice Honda."

"A Honda!" Harold said, surprised.

"Yeah, and it's an automatic," Jerry said.

"What's an automatic?" Harold asked.

"Well it's fully loaded, with a windshield and hard saddle bags," Jerry said. "And you don't have to change gears."

Harold was silent for a few seconds, very disappointed that he would be riding a motorcycle built for a 65-year old guy touring the U.S. after retiring. He had spent several months imagining himself on a Low Rider or even a Sportster but definitely not a Honda-matic.

"I guess, it'll do for now. Thanks, dad," Harold said.

"Oh, by the way, Kenny's first appeal was denied," Jerry said.

"Great news! He's not gonna get outta prison for a long time," Harold said.

"Well, one down but two more to go. Still, I think you're right," Jerry said.

Foxy had retained Clay Lee and his firm to carry out three appeals for Kenny. Clay Lee was happy to continue taking money from the Winkler family for each of the appeals that Kenny was allowed. They all knew that in the state of Georgia a convict is given only three chances to appeal his case before a Georgia judge.

Harold traveled by train and bus to Morven to pay back his father and pick up his Honda one weekend in May. Scott spent a few days with Sheila while Harold was gone.

He drove the big blue Honda-matic back to Norfolk, traveling up Interstate 95 with all its smooth glory. It was a silky ride, with its windshield, cruise control and automatic transmission, but it wasn't the bike Harold had been dreaming about.

*     *     *     *

Maria was babysitting Scott during the day while Harold was at work. She seemed perfectly happy to take him back over to her apartment every day. Harold didn't own a telephone or TV and she liked to watch soap operas to improve her English. Scott spent the next several months with her and even began to pick up a few French words.

Harold's hope of working for Georgia Power vaporized because he needed a job right away and they weren't hiring. With head-hunters often calling him at work with offers, he felt it best to get a job somewhere and come back to Georgia later.

He sent a letter of application to Grand Gulf Nuclear Power Station located in Port Gibson, Mississippi. It seemed to be the closest plant to his hometown in Georgia and it was offering him an immediate job.

Grand Gulf was finishing upgrades required of all nuclear power plants under construction because of the accident at Three Mile Island. Several emergency systems were redesigned at plants around the U.S. and the world because of problems that were experienced during the partial meltdown of the reactor core.

In an effort to establish a base of Nuclear Operators, Grand Gulf offered prospects like Harold a chance to fly out to Mississippi and take a look at the plant. His tickets arrived as promised and Harold flew to Jackson.

Grand Gulf was located at the end of two-lane road, deep in the forest along the Mississippi River. The very small winding road to the nuclear power station was more of a challenge than it should have been. Experienced drivers passed him around curves and near oncoming traffic, but that sort of driving seemed to be normal for the little road.

Harold pulled up to something that passed for an administration building and met with Bob, who had sent him the plane tickets. Bob was a retired Navy personnel officer with a good working knowledge of what a Navy Nuke was looking for in a career, a Reactor Operator's License.

"Hello, Harold," Bob said. "I'm glad you made it."

"Yes, thanks for your invitation," Harold replied. He was a little nervous knowing that this interview could change his life's direction.

"We've got you scheduled for a simple entrance exam tomorrow. So, you can spend the day looking around the plant," Bob said.

Harold was dying to get into a civilian nuclear facility—he had heard about them for several years. Grand Gulf was currently the largest boiling water nuclear power plant in the world and he couldn't wait to get inside.

"That sounds great," Harold said.

"Okay, I'll call the Main Control Room and get you an Operator to guide you around," Bob stated.

A few minutes later a very tall, thin man came into a small waiting room. Harold had been moved there while Bob interviewed two other Navy nukes.

"Hey ya'll," Hambone said shaking Harold's hand with authority. "Name's Helmut Bonner, but people call me Hambone."

"How're you doing?" Harold replied.

Hambone took Harold through his processing into Grand Gulf, which took about an hour, then began a tour through each building of the huge facility. He was impressed by the sheer size of equipment positioned over several acres of property. Reactor rooms aboard the Nimitz could not compare in size to something like the civilian nuclear facility which had absolutely no space restrictions.

Hambone returned him to a small room full of Operators located just outside of the Main Control Room, after his extended tour. The men were talking about the latest gag that had been played on one of the pipefitting contractors working near the main turbine.

"What's up, Skillet Head?" Hambone shouted in his country twang.

"Hambone, Hambone," Skillet Head replied, two octaves above his normal baritone voice.

It must have been some kind of name calling code Harold thought, but the sound of it was truly hilarious.

"What ya'll doin'?" Hambone shouted.

Skillet Head sipped a cup of freshly brewed coffee and replied, "We're just hanging on."

It was about two o'clock in the afternoon and everyone sitting in the small room had been working on valve line-ups earlier that day. Hundreds of valves had to be lined up before the very first plant start-up for Grand Gulf, scheduled for 1985, if all its equipment finally tested satisfactorily. Concrete for its foundation was poured ten years earlier in 1975 under a cloud of resistance from the locals.

"You find that there French horn again, Skillet Head?" Hambone asked.

"Yep, seen it down near a pipe fitter, on the one thirty-three foot elevation," Skillet Head replied.

Rocked back in his chair one could see that Skillet Head was a portly man about forty, trained in Southern man-child lack of etiquette. His belly was captured with a wide black belt, impressively holding his tight fitting company shirt inside his Jeans. He wore a Redman Chewing Tobacco ball cap that was a one size fits all by adjusting a plastic tab in the back.

Hambone had nicknamed the man Skillet Head for good reason. His ball cap sat snugly atop his large head, held there only because he had extended its tab with a piece of high pressure tape. Skillet Head's nickname was perfect, Harold conceded.

Skillet began to tell his French horn gag as Harold found a coffee cup in the metal cupboard. When he pulled it from its upside down position on the bottom shelve of the cabinet a raw egg fell from underneath onto the laminated countertop. A roar of laughter circled around the room. Harold smiled realizing the group of operators had been waiting most of the day for that gag to unfold.

He turned to the group, gave a salute with his cup in hand as another Operator came to assist in the cleanup.

"You ain't gonna believe this," Skillet said.

"Gimme a chance, Skillet Head," Hambone replied.

"I took my French horn down, to show dem dummies down doin' pipefitting around that feed pump, how it works," Skillet said.

Another Operator, who had been onsite for about six months asked, "How'd you make a French horn?"

Skillet chuckled. "I bent quarter-inch copper tubing around my shoulder and chest about three times, then glued a big ol' funnel into one end. But that funnel was turned so that it pointed directly into the side of somebody's right ear. The other end was fit with an old trumpet mouthpiece that my boy ain't using no more. Then I filled the funnel end with line chalk."

"You ain't no good, Skillet Head," Hambone called out.

"Yeah, but my ol' lady don't care," Skillet retorted.

"Go on, finish your story," Hambone demanded.

"Well, this ol' boy down there takin' a break with a couple of his buddies wanted to look at my horn. I had already loaded it earlier with the blue line chalk and it was ready to go. I told him to be sure to blow real hard cause it took a lot of wind to get a sound outta that funnel. He said he was in the band in Vicksburg, and he began to blow as hard as he could," Skillet explained.

The room filled with laughter as everyone imagined a young pipe fitter covered in blue line chalk.

"Man, Skillet Head, you ain't right," Hambone stated. "What do you think about that, Stretch?"

Stretch was about five feet tall with a great sense of humor, born and bred in Mississippi. Having been recently saved at the First Baptist Church in downtown Vicksburg, he thought for a minute before answering.

"Did he pass the audition?" Stretch asked Skillet.

"Yep, sounded like Lawrence Welk," Skillet replied. Another round of laughter broke out.

Harold finished his coffee and gave Hambone a head nod that he was ready to go.

"Hurry back to see us," Skillet said. "We work around here sometimes, so next time you come we'll have you a few jobs lined up."

"Thanks for the invitation," Harold replied.

He and Hambone left for the elevator back down to the ground level where Harold thanked him for his tour.

Harold took his exams the next day, met a few of the new hires also taking the series of tests and completed his physical exam. He was in excellent shape from his years of working out with weights on the Nimitz, so his physical exam went by quickly. Even his hearing exam went well, which consisted of the local doctor from the Port Gibson Hospital holding two quarters behind his back and tapping them together.

"How many clicks did you hear?" the doctor asked Harold.

"Three," Harold replied.

"Okay, you look to be in fine health," the doctor said.

After a long meeting with Bob and assurance that he would contact him when he made a decision, Harold boarded his plane that afternoon and flew back to Norfolk, not knowing whether he would be offered a job or not. He couldn't imagine himself working so far from his home in Georgia, but he'd really enjoyed meeting the guys working in operations. If he was offered a job, he thought that he would work there long enough to get his civilian reactor operator's license and then move back to Georgia.

Harold picked up Scott on Saturday morning and returned to his apartment. Sheila was more than ready for Scott to go with Harold. She had a party to go to that night and wanted to spend the day sleeping so she could stay up all night.

Harold made three more calls to Georgia Power Company, still hoping to get a job at their operating nuclear plant, but they weren't hiring operators that summer, and the woman he spoke to told him to come early and stand in line like everyone else, very much unlike his welcome in Mississippi.

August finally arrived and Harold hadn't heard anything from Grand Gulf yet but he carried out his plan to leave the Navy at the end of his six-year hitch anyway. It took him about a week to complete his check-out sheet, which included signoffs from every major facility on the Nimitz. Beginning with the library and ending with his Department Head.

"Is there anything we can do to keep you in the Navy?" his Department Head asked.

"No, I've spent too much time away from my family already," Harold replied.

"Well, I have to ask that question. I know that some of you guys have been out to sea a lot," the officer stated. "Good luck."

"Thank you, sir," Harold replied.

Harold left the Nimitz that day, feeling great. Although his car had been towed from where he had parked it that morning, there was nothing that could ruin his day. He jumped on a bus and paid the fine with a smile on his face.

He was free for a couple of weeks before returning to Georgia so he thought that he would visit Atlantic City before returning home. It'd be a good place to relax and Scott would enjoy the trip, he told Rob, when he stopped by his apartment to say farewell.

"Where you gonna be in about six months, Rob?" Harold said.

"Cindy and I are gonna be living in Florida," Rob replied. "How about you—what are you gonna be doing?"

"I'm gonna take a little trip up north, then go home for a while," Harold said. "Then, I guess I'll wait for a decent job offer. If none come, I'll work on the farm for a while."

"Take care, brother," Rob said.

Harold shook Rob's hand, "You too, bro."

Harold drove over to Sheila's apartment. She pretended to resist Harold's plan to leave Norfolk with Scott, but her motives were money driven—he was her meal ticket and didn't want it to be too far away, especially if she needed some quick cash.

Before leaving for Atlantic City, Harold helped her buy a car by trading in his Mustang and Honda-matic 750 for a pickup for him and a Chevrolet for her. It later turned out to be a big mistake signing a loan for her on a car that she never intended to pay for.

Harold kept Scott entertained as much as possible as they drove to Atlantic City, pointing out road signs and storefronts, trying to get him to recognize the letters on the signs while they rode. Eventually Scott was able to pick out words posted on billboards during their trip through Washington and New York.

They stopped along the way at a McDonald's restaurant, Scott's favorite place to get hamburger meals boxed together with a cheap toy. Harold bought a newspaper and began reading while Scott played on a large colorful tubular playground beside their table.

He pointed to a headline on the paper that read, "SALT Treaty Underway."

"Do you know what this word is, big man?" Harold asked.

"Salt Treaty," Scott said.

Harold was amazed that he could read the word salt, but even more surprised that he said "treaty." He had never taught him anything close to a word that sounded like treaty.

"Hey, where did you learn that word?" Harold asked.

"I don't b'no," Scott stated.

"Okay, let's go, smart guy," Harold said.

While in Atlantic City they went to the beach and the boardwalk amusement park that Harold had promised his son. It was a good chance for the two to get away from Sheila and begin their lives together outside the protection of the military umbrella. Harold was looking forward to their life back in Georgia or Mississippi, whichever place he decided to live.

A few days later the two pulled back into Norfolk and gathered up Scott's belongings from where Sheila was staying. She was ready for Harold when they arrived.

"Where are you going with my son?" Sheila shouted it was the beginning of a confusing tirade.

Harold had been packing his truck with Scott's things for at least an hour, when she started to lose control of herself.

"Why don't you stay in Norfolk?" Sheila asked.

"I want to move closer to home and Scott is going with me just like we agreed and have been planning for the last three or four months," Harold replied.

"I know that he will be better off with you," Sheila stated.

"Yeah, that's what we agreed," Harold said.

Her emotions were swinging wildly between trying to be a mother and not, "But you can't have him!"

"No, I'm taking him as I told you," Harold said. "Don't you remember what I said the first day I returned from my cruise?" Harold reminded Sheila of how she had kept Harold from knowing where Scott was for over six months.

"Yeah, I remember. But I need my freedom," Sheila said.

"I am really confused!" Harold retorted. "What are you talking about?"

"I believe that Scott will be better off with you, but I can't stand to see him leave," Sheila said.

"Okay, just let us go, goodbye," Harold said empathically.

Sheila was wailing by this time. Scott, visibly upset, began to call out for his mommy, then his daddy. It was a heart-wrenching sight to see them standing in a small parking lot finishing a break-up that should have ended a year earlier when Harold caught Sheila cheating on him.

Harold closed Scott's truck door, climbed into the driver's side and left Ocean View for the last time.

# CHAPTER 21

▼

Harold left Norfolk, Virginia and the Navy behind him in September of 1983 and with Scott traveled to Morven where he had started out six years earlier. Jerry and Betty met them at the door of the Harmon house, very glad to see both of them.

Scott entered into the house like he owned the place, Betty right behind him lovingly watching his every move.

"Where've you been?" Jerry asked Harold.

"We took a little trip to Atlantic City," Harold replied.

"A guy from Mississippi has been calling here every day for the last two weeks," Jerry said.

"Really! Was his name Bob?" Harold asked excitedly.

"I don't remember," Jerry replied.

It was Sunday and Harold could hardly wait till Monday morning rolled around. He telephoned Grand Gulf at nine in the morning and spoke to Bob.

"Hey, Harold, you're a hard man to find," Bob said. "Are you interested in coming to work for us?"

"Yes, I am. I believe I would enjoy working with you and building my career at Grand Gulf," Harold responded.

"Okay, well, get here as soon as you can. We have a new Operator's class starting in about a month or so, and we want you in it," Bob stated.

"I'll be out there in about two weeks," he replied.

Bob offered him an acceptable salary before their conversation ended and when Harold hung up Jerry's old blue wall phone he felt like a new man.

He told his father the good news and Jerry was happy for him, but Harold could tell that his father was a bit unhappy knowing that he would be living that far from home, so he assured Jerry that he would come home as often as he could. "Besides," Harold said, "I won't be stuck at sea for six or nine months and never get to see my family."

Harold and Scott spent the next two weeks hunting and fishing with Jerry as often as his father was available. He felt that they were closer now than they had ever been. Jerry was proud of his son and introduced him to everyone as a nuclear engineer. Of course, Harold didn't have a degree in nuclear engineering, but it didn't seem to matter to Jerry.

The two weeks flew by and Harold left Morven with Scott for Vicksburg, Mississippi, where Bob had arranged for a hotel until they found a place to live. Harold picked up the latest Bruce Springsteen album when passing through Tallahassee and played it a couple of times on his stereo for Scott to dance to while they traveled. It didn't take long for Scott to memorize every song and repeat back most of the words.

The two checked into Vicksburg's Holiday Inn late the night they arrived and began looking for an apartment the next day. Three weeks later they moved into a place near the edge of the city, not fancy, but liveable. It had a sunken living room and upstairs two bedrooms. Harold found a babysitter for Scott through the Vicksburg newspaper. She lived close by and was very good with kids.

Harold walked into a newly furnished classroom the first morning of training and saw about twenty other young men in the room who would, like him, be trained as operators. A contracting instructor from a company called Quadrax entered and they all sat down in the brand new chairs stretched out behind three rows of wooden tables.

Everyone introduced himself one at a time, standing and addressing the group. Harold was last in the room after two other ex-Navy nukes spoke about their six years of enlistment. The course was designed to be twelve months long, six in classrooms and six in the plant filling out a very long qualification card.

Harold took the classes until Christmas break when he and Scott went back to Georgia to spend the holidays with Jerry, Betty, Lisa and Polly who were all in Morven for the holidays. December weather had moved into South Georgia with a chilling vengeance, causing an early frost.

The Harmons had a Christmas dinner of turkey, cornbread dressing with giblet gravy, sweet potatoes, and biscuits, green beans cooked with fatback, fried chicken, cranberry sauce, squash casserole, pecan pie and chocolate. Jerry asked the blessing and they ate the meal with gusto, little Scott chomping on a turkey leg almost as big as his arm.

The Harmons began reminiscing about childhood memories and Polly told a story she remembered that included their mother. Betty was clearly upset and left the table within minutes, excusing herself and heading to her bedroom. It was a rule Jerry had discussed with them when Betty first moved into their house and Lisa moved out. They were not to discuss Helen when Betty was in the room. But Polly or Lisa didn't like the rule and made a point to disobey it this Christmas day. Jerry finally said that it was time to watch TV and he went back to the bedroom where Betty was already on their bed. Jerry had installed a wall-mounted TV in the room many years earlier and she was watching the 1940's movie, "White Christmas."

The two hibernated in their room together, hiding from ridicule and embarrassment by anyone who still challenged their living arrangement. Jerry's self-induced reclusion made him happy when he was with Betty, but they had few outside friends. None of Helen's lifelong friends ever came by to visit Jerry after Betty moved in; isolating him from family friends he had known before her murder.

Polly, Lisa and Harold sat around the same table where they remembered eating many Christmas dinners when growing up. Helen always said she wanted to spend her retirement years in her home with her children and grandchildren around her at the dinner table. The three siblings talked for a long time—and mostly about things Helen wanted for them. Her influence was a very dominant force in their lives.

Lisa began to cry a little when Polly started to talk about Christmas in 1966. It was a great event, Polly recalled. She remembered that Lisa had gotten a Mary Poppins music machine that looked like a merry-go-round, horses with people mounted on top. She loved to listen to the music and watch the top slowly rotate.

Polly received a new set of pajamas that included sewn-in feet to protect her from the cold black and white tile floor of the old dentist office. The tiles were very cold in the winter. Sitting on a concrete slab the block building they lived in became very cold when the propane freestanding heaters were turned down at night. Polly loved her new pajamas and wore them every night after taking her bath in a small white tub located in their only bathroom.

Harold remembered getting his first electric train. It was truly an amazing achievement when Jerry first put it together. The black train started to move around its three-wire track very slowly at first but the speed was adjustable by a small controller wired into its circuit. It had three small wooden logs that sat atop a flatcar, engine and red caboose. Harold said that he remembered playing with the train for a week every day, then on Sunday afternoons until it finally quit working.

For dinner that Christmas in 1966 Helen baked a hen she bought at the J&I Super Market. The chicken was golden brown and sitting in a metal pan of cornbread dressing that had been baked together, perfectly. It looked like a meal for royalty, Polly recalled. Helen had placed the meal on their laminated table with shiny aluminium legs in the small kitchen that doubled as a dining room. It was a far cry from Helen's new wooden table and hutch that she purchased when they moved into the dream home that she and Jerry built the following year.

Helen had made their early life so much more exciting than it really was. She was a master at making small things seem to be extra special, which carried over into her children's adult lives.

*       *       *       *

Arriving late at night at their Vicksburg apartment, Harold felt exhausted. Scott had fallen asleep in the truck, so Harold decided to get their bags inside and then carry Scott to bed.

All the lights in the apartment were out as Harold swung open the door. Carrying his Nike gym bag, Harold stepped onto a wetted carpet. Feeling its fibers shift underneath his tennis shoes, he thought some of the rain that was now falling heavily had leaked underneath the door.

Reaching for a light switch near the front door, Harold flipped the switch but no lights came on. He also hadn't turned on the heat before leaving for Georgia and the air temperature inside his apartment was very cold.

A streetlight was shining through his back door window and most of the light was channeled into the living room. The sunken living room floor seemed to have become level with his kitchen floor. What's more it was strangely glistening.

There was no furniture in the living room except a stereo cabinet, with a dbx decoder resting on its bottom shelf. Harold noticed that its power light was on but seemed to be underwater. Looking back across the room Harold realized that he could hear water running. Suddenly he realized what he was looking at in the streetlight's opaque intensity.

His living room had become filled with water that he now realized was coming from a broken pipe in his wet bar. He walked through the knee high water and opened the wet bar lower cabinet doors, water streaming underneath his feet.

Luckily, the pipe had broken above a cut-off valve and he was able to stop the water by closing it.

Not recognizing that his apartment's temperature would drop below thirty-two degrees while he was away, Harold now saw that the wet bar copper water pipes had cracked under pressure of swelling ice within. Physical science was enlightening him to his findings, but the real treat was when he stepped over to his dbx noise reduction stereo component.

Located under nearly eight inches of freezing water and still plugged into the wall, Harold reached down to turn off its switch. He figured he must have left the component on when he and Scott went to Georgia. As he got close enough to turn off the dbx, a jolt of electricity rudely penetrated his skin.

Resistance to current flow caused by the clean water had allowed him to walk through it toward the stereo cabinet and close enough to reach the dbx, and not feel any electrical current coming from the device, until he got closer.

Its power supply created a temporal electrostatic field about four or five inches through the surrounding water. It had generated enough power to illuminate the 'power on' light and give Harold a nasty shock when he infiltrated the field's outer rim. He stepped slowly away and toward its plug, which he quickly pulled from the socket.

Harold went back to his truck where Scott was still sleeping soundly to the sound of freezing rain falling onto the truck's cab and a plastic trash bag he had used to put some clothes in for protection. Now resting in the pickup's bed, the black plastic trash bag was protecting Harold's things quite nicely.

Harold carried Scott into their apartment and up to his room. He barely moved when he put him into his bed covered with two large handmade quilts. Harold turned on the heat and adjusted the thermostat to 68°F. He heard the electric heater come on as he went back downstairs to put some light on his problem.

He replaced the bulb in his overhead light fixture, turned on the living room light and let out a long sigh. Luckily, water damage to his belongings was minimal. There was no furniture downstairs except a small breakfast table and two chairs, which they used for everything. The concrete encased sunken living room looked like a twelve-inch swimming pool now that everything was stable.

It was late and Harold had already cleaned out all the water that was left in the kitchen, so he turned off the light and went upstairs, leaving the bulk of the work until the next day.

When Scott woke up in the morning, he rushed into Harold's room, which was across the small hallway upstairs.

"Dad, I want to go fishing," Scott said in his very loud two-year-old voice.

"It's too early, go back to bed," Harold replied.

"But the water is here," Scott answered.

"Oh, yeah," Harold remembered last night's events. "Okay, let's get ready."

"But I want to go fishing," Scott said.

"I know, big man, but the fish aren't in our apartment," Harold replied.

He got Scott dressed and they went downstairs to take another look at their water filled living room.

"See, we can find fish here," Scott said.

Harold smiled. "Well, I think we should call somebody to clean this mess up, don't you?"

"Yeah, I reckon," Scott replied, disappointed.

Harold called into work to let them know that he'd need to stay home while a cleaning service came by to drain the water from his apartment. When his landlord refused to hire a cleaning service Harold said, "Well, then what should we do?"

Walking out the front door the landlord paused and said, "I'll be right back."

He returned with his wife and several buckets. The landlord's wife began bailing water from their indoor swimming pool and throwing it through an open window as quickly as she could. Harold watched for a moment in disbelief, then began bailing, too. He spent the rest of that day bailing out water with a bucket alongside his landlord and his wife.

The next day Harold had to return to work, but notified his landlord that they could finish while he was out. When he returned that evening with Scott in tow, he found all the water dried up and his carpet missing. It was a thin green indoor-outdoor cheap carpet, but it kept Scott from having to walk on concrete flooring. The landlord refused to replace it and said, "You should be paying me for the damage. I'm gonna deduct it from your security deposit."

Harold decided it was time to stop dealing with landlords. Within a couple of weeks he had discovered a decent mobile home park that was owned by a guy who was very proud of his place. Sunrise Trailer Park was Harold and Scott's new home.

Scott was thrilled to have his things in his new room in the single-wide mobile home that he and his father moved into. He had built-in drawers for his clothes under his closet and enough floor space for him to play with a few toys. His tricycle fit nicely on their patio, where he rode in circles and played for hours with his toy trucks.

Work was going well for Harold at Grand Gulf Nuclear Station. Being more experienced in power plant operations than most of the other Operators he was working with, Harold found himself tutoring them on several occasions during their initial training classes.

And now that Kenny's first appeal was turned down, Harold felt that soon there would be some sort of closure. Justice had finally been done.

# CHAPTER 22

▼

Scott's third birthday in June of 1984 was celebrated in Georgia with the rest of the Harmon family. Sheila even came down to see her son for the first time since they left Norfolk the previous August. She begged Harold to let Scott come back to Norfolk with her for six months. Harold agreed.

Harold returned to Vicksburg and began standing watch on rotating shifts at Grand Gulf in order to finish his training. It was a seven-day rotation, eight hours per shift—a work schedule that was not conducive to Harold's needs, as a single parent. He would have to arrange for Scott to stay overnight with a babysitter when his son returned from Virginia. And this turned out to be sooner than later.

Within two weeks of Scott's departure from Georgia, Sheila brought him back to Morven and dropped him off at Jerry's house. She made up some kind of excuse, but the fact was she couldn't manage being a single parent. It was impossible for her to have a life of freedom with a three-year-old hanging onto her.

Harold drove nine hours after working off his last midnight shift to pick up his son in Morven. Scott was very happy to see his father and return home to their life in Mississippi—it had become his anchor.

Harold found a young woman who lived in his trailer park and who agreed to keep Scott overnight while Harold was working. She had two children of her own, but in the end, she was unable to adjust to having another small one spending fourteen nights in a row with her. By September of the following year, Harold's shift work was creating a very difficult situation for him and his little boy.

Harold tried to keep things going, getting Scott ready for bed and delivering him to his babysitter, then working from midnight until 7:00 a.m., arriving home an hour later, sleeping until noon and then picking Scott up. He had been working through his rotating shifts for four months when he finally mentioned to his sister Lisa how hard it was on him.

Lisa had married a Guatemalan that she met in Miami on a luxury cruise while Harold was still in the Navy. She and her husband Gorge De Elaurdo had been happily living in Guatemala City for a few years now. Her house and property were surrounded by a ten-foot stone wall, patrolled by hired guards. Gorge's uncle and father had been kidnapped eight years earlier by guerrillas after a coup d'état, holding them for ransom in a spider hole underground until being paid. The guerrilla activity had receded now, but Gorge remained cautious.

Lisa offered to take care of Scott until Harold could resolve his shift-working dilemma or find another job.

Harold tried to explain to Scott that he would be staying with his aunt Lisa for a while at her home, but Scott never really got the message. Harold told his son that he would always love him and no matter what, he would come home to Mississippi after his visit.

Lisa and Gorge arrived in early November to pick up Scott. At first the boy was excited to see his aunt Lisa. Harold watched as he hugged and kissed her when they met—they were bonded almost as close as mother and son. He knew that Lisa would take very good care of Scott; he also knew that he couldn't continue on his current work schedule and raise Scott alone.

Harold packed Scott's clothes, a few toys and some apples that he loved, into his bags while Lisa and Gorge played word games and read books with him.

"Okay, Scott, you ready to go?" Harold asked when he had finished the packing.

Not really knowing where he was going, Scott replied, "Yep."

"Come with us to the hotel, Harold," Lisa said.

"Yeah, that's a good idea," Harold replied.

Harold began to regret what he was about to do. Scott's anchor was about to be ripped from beneath him, sending his short-lived stability into nothingness.

He now wondered what on earth he was thinking when he agreed to take a job doing shift work, as a single parent with a small child.

"You want to take a bath, Scott?" Lisa asked when Harold and the boy arrived at the hotel room where Lisa and Gorge were staying. They had an expensive suite with two bedrooms.

"I think so," Scott replied.

Lisa took Scott into the bathroom and filled the large tub with warm water. A few minutes later, while Scott happily played with his favorite toys in the bathtub, Lisa came out of the bathroom and said to her brother, "Harold you should probably go."

"I know, it's just hard to leave," Harold replied. "Scott will be upset and think that I'm coming back to pick him up."

"Daaaad?" Scott called.

"Scott, I have to go now, I love you. Aunt Lisa is taking care of you," Harold called out.

"Okay," Scott replied. "Love you, too."

As Harold walked slowly to his truck in the hotel parking lot, tears streamed down his cheeks. Scott needed some stability in his life he told himself. The boy's bedwetting was proof of that.

Harold went into his trailer and sat in front of his stereo. He had put on a recording of Neil Young singing "Helpless," which was exactly how Harold felt.

The chair he was sitting in felt like a magnet and his body felt like iron. An unexpected rush of depression made him weep uncontrollably.

After an hour of constant tears, he began vomiting. Harold spent the rest of the night alternating between tears and heaving. He finally collapsed in the narrow trailer's hallway and fell asleep for a few hours.

It was still dark outside when Harold awoke in the pre-dawn morning and boiled some water for instant coffee. After drinking a cup of strong dry roasted bean, he walked to a twenty-four hour Quick Stop about a mile from his trailer. The sick feeling was still in his stomach and he thought a walk might improve how he felt—it couldn't hurt.

By the time he arrived at the twenty-four hour store a red sun had risen in the east. "Red Sun in Morning, Sailor take Warning," came to his mind as Harold bought a newspaper and a Coke then walked back home.

As soon as Harold opened the door of his mobile home he had a desperate need to talk to Scott one more time before his flight out of the country.

Harold telephoned Lisa's hotel room, but they had checked out very early that morning. Lisa had told Harold the night before that she had already made arrangements for the boy's passport in New Orleans. However, the passport office was closed when they arrived in New Orleans, so she decided to try to get Scott onto the plane without it.

\*        \*        \*        \*

Lisa and Gorge had an eleven o'clock flight to Guatemala City. A short discussion with the flight check-in attendant ended when Gorge offered the attendant two one-hundred-dollar bills, to overlook Scott's lack of passport. Their tickets were quickly printed and they boarded the flight home.

Upon their arrival in Guatemala City another fifty dollars got them into the country where Lisa's brother-in-law picked them up in his Jeep Cherokee. Lisa and Gorge's new home was within the city limits, but away from the main thoroughfares of downtown. The city's main roads were mostly stone and dust, dotted by an occasional guerrilla terrorist.

Scott soon began to adapt to living with his aunt Lisa; learning Spanish came easily to him and he really liked the way she cooked. After about a week, Harold was finally able to get through the seriously inadequate phone system and spoke to Scott for a few minutes.

"Hello, son."

"Hey, dad," Scott replied.

"Do you like it at your aunt Lisa's house?" Harold asked.

"Yeah, I am going to Chochi's party!" the boy exclaimed.

"Oh, that sounds like fun," Harold said.

"Here's aunt Lisa," Scott said.

Harold's conversation with his sister was reassuring—they were taking good care of Scott, and since they couldn't have children of their own because Lisa was barren, he quickly became part of their family.

Harold was never more grateful for having a wonderful sister like Lisa. But it was tempered with the deep resentment he now constantly felt toward Sheila and her extreme inadequacy as a mother. It often left him in an "if only …" state of self-pity, and feeling this way made him angry with himself. There were no easy solutions.

# CHAPTER 23

▼

Lightning streaked through a rainy afternoon sky as Harold sat in a Brumby rocking chair on the Harmon's front porch. He had come home for a much needed four-day visit. It was Thanksgiving and he was sitting alone watching the rain start to wash across the front yard that his father had mowed the day before. Thunder came ten seconds after the sky blinked from another bolt of electricity.

White flashes of light occasionally brightened a now dark sky, caused by heavy cloud cover. Harold watched as mother earth brought about an atmospheric cleansing. A theater of thunderous noise and lightning became loud entertainment for the young man, twenty-five years old, a father, and now divorced from a wife who made Harold wonder whether marriage was even worth it at all.

Sitting on the front porch and sipping iced tea while he watched the storm, Harold felt a deep relaxation. He could see peach trees growing across the dirt road. Leaves had fallen from the trees, which were trimmed yearly across their tops so that field hands could reach the fruit hanging from branches intentionally grown closer to the ground.

Pine trees that Helen and Harold planted around the Harmon farm were still evident in all directions. Rainfall began to slacken as he finished his glass of tea. He could see clearly through the brief interlude in the downpour, a large pine tree that was on the corner of the dirt road and the white gravel driveway leading up to the Harmon house.

He had climbed that pine tree many times. Harold knew every branch up to about thirty feet high, where his nerves had always run out.

The old pine tree had been on the farm for as long as Helen could remember. Helen told him that she had climbed it as a child, along with the pecan trees across the dirt road. But the old pine tree was special, because her brothers had all fallen out of it, yet she had never been thrown from its branches. It was her favorite tree growing on her land, well rooted and forever green.

Visible now that the rain had turned into a drizzle Harold could see the pecan trees, still with pecans hanging on their branches even though all their leaves had already fallen. He remembered spending afternoons and Saturdays picking up pecans for sale when he was still in grammar school.

Clouds brought in with the storm began to break a little, allowing the sky to change from almost black to greyish blue, a strange sky color for five o'clock in the afternoon. Harold walked back inside, got another glass of tea and spent the evening alone watching satellite TV while Jerry and Betty slept. It had been a very long day without Scott, whom he really missed being with on Thanksgiving.

Early the next morning Harold awoke to a tractor passing very near his bedroom window. It was seven o'clock and Jerry was already out on his John Deere, using his harrow to turn under some brush growing around his yard.

Jerry was wearing a Levi jacket and baseball hat while wheeling about on the green tractor. His hat read USS Nimitz across its front and had scrambled eggs on the brim like those of an Admiral. Harold had given his father that souvenir after his last Mediterranean cruise almost two years ago. Jerry out working on an early Saturday morning was a sight he had seen many times. Harold smiled as he watched his father on the tractor. Some things never change. It was a comforting thought.

Harold found Betty in the kitchen cooking thick-cut salt bacon on a new griddle. Eggs were sizzling in an iron skillet on an electric stove and homemade biscuits were in the oven. Harold took a slow, deep breath so that he would long remember the smell of a real Southern country breakfast—a far cry from the sausage and biscuit sandwich he'd grab on his way to work, when he was pulling a dayshift at Grand Gulf, washing it down with coffee from an institutional coffee machine with powdered milk and two packs of sugar.

In the afternoon Harold went outside to help Jerry clean up the brush that had grown up around some fence-rows. Working alongside each other gave them a chance for some private time to talk.

"Look, son," Jerry began, "I'm really worried about Scott being so far away from you."

"So am I, dad," Harold said, stopping at a pile of brush to look at Jerry. "But what am I gonna do?" He shook his head. "I can't take care of Scott and work these impossible shifts that I have. I'm really between a rock and a hard place."

"I know it's very difficult, and you're doin' your best," Jerry said. "It's just that he may be in a place that's not so safe. I trust Lisa's judgment and all that, but Guatemala City is full of guerrillas, and—."

"Dad," Harold interrupted, "let's stop talking about this. I'll stay in very close touch with Lisa."

"Okay, son," Jerry said reluctantly, and decided to change the subject. "Got any plans for tonight?"

"Matter of fact," Harold said, "I thought I'd go into Valdosta tonight—for a little R and R."

"Good idea. There's a place near Shoney's, in a strip mall, that's real popular."

Harold nodded. "Thanks; maybe I'll even run into some old high school buddies."

"That'd be nice," Jerry said as he started cleaning brush again.

Most of the late night places to visit around town were being renovated because of a city ordinance requiring handicapped access to all its passageways and toilets. But the small bar Jerry suggested had a lot of cars parked near its entrance and a "Live Music" sign pasted to its front door.

Harold parked his truck and went inside. Music blared through at least six JBL studio monitors. Everyone seemed to be enjoying themselves at the twenty-five or thirty tables scattered throughout a maze of half walls and nooks. He found a stool near a television at one end of a long dark wooden bar and ordered a beer.

He didn't recognize anyone sitting near his perch that he might know, so he turned to watch television as a boxing match came to an end and arm-wrestling world championships began. Harold watched for a few minutes, then finished his second beer and headed to the men's room, marked by a small brass cowboy nailed above the door. Walking over to the sink to wash his hands after relieving himself, Harold saw one of his old friends from the high school football team.

"Rusty?" Harold asked with total surprise.

"Harmon!" Rusty exclaimed, instantly recognizing his old buddy.

Rusty stepped over and shook Harold's hand as the hand dryer wound down, using an around thumb grip they had learned at summer football camp.

"What's up, man? It's been a while!" Harold said with genuine excitement.

"Yeah, it has. What's been goin' on man?" Rusty asked.

Russell Carr—everyone called him Rusty—lived in Quitman where his father owned a Chevrolet dealership. His friends thought it was somewhat comical having a father with a car dealership whose son was named "Rusty Carr," but everyone liked Rusty and he was a great offensive tackle on his college football team.

"I'm checking in on the folks for Thanksgiving; and you?" Harold replied.

"Taking a little break," Rusty said. "Hey look, I'm here with some people tonight, but what do you think about going to Tallahassee tomorrow night?"

"That sounds great, what time you want to head out?" Harold asked.

Tallahassee was an hour's drive from Morven and very near the Georgia-Florida state line. It was the closest large city to them while growing up in one of the most southern parts of Georgia.

"Hey, do you remember my cousin Anne?" Rusty asked.

"Of course. How is she?" Harold replied.

"Let me tell ya, she's hot man," Rusty replied, "I know she's my cousin, but I'm a very good judge of women."

They both laughed and Harold said, "That you are."

"I've got a date with a girl from over in Cummings; do you want to double?" Rusty asked.

"Sure, sounds great!" Harold replied.

"Okay, man, I'll call you at your dad's place," Rusty said.

"Alright, see you tomorrow," Harold said.

Harold and Rusty shook hands and Harold was back in Morven by midnight. He walked right into the Harmon house, which was never locked. In fact, he couldn't remember locking the front door since his mother had gone missing in 1972. She seemed to always lock house doors when they were coming and going, but not Jerry, who was much more relaxed about leaving doors unlocked, knowing that he had a loaded pistol in the nightstand next to his bed.

Rusty called about ten o'clock Saturday morning and said that he had set everything up with Anne. Harold was delighted—it would be his first real date since the divorce from Sheila. Harold met Rusty at his parent's home in Quitman and it took about five minutes to reach the Johansson house where Anne's mother met them inside her empty garage. The home was one that she and her husband had built together, before beginning their divorce proceedings almost two years ago. The final nail in their marriage's coffin was pinned and ready for the hammer to fall any day now.

Anne too had had a difficult marriage that ended in a break-up and a return trip to Georgia from Texas. Now Anne was living just outside Atlanta in Marietta, with her daughter. Louisa, who was five years old and shyly standing behind her grandmother as Harold spoke to Anne's mother for a few minutes. Anne came into the garage. Rusty was right. She definitely looked "hot."

"Hey, Harold," Anne said smiling.

"Hello, Anne, it's been a long time."

"Yeah, it sure has."

Anne gave Harold a hug around his neck as Louisa watched her mother with wide eyes soaking up everything. Anne was careful to hug Louisa much longer than she had Harold to demonstrate who clearly, was the most important person in Anne's life. And in fact, Louisa was the only salvageable benefit of Anne's traumatic marriage.

Rusty said a quick hello to Anne's mother and then Anne and Harold piled into the blue Mazda sports car with a sunroof and small back seat that Rusty borrowed from his father's used car lot.

"Rusty, where'd you meet this girl we're picking up?" Harold asked

Playing on the car's radio was an original version of Lynrd Skynrd's "Free Bird," which needed a little respectful volume. So everyone had to shout in order to be heard over an awesome duelling guitar riff.

"She bought a car from me the other day at dad's dealership," Rusty replied.

"Not supposed to mix business with pleasure," Anne said, shaking her finger in mock scolding.

"Yeah," Harold added, "but if anything goes wrong with the car, she'll know who to call!"

They picked up Rusty's date, a pretty girl named Wendy, and finally arrived in Tallahassee at nine that evening. Rusty pulled the car into a popular restaurant where they recognized two high school football buddies. Harold said, "Seems to be a meeting place for Brooks County graduates."

Dinner over, they headed to a local disco, where at eleven o'clock it was just beginning to rock. As they made their way through a sea of young people Harold couldn't help noticing how many guys were checking out Anne, who was wearing tight-fitting Jeans, boots and a pretty red blouse.

Rusty and Wendy pushed themselves onto the dance floor and joined the small ocean of gyrating bodies. Harold and Anne decided to sit this one out, a very loud Allman Brothers tune. He and Anne sat at a small table and had to shout in order to communicate.

"Where are you living, exactly?" Harold asked.

"I'm living just outside of Atlanta, in Marietta," Anne shouted. "Where are you living?"

"In a small trailer outside of Vicksburg," Harold replied.

"What was your wife's name? I don't remember her," Anne asked.

"We met after high school, and then I went into the navy."

In high school Anne had been a majorette, marching with the band while Harold played football, so they saw each other at the games and other school events, but never really got to know each other.

"My years in the Navy worked out, but not my marriage," Harold said.

"Rusty told me your marriage didn't go too well, either." Harold said.

"Yeah, he turned out to be a loser," Anne said. "But Louisa has been a blessing."

"I feel the same way about my three-year-old son. He's in Guatemala right now."

"What's he doing there?" Anne asked.

"It's a long story and I can't yell anymore," Harold replied. Anne nodded in agreement.

Anne finished drinking a watered down Amarctto Sour and Harold a black label Jack Daniels while Rusty and Wendy made there way back to the table. Anne and Harold managed to make their way onto the dance floor where by now there was barely room to breathe, let alone dance.

Anne said as they drove home from Tallahassee, "Nice place that disco, Rusty, but let's find a less popular place next time." Wendy agreed and then dozed off on Rusty's shoulder as Harold took his turn driving.

Anne talked about how she had completed architectural drafting school and gotten a job with a good company in Marietta, as they cruised north at between eighty and ninety miles per hour, the wide tires of the sports car holding to the narrow road's asphalt surface like glue through its many tight turns.

Harold gave Anne a quick kiss at her mother's front door. "It was so good seeing you again," he said.

"Maybe we can make up for lost time," Anne said, almost shyly and hurried into the house.

That night as Harold lay in bed he couldn't fall asleep—all he could think about was how beautiful Anne was and wondering why he had never dated her in high school.

Over a hearty breakfast the next morning, Jerry asked, "When are you coming home again, son?"

"I think I have to work through Christmas this year because I took off Thanksgiving," Harold replied. "It's a gentlemen's agreement that we use at the power plant."

"Well, I know that you can't get a job like that here," Jerry said, "so you should stay with it."

"I know," Harold said. "And I believe there's room for advancement."

"What are you gonna do about Scott?" Jerry asked.

"I have to find a way to take care of him while I'm working shifts," Harold replied. "It's almost impossible though until next year. I go back into training again for about six months."

"Well, I know that he'll be safe with Lisa and I really like her husband," Jerry said. "But he needs to be with his father."

✳     ✳     ✳     ✳

Anne tried to phone Harold that Sunday afternoon, but Jerry said, "I'm afraid you just missed him. He's on the way back to Vicksburg."

After Anne hung up the phone, she told herself that it was probably best that she missed him. He lived too far away to get involved with in some kind of long distance romance. Although the message she left might generate a little interest, she pondered.

Anne hadn't seen Harold in such a long time that she really didn't know how she felt about the whole situation. It was like they were still in high school, she thought as she drove through Macon, Georgia on her way back to Marietta. Louisa, in the back car seat was chattering away.

How would she react if he called her that night or maybe he won't call at all. Maybe he didn't want to have a long distance relationship either. And what about Louisa? Relationships are hard enough, she thought, but when both parties have a young child, it can really put a damper on things. They arrived home in time for Anne to get Louisa ready for bed and check in with her mom by phone one more time, before calling it a day.

Anne started her week as usual on Monday morning at five o'clock, getting Louisa fed and dressed and dropped off at kindergarten. Anne usually got into work at eight. The surveying company where she worked as a drafter was the best job she had ever had. The pay was good and she'd made many friends there, even dated a couple of the survey crew guys, hoping for a decent relationship. But it wasn't easy as a single parent, to balance what she wanted to do with what she had to do.

Anne shared an office with a young man who had spent two years in Vietnam during the war as a Navy Seabee, building temporary housing for troops moving into and out of the jungles. The Viet Cong had bombed his position so many times that he became accustomed to napping under a table for protection from falling objects. Even after several years of therapy, this habit continued to haunt him even in civilian life. At lunch every day he would take a nap under his drafting table for at least an hour. Anne would wake him about one-thirty in the afternoon, where he would be refreshed and ready for the rest of the day.

For the next week Anne hoped she would hear from Harold, but when she arrived home each night there were no messages from Harold on her answering machine.

In Vicksburg, the week went by quickly for Harold as he worked through his normal training cycle. Everyone in the Reactor Operations Department was required to attend continuing training once every five weeks for at least five days. At the end of these training weeks an exam was given to each member of the crew. Fortunately, Harold usually didn't have a problem passing his courses.

He called Jerry on the following Saturday morning and the first thing his father said was, "Good news. Kenny's second appeal has been denied."

Harold was elated, but cautious. "He's still got one more, dad. And Clay Lee will pull out all the stops."

Kenny's next appeal hearing would be held inside the Valdosta Division of the District Court responsible for Lowndes County. A judge would make the final decision on whether Kenny would fulfil his life sentence or be released. It seemed to everyone in the Harmon family that it would be just a formality and Kenny's last appeal would be denied. The thought of a possible reversal in Kenny's conviction was unthinkable to the Harmons.

"Don't worry, son," Jerry said. "It'll be over soon." There was a pause, then Jerry finally mentioned that Anne had called the previous Sunday. "She said she enjoyed your date and you should give her a call when you come to Georgia."

When Harold hung up the phone, he let out a loud "Yeah!"

His three to eleven p.m. shift was starting that night; he'd be able to call Anne from work during his break.

Inside Grand Gulf's main control room were controls for safe operation of the reactor and its supporting equipment. Post Three Mile Island designs brought many safety features to the nuclear power industry. Each emergency system associated with plant recovery after either an accident or sabotage was backed up by at least one other system.

Sitting within a horseshoe of panels, the on-shift Reactor Operator is accompanied by two other qualified Reactor Operators who can take over reactor controls should the need arise. At Grand Gulf there were between ten to fifteen men or women assigned to each shift for operational responsibility of the reactor. But the Shift Manager was considered Site Emergency Director, and overall license holder at night, during holidays and through the weekends.

Rounds were divided between three men separated into three different buildings or areas. Harold had qualified more quickly than any other Operator before at Grand Gulf because of his Navy nuclear power operations training coupled with his desire to be the best.

Rounds on this night consisted of touring buildings outside, structures near the Mississippi River, and main transformers that raised the output of Grand Gulf's generator from twenty-two kilovolts to five hundred kilovolts, unlike Europe's electrical power grid that criss-crosses through various countries at four hundred kilovolts. Steel-girded power line support structures, carrying large electrical cables, could now be seen all over America bringing electrical power to businesses and homes.

Nuclear power from the reactor was converted into an average output of 1250 megawatts of electricity using one of the largest turbine-generator sets ever designed and built. Turbine, generator and its supporting components were situated inside a large concrete reinforced building that had two floors underground and two floors above ground.

East of Grand Gulf's turbine building were giant conduits, carrying three phases of current from its generator to three large transformers. Electrical power transmitted into the transformers create significant amounts of heat and during the summer months banks of large cooling fans were run in order to cool the transformers.

Winter was now on its way, causing the weather in Mississippi to finally turn cold that December evening. A shorter day gave way to darkness by about five o'clock and Harold's drive in the company truck to the radial wells down by the Mississippi River required energized headlamps. His headlights prevented him from running off either side of heavy haul road and into a swampy area that might swallow his truck.

Harold drove slowly down a very bumpy road that was once used by a transport truck to haul the reactor vessel from a barge to its current location in a containment building. Barge transport was employed in the late '70s to bring the huge reactor vessel from its manufacturing plant upriver to an off-loading ramp located about one mile from the power plant. Potholes in the concrete had been filled in many times between spring floods and summer rains.

Harold parked the company truck at one of three tall caissons, which housed two huge pumps each. Mississippi River water taken from pipes laid underneath the river, imbedded in its riverbed, passed through each pump's twelve-stage impeller. Water was sent in copious amounts to the power plant through fiberglas underground pipes.

Some of the water was used as makeup water to a large cooling tower shaped in a recognizable design and used at nuclear power plants all over the world. The balance was used for cooling plant equipment, which generated heat while operating.

Harold climbed on top of the first well, taking a breather at the top of the high ladder mounted to the caisson. He gazed out across the Mississippi where he could see the swift, vast artery of America cutting its way to New Orleans. He could also see cross-currents powerfully churning large trees underneath its surface, remnants from a tornado upriver. The Mississippi's might was awesome, Harold thought, as he watched it from each of the three wells while completing his rounds.

Slowly driving back to the plant, after taking his switchgear house rounds, also located at the river, Harold saw six deer standing in a clearing about a hundred yards from the heavy haul road. Headlights from his Dodge pickup broadsided an eight-point buck and four does nursing two fawns. It was a beautiful sight to see, but ended quickly when the deer noticed that they were being spotted with the company's truck lights.

The buck was first into a thicket of high briers and small trees followed by the does and fawns, disappearing hurriedly out of sight. It wasn't too unusual to see a few deer standing around the heavy haul road or other small dirt roads that crisscrossed through the company's property. Small herds of deer were scattered up and down all the slues near Grand Gulf Nuclear Power Station.

Upon his arrival at the security gate and subsequent entry into Grand Gulf's protected area, Harold made his way to a small conference room where he found a telephone. It was time to call Anne, but he had to decide what he wanted to say first.

He searched his memory for commonalities between them. Most prevalent was being a single parent, but that made Harold feel guilty about Scott's living in Guatemala.

"Hello?" Anne said, when Harold finally decided to stop thinking and just call her.

"Hello. Uh, Anne?"

"Hey Harold!" Anne exclaimed. "What are you doing?"

"I'm at work tonight, but I found a little time to take a break and give you a call," Harold replied.

"When are you coming to Georgia?" Anne asked.

"I don't know, maybe after Christmas—it's almost here you know."

"And when is Scott coming home? I really want to meet him. I imagine he's a lot like you."

"I suppose so. I don't know when he'll be coming home, but I do miss him."

"You should ask Lisa to bring him back. I can tell that you're lonely without him," Anne said. "He's all you talk about."

"Yeah, you're right. I will, I'm gonna call Lisa tonight. Thanks for the push."

"Well, I'm just one of those pushy broads," Anne said with a laugh. "I would like to see you again, Harold."

"I'd like to see you again, too. I had a really good time the other night," Harold replied.

"Okay, well, come on up here after Christmas and we can spend the weekend in Marietta," Anne said.

"Sounds great, but I want to get Scott back first, so that you can meet him and he can meet Louisa."

"I'd like that, Harold," Anne said. There was a pause, then Anne said she'd have to get off the phone—it was past Louisa's bedtime.

"Talk to you soon," Harold said, and when he hung up, he felt a rush of excitement that he'd never felt before.

After an hour had passed, Harold made up his mind. He telephoned his sister in Guatemala City.

Over an echoing phone line a voice on the other end of the line said, "Saludo?"

"Hello, Lisa de Elaurdo," Harold said.

He repeated Lisa's married name until finally someone fetched her and he heard her voice.

"Harold?" Lisa said.

"Hello sister, how're you doing?" Harold asked. "And how's Scott?"

"He's fine His friend Chochi is here and they're playing hide and seek," Lisa replied.

"Listen, Lisa, we need to talk for a minute about Scott. I want to bring him home to Mississippi. I need him to live with me."

It was going to be hard for Lisa to give Scott back to Harold; she had become very attached to him—he was now like a son to her. Feelings of sadness could be felt through thousands of miles of telephone lines, phone exchanges, and satellite connections. Harold could hear her begin to choke on her words as she tried to talk.

"I thought you would leave Scott here longer, Harold. You never said when you wanted to take him back. I love him very much," Lisa said in a shaky voice.

"Lisa, can you hear me?" Harold asked.

Suddenly, silence consumed their conversation, which ended with a sharp click. It sounded to Harold like the housekeeper was cutting off his telephone calls every time he tried to phone back that night. Finally, he gave up after a couple of hours of trying.

Harold ended his shift that night and drove back to his mobile home around midnight. He continued to work evening shifts for two more days, then he worked the midnight shifts from eleven to seven each morning. Seven straight nights of midnight shifts and Harold had a hard time adjusting to sleeping all day. Exhaustion from not sleeping well becomes a natural feeling.

When Harold arrived on his first day of midnight shift, he called Lisa straightaway, even before his briefing normally scheduled at each shift's beginning.

"Lisa," Harold said.

"Yes, Harold, is that you?" Lisa asked.

"Yeah, have you had time to work out when you can come back to the States?"

"Yeah, we've decided to come to Miami for Christmas and then go to Daddy's," Lisa replied. "Can you meet us in Morven?"

"I have to work through Christmas this year, but you can leave Scott with dad and I'll pick him up a couple of days after my shift is over," Harold replied. "Lisa, I'm so grateful for all you've done for Scott and me. I miss him so much that nothing matters without him."

"I know, Harold. Thanks for saying so," Lisa said.

Eventually their conversation tuned to lighter matters.

"Do you remember Sheriff Johansson?" Harold asked Lisa.

"Yeah, of course. Daddy used to meet him down under the shade tree near where highway 94 intersected with highway 76. It was a good place for them to sit in their patrol cars and discuss how things should be done in Morven, concerning law-breakers. Why do you ask?" Lisa replied.

"Well, his granddaughter and I are starting to date," Harold said. "She lives in Marietta, you know, just outside of Atlanta. I think I'll visit her after Christmas."

"That's great, Harold, I hope everything goes well for y'all," Lisa said.

"I do too. I think we're on the same page."

"Take your time getting involved with someone again. You don't want to rush into anything," Lisa warned.

"Don't worry, I won't rush it. I think I learned my lesson," Harold said with a chuckle, but mostly he felt relief that he would soon have his son back with him.

# CHAPTER 24

▼

Highway 61 near Grand Gulf was a two-lane road, winding and narrowing as it traversed pasturelands through small hills on its way to Vicksburg. The highway connected New Orleans to Tennessee through the heart of the Mississippi Delta, passing through several small river towns along its way. Many blues songwriters have mentioned the famous highway, but this short stretch between Grand Gulf and Vicksburg was more legendary to locals for taking lives

Nuclear power plant workers frequently traveled north from the plant to their home after working all night. Harold was no exception this particular morning, tired from lack of sleep and completing his first midnight shift. His eyes felt like two steel doors trying to be drawn together by an electromagnet.

When he turned onto Highway 61 from the Grand Gulf road he felt as if he would fall asleep before going his first mile. He pulled off the road near a park and close to a small bar that had been built during a shutdown and plant outage. Contractors and plant personnel would stop at the little bar on their way home after evening shift to grab a couple of beers. But the parking lot was empty at seven thirty in the morning, which is when Harold got out of his truck and walked around for a few minutes as he shivered in the frosty morning air. He felt more awake and decided that he had better try to get on home before traffic got worse. People would be using the road soon to come into work and he would be meeting much more traffic, as he got closer to Vicksburg.

As he got into his truck he glanced back at the sign located by the bar. He remembered that it read, "First Chance" when he drove by on his way out from the plant toward home. Now the sign read "Last Chance," as if to say this is your last chance to get a drink before going into the depths of a nuclear holocaust. Harold laughed at the thought.

Harold began his slow pace home and focused on staying between the lines on his side of the road. Occasionally, something that looked like an animal would run in front of his truck, guys on shift called them "ghost bunnies." This was caused by a very tired imagination creating images, sometimes triggered by an eye closing momentarily. He hit his brakes often, trying to avoid the ghost bunnies that crossed his path.

Ahead of him he noticed a blue flashing light slightly off to one side of the highway. He thought that it must have been an accident of some kind because he hadn't seen any traffic coming toward him in a while. As he came closer he could see that it was one of his colleagues from his shift that had been involved. It was a motorcycle rider who loved to ride Harley Davidsons. The guys at the plant had nicknamed him Harley One because he was the most prolific Harley Davidson motorcycle rider on the reactor site.

Harold looked toward the embankment of Highway 61 as a state highway patrolman slowly waved him through the scene. He could see that a rescue team was already there putting Harley One into a meat wagon.

Harley One rode motorcycles all his life and was an excellent rider, but when a person is tired from losing a lot of sleep, they're unable to react to a small pothole or a spot of cat pee in the road. Harley One had been in that situation many times, but his luck finally ran out and he was now being rushed to the hospital with major injuries caused by his direct impact with a metalic sign pole.

Harold drove on toward home, thinking how lucky he was that morning to have stopped and taken a little walk in the cold morning air. When he pulled into his driveway at the trailer park he said aloud to no one in particular, "Guess I'll live to see another drive to work."

His new-found relationship with Anne was beginning to be in his every waking thought. He remembered that they'd both been part of the student council in high school, that they'd worked on a Christmas parade float together and he remembered seeing her at a homecoming dance. Now she was back in his life and he suddenly felt extremely lucky.

Harold crashed the moment he got inside his mobile home and slept until five in the afternoon, but before he headed back to Grand Gulf for the next midnight shift, he telephoned Anne. "I'll be coming to Georgia to pick up Scott in January," he told her.

Anne was thrilled and said she would arrange a trip down to south Georgia so that they could see each other again. His midnight shifts would last through the Christmas holidays, keeping him busy but not having much fun.

Christmas Eve was especially lonely with no one to celebrate with at home. Nuclear reactors are attended at all times, whether at night or during holidays, so everyone working at the power plant must perform his or her duties with dedication in order to ensure safe and efficient operations of the nuclear reactor.

But still no one wants to spend a holiday working, so management usually made arrangements for food to be delivered by a caterer in order to thank everyone for their performance. However, the nearest official catering service to Port Gibson was over an hour away in Jackson. Because of the special occasion, the Piggly Wiggly market located in Port Gibson made a special meal for everyone on shift, for his or her holiday dinner.

Harold ate, after completing rounds, along with everyone else about two o'clock Christmas morning. Brought together because of their occupation, fifteen men and women, rotated through a kitchen just off of the main control room of the operating facility, eating whenever they could manage to take a few minutes away from their constant monitoring of the plant.

Harold now had to work one more night before traveling to Georgia to see Scott for the first time in four months. Leaving right after work the next morning Harold's excitement could barely be contained.

When Harold arrived in Morven he drove down the short stretch of dirt road leading to the Harmon farm, now with a new name "Peach Road." Groves of peach trees on either side of the hard red clay and iron rock road were not in bloom yet, but within two months small pink flowers would pop out all over the trees.

His pickup truck bounced up and down as he drove over the road's washboard bumps that went on for nearly two hundred yards. The washboard bumps were most prevalent on dirt roads that endured a great deal of tractor-tire traffic. Peach Road frequently hosted tractors hauling peaches, watermelons, tobacco or some other crop. The bumps were in rare form that day, because icy rains had fallen over the last several weeks.

Scott came running out of Jerry's house as his father drove up the familiar white gravel driveway. Harold jumped out of his pickup truck, meeting him halfway. His three-year-old son hugged Harold's neck with all his little-boy strength for a long time. The reunion was joyful for both of them. Scott learned to speak some Spanish while he was living in Guatemala, which got tangled through his English as he told his dad all about his stay with aunt Lisa and uncle Gorge.

As Betty made Harold and Jerry some coffee in their new percolator, sitting by the old toaster in the kitchen, Jerry said, "Lisa was really upset when she dropped off Scott."

"I know she got very attached to him while he was there," Harold replied.

"Yeah, I believe that it was more than that. She really wanted to raise Scott, as her own," Jerry said.

"Dad, my feelings for him are too strong. I couldn't imagine someone else raising my boy," Harold said emphatically.

Their conversation continued as Scott played with some of his Mayan Indian toys that he brought back from Guatemala. A wooden monkey tied to a four-inch pogo stick, which moved up and down as if it wanted to jump on his command was one of his favorites. And another handmade toy he loved to play with was a yellow and blue wooden top with a sharp metal tip. Its string was too long for him to make it work, so he just turned it with his hand as fast he could. Harold watched his son with intense love and said to Jerry, "Look what Sheila's missing."

Betty came into the living room where the guys were sitting, still wearing her apron from preparing Jerry's lunch. "I can't remember if I told you Harold but Maxine got married two weeks ago."

Harold had lost all contact with Maxine over the years. "That's great, where is she living?"

"Florida, near Orlando," Betty replied. "I really like the guy she married, he's a hard worker."

Sipping from his coffee cup, Harold briefly thought about his adolescent experience with Maxine and how smart she was to end things when she did. "Well, I wish her all the best," he added.

Anne called Harold at Jerry's that afternoon from her mother's house in Quitman. They agreed to go back to Marietta together the next day. She and Louisa wanted to spend some time getting to know Scott. When Harold and Scott pulled out of Jerry's driveway around ten o'clock the next morning Scott waved and yelled goodbye to his grandfather. They arrived in Quitman a few minutes later and walked up to Louisa standing in her grandmother's yard.

"Hello Scott," Louisa said.

"Hey, what's your name?" Scott replied.

"Scott, her name is Louisa," Harold said. "Remember I told you about her in our truck."

"Hey 'ouisa," Scott said. "My dad is taking me back from Mis-sippi."

"Mom is taking us to our house first," Louisa said.

"Okay," Scott said.

Anne came outside carrying her last bag, placing it into a Silver Ford Escort sitting in the garage. She came over and kissed Harold lightly, then turned to Scott.

"Hello, big man," Anne said.

"Hey, you're pretty," Scott said.

"Thank you," Anne exclaimed. She looked to see if Harold had a guilty look on his face. She thought that he might have set Scott up to say something like that, but it was in Scott's character to say exactly what he was thinking.

Anne suggested to Harold that Scott ride with her and Louisa. "It'll be a good chance for the kids to bond," she said and Harold agreed.

On their first day in Marietta, Anne had arranged for them to picnic at Stone Mountain Park. The park's attractions and the granite mountain were famous tourist spots and the massive carving onto the granite of Robert E. Lee and other Confederate leaders, was particularly popular in Georgia. Harold, Anne and the kids spent a day hiking along the park's old American Indian trails and Harold regaled them with his best rendition of Robert E. Lee's leadership during the Civil War as they all paused and looked up at the great granite mountain.

On the way home, the exhausted children fell asleep in the car and Anne snuggled up to Harold as he drove.

They woke Scott and Louisa when Harold pulled into driveway around eight o'clock. As Anne hustled the children off to bed, she called to Harold over her shoulder, "Pour us a couple of glasses of Chardonnay; I'll be right down."

In the guest bedroom, Louisa and Scott announced they wanted to sleep together and Anne put them down on the comforter and kissed them both goodnight. They were asleep again instantly.

In the small living room, Anne went up to Harold and took the glass of wine he held out to her. "I think the kids really had fun today," she said and gave Harold a gentle kiss.

"They loved it," Harold said, relieved that her feelings were becoming as strong as his. As Harold pulled Anne toward him, he felt a sensation of falling when the adrenaline rushed through his body.

"What did you think when you first saw me a few weeks ago?" Anne asked, smiling and sipping her wine. She sat down on the couch and Harold immediately joined her.

"I thought you looked awesome," Harold replied.

"Thank you. But what I meant was, how did you feel?"

Harold paused and took a deep breath. "I felt like an idiot for not having dated you before. And that if I ever had a chance to correct that mistake, I would."

"I want you to know that I trust you, Harold," Anne said as she got up, went over to a pretty candle on a table across the room, and lit it with a match. She turned back to Harold. "And that's not easy for me to say. Louisa and I have been through hell getting this far, and I don't ever want to go back down that road again." She came back to the couch and sat closer to Harold.

"I want you to trust me, Anne," Harold said as they looked deep into each other's eyes.

Their conversation lasted several hours, each rediscovering the other. The years since high school now melted away and the two could not have felt more connected and grateful they'd found each other again. That night they made love in a bedroom on the other end of the house, away from the children.

The next morning Scott was up by six and Louisa followed soon after. Harold helped Anne serve breakfast as Louisa asked, "Where are we going today?" and took a last bite of her donut.

"How about we all stay home today and play games?" Anne offered.

"Oh, I know, let's play hide and seek," Louisa said excitedly. "And, then we can play checkers."

Anne finished putting away the breakfast dishes as Harold organized several games for them to play. Including hide and seek, which Scott was exceeding good at playing. Evidently Lisa and Gorge had taught him an extreme version of hiding, in case they were ever threatened by kidnappers. Scott would stay hidden for up to an hour, before finally coming out, never saying a word or making a sound.

The day flew by and all four had the best time any of them could remember in years. Harold and Anne spent their last night together, each wondering when they would see the other again.

The next morning before leaving, Harold held Anne in his arms. "Come to Vicksburg in February and let's go to New Orleans for Mardi Gras—how does that sound?"

"I thought you'd never ask," Anne teased and hugged Harold tighter.

On the nine-hour drive back from Georgia to Mississippi, Scott fell asleep on the front seat next to his father, but awoke as Harold carried the boy into their mobile home. Scott noticed all his old toys scattered around.

"Dad, I never want to go away," Scott said.

"I promise you won't," his father replied.

The next morning after they finished their breakfast Harold took Scott with him to the nearby laundromat in Vicksburg. Scott happily played with his yellow tow truck while Harold did their laundry.

Outside the laundromat's large windows, Scott watched an unusual sight. Snow had begun to fall and was piling a little on car roofs and hoods.

"Dad, I wanna go outside," Scott said, excited about seeing the snow.

"We have to finish this job first, young man," Harold said.

"Where does snow come from?" Scott asked.

"Well, it's rain that comes down frozen in very tiny pieces," Harold explained.

"Oh, like an icy," Scott stated.

"Yeah, kinda like an icy without the Coke flavor," Harold chuckled.

The snow looked strange through a sudden ray of sunshine from the east. It was a brief moment that brought Harold an unexpected feeling of euphoria—seeing the sun, thinking about how things were going so well with Anne, and with Scott home to stay.

With clothes folded and in the laundry basket, and while driving to the local carwash to give his truck a much-needed bath, Harold explained to Scott that he had found his original babysitter and that he would stay with her while his dad was working. He might even get to spend the night sometime, because his dad would need to work at the power plant. Scott was excited about seeing his old friends and spending time with his babysitter again, but looked a little concerned about the spending the night. Harold reassured the boy that everything would be fine. "Okay," Scott said, "you the boss." Harold broke up laughing.

The expansion of Operator's training at Grand Gulf, allowed Harold to work day shift for six months, beginning in January of 1985. Six months felt like an eternity off shift work or duty days back on the ship.

*       *       *       *

Mardi Gras created an atmosphere of celebration throughout Louisiana, which sometimes spilled over into Mississippi. New Orleans was only a couple of hours drive from Jackson where there were usually parades comparable to the New Orleans spectacle. Harold looked forward to spending a few days with Anne in the Big Easy, watching parades and enjoying the great Jazz music, which was much more pleasurable for him when accompanied by a beautiful woman.

Louisa came with Anne to Vicksburg the weekend before Fat Tuesday. Harold had already found someone to watch both kids for a few days. Anne contacted her cousin Rusty to let him know that she and Harold would be down for a visit.

Rusty had moved to New Orleans to open his own car dealership, along with his brother Johnny.

Johnny was also an old friend of Harold's—he had played football with him and Rusty in high school.

The magic surroundings of Mardi Gras and being with Anne created more joy for Harold than he thought he'd be able to contain. But remembering what he had learned about life from his marriage to Sheila—now becoming more and more just a bad memory—Harold vowed not to make any hasty decisions about his relationship until he was sure it would work.

When Anne and Harold arrived at the hotel in New Orleans, she phoned Rusty and Johnny to meet them at Café Beignet where they could grab a chicory-flavored coffee and beignets before going down to Bourbon Street.

People were everywhere—Anne and Harold could hardly move when they walked downtown from their hotel near the Superdome. Partying patrons carrying "Hurricane" labeled drinks stumbled by.

Rusty and Johnny soon showed up at the café and after coffee and those delicious beignets, Rusty said he wanted to try the gondola. The ride had been left in New Orleans after the World's Fair—it spanned the Mississippi River just before it emptied into the Gulf of Mexico. The decision was made and they all walked through a massive crowd of celebrating people to get down to the harbor.

Harold, Anne, Rusty and Johnny all got into one large car that crossed high above New Orleans' port structures and the muddy waters of the Mississippi River.

Harold hadn't been much of a conversationalist with other women he had known since Sheila, but now with Anne talking over problems seemed almost easy. He had never felt happier or more compatible than he did with a lovely young woman.

After saying goodnight to Rusty and Johnny, promising to keep in touch, the two returned to their hotel room overlooking Bourbon Street. Despite his promise to himself to be very sure about a relationship with Anne, Harold knew one thing: he had fallen in love with her. The several months of telephone calls and their visits together had cinched it. He loved Louisa as a daughter and sensed Anne felt the same way about Scott.

"I had fun tonight, did you?" Anne asked.

"Yeah, and it was good to see Rusty and Johnny again," Harold replied.

Harold knew he wanted to ask Anne to marry him in some kind of romantic way, but fumbled with his words until, finally, he blurted out. "Anne, I love you very much."

"I love you too, Harold," Anne said.

"Anne, will you marry me?" Harold said suddenly.

Sitting down on a corner of the bed, Anne replied, "What did you say?"

Harold sat down in an antique chair by a window in their hotel room and repeated, "I said, would you marry me?"

Anne looked at him to see if he was just kidding, or actually asking her to marry him. Her feelings for him were clearly shown by a smile that slowly came across her face.

"Yes," Anne answered.

Harold's search for someone he knew he wanted to spend his life with had ended and a great feeling of bliss came over him as they kissed.

Thinking about their life together and Scott's future with Anne and Louisa, Harold was finally able to relax. He and Anne spent that night talking about how they would tell their kids, and how they would let everyone else know that they were getting married.

Getting absolutely no sleep the night before, Harold felt as though he was in some kind of dream as he and Anne watched the passing Mardi Gras parades along the streets of New Orleans. They held each other constantly with very few words passing between them, feeling totally in love.

Harold brought Anne back to his place that evening, picking up Scott and Louisa from their sitter along the way. Louisa was thrilled to find out that her mom would be getting married to Scott's father, but Scott was slow to come around to the idea.

He had finally gotten to live alone with his dad after spending four months in Guatemala and now he was going to have to share him with others. It was hard for the now four-year-old to understand why Harold wanted to get married to someone other than his mom, Sheila. After hearing the news, Scott went into his bedroom and in protest smashed his favorite yellow tow truck with his small baseball bat.

"Let me talk to him alone," Anne said to Harold.

Anne spent as much time as she could with Scott, reassuring him that she was not going to take his father away. "You're the most important person in your dad's life," Anne said to Scott as she sat next to him on his bed. "It's always going to be that way, just like Louisa is to me. But now we're just going to be a bigger, happier family—a real family. We'll have great times together, you'll see."

Scott gave Anne a little smile of acceptance. Anne picked up the broken tow truck. "Let's get some glue and see if we can fix this, okay?"

# CHAPTER 25

▼

Marietta was steamy hot by the time Harold arrived in June of 1985 for the wedding. He and Scott had driven through the night, along the Gulf of Mexico on highway I-20, arriving at Anne's place around ten in the morning.

It was a long night for Harold, having finished work late the day before leaving Grand Gulf and packing all his and Scott's things for their trip. But the next day was to be a new beginning for them, blending two families together. Harold and Anne's marriage meant a lot of work lay ahead, for everyone.

Scott was ill as a sore-tailed-cat from the ride and only wanted to go back to sleep for a while, so Anne put him on her bed for a nap. He revived himself about two that afternoon and found Louisa in the garage watching Harold trying to make homemade ice cream in an old churn, with one broken hold-down latch.

Anne added fresh peaches into the electric churn, which was rotating inside a small bucket of ice. Harold tried to keep everything together while adding more ice and rock salt as needed. A few minutes later, delicious peach-flavored ice cream came out of the small metal cylinder that had been the center of attention for the last hour. Everyone began tasting the mix, which actually turned out to be pretty good—it promptly disappeared.

The day went by much too rapidly for them, everyone anxious about the wedding, wanting to get on with it as soon as possible. Early the next morning, Anne got the kids ready and drove them over to her friend's house where she and Harold were to be married. The house had been decorated for the wedding and people began showing up about an hour before the ceremony.

Jerry came up from Morven to be Harold's best man. Lisa had flown in from Guatemala and Polly drove in from Georgia Southeastern College. Anne's immediate family members were all present except for her father, who chose not to attend because Anne's mother—his ex-wife—would, of course, be there. Anne's parents' divorce left bitter feelings all around.

It was ninety-nine degrees by eleven-thirty that morning when the preacher finally pronounced Harold and Anne husband and wife. Scott's shirt was soaked with sweat from standing in the sun alongside his father during the ceremony. Louisa, whose face was red from the heat, quickly went inside to change into a summer dress and out of her Sunday clothes. Everyone else headed for the shade of a few large trees planted along the driveway.

Harold and Anne left the reception about three o'clock for their honeymoon in Daytona Beach, Florida—leaving both children with Anne's mother. They spent a week on the beach thanks to Anne's father who made up for not attending the wedding by paying for the honeymoon. Harold could not remember ever being so happy in his life. They returned to Georgia, picked up their children and a U-Haul moving van, then drove to Mississippi to begin their new lives together.

Harold had found a house for the four of them between Vicksburg and Grand Gulf before their wedding, closing the deal by using his military veteran's benefits. Everything was going really well for them. They settled comfortably into the house, and the children got along so well that it was a constant source of joy for both Anne and Harold. But all their happiness was soon tempered by news that Kenny Winkler's third appeal was coming up soon.

✳     ✳     ✳     ✳

Anne's mother mailed newspaper clippings from the Valdosta Times declaring that Kenny's last appeal would be allowed. Harold knew that this campaign to get him released from Reedsville State Prison would be much more fervent than in the past. The appeal created an impressive resurgence of media coverage.

Photos of Helen, looking forever young, were shown as often as photos of Kenny, who now appeared more haggard from having been in prison for three years and seven months.

Kenny felt that, no matter what, he would not admit to murder and blemish the Winkler family name. Moreover, his lawyers told him that because Georgia prisons were overcrowded, he could be out in a couple of years anyway.

Thanksgiving dinner that year had to be postponed one day, because Harold was working the day shift at Grand Gulf on the holiday. But it didn't make much difference to the kids—they were very excited about being together as brother and sister, with a mother and father.

Anne prepared a great meal for their first Thanksgiving as a family. She also tried to involve Louisa as much as possible in the preparations, but Louisa was more interested in watching the parades on television than cooking.

While cleaning up after dinner Harold got a phone call from Polly. She said that Judge Dickson was the judge who would hear Kenny's request for release from prison. Harold sighed on hearing the news. Judge Dickson ran a very liberal courtroom in the Valdosta Division of the District Court. He overturned five convictions during his ten years on the bench, based primarily on *his judgment* of their being a lack of evidence. Dickson was scheduled to hear Kenny's request for a Writ of Habeas Corpus in December of that year.

"Looks like Winkler is gonna have his last appeal in a couple of weeks," Harold said to Anne as he hung up the phone.

Ann was washing the last of her pans from the cornbread dressing. "What does that mean?"

"It means that when this appeal for dismissal of the charges has been denied, he will be in prison for a long time," Harold replied. "I think that he might come up for parole after seven years or so, but that doesn't mean that he'll be released."

"Good." Anne dried her hands on a kitchen towel and hugged her husband. "Honey, it'll soon be over."

"Yeah, it's been too long. Seems that every year for the last thirteen years something comes up about my mother's disappearance or murder," Harold said.

Harold went outside to play catch with Scott's old football while Anne and Louisa stayed in the kitchen to bake a pecan pie.

As Harold tossed the football to his son, he couldn't quite ignore the gnawing feeling in the pit of his stomach. "Please, God," he muttered, "let this be the end of it. Let my mother rest in peace."

# CHAPTER 26

▼

Kenny's defense attorneys planned their appeal carefully. It would be important for Clay Lee to win this one; his reputation had been tarnished by a short string of losses and failed appeals. Not because his methods were lacking, but because his clients were criminals who deserved to go to prison.

Clay Lee intended to present their appeal in person on a Friday afternoon to Judge Dickson. He felt it would have a greater impact if he conveyed the message himself. His Southern gentleman demeanor was still getting him plenty of press throughout Georgia. He planned to ride his fame into Judge Dickson's court-room, demanding righteous redemption.

Clay Lee, in an elegant thin pin stripe suit complemented by Italian shoes, approached the bench of Judge Dickson.

"Your honor," Clay Lee started, "I would like to present to you a document explaining reasons why a jury of so-called peers in the Kenny Winkler murder trial, could not have been justified in their decision of guilt."

"Yes, Clay Lee," Judge Dickson said with a hint of a groan. He viewed the Writ with half glasses.

"Your honor, I believe that after you read this text, and our points of conten-tion, you will definitely understand why this jury should have had reason to doubt Mr. Winkler's guilt," Clay Lee stated.

There was a smug smirk on Judge Dickson's face as he said, "I have already read this document and have made my decision concerning this case."

"If you please your honor, I would also mention that this is Mr. Winkler's last appeal, granted by the state of Georgia," Clay Lee added.

"I am quite aware of the particulars of this case. And that is why I am accepting the motion for release of Kenny Winkler on bail, until such time as a full pardon can be arranged," Judge Dickson said.

Kenny, who had been sitting in the courtroom watching Clay Lee struggle for his release, maintained an expression that did not change as he stood up from his chair and faced the judge.

"Kenny Winkler, this court will release you on five hundred thousand dollars bail until further notice," Judge Dickson stated.

"Thank you, your honor," Clay Lee said.

Kenny smiled to his lawyers and nodded as if to say, "It's about time you clowns got me out of prison."

The date was Friday December 20, 1985. Kenny had been in jail for less than four years when he was released. Not only released, but if Judge Dickson's decision was not addressed by the State of Georgia's Attorney General, his record could be expunged of ever having committed Helen's brutal murder.

Judge Dickson's ruling that afternoon became front-page news in Saturday's newspaper. But it was Kenny's entire life and so-called vindication, printed in the Sunday papers that really offended Helen's family. The Harmon and Grantham families' Christmases were completely overshadowed by Kenny's release.

Harold was working midnight shifts over the weekend, so he didn't get news of Judge Dickson's decision until he awoke from his nap Sunday afternoon. Polly telephoned crying. Kenny would be a free man a few days after Christmas and there was nothing they could do to prevent it from happening. Anne could see Harold's sudden change as he listened to what Polly was saying. He hung up the phone and turned to Anne.

"What's going on?" Anne asked fear and worry on her face.

"Kenny is gonna be released in a couple of days," Harold replied.

"I can't believe that!" Anne exclaimed. "How can they possibly release him after a trial and two disallowed appeals?"

"Seems there's still some politics being played with this case," Harold said.

"Will he be able to get his family inheritance?" Anne asked.

"Yeah, I suppose it's up to six or seven million dollars by now," Harold replied.

"I'll bet that he starts his business again, too," Anne said.

"I'll have to contact the Attorney General's office in Atlanta to get more information," Harold stated. "I'll do that after they actually release him, sometime next week."

"And we were hoping for a normal Christmas this year," Anne said.

"Yeah, well, we can get through this," Harold said, without much conviction.

He didn't want to let something like Kenny's release ruin his family's first Christmas together in their new home. Harold tried not to talk about it too much, but his thoughts about what he needed to say to Georgia's Attorney General, were uppermost in his mind throughout the holidays.

The court's records department couldn't process the paperwork for Kenny's release quickly enough for him to get out of prison before Christmas, so his actual Writ of Habeas Corpus wouldn't be granted until December 30th.

Christmas Eve in 1985 brought with it an unexpected light snowfall that delighted Scott and Louisa as they watched snowflakes gently coming down.

Anne finished wrapping a few presents on Christmas Eve after Scott and Louisa finally went to bed. She baked a sweet potato pie and finally went to bed herself at one in the morning. Harold was working a midnight shift but, fortunately, it would be his last for a while.

Christmas morning came early; it was six-thirty when the hall lights came on. Anne heard Louisa jump up and run to Scott's room to wake him up. Ann was relieved to get out of bed; she had been tossing and turning for hours.

Harold returned from work around eight a.m., dead tired but ready for the excitement he expected to see from Scott and Louisa. They were already awake and waiting for him to come up the driveway. Both had by now seen some of what Santa Claus had left them under a fully decorated Christmas tree, but they had several more presents to open when he arrived.

"Look what I got," Louisa squealed. "It's a new bicycle!"

"I got one too!" Scott shouted.

Louisa's bike came assembled, complete with multi-colored tassels hanging from its grips. The seat would have to be set a little higher than Scott's, because she was about six inches taller than him. She basically knew how to ride her bike already—Anne had taught her while they were living in Marietta.

Harold's biggest job on Christmas Day was to put together Scott's new bicycle—it was still in the box because he didn't want Scott to find it before Christmas morning. Harold worked for an hour putting every small screw in its correct location, ensuring its seat height was close to Scott's leg length.

The kids were very excited picking up each present, playing with it for a few seconds and moving on to the next until all were opened.

"Open your present, dad," Louisa said.

"Okay," Harold replied.

Scott went over to a square-shaped box sitting under the Christmas tree and said, "I'll get it for you."

He handed Harold the box still wrapped in red paper with Santa Claus figures in white dotted across its surface.

"What is it?" Harold asked Scott, jokingly.

"It's a basketball!" Scott exclaimed.

Everyone laughed as Harold opened his present, including Scott, who finally realized he wasn't suppose to spoil the surprise by telling a present's contents.

Morning broke as the sun finished its rise, shining reddish-orange through a bedroom window. Snowflakes imprinted on windows a day earlier had disappeared, leaving some light moisture in various locations around the yard. A radical change in weather had occurred between breakfast and lunch allowing outside temperatures to rise high enough for Scott and Louisa to go outside.

Harold watched the kids play with their new bikes. He tried to remember how he learned to ride his first bike, so that he could give Scott better instruction. His memory quickly flashed back to watching his mother ride a blue Sears bicycle on a street in Morven when he was a very small child.

Harold suddenly remembered that he had forgotten to put on the training wheels and got Scott to hold up long enough to attach the small, white side-walled tires to his rear bicycle wheel. Things began to go much smoother for Scott once some balance was added to his bike.

Anne came outside, taking a break from cooking Christmas dinner.

"What are you thinking about, Harold?" Anne asked.

"I don't know, I guess about mom," Harold replied. "I can't believe that Kenny is gonna get outta prison in a few days."

"We'll have to contact somebody about this," Anne stated.

"Yeah I know. I just want to forget about it for today," Harold said.

"Come inside, honey, I've made some fresh coffee."

Harold kissed his wife as they walked back into their house.

In a few minutes, the kids rushed in looking for a snack, and eventually Harold put away his memories.

On Monday December 30th, Kenny was released from prison. Word of his release came from Anne's mother by telephone on New Year's Day, as expected. According to Clay Lee's statement in the Atlanta Constitution, Kenny Winkler was a victim of circumstantial evidence and would never be put back in prison on charges of having murdered Helen Harmon.

Harold contacted the Attorney General's office in Atlanta on January 6th. "My name is Harold Harmon," he said to the female secretary who answered the phone. "My mother was Helen Harmon who was murdered by Kenny Winkler in 1972. He was released on appeal in December and I want to protest his release."

The secretary said she would pass Harold's information to the attorney general's office. Within an hour, Harold's phone rang.

"Hello Mr. Harmon, this is Andrew Balsam from the Attorney General's office in Georgia."

"Hello Mr. Balsam, thank you for calling me back," Harold replied.

Andrew Balsam was an administrative assistant in charge of public affairs. He described to Harold the necessary formalities that had to be completed for an official protest to be considered. He then assured him that everything would be re-examined very closely once they received the proper paperwork.

*        *        *        *

The CBS program "60 Minutes" aired a story about Kenny's return to the Valdosta community in the early spring of 1986. He constructed his new house and became a celebrity to some close Winkler family friends, who were still hanging around, waiting for his considerable inheritance to kick in. His business selling advertising began to see some expansion as people around town were asked to ignore his conviction by the media.

*        *        *        *

On April 26th 1986 the number four nuclear reactor at the Chernobyl nuclear facility in the Ukraine experienced a catastrophic steam explosion and fuel meltdown. The subsequent fire, radiation, and radioactive fallout killed hundreds of people immediately, and many more were expected to die from radiation exposure. Effects of the cancer-causing radiation, sometimes delayed for years before actually becoming detectable, were every so often passed on to the next generation.

Grand Gulf Nuclear Power Station like, every other nuclear plant in the U.S., monitored events occurring in the Soviet-owned territory, located close to the northern Scandinavian countries of Finland, Sweden and Norway. Even though the Soviet Union did not report the event to the world for at least two days, it was obvious from radiation detectors located at nuclear power plants distributed around Europe that a major accident had occurred somewhere to the east.

Radioactive contamination spread over crops and livestock, being carried by the trade winds from Chernobyl westward. It reached as far west as the northeastern part of the United States, setting off radiation detector alarms in ventilation systems located in several power plants.

Firefighters in the Ukraine worked to put out an inextinguishable fire as the world watched on twenty-four hour news programs, for several days. International help was called for to investigate the best course of action to contain some of the release. However, it was a mismatch of politics versus science, as assistance was offered from the West and denied.

Finally, the molten mass of supercritical self-propagating nuclear material melted through the reactor's containment into a lead-lined basement and spread itself thin enough to become subcritical. Not being able to feed itself neutrons, the monstrous elephant's foot-like mass of graphite and uranium mixed with undiscovered elements, lost some of its heat. The effects eventually diminished enough to start construction of some basic containment building in order to stop the continuous release of radioactive gases to the world.

Harold watched the event unfold on television every day before and after work. The U.S. Nuclear Regulatory Commission, issuing one bulletin after another about the accident, was tracking Chernobyl every day during the accident and feeding information to all nuclear reactor operators throughout the country, followed by information from another organization in the U.S. established after Three Mile Island's partial meltdown, called the Institute of Nuclear Power Operators or INPO. These organizations made it obvious that an international organization would be needed in the future to handle events as international as Chernobyl had been.

The accident took Harold's mind off the nightmare of Kenny's release. News articles and media coverage of Chernobyl kept Harold and Anne talking about what it would mean to the future of nuclear power and his job should everyone see this as the last nail in the coffin of nuclear power plants.

\*        \*        \*        \*

Harold and Anne decided to move and put their first home up for sale in August. They both agreed that life in Vicksburg was not what they wanted and that living closer to Jackson would be much better for them and their children. Anne had also gotten a great job drafting for a growing civil engineering firm in Jackson and the drive into work from Vicksburg every day was too long for her to do the things she wanted to do at home.

Harold would now have an hour-long drive to Grand Gulf, but he was willing to make the sacrifice, especially since the kids would be in much better schools than they were in Vicksburg.

He also heard a rumour that college classes might begin soon at Grand Gulf in order to give operators a chance to get a Bachelor of Science degree in Nuclear Engineering. Chernobyl had by default raised the bar for Senior Reactor Operators in nuclear plants across the country, and the Nuclear Regulatory Commission was pushing very hard for utilities to get more university degrees in nuclear reactor control rooms.

Some extra classes were being taught at Mississippi College in Clinton, which was right outside of Jackson. Harold kept himself as busy as he possibly could to block out Kenny's release from prison. He even found time to work out with free weights every day, in their garage. But news of Kenny's increasing business net worth, along with a constant barrage of barriers from Georgia's Attorney General's office, kept Harold on edge most of the time. After many telephone calls to Atlanta, he finally contacted an Assistant Attorney General by the name of Hillar, who began to answer some of his questions.

"Mr. Hillar, will we be able to get Kenny put back in jail?" Harold asked.

"I believe that's a very good possibility," Hillar replied. "Because of evidence presented during his trial and Judge Dickson's poor reputation, we may have a good chance for a reversal of the judge's decision,"

"When are we gonna know more about what we should do next?" Harold asked.

"We have a lot of work to do before we can get this case up to the Fifth Circuit Court," Hillar stated. "I'll send you some documents this week that you'll need to sign and return to me as quickly as possible."

"What kind of documents are you talking about?" Harold asked.

"It's a request to have Judge Dickson's ruling overturned and Kenny Winkler put back in prison," Hillar replied.

"No problem, just send them to me. I'll sign them and get them right back to you," Harold said emphatically.

"I'll keep you informed about our progress, but I may need you to come to Atlanta for the hearing. We must have someone present to represent Helen's family," Hillar replied.

"Just let me know when to be there and I'll make it my number one priority," Harold stated.

He was willing to do anything that was needed in order to stop the burning sensation in the pit of his stomach that seemed to heat up every time he thought about his mother's killer walking the streets of Valdosta. The doctor told him it might be the beginning of an ulcer, caused by stress or his eating habits.

Harold began to watch everything he ate very closely for months in an effort to end the pain in his abdomen. He even bought a computer program that helped him track his caloric intake. He logged everything into the computer program daily and was able to print out a complete list of all the vitamins, proteins, fats and carbohydrates he had eaten. It gave Harold a chance to learn his body's daily caloric needs, but it didn't totally relieve his anxiety about getting something done about Kenny's release. Putting him back in prison where he belonged would promptly clear up Harold's agonizing.

Harold called his family to let them know the latest developments and was happy to hear that Lisa said she wanted to be at the hearing. Polly, too, who was married to a Navy man and living in Annapolis, Maryland, said she would attend. But Jerry declined, saying he didn't want to get involved because it would be too hard on Betty. "Yeah, sure," Harold said. "I understand." But he really didn't. He told Anne it was "just a cop-out."

"Please, honey," Anne said, "let it go."

# CHAPTER 27

▼

Harold had the next day off, so after the kids went off to their schools and Anne left for work, he took the opportunity to work out at a real gym in Vicksburg.

Posted on a bulletin board at the gym was an ad for an open weight-lifting competition to be held at the mall in Vicksburg. Harold signed up, deciding to test himself against some local talents. There were several types of lifts required for the competition, but Harold's favorite was the dead lift—standing up with the bar holding as much free weight as one could lift and locking his shoulders back in place.

There wasn't time to prepare properly for the competition, so Harold just practiced the dead-lifting technique he learned in the Navy, for the two weeks leading up to the competition.

The competition started at nine on Saturday morning. Patrons, shopping at the Vicksburg Mall, gathered to watch the athletes. Soon, a crowd formed around the lifters that included three weight classes: under 150 lbs, 150 lbs to 200 lbs and over 200 lbs. At six feet four inches tall, Harold weighed in at two hundred and fifty pounds that morning.

Light and middle weight lifters went through their lifts, winners ending with their heaviest lifts around one and half times their body weights. The first of five heavy weight lifters that Harold lifted against, weighed in at close to three hundred and thirty pounds.

Harold and another lifter he saw in a Mr. Mississippi body-building contest a month earlier, made their first lift at 400 lbs. The weight felt easy for Harold on that day, unlike other times when his energy was low, from not watching his diet. Anne and the kids watched from a still growing crowd.

Bodybuilders sometimes get chastised by power lifters for not being as strong as they look in their small Speedos, but the bodybuilder put another fifty pounds on the bar, raising the total weight to an even 500 lbs. He walked over to the bar, now covered in white chalk from a full four hours of use by twenty-five contestants. He gave a little smirk toward his bodybuilder girlfriend and strained with all his might to lift the weight.

Slowly the bodybuilder grunted loudly as he shook from muscle spasms traveling though his body. A coach from the high school weightlifting team blew a silver whistle a couple of seconds after he locked out his shoulders, to signal a good lift. The weight crashed back down into the platform making a loud banging noise that could hardly be heard over his yelling, "Yeah!" Cocky now, feeling that he had won the contest, he waved to the crowd.

Harold couldn't believe that he was the only other contestant left that might have a chance to beat this guy. He had never lifted anything this heavy in his life, but to win he would have to lift something heavier.

Harold turned to Anne. "Do you think I can lift that much?"

"Yeah, you can do it, Harold. Just think about Kenny Winkler and it'll give you more strength!" Anne exclaimed.

Harold walked over to the loaders handling the steel free weights and said, "Five twenty-five."

It was an intimidating sight for him to see and think about. Five hundred and twenty-five pounds was over twice his body weight and he had never lifted over 400 lbs, but he was focused. He wasn't thinking about the weight itself, but the feeling of finishing a lift that would push his body through a wall that he had never been through. He knew that it would feel heavy when he lifted it from its resting position into the air, but that was second to his sudden rush of hatred that he felt for Winkler. Anne's words were an inspiration.

Thoughts of his mother's murderer being released from jail had intruded on his subconscious long enough. It was time to flush it out of his mind and get over the depression that had returned.

Harold walked over to the bar and after a quick chalk rub on his palms, he grabbed the bar with an over-under grip and paused for a moment to gather his strength. If there was one time that he wanted to feel flushed with adrenalin, this was it.

Tightening his body, Harold snatched at the bar. The weight began to move slowly upward, powered by Harold's muscles now bulging from every part of his body. He could feel a sudden rush of blood flow through his arms and back, which felt like they would explode if somehow he were unable to complete this lift. Not willing to give up, Harold continued to raise the bar until it was past his knees and his shoulders were nearing lockout.

To be a good lift he knew that he had to roll back his shoulders and hold the weight long enough to allow the coach to call it good and blow his whistle. But he wasn't thinking about the weight at all, when his shoulders finally locked into place. He was thinking about what his mother might say if she were watching this lift. It would be, "Good job, Harold, and I knew you could do it!" It was sufficient to give him strength to hold on, until the whistle blew and he released the bar. It crashed into the platform, but could not be heard over the enormous roar coming from the huge crowd that had now gathered in the promenade of the mall to watch the event.

Anne, Scott, and Louisa screamed the loudest and rushed up on stage as Harold slowly waved to the crowd. All three hugged him. He'd never seen Scott so excited. Harold stepped down off the platform and went into a small waiting room. He was so relived to have finished the meet with a win in his column, but it was a handshake from the bodybuilder that gave him pause. Harold knew that the man was opening a gym in a few months and a win would have been good for his membership drive, but he was generous enough to congratulate Harold and offer him a free one-year membership at the gym when it opened.

*        *        *        *

A sudden decision by the top management of Grand Gulf's parent company in Jackson permitted the program of work-study to be introduced at all its nuclear power plants. The program allowed anyone in plant operations who wanted to obtain their Bachelor of Science Degree in Nuclear Engineering to attend classes on site, at no cost to the employee.

The Nuclear Regulatory Commission released its preliminary edict to have all Senior Reactor Operators working in any nuclear power plant control room to obtain a Bachelor of Science degree in a nuclear power-related field. The NRC was making policy decisions based on statistics made by college graduates versus non-graduates, in an effort to avoid anything like Chernobyl happening in the U.S. which had about ninety operating nuclear power plants within its borders.

An organization based in Memphis, Tennessee established an institute that offered the B.S. degree to several utilities throughout the nuclear industry, including those owned by Grand Gulf's parent company. Plant management bought into the idea, giving Harold the opportunity of a lifetime. After brief discussions with Anne, he immediately signed up for classes.

Classes were set up for Operations Department shift workers, allowing them to come in before work or stay after their shift in order to attend classes taught by professors brought in from all over the world. Professors working towards their citizenship in the United States were hired from countries like India, Pakistan, Iran and England. Professors from countries that had circumvented the Nuclear Non-Proliferation Treaty and had attained expertise in the nuclear field were very willing to take temporary positions as a university lecturer with the institute.

It wasn't a big concern of Harold's where professors were from, as long as he was able to learn what he needed to get his degree. And once it was obtained, he was assured that he would be able to go directly into a Senior Reactor Operator's (SRO) training program at Grand Gulf.

Licenses issued to SRO's by the Nuclear Regulatory Commission were not easy to come by, but Harold felt confident that he could pass any exams necessary to achieve his ultimate goal of working in the main control room. Anne was behind him one hundred percent, even knowing that she would have to work hard at home to keep things running smoothly.

The winter semester started in January. Harold began attending his first two weeks of classes, being held over his midnight shifts, which were the most difficult to complete. He would work off shift at seven-thirty in the morning, then make his way over to Grand Gulf's training building for a three hour class in college level heat transfer two days a week.

Grand Gulf had just started a twelve-hour shift rotation for its operators, so Harold was attending class after working from seven p.m. to seven-thirty a.m. on midnight shift and vice versa on days. But even with the horrible hours, he was enjoying going through the program no matter how physically and mentally taxing the classes were. Harold knew it would all be worth it once he had the degree in hand.

Anne and Harold worked hard together to keep up the grueling pace of their lives. Eventually, they bought a house in Clinton and put Scott and Louisa in their new school. Everything was going well for them and Harold felt even better when he received a phone call from Atlanta in March of 1987.

# CHAPTER 28

▼

Harold was sitting on the couch watching the TV news, studying his heat transfer notes from the lecture he attended a day earlier, when the telephone rang. He walked over to the wall-mounted phone and lifted the receiver.

"Hello, Mr. Harmon?" the male voice said.

"Yes, this is he," Harold replied.

"This is Assistant Attorney General Hillar."

"Hello, Mr. Hillar. I've been waiting for your call."

"I have some good news for you and your family," Hillar stated. "We'll have a chance to present our petition to put Kenny Winkler back in prison to the Fifth Circuit Court, in three weeks."

"That is fantastic news," Harold said.

"Yes, and I need for as many of your family members to be there as you can possibly get to come," Mr. Hillar explained.

"I'll contact them right after we're through with our conversation," Harold assured.

"Okay, great. I'll send you details of what building the hearing will be held in by mail, but please make plans to be in Atlanta on April 3rd," Hillar said.

Confident that there was nothing that would keep him from making it to Atlanta, Harold said, "Not a problem."

Their conversation ended and Harold turned to Anne with a smile. She had overheard their discussion and was ecstatic about Harold's news. She, too, had wonderful news to tell him—she had taken a pregnancy test and the results were positive. But she decided to wait to tell Harold until the hearing was over.

Anne knew there were two possibilities: one, that Kenny would be sent back to prison and everything would return to normal for them, and the baby would be an added bonus. Possibility number two was that his appeal would not be overturned and Kenny would be a free man. Anne thought that the latter was the worst possible scenario, but if it happened, telling Harold she was having a baby might help to soften the blow.

Harold put in a call to Lisa. Although she had promised to travel to Atlanta from Guatemala City when the time came to show how strongly Helen's family felt about putting Kenny back in prison, she declined to attend, saying, "I can't take any more of this, Harold. The trial took too much out of me." Stunned at her answer, Harold said he understood her position and called Polly.

Polly's excuse was that she didn't have time to get to Atlanta from Annapolis. Her new position with the Federal Bureau of Investigation was keeping her very busy and she hadn't built up any vacation time. Harold explained to her that Hillar thought it was essential for them all to show a consolidated family endorsement of the petition to have Kenny put back in prison. But finally Harold relinquished his argument and said that he understood.

He called Jerry with one last plea for him to help. Jerry said that it would be too hard for him to come and that Betty would feel extremely uncomfortable escorting him to Kenny's appeal review.

Harold said to Anne after he hung up the phone, "Lisa won't come. I believe the trial took away some of her fight, Anne. She's not the same."

"I know she'd be there if she could, Harold," Anne said.

"And Polly says she can't get here in time, and well, you know my dad's usual excuse. So, I guess it's just me squaring off against Kenny."

"For the last time," Anne said.

The next afternoon Harold called the Attorney General's office in Atlanta to explain to Hillar that he would be the only family member present, but that he would definitely be there as planned. Hillar assured Harold that his attendance would make all the difference—it was crucial that he come.

That evening the fire was roaring in their new home in Clinton, while Anne finished making arrangements for them to stay two days with her aunt Ouida and uncle Mike. She turned to Harold occasionally to get agreement on times and dates as he watched the flames of the fire slowly die down. He and Anne sat in front of the fire until it had turned to ash, and then went to bed.

Within a few days, Harold and Anne along with Scott and Louisa, arrived in Marietta. Ouida and Mike were happy to see them and made their stay as pleasant as possible under the circumstances.

As Harold retired early to the guest room he lay in bed mulling over what might occur the following day. Would he be asked to say something or would Hillar take the lead in representing the family? He was still upset and a bit angry that Lisa and Polly wouldn't be there.

"Harold, are you still awake?" Anne asked as she got undressed.

"Yeah, I can't sleep," Harold replied.

She already knew the answer to the question before asking, "Are you thinking about tomorrow?"

"Yeah, just trying to sort things out."

"Well, Mr. Hillar said that you should not have to make a statement. But you need to be ready, remember? In case they ask you personal questions," Anne said.

"I've been thinking about that and I believe I'm ready." His voice began to show a little anger. "What bothers me the most, though, is being in a courtroom with that killer."

"I know, but you have to be there," Anne said.

"Yes, and I'm very grateful for the chance to put him back in prison," Harold said. "Guess I'll keep my anger in check."

Harold lay in bed trying to go to sleep for several more hours, but couldn't. He finally resorted to a method of muscle relaxation he learned while in the Navy's nuclear power school, trying to fall asleep the night before an exam. He concentrated on relaxing each of his muscles from the top of his head down to his toes, one at a time. Usually by the time he got to his fingertips he was out, as was the case this night.

\*     \*     \*     \*

Louisa and Scott stayed home with Ouida while their parents maneuvered through heavy traffic on Interstate 85. Traffic to downtown Atlanta was insufferable at eight o'clock in the morning, but they needed to be in the courtroom by nine.

As they drove, Harold discussed with Anne what they could expect for the final time. Hillar had described an environment where lawyers would be discussing legal procedures more than innocence and guilt. Also being argued was how Judge Dickson had overstepped his bounds by declaring a jury incompetent to pass judgment on a murder case that had been proven beyond a reasonable doubt back in 1982.

Hillar met them at a restaurant just outside the courthouse at eight-thirty as planned in order to brief them again. Within minutes their discussion was over and they made their way together to a large area in front of the courtroom reserved for Fifth Circuit Court hearings.

Blazing white painted walls and columns in the foyer outside the courtroom were in high contrast to maplewood trimmed doors, staircases and windows. Stepping off the elevator onto the black and white tiled floor, waxed to a dazzling shine, the three walked slowly toward the courtroom.

Hillar paused briefly before entering, pulled aside by his assistant waiting at the doorway. Harold and Anne looked inside to see a wide open courtroom with paintings of dead governors and a Georgia state flag flanked by Old Glory. Three judges spaced at arm's length were seated behind an extra large desk.

Harold and Anne were escorted by Hillar to a second row seat, adjacent to a podium located in the middle aisle. Hillar and his two assistants sat at a table located toward the front of the courtroom. Clay Lee Barker and three defense lawyers sat opposite to Hillar's table.

Foxy was no where to be found. Clay Lee thought it best to minimize the hearing as much as possible—Foxy's presence might have added credence to the affair.

Kenny entered the courtroom, with George McMillan, his family lawyer from Valdosta, and sat boldly in the same pew as Harold and Anne. Kenny's arrogance in sitting just five feet away from Harold was an attempt to smack the Harmon family in the face one more time. Kenny wanted everyone to know that he was a free man and there was nothing anyone could do about it.

Anne grabbed Harold's hand and squeezed it tightly, looking up to him as he turned his stare in her direction. She could see that veins were popping out around his temple and neck. Muscles rippled through his face, especially around his jaw showing that he had begun to clench and grind his teeth. Smiling at him, Anne shook her head slowly and looked forward. Harold hesitated for a moment and then turned his gaze back over to Kenny.

Kenny had a half-assed smirk on his face, but never turned toward Harold to make eye contact. It was obviously a ploy he had planned with his attorneys to demonstrate to the judges that he was not intimidated by today's proceedings.

Living in Mississippi had its advantages while Kenny was out on bail, after Judge Dickson granted his last appeal because it kept Harold from ever running into him on the street. Harold was now facing his nemesis. Anne took her hand back slowly; Harold's grip had tightened beyond her threshold for pain.

Judge Grayson sitting in the center of the three-judge panel began the proceedings promptly at nine o'clock.

"Ladies and gentlemen, we're here today to review the case of Kenny Winkler's release by Judge Dickson of the District Court, Valdosta Division. Do you have a motion, Mr. Hillar?"

Hillar took the non-verbal exchange between Harold and Kenny as inspiration. He began his statement with the vigor of a man on a mission.

"Your Honors, I am here representing the Georgia Attorney General in protesting by petition to have the appeal decision granted by Judge Dickson reversed, based on evidence presented during the murder trial of Kenny Winkler," Hillar stated. "This protest was requested by the Harmon family and we fully support its discharge."

Hillar went on to review the details of Helen's murder. He was extremely well prepared to present every aspect of the discovery of her body, investigation by Detective Starnes, and trial by jury, then conviction of Kenny for her murder. Subsequent to his description of Kenny's trial Hillar described Judge Dickson as "a very conceited individual with little respect for due process."

Hillar concluded his statement with another plea to the court to retract Kenny's granted appeal.

"Thank you, Mr. Hillar," Judge Grayson said. "We will take a ten-minute break before hearing remarks from the defense."

Everyone stood as the three judges left for their chambers.

"I'll be right back," Harold told Anne. "I need to find a toilet."

When Harold turned to leave, Kenny quickly made his way to his attorney's table. Harold smiled at Anne and started moving out when he noticed several members of the press scattered around, sitting between many empty seats of the large room. As he walked toward two large doors leading out of the courtroom, a woman followed him into the lobby.

"Excuse me, sir, but are you a relative of Helen Harmon?"

"Yes, I'm her son," Harold replied.

"I was very sorry to hear about her death and I wish to express my sympathy to you and your family," she said.

"Thank you very much," Harold replied.

"Would you like to make a statement?" she asked. "I'm with the Atlanta Journal Constitution."

Harold turned around slowly and looked into her eyes. "I believe that justice was served over five years ago and I believe that we will be vindicated again today. Judge Dickson had no right to release Kenny," Harold stated.

"Thank you, Mr. Harmon," she said. "I wish you all the best."

Harold turned away and went into a nearby men's room. After using a urinal at the end of a long row of stalls, he turned away to see Clay Lee entering with one of his associates.

"Good morning," Clay Lee said with a big smile on his face.

Harold was taken aback, but composed himself quickly. "Yes, it is."

Harold knew that Clay Lee was on the ropes with this case's appeals and was looking for any indication of weakness in the Harmon family.

Washing his hands for several seconds Harold waited for Clay Lee's follow up comment, readying himself for an attack.

Looking in Harold's direction, never calling him by name, Clay Lee asked, "What do you think is going to happen in there today?"

"I believe that a killer will be put where he belongs. In prison," Harold replied.

Clay Lee walked over to the end of the long row of stalls and hesitated a moment while Harold dried his hands.

"It'll be a cold day in hell, before they put Kenny back in prison, I'll see to that," Clay Lee stated.

Harold stared at Clay Lee Barker with anger, commitment, and an ever-present need for justice.

"It's gonna take more than a ride on a pompous ass to prevent us from sending that bastard back to prison," Harold said as he left the men's room.

Clay Lee was somewhat surprised—perhaps he had underestimated the Harmon family resolve.

Harold made his way back across the lobby avoiding another reporter who was approaching him. Just as he sat back down beside Anne in the courtroom, Clay Lee entered carrying a large glass of ice water.

Kenny returned to his seat next to McMillan, near Harold and Anne. Harold moved closer to Kenny, his stare on him constant and intimidating. Especially since Harold was twice his size. Kenny's smirk was replaced with a solemn frown.

"Everyone rise," the bailiff called out.

The judges filed in and resumed their original positions behind the large desk.

"Does the defense have a statement?" Judge Grayson asked.

"Yes, your Honor," Clay Lee stated.

"But before you begin, Mr. Hillar, is there a member of the Harmon family present today?" Judge Grayson asked.

"Yes, your Honor, Helen's son is here today." Hillar turned and pointed to Harold sitting in the second row.

Harold stood up to show himself, then sat back in his seat after Judge Grayson's acknowledging head nod.

"Thank you, Mr. Hillar. Defense may continue," Judge Grayson said.

Verbal fencing against each of Hillar's statements began, with all of Clay Lee's strength. "I would like to challenge each judge sitting on this panel of the Fifth Circuit Court to remember that Kenny Winkler was convicted by a jury in a court located in Valdosta, Georgia. Education being what it is in that part of the country, complicated evidence evaluation is uncertain. Evidence which consisted of memories of very old black men, coerced by detectives investigating the case into stating they had participated in hiding Mrs. Harmon's body, cannot be used against my client.

"Any respectable prosecution sending a man to prison for a life sentence would never use uncertain evidence that was nearly ten years old. I have never in all my years of practicing law in the great state of Georgia seen such misuse of the judicial system," Clay Lee said.

He went on, justifying his own opinion and that of Judge Dickson. When he was done with his rant, attacking every phase of Kenny's trial, Judge Grayson spoke.

"Mr. Hillar, you may have a rebuttal to the defense's statement if you wish."

"Your Honor, I do wish to single out several dominate features of this case. One being that two eye witnesses stated that they helped bury Mrs. Harmon's body in a box near the Valdosta airport in a once-wooded area, although one recanted at the trial.

"Two, opportunity to perform Helen Harmon's murder was presented to the jury by a confirmed timeline, using eyewitness accounts of Kenny Winkler's travels to Valdosta. And most importantly, motive for the heinous murder of Helen was presented and confirmed as being an extreme case of sexual harassment culminating itself finally, in murder," Hillar intoned.

"We will recess until three o'clock, for our final decision," Judge Grayson stated and pounded his gavel.

Everyone stood as the judges left the courtroom. Harold and Anne went to lunch with Hillar at a restaurant near the courthouse, but far enough away to ensure they would not see Kenny or Clay Lee. He wanted to know all about Harold and Anne's life and told them it was a privilege to be working on this request for appeal reversal. Harold thanked Hillar with grateful words and tears in his eyes.

Entering court just before three o'clock, a larger group than had attended the morning session took their seats on both sides of the aisle. Everyone rose as the three judges filed in, each caring files and assorted documents.

Judge Grayson opened the afternoon with a solemn tone. "Would the defendant rise," he said looking at Kenny Winkler.

"We have reviewed this case thoroughly and it is our opinion that Judge Dickson violated his powers and authority in releasing Kenny Winkler from prison. Therefore, through the powers vested in this Fifth Circuit Court, we reinstate Kenny Winkler's life sentence, which he will fulfill in the correctional institutions of Georgia."

Harold looked over at Kenny, but Kenny would not look in Harold's direction. It didn't matter though; Harold could see from his cowed body posture that Kenny knew he was defeated. He began to cry.

Clay Lee glanced over at Hillar, who knew all about Barker from previous trial transcripts he had spent hours reading while in law school. Hillar met Barker's eyes and smiled.

Judge Grayson looked toward Harold. "I want to express our deepest regrets to the Harmon and Grantham families for the pain they tolerated because of Judge Dickson's decision. I can assure you that this court intends to follow up on the abuse of power from his bench."

"Bailiff, remand the prisoner," Judge Grayson demanded.

Harold stood with Anne as the bailiff handcuffed Kenny and escorted him through doors located in front of Clay Lee's desk. Suddenly a sense of euphoria came over Harold when Anne turned to hug and quickly kiss him.

"I knew he was going back!" Anne exclaimed.

"Watching him go through those doors with handcuffs on will forever be etched in my mind," Harold said, hugging his wife.

Walking from the courtroom, escorted by Assistant Attorney General Hillar, they made their way to an elevator. With Hillar's help they were able to avoid reporters who were temporarily surrounding Clay Lee. Even after losing his appeal in a higher court, he maintained his cool composure, answering questions quickly and with his usual charm.

"Thank you, Mr. Hillar," Harold said as they waited for the elevator doors to open.

"It was my pleasure. I'm just sorry that you had to go through this ordeal," Hillar said.

The elevator doors opened and Harold and Anne waved a last goodbye to Hillar as they got in the elevator.

"Thank you again," Harold said.

"I'll send you a copy of the decision," Hillar called out.

The elevator doors closed.

*     *     *     *

Inside the elevator, Harold and Anne looked at each other and smiled. Kenny was in prison again and would be there for a long time before his first parole hearing, due in about five years. They knew that they would have to continue to show interest in keeping Kenny behind bars to the state of Georgia, but that seemed to be too far in the future for them to think about today.

"Harold I've got something to tell you," Anne said as they got off the elevator and walked through the lobby.

Still feeling high from what had just occurred back in the courtroom, Harold asked, "What is it?"

"We're gonna have a baby!" Anne exclaimed.

"Wow, that's great!" Harold shouted and grabbed her up to kiss her.

Several people walking past them in the lobby overheard and one called out, "Congratulations."

Ann blushed and turned back to Harold, lowering her voice. "I've been waiting to tell you, but I knew that your mind was completely focused on today," Anne said.

"How far along are you?" Harold asked.

"Well, the doctor says around three months."

Harold kissed her again. They walked out of the courthouse and into a bright sunny day. Gentle breezes blew as they headed toward their car in a parking tower around the corner. On Peachtree Street they passed a woman in her mid-thirties with three children.

She looked happy walking through Atlanta in her summer dress with her three children following behind her. For a brief moment her expression reminded Harold of 1972. The woman's demeanor was as confident and bold as his mother's had been.

They passed by and Harold overheard the boy say, "I don't want to wear a tie on Easter; it itches my neck." Something he could have easily said, thinking back on how he hated to dress up for Easter Sunday.

"Yes, I know. But you'll be fine," his mother said in a loving voice. Just like Helen.

# EPILOGUE

▼

Harold and Anne's daughter was born in Mississippi and they named her Helen. Scott and Louisa were both thrilled to have a baby sister to play with while growing up in Clinton.

In the year 2002, Harold ended his long and successful career with Grand Gulf Nuclear Power Station. He was appointed to the International Atomic Energy Agency (IAEA) to work as an International Nuclear Safeguards Inspector, traveling to countries around the world, and monitoring them for undeclared nuclear materials or activities.

The IAEA is headquartered in Vienna, Austria; consequently, Harold, Anne and Helen moved there in 2002 and have loved living under the United Nations umbrella in that historical city. Vienna, with its magnificent architecture, music, art, and wonderful coffee houses, is a feast for the senses.

Harold's work with the IAEA has been rewarding as well. But his most prestigious honor, by far, came when Harold and his colleagues were awarded the Nobel Peace Prize in 2005. Harold's participation in ensuring the non-proliferation of nuclear weapons, mandated in the Atoms for Peace Statute (established by the United Nations) is important and still challenging.

It was also in the spring of 2005 that a parole hearing was held for Kenny Winkler by the Georgia parole board. Kenny's parole hearings have come up through the years since his final incarceration in 1986 on three occasions, each publicized by the local media. But it was the parole hearing of this spring that rallied the interest of the community most.

News of a hearing created a stir in Morven; one that spread throughout south Georgia. A petition was circulated by friends of the Harmon family that called for

Kenny to remain in prison—it was signed by hundreds of people in Morven, Valdosta and around South Georgia. Letters of objection were also sent by Harold, Lisa, and Polly in addition to letters from friends and family from other regions of the United States—all of which helped to dissuade the parole board once again.

Jerry died in 2001, losing his battle with cancer and leaving Betty to live out her days at the Harmon house. While Jerry was able to witness the prosecution of Helen's murderer, Granny never knew what happened to her only daughter before passing away in 1979.

Scott now lives in Valdosta, since his honorable discharge from the Navy and Louisa has two children of her own. Even though Louisa lives near Atlanta, she and her brother are very close—spending their holidays together when possible.

Constantly reminded of their beloved mother's murder, Helen's children continue to keep Kenny Winkler in prison. But reliving the ordeal, digging up painful feelings and wrestling them to bed each time a parole hearing is scheduled, is something they have had to face many times over the years. It's a fight that Harold has come to understand and accept as necessary, because it's not the man who remains in prison, but the murderer.